Dancing Deer

DANCING DEER

A Glimpse into Small-Town America

Book One of the Dancing Deer Series

By *Ron Lambert*

Copyright © 2012 by Printers Guild Publishing House, llc

All rights are reserved. No part of this book may be reproduced or transmitted in any form by any means: electronic or mechanical. It may not be photocopied, recorded, or otherwise without the prior written permission of the publisher. For information on getting permission for reprints and excerpts contact Printers Guild Publishing House at printersguildpublishing@gmail.com.

Published in the United States by:

Printers Guild Publishing House

425 Spring Street, Suite 101
Columbus, Texas 78934-2461
(979) 732-2962   Fax (979) 733-0015
www.printersguildpublshing.com

ISBN 978-0-9855083-1-9

Contents

CHAPTER 1—JEDIDIAH............................... 9
    Possum Point, Arkansas - October 1919

CHAPTER 2—TRAVELLER........................ 25
    Lee Mountain, Arkansas - Early Spring 1933

CHAPTER 3—RESIGNATION..................... 47
    Dancing Deer - Spring 1933

CHAPTER 4—EMILY.................................. 55
    Possum Point - Spring 1933

CHAPTER 5—PHILIPPE.............................. 63
    France - 1940

CHAPTER 6—JESSE................................... 77
    Dancing Deer - September 1941

CHAPTER 7—ROSE..................................... 85
    Dancing Deer - April 1942

CHAPTER 8—BASIC TRAINING.................. 101
    Little Rock - June 1942

CHAPTER 9—BALDER................................ 113
    Lee Mountain - Late October 1942

CHAPTER 10—NADINE............................... 125
    Dancing Deer - November 1942

CHAPTER 11—HMS *QUEEN ELIZABETH*..... 147
    Fort Devens, Massachusetts - November 1942

CHAPTER 12—ALGIERS.......................... 157
   The Southern Shores of the Mediterranean - November 1942

CHAPTER 13—STATESIDE........................ 165
   Virginia – February 1943

CHAPTER 14—LEAVING TOWN................. 189
   Dancing Deer – March 1943

CHAPTER 15—CLAUDE........................... 203
   Springfield, Missouri – March 1943

CHAPTER 16—SICILY............................... 229
   An Island in the Mediterranean – July 1943

CHAPTER 17—ITALY................................ 251
   The European Theater – July 1943

CHAPTER 18—GENEVIEVE....................... 265
   Provence, France – Middle of May 1944

CHAPTER 19—FRANCE............................ 291
   Northeast France – Late July 1944

CHAPTER 20—PARIS............................... 303
   City of Light – Early August, 1944

CHAPTER 21—THE TRIP.......................... 317
   Springfield, Missouri - October, 1944

CHAPTER 23—COMING HOME................. 341
   Reims, France – November 1944

AUTHOR BIO... 359
ADDITIONAL NOVELS................................ 361
Order Form... 363

Dancing Deer is a work of Fiction

The book's World War II battle scenes are in correct chronological order as they occurred and as outlined in the history of the US Army's Forty-Fifth Infantry Division. No other claim is made as to the accurate depiction of battles, skirmishes, or other incidents of war except through the author's best effort.

Except for some historical personages the names, characters, and incidents of the story are used fictitiously and do not represent any actual person or event.

Some of the towns, cities, or geographic localities are real. The author grew up in a small rural community and saw wonder in all living things. He wrote this story using the hazy remembrances of a child's fertile imagination and a burning desire to tell how his uncle, Staff Sergeant Troy Hottinger, won the Army's Distinguished Service Cross. The events in the sergeant's life, other than that one heroic achievement, have been fictionalized.

Trademarks

Red Wing Shoes, *The Courier Democrat*, *The Kansas City Star*, *The Arkansas Gazette*, *The Memphis Globe*, Sears and Roebuck, Montgomery Ward, and all other trademarks are property of their respective owners. Printers Guild Publishing House, llc is not associated with any product or vendor mentioned in this book.

CHAPTER 1—JEDIDIAH

Possum Point, Arkansas - October 1919

Jedidiah pulled the covers over his head. He had to find a place to hide. Anyone getting him out of bed before daylight better come loaded for bear. Out the window. Wait a minute, grab some clothes, then out the window.

"Jedidiah, come on. Your breakfast is ready. You have to take your brothers their lunches." He could hear his mother's dress rustle. She was probably shaking a wooden spoon his way. "Jedidiah, it's ten o'clock. Boy, how long you gonna sleep?"

He wasn't a boy. He'd already graduated from school. Why does his mother refer to him as if he were still a child? He squinted at the window. She's got to put up thicker curtains.

Jed's older brothers, Claude and Rupert, were helping a neighbor rebuild a barn. The doddering old fool dropped a lantern while trying to feed his livestock. He barely escaped. Crawling out behind frenzied animals, the old man watched his barn burn to the ground. Now it was late October and he had to rebuild before winter blew in. Without the barn he wouldn't have a place to store his hay and without hay his horses and milk cow would starve. Jedidiah's brothers worked every moment they could spare with the old man. Today they would be tackling the most difficult part.

When Jedidiah arrived, he was astonished to find every able-bodied man in the county helping his brothers and the old man. Their women-folk had set up tables and were scurrying to and fro bringing food to each. It was a beehive of activity. Jedidiah could see steaming bowls of food decorating long wooden planks set atop saw-horses. One woman brought yeast rolls. The heady aroma encircled her as she walked to the table, carrying it in front like manna from heaven. The men salivated when an occasional whiff came sneaking them out.

A slender girl of eighteen or so, wearing a flowery bonnet and carrying a bucket of water, wound her way through stacks of lumber, kegs of nails, and assorted scaffolding. Jedidiah had never seen her before. He watched. He decided she had to be the prettiest girl in the county. She had a wisp of light brown hair poking out from her bonnet and a happy, animated way of responding to the workers' kidding. He began to feel uneasy. Ashamed of his appearance: an old pair of overalls, tattered work shirt, and dusty boots, he was also ashamed for showing up in the middle of the day with a piddling amount of food. He stowed the satchel of sandwiches and thermos of sweet tea, ran his fingers through his hair, and went looking for his brothers.

Rupert and Claude were hanging from a rafter. He started to climb up, decided against it, and called out, "Hey guys, come on down for a minute."

"What's up, Jed?" asked Rupert.

Claude said, "Jed, You see all these folks? They've been arriving since early this morning."

"Gimme a hammer and some nails."

The two brothers looked at each other with perplexed expressions. Claude reached down to the loop in his overalls and withdrew a hefty framing hammer; Rupert forked over a fist of sixteen-penny nails.

A young lady walked up and asked, "Would anyone like water?"

Jedidiah wiped the sweat from his brow. With his two feet planted far apart, he managed to blurt out, "Thank you, miss, I'm almost dehydrated."

Rupert rolled his eyes. With a delicate hand, the young lady reached into the pocket of her apron, withdrew a scented piece of lace, dipped it deep into the bucket of water, and pressed its dampness against Jedidiah's forehead. He dropped the nails. What followed was an awkward moment of silence. It was at this point in Jedidiah's life when he was transformed from an arrogant youth, full of himself, into an incoherent puddle of manhood. Jed couldn't remember his name. A passing worker kicked a nail, the young lady lowered her head, and the spell dissolved like mist evading the sun.

Rupert said, "Boss, where would you like me to work next?"

Claude slapped Jed on his back and said, "Your suggestion of increasing the pitch of the roof will probably solve our problem. I'll get right to it. I should have thought of it myself."

Jedidiah steadied himself. He and the young lady bent down and, on their knees, began picking up the nails. It was at this inopportune moment when Bill Potter walked up asking for water. Extending his hand to the young lady, Bill offered to refill her bucket. She climbed to her feet clutching a handful of nails. Jedidiah was speechless. He took the nails with barely a thank you.

Bill turned to Jed. "What brings you out this early in the morning, Jed?"

Jed stammered, "Just . . . just trying to help my brothers finish this barn."

"You mean you're actually working? No one's making you?"

Jed felt his blood rise. He had a right to work if he wanted. Before he could make a proper retaliatory remark, Claude said, "Jed, when you get off break I could use your keen eye on something."

The young lady took the bucket to be refilled, Potter spun around and went after her at a fast clip, and Jedidiah picked up the remaining nails. Jed thought how pompous that fool Potter was. He wasn't dressed for work. Wearing dress shoes and tight-fitting jeans and shirt, he only came for amusement or to gawk at any pretty girl who might show up—like the girl with the water. The Potters were too well-to-do. Bill's father bought him anything he wanted. Jed pondered for a moment and wondered if he disliked Bill for his family's money or because he'd shown an interest in the girl. Bill usually treated Jed like he was a nobody. Jed was amazed Bill knew his name. They'd gone to school together but Jed graduated earlier in the year at the bottom of his class and Bill will graduate next spring at the top of his.

Jed could have done better. He wasn't motivated. He was, however, the first in his family to actually graduate. Come to think of it, he didn't dislike Bill. No, he was envious. They certainly didn't travel in the same circles. Jed wondered if the pretty girl would be mesmerized by the glitz surrounding Bill or if she would be astute enough to judge a man by his character. But then again, what kind of character does a man show when he graduates at the bottom of his class, stays out drinking all night, sleeps till noon, and several months later still hasn't found a job?

Jedidiah joined his brothers and learned the exhilarating experience of being useful. He took only short breaks when one of the women offered him food or the many times when the young lady came by with water. He drank a lot of water.

During the afternoon of work, Jed asked around and found she was the oldest in a large family, she lived in Possum Point, a small town a couple of valleys distant, and her dad owned quite a bit of property. He made a living by renting his property to tenant farmers.

The women left after everyone was fed. The men worked until dusk when the old man, his hand on Claude's shoulder, graciously thanked them. He was teary-eyed as he said how blessed he was to have such good neighbors. Jedidiah felt pretty good himself. He'd actually put in a hard half-day of work, developed a deeper appreciation for his brothers, and come face-to-face with the prettiest girl he'd ever seen.

Early the next day, Sunday, Jedidiah saddled his major—no, his only—means of locomotion. With a vague list of directions, he headed out to find her. Carrying the piece of lace, he felt like Cinderella's prince with the glass slipper. He arrived at her house late in the afternoon. Too nervous to actually knock on the door, he paced back and forth in front. He soon decided no one was home. With his resolve bolstered, he sneaked onto the front porch. He didn't knock and he didn't tarry as he quickly left a handwritten note and walked away at a much faster and more spirited gait.

In town, he asked around and found she was at church. On Sunday she and her family attended services, ate picnic-style on the grounds followed up by some sort of singing, and ended with a long-winded prayer service that, according to his source, lasted for hours.

The following Sunday Jedidiah strolled into her church in his best clothes. He found the girl sitting three rows from the front beside an empty space. It must be an omen, he thought, as he slipped into the vacant seat. She looked surprised to see him but didn't have time to say anything before the minister asked everyone to stand and to turn in their hymnals to page 105. Jed had never read anything on music and now found himself at a disadvantage trying to understand the scribbling on the page. Jedidiah had more or less floated through school. His entire education had been accomplished with less than a dozen textbooks gracing his doorstep.

A hand tapped him on the shoulder. An angry voice whispered, "Get the hell out of my seat."

It was Bill Potter. Jed wasn't going to just give up the seat. "Find yourself somewhere else to sit."

Bill leaned forward and whispered to the young lady, "Sorry to be a little late. Now tell this jackass you were saving the seat for me."

A lady from the row behind began shushing and, when Jedidiah didn't budge and the young lady kept singing, Bill had to retreat a few rows. Jedidiah stood entranced. The girl he was standing beside sang with a clear soprano voice that quivered and trilled and made him think she was a nightingale in disguise. The minister spent the rest of the morning giving a torturous sermon. He said all manner of bad things about the activities making up the better part of Jedidiah's routine day.

After the service ended, Jedidiah turned to the young lady and said, "Hello. My name's Jed Calhoun. We met a week ago yesterday at the barn-raising."

"I remember. I'm Emily Sinclair, Mr. Calhoun."

Jedidiah thought Emily was the most beautiful name he'd ever heard. Potter walked up, grabbed her by the arm, and said, "Let's hurry outside so we'll have our choice of shade trees and picnic table."

Emily pulled loose. "My family eats together," she said as she looked at Jed. "Would you join us, Mr. Calhoun?"

"Please, call me Jed. I'd be delighted." Jed beamed. Bill bristled.

Emily introduced Jed to her parents and siblings. Jed surmised everyone must've already met Bill as he was not singularly introduced.

Mr. Sinclair was rather corpulent. He probably didn't do much manual labor. Emily was the oldest of five with two brothers and two sisters. Mrs. Sinclair unrolled an oiled gingham tablecloth over a wooden table and set out covered bowls the children had retrieved from their automobile. Jedidiah's family didn't own an automobile and this was the first time he thought he might've jumped into a river too deep for wading.

Mr. Sinclair turned to Jedidiah and asked what kind of work he did. Jed blushed, stammered a little, and then said he'd recently started work at the sawmill in Moccasin Gap.

Bill laughed and said, "You don't work at the sawmill. You don't work at all. Rupert and Claude do but you spend your time in jail or playing ball. You still selling that concoction you made of the fermented apple cider and raisins, or did the Skunk Hollow Sheriff relieve you of that?"

Jed turned crimson red. It took a moment for him to regain his composure. "Bill, I've changed my ways. I've seen the error of my judgment and, with my brothers' help, I'm beginning a career in joinery. They're not paying me for any work I do at the sawmill. I'm just learning as much as I can about the properties of different varieties and cuts of wood."

Mr. Sinclair spoke. "Well said, young man. I can appreciate someone who pulls himself up by his bootstraps, someone who can learn from his mistakes. I've heard what wonderful workers your two brothers are and, if you're learning from them, you'll be able to take care of yourself. Now let's bless the food and get down to business." Under his breath Mr. Sinclair continued with, "Nice comeback, Mr. Calhoun. I think this is going to be quite interesting."

With an occasional glance from her father, Emily spent the afternoon entertaining Jed and Bill. Neither would leave her side for fear the other would increase his standing at the expense of the one who had left. Bill wasted the first hour impressing Jed and trying to impress Emily. He talked about the things he owned or would own, the places he had been or would travel to, and the things he had done or planned on doing. He spent the second hour talking about the same things.

When prodded, Jed said, "I haven't traveled to many places. I live on a farm with my parents and two brothers. My best friends are Balder and Traveller. Balder's a big coon hound that follows me around. We hunt and fish together. Traveller's my horse. He was a year old when we met. I'm not sure if I take care of him or if he takes care of me. It's pretty much a two-sided affair."

"I do odd jobs, mostly for my brothers. So far I haven't found a vocation that suits me. In my spare time I listen to the birds sing and watch squirrels hide their acorns."

Emily took everything in but was reluctant to express an opinion on the attributes of either young man. She told them, "My days are filled with looking after my brothers and sisters and helping my mother with the meals, laundry, and housework. I read to my father in the evenings and listen to the radio when allowed to do so. Our life was easier, but less fulfilling, when we had the maid and cook. Dad asked them to find other employment a few months back. We then had to decide what we could do to help. We are more of a family unit now, each being more considerate of the other."

Bill said, "That's preposterous. I've always had someone else do my work. I can't see a life of manual labor. I've never had a list of chores. To me, the rewards for having money more than outweigh whatever means are necessary to acquire it. Everything is measured by its monetary worth and I'm going to have plenty of money and plenty of everything it provides."

By the time the singing started, Jed knew more about Bill Potter than he cared and not enough about Emily. However, his judgment was muddled by the fact that he really needed to visit a tree. Bill didn't seem to be suffering from the same affliction.

It was getting late and Jedidiah had a long ride home. He needed to say good-bye and it looked like he would be the first to leave. Bill, on the other hand, had his father's car and no particular time requiring his departure. Jedidiah shook hands with Bill and Mr. Sinclair and told Emily what a wonderful time he'd had. His horse was nearby, grazing on lush grass. He loosed the tall gelding, mounted, waved, and trotted off wondering if he could get his brothers to let him watch them at the sawmill for a few days.

On Friday of the following week, Jedidiah paid a visit to Mr. Sinclair's office. "Mr. Sinclair, I've come to ask your permission to call on Emily."

Mr. Sinclair paused then stared at a man who wanted to steal his daughter. He said, "Well, I respect Emily's judgment and, if she wants to see you on occasion, I have no objection. However you should be aware, other young men have also asked me for the same opportunity and I've granted it to them as well. Mr. Potter is having dinner with us this very evening. If you're so inclined, you should join the party and make it even more entertaining."

The excitement of being given her father's permission was countermanded by the realization he might already be too late. What did he have to offer? He didn't have a job. He didn't have any money. In fact, his entire family didn't have any money. In comparison to the Potters they were damned poor.

He started off the remainder of the day at the Possum Point Mercantile. A nice elderly lady helped him pick out a new shirt and straw hat. Without any money in his pocket he asked if he could open an account for his dad and was surprised when the lady said his father already had one. The woman looked it up and said his father purchased a purse a few months back, right before Mother's Day. He still owed for it but the shirt was only three-fifty and another two dollars for the hat. She'd add it to the outstanding bill. Jedidiah decided, while she was at it, she should tack on a pair of calfskin riding boots for an additional nine dollars.

Jed shaved that morning but hadn't bathed. Life was just solving one problem after another. He rode his horse to the Buffalo River and walked upstream in the shallows until he came to a secluded spot. He bathed the horse first and then let him graze tethered to a tree close to the bank. Jed had named his tall, silver gelding after Confederate General Robert E. Lee's horse. Traveller knew everything about Jedidiah. Jed might lie to someone else, or even mislead himself, but to Traveller he told it exactly as it was. Somehow, the two of them, with unclouded information, could come up with better solutions to Jed's problems than Jedidiah could by himself. They decided Jed should be polite, answer when questioned, offer opinions on safe subjects, and let Bill continue to dig his hole. He had a pretty good one started the previous Sunday afternoon.

The water was brisk and Jed didn't stay in long. After swimming, he dried off by standing and soaking up the warm November sun. Freshly bathed and with a new shirt, boots, and rakish straw hat, Jedidiah knocked on Emily Sinclair's front door. Silas Sinclair had already informed everyone he had invited Jed to their evening meal. Bill was livid. Mrs. Sinclair and Emily were busy in the kitchen while two little girls set the table. Silas took Jed's hat and invited Bill and Jedidiah into his study while they waited for the meal preparations to be completed.

Mr. Sinclair asked Jedidiah, "Tell me about your job at the sawmill."

"I've only worked there a short while, but it's been interesting. My brothers cautioned me about sawmills being dangerous and it seems a lot of workers are missing fingers. The noise is terrible and sawdust fills the air, so there's plenty of fear of sparks starting a fire. I'm only going to work there a few more days as my father's seeing about getting me an apprenticeship at a cabinet maker's shop."

"You might go see Mr. Morrison, the undertaker," said Bill. "I understand he's looking for someone to make coffins." Bill let out a hearty chuckle.

Mr. Sinclair grimaced and asked, "Bill, how did you spend your summer?"

"Well sir, I certainly didn't have to work." The hole grew deeper.

Jed sat with his back to the door while he listened to Mr. Sinclair and Bill. Instantly he sensed Emily's presence. Drinking in the bouquet of her being, he became intoxicated by her nearness. Standing in the doorway, she announced, "Dinner's ready."

Once they were seated, each person looked to Mr. Sinclair, expecting him to say the blessing. Instead he said, "Mr. Calhoun, would you bless the food?"

Jedidiah looked down, closed his eyes, and prayed. After a moment of silence, Mr. Sinclair said, "I meant aloud, Mr. Calhoun."

Bill laughed. Emily squirmed. The children giggled. Mr. Sinclair cleared his throat. Jedidiah closed his eyes hard and tried to remember his mother's words. Slowly he said, "Dear Lord, our protector and deliverer, our savior, we give thanks for the bounty you have provided. We ask that you be with us, watch over us, and that we are pleasing in your sight. Amen."

There was small talk at the table but Bill was surprisingly quiet. Mr. Sinclair asked Emily how her day went and then turned to Mrs.

Sinclair and commented on what a fine meal she had prepared. Everyone agreed. Mrs. Sinclair blushed.

After the meal, Mr. Sinclair said, "Gentlemen, let's go onto the front porch and discuss politics while the women clear away the food."

When they were seated, Mr. Sinclair lit a cigar. Jed realized the day had slipped away and said, "I'll have to leave soon. It's getting dark and I have a long ride home."

Mr. Sinclair asked, "Do you live close to Dancing Deer, where Bill lives and where his father has his bank?"

"No. I live on a farm about halfway between Possum Point and Dancing Deer."

"If you could wait a few more minutes, the three of us should be able to talk Emily into playing the piano." Mr. Sinclair turned to Bill. "Is your father considering running for the state legislature?"

"Father hasn't said anything about it to me."

"That's odd. I've heard rumors there's soon to be an announcement."

"Father and I are not that close. We seldom talk." The hole grew wider.

Emily played for them and Jedidiah was completely spellbound. Bill talked about going to a piano concert in Little Rock and said Emily's performance was the superior of the two. Jed said it was the most beautiful music he'd heard since he'd listened to her sing in church.

Jedidiah rode Traveller into Dancing Deer the following Monday and asked about any available work. During that winter and through the next spring Jedidiah worked at several jobs in Dancing Deer and the surrounding area. He mucked-out stalls at the livery stable, washed dishes at the local diner, cut railroad timbers, laid brick on the bank's swank new building, and trimmed horses' hooves at the veterinarian's clinic. He couldn't hold on to any one job for long. He did however, save most of what he made. His family couldn't believe the changes that had come over Jed. He was up at daylight every morning. On the days he didn't work, he spent looking for work. No more nights incarcerated in the Marsden County Jail. No more irate neighbors complaining of some stupid prank—like that Halloween when he disassembled a wagon and reassembled it in a hayloft. And no more staying out all night with the town riff-raff. He had actually purchased a Bible. Although he hadn't read anything in it yet, it was showing wear from being hauled around in his saddle bags.

Each Sunday, and occasionally during the week if he needed a rest between jobs, Jed rode Traveller to see Emily. He thought her preacher knew him or at least of him. He couldn't see how, but more than a few of the sermons seemed to be addressed directly toward him or his past behavior. Bill stopped coming around after that first evening and the other men Mr. Sinclair alluded to never materialized.

When Jed finally accumulated the magical number of one hundred dollars he went to Mr. Sinclair. "Sir, I love Emily and would like to ask for her hand in marriage."

"Son, I'll agree with whatever Emily wants. But first, how are you planning on providing for her?" Jed shrugged his shoulders. He stopped just before saying he was buying a wagon and would be selling pots, pans, and bolts of fabric from farm to farm. Jed was trying to stop his lifelong habit of fabricating likely scenarios which never panned out. Instead, he said, "I have a job and a little savings. Whatever else we need, God will provide."

Mr. Sinclair looked at Jed long and hard. He then said, "I might also offer some help. I own a piece of land on Lee Mountain close to Dancing Deer. If you agree, and when you've built my daughter a house on it, you can be wed—allowing of course it's what Emily wants."

Jedidiah was walking on clouds. Mr. Sinclair slapped him on the back and said, "All you've got to do now is convince Emily."

That evening, sitting on the front porch swing and listening to the cicadas, Jed took Emily's hand and gazed into her beautiful face. He said, "I love you, Emily."

Emily looked around to see where her father was. She looked back at Jed and said, "Jedidiah, I know."

Jed expected her to say she loved him as well and he would then easily wind his way into asking her to marry him. Jed wondered if Emily did love him. He opened his mouth to say something and Emily kissed him. Jed had received his answer in a most definite way.

"Jedidiah Carson Calhoun, I love you more than anything in this world."

"I don't have much money." Jed shifted his weight. What's the matter with me? I can get this out. "But if hard work and a desire to provide the best I can mean anything to you, maybe you could take a chance on me."

Emily asked, "Jed, what exactly are you saying?"

"Emily, will you marry me?"

Quite shaken, Emily paused then asked in a faltering voice, "Have you talked to my father?"

"Yes. And he's agreed, as long as it's what you want and on the condition that I first build you a house."

"Then, I will."

Immediately, the door swung open and the entire Sinclair family stepped onto the porch and started hugging the couple. Mrs. Sinclair told Emily they would have a grand time planning the wedding. From this point on Jed was completely out of the picture. The women took over. He had to build their future home and show up on time for the service. That was it. It turned out to be all he could handle.

On a beautiful early summer Sunday, they rode in Mr. Sinclair's car to see the property. A dirt road wound up Lee Mountain. With all the rocks, thinly soiled crevices, and small rivulets of water seeping out between various rock formations, Jedidiah wondered how in the world he could build a house on the side of a mountain. On top, it leveled into a plateau. Two other families already lived there with farms. Mr. Sinclair said each owned eighty acres of flat land on the plateau and more on the adjoining mountainside down to the valley below. He said the land he owned was a hundred acres of flat land at the far end of the plateau and two hundred more on the back side of the mountain. He said the mountain was made primarily of limestone with a few large deposits of shale. A portion of the shale, located on Mr. Sinclair's back side, jutted up like the back of a razorback hog. He called that area the ridgeback.

The dirt road ended at Mr. Sinclair's land. There, under an oiled tarp, sat lumber, nails, shingles, windows, doors, hinges, a few miscellaneous items, and a ladder or two. There was also a large stack of bricks and sacks of mortar for lining the well. They ate cold fried chicken and talked about how the house should be situated and where the barn and privy should go. To Jedidiah and Emily it was heaven. To Mr. and Mrs. Sinclair it would be a place of refuge where they could come and help raise their grandchildren.

That night Jedidiah talked to his brothers. They gave him rudimentary instructions on how to get started. Jedidiah spent the first day marking the house perimeter with sticks and string and beginning the excavation of the well. That evening, Claude asked him about the house's elevation. Would the water flow around it, away from it, or toward it? Would shade trees shelter it from the afternoon sun? Was it facing the east so he could sit on his front porch and watch the sun come up in the morning and be in the shade in the afternoon? Was there a spot behind the house, at a lower elevation, for building the privy? How far was the privy from the well? How about the barn? Was runoff from the barn going to stink up the front porch area? Contaminate the well?

The next day, Jedidiah pulled up his sticks and string and spent the morning pondering the questions Claude had raised. That afternoon, he had it all figured out and re-staked. He spent the rest of the day digging on the well. The second night, Claude asked him if his measurements were square. Claude said a famous Greek mathematician determined that the square of the side opposite a right angle was equal to the square of the two adjacent sides added together. Jedidiah was dumbfounded. How was he going to use this? Rupert came in from outside carrying a triangle he had built from three pieces of lumber. He said to set it in the corners and make the string go down the edges of the wood. With a worried look Jedidiah asked them if they might have a little spare time on Saturday to check his work.

Jedidiah, Rupert, and Claude eventually got their efforts coordinated. Each evening Jedidiah informed his brothers of his progress that day. Rupert and Claude then told Jedidiah what to do on the following day. They drew diagrams, listed steps in the order they wanted them accomplished, and laughed their heads off when they showed up Saturday to check their younger brother's work. They arranged the material into piles. Then they labeled and made a list of what was in each pile. Usually, on Saturday, they had to redo everything Jedidiah had worked on during the week. Eventually, Jedidiah caught on. After eight months they finished the house to their satisfaction.

Emily had other ideas and it took the three men another two months before she was satisfied.

Mr. Sinclair said it was a wonderful house but a little small. Mrs. Sinclair said she liked it but wondered why the well was in the front yard. The children thought it had a marvelous privy—a two-seater.

On a pleasant Saturday evening in April of 1921, Emily became Mrs. Jedidiah Calhoun. Over a hundred people attended the wedding. Bill didn't show. They had a shivaree where a large retinue of well-wishers accompanied Jedidiah as he pushed Emily from house to house in a wheelbarrow. Each house deposited canned goods or some kitchen implement into the wheelbarrow with Emily. Eventually, they had to quit. Jed was tired, the crowd was getting rowdy, and the wheelbarrow was full. They were both ready to go to their new home.

In early June of the year 1920, Bill heard that Emily and Jedidiah were engaged. He sequestered himself in his bedroom and wouldn't eat or bathe. He'd always been given everything he wanted. Now all he wanted was Emily. To his way of thinking a country idiot had stepped in and stolen her. No one before had ever been able to keep from him anything he really wanted. Jed would pay.

Rumor had it that Bill's dad, who owned not only the bank but a lot of everything else located in Marsden County, lost his temper with his son's inability to come to grips with the situation and sent him on retreat to a monastery near Fort Smith. With the help of some concerned monks, Bill pulled himself together. He learned how to meditate, how to apportion his time, how to determine what was important, how to set goals, and how to concentrate his efforts to achieve whatever important goal he had set. The monks worried over Bill. Thinking they were ineffective in bringing harmony and balance to a troubled soul, they tried desperately to instill Christian ethical and moral values before they lost him altogether. But Bill became separate and independent. He decided he could take care of himself and kept his emotions, his ambitions, and his feelings bottled up. He festered with hatred toward Jed and was rude to the monks when they tried to pry into his inner battles.

Bill's father sent him from the monastery to a college back east. Getting a girl pregnant, he married during his sophomore year. Three years later he graduated with a business degree. He settled in with his eastern in-laws only to return to Dancing Deer to take over his father's bank on his death. Bill came back leading a daughter and dragging a reluctant wife.

Bill's wife only tolerated the loneliness of small-town, rural America for a month before she packed up and escaped. Bill was glad to be shed of her but now he had a young daughter to raise by himself. He thought of Emily constantly.

Over the next few years, Jedidiah never did get a steady job. He made what little money he needed by breaking horses to pull a plow or a wagon and hewing railroad timbers. He sold the horses to the Army. The timbers he sold to the railroad that went through Russellville. After a year of marriage Emily told Jed she was pregnant. On April 25, 1923, Emily gave birth to a beautiful blond-haired, blue-eyed boy. They named him David Blaine Calhoun. Three more children, all little girls, followed. Emily had Jed prepare a big garden which she tended each year to feed her growing family. She also had Jedidiah dig a root cellar where she stored the potatoes and other produce needing to be kept in a dark, moist place. They had a wonderful life and not much money, but it's not money that provides happiness and what does was in wealthy abundance.

CHAPTER 2—TRAVELLER

Lee Mountain, Arkansas - Early Spring 1933

Jedidiah opened the screen door and carried his coffee and a letter onto the front porch. His family was still asleep and would be for another hour. He looked over the grassy area, past the hand-dug well, toward the woods. A misty fog enveloped his farm, giving everything it touched a wet and baleful appearance. Removing his son's book from his rocking chair, Jed settled in. He looked at the envelope. It was from the First Bank and Trust of Dancing Deer. He set his coffee cup on the rocking chair arm and removed the folded letter. It was a short note on letterhead stationery. It said, Jed, I need to see you. and was signed, Bill.

Just a few years back Jed knew he'd been a good-for-nothing drunkard and a liar. His dad patronized him, his mother protected him, and his brothers fought his battles for him. There hadn't been anything for him to do, so mostly he stayed in trouble. But now—well, just look at him now. He owned a chunk of land on a mountaintop, he was married to a wonderful woman, he had a brood of hard-working children, and not an enemy in the world except Bill. What could Bill possibly want?

Jedidiah thought about saddling up his new stallion. Traveller was getting along in years and wasn't as spry as he used to be. But then again, Jedidiah wasn't in any hurry and Traveller had been his steed of choice these many years.

Soon after breakfast, Jedidiah whistled and Traveller's head raised, his ears twitched, and he trotted over to Jed expecting a green persimmon or a lump of sugar. When Jed slid on the bridle and talked to him in the soft, affectionate manner that was his style, the horse started prancing about, pawing at the dirt. He couldn't wait to get started. It didn't matter where they were going, what time of day it was, or what the weather was like. He and Jed were heading out and Traveller was excited with anticipation.

Jedidiah slipped a red Navajo blanket on Traveller's back and slung on a hand-rubbed, oiled saddle. He then put the stirrup on the saddle horn and cinched it up. Traveller took a gulp of air. He held it as Jedidiah tightened the cinch. Jedidiah lowered the stirrup and eased into the saddle.

As they left the confines of the barn, Jedidiah waved at the children, Traveller exhaled and Jedidiah, holding onto the saddle horn, slowly slid with the saddle down Traveller's side. He tumbled into a puddle of water. The children thought their daddy did it on purpose. They laughed and giggled and, between squeals, suggested one of them fetch Mrs. Miller's carriage. Jedidiah was now sitting in a small pool of standing water. Traveller nuzzled him in the face. Jedidiah had all day to figure some prank to play on Traveller in retaliation. Traveller knew something would happen but didn't know what or when. Jedidiah and Traveller had acted this way toward each other since Jedidiah's dad gave him the gelding on his sixteenth birthday. They were two buddies out exploring and having one adventure after another.

Jedidiah repositioned the saddle, tightened the cinch strap, and went inside to change clothes. He was going to meet with Bill Potter, the county's wealthiest man, and thought he should be somewhat presentable. Emily didn't have to be told. While he was locating another pair of trousers, the children located their mom and supplied her with all the information she needed. She came into the bedroom and asked Jed how he'd soiled his pants.

Jedidiah laughed and said, "As of right now, its one-to-nothing, Traveller."

"It's a good thing you came back to the house because I've prepared a small list of things we need from the mercantile. Also, if you'll bring me and David Blaine a book each from the library, you'll be properly rewarded."

"What kind of reward?"

"That'll be my surprise."

Life is full of unexpected pleasures and having a little fun in a relationship is one of them. Jed finished changing his clothes, took the list, and headed outside.

When Jed had first gone in for new trousers, Balder, Jed's big coon hound, ran out to Traveller. He wanted to play pull-the-dog. If Traveller had his bridle on, Balder would get a good grip on the reins with his teeth. He would then sit down and lean back. With Traveller walking backwards and turning in fast circles, Balder would slide all over the pasture, sometimes getting airborne. The children marveled at the two animals playing and usually brought out a piece of slick tarp for Balder to sit on in the grass. If provided with the tarp, Traveller could get going pretty fast before Balder would go sprawling. Then they'd stop, get re-situated, and do it again. After a few minutes Balder would be so dizzy he couldn't stand up. If the kids weren't around to supply the tarp, the grass and occasional weed rubbed the hair off Balder's rear-end—hence the name. The game ended with a dizzy dog that somehow had to find the house so he could recover under the porch for a spell. Besides Jed, Balder was Traveller's best friend and they bunked together in the barn during inclement weather.

When Jed stepped off the porch, Traveller came prancing up, full of himself, and ready to tackle with Jed whatever the world could throw. They were a team and there wasn't anywhere they couldn't go or any problem they couldn't solve. When they reached the back side of the front gate, Traveller used his teeth to take hold of the leather strap hanging from the sliding board locking the gate. He pulled it to the right. Unlocked, a spring and a weight on the end of a rope opened the gate wide enough for a carriage to pass through. Traveller backed up from the opening gate. He then turned to the right facing the gate's open front side. Traveller took hold of a second leather strap and pulled the gate shut as he backed through the opening. He then slid the board to the right again, locking it. All Jed's gates were made in the same manner and Traveller could go anywhere he pleased. Jed had originally designed the gate at his father's farm a few years earlier and, riding home from Emily's, he often dozed while Traveller loped in. He'd wake with Traveller pawing the watering trough. Five minutes later he had the bridle and saddle off and himself in bed. It was up to Traveller to figure his way into the barn.

Jed even had a feeding contraption set up so all Traveller had to do was hit a sock bag with his muzzle and a lever would drop a portion of sorghum-based sweet feed into a bin. Jedidiah was afraid Traveller would overeat and founder so he added small pieces of spinach leaves and stems to the sweet feed. Traveller could take just so much spinach. He never once foundered.

When Jedidiah and Traveller reached Dancing Deer, Jed was astonished at how many cars there were. "Traveller, it wasn't so long ago that everyone rode horses or traveled in carriages pulled by horses. The automobile was only a curiosity. Now, just about everyone has one. What's your take on the matter?"

Maybe he should get with the program. Compared with a lot of people he was doing pretty good. Times were hard right then with unemployment at record levels. Even his brothers had trouble finding steady work. But he had a way with horses and a ready market when they were trained to drag or haul something. He also hewed railroad timbers but that was hard work and he preferred making money with horses.

Jed came into town occasionally to cash checks or to get supplies. He didn't have a bank account. He didn't want Bill Potter to have a hold on his money. Instead, he cashed his payment checks and took the currency home to Emily. She was good with money and if he didn't see it, couldn't find it, and didn't know if it was even there, he was better off.

Jed took Traveller to the livery stable where he instructed the man in charge to give the tall grey gelding a section of alfalfa and to curry his coat. Jed then headed to the bank. Once Bill was informed that Jed had arrived, he came striding through his office door with his hand outstretched. Jed was surprised at Bill's demeanor. Jed offered his hand in return and followed Bill into a plush office filled with comfortable, overstuffed leather wingbacks. There were pictures of Bill shaking hands with important-looking people, pictures of men in long narrow row boats, trophies with Bill's name engraved, a signed baseball, and other trivialities Jed filed away as things unimportant.

Bill said, "Jed, I'm so glad you came. I know how you like horses and I have an opportunity for you that needs attention as soon as possible."

"How's your little girl, Bill? I guess she must be about ten or twelve by now."

"Oh yes, well, she's ten, the same age as your son, David Blaine. They're in the same class. She says he's always getting into trouble. Do you Calhouns have the market cornered on orneriness?"

"Yes, as a matter of fact, we do. I portion it out each morning with the oatmeal."

"Jed, I know you and I haven't seen eye to eye over the years but I truly believe that right now we both can benefit each other. Much as I'd like to talk about our families, I'd rather get the business out of the way first."

Jed stared at the man he had contended with in his courtship of Emily.

Bill continued. "I've foreclosed on a farm that had a herd of a hundred and ten horses. The farmer's fallen on hard times for two years running and this last winter he barely had enough resources to feed his family. His horses suffered and I'm afraid if I don't find someone fast to take them off my hands I'm going to lose the whole herd. I don't know anything about horses other than as collateral. I was hoping I could make you a bargain-basement price and you, with your ability at animal husbandry, and with a ready market, could turn a handsome profit. We both benefit."

"Bill, in case you haven't noticed, people are buying cars. A horse is only a plaything. And, I haven't got a ready market. If I bought the horses from you it would only be because I couldn't stand to see an animal mistreated. Besides, if the horses are in such a sad state I don't know if I want to be saddled with the responsibility."

"Well, Jed, let's put the pencil to it and see what happens. Say I sell you the horses for $40 each. You fatten them up on your pasture this summer, break as many as you can to work, and sell a third of them—no, let's make that 40, all colts or geldings—to the Army before winter for $120 each. Your cost would be $40 times 100. I'm going to throw in the extra 10 for free. That equals $4,000. So you pay me $4,000. Now let's see, you sell 40 horses at $120 each to the Army. So they pay you $4,800. That makes $800 profit in your pocket and you've got 70 brood mares free and clear to breed to that new stallion. I can't see how you can go wrong."

Jed countered with, "Well, let's try this on for size. I pay you $4,000 for 110 horses, I'm out $20 each in vet bills, half the horses die anyway, and the Army pays me the going rate of $100 per horse. Let's see, that's $4,000 for you, $2,200 for the vet, and $5,500 for me. By my calculations I lose $700 out of my pocket and half a year busting my butt."

"I see your point. How about I alleviate some of your concerns? You don't have to pay me until you dispose of them. I'll pay for a vet to come out and for any medicine he thinks they need. I'll even see to it that you get 50 pounds of sweet feed per horse from the Livery Feed and Seed. And I'll give you credit of the $40 purchase price, for any horse that dies from the long-term effects of nearly starving to death this past winter. Except for the first 10 I'm giving you as a fudge factor."

"Bill, I'd agree to that if the Army was actually paying me the $120 you think. But the truth of the matter is the going rate is $100 per horse."

"Yes, I know the going rate's $100 per horse, but the Army pays you more because you do such a good job." When he said this he pulled from his desk drawer a bound journal. He flipped it open and the top page had a series of dates in the first column and dollar amounts in the second.

"Let me read off these amounts of government checks you cashed during the last three years: $600, $700, $500, $900, $1,100 and then the price they paid you per horse changed and your checks are $480, $960, and $840. Since these are all for sales of horses. That is all you sell to the Army, isn't it? And no half or quarter of horses are sold, then all these amounts have to be divisible by the dollar amount you're paid per horse. At first you were paid $100 per horse then you either got an increase to $120 or a decrease to $60. And since the going rate almost everywhere for a horse trained to work is $100 they must be paying you more since your horses are so well trained."

Jed threw up his hands in defeat and said, "May I see the horses first?"

"Sure thing. There are fifteen at the livery right now. The rest are in the same condition. When I had these brought in I told the wrangler not to pick and choose but to be random in his selection. And, since I'm now the Marsden County Republican Party Chairman, the County Agricultural Extension Agent owes me. If it's all right with you, he'll be the one checking the animals. That way I get a break on the labor and on the meds.

"If you like them I'll need both you and Emily to sign the contract. It's not that I don't trust you, but I believe Emily handles the purse strings in your family and she'll be the one making payment. Besides, that lets me come out and see Emily and your son, David Blaine. Can I bring Rose? She's never met Emily."

"That's fine with me, Bill—unless I come back after seeing the horses and tell you differently. How about this Friday, say around five in the afternoon? That way you can find out what a great cook Emily is. We can eat, sign the papers, and you and your daughter can be back at just about dark. Now, if you'll excuse me, I'll go see what kind of mess I've gotten myself in."

Jed was expecting fifteen pathetic and emaciated horses but what he saw were horses that had lost a little weight and weren't sickly at all. He found the livery man and asked, "Pardon me. Who brought these horses in?"

"I did. Potter bought the Livery Feed and Seed a few months back. Now I work for him. These are his horses."

"Well, I understand they're part of a larger herd. Are the rest in the same shape?"

"Yeah. They're all a mite underweight. I think they'll soon be back up to speed if they're put on good pasture. Potter told me not be choosy, just to bring in fifteen average horses."

Jedidiah went by the library and told the woman at the counter, the same woman his brother Rupert had recently taken to a political rally on the town square, that he wanted to pick up a book for his wife and another for his son. She had done this before. She said if he could give her a few minutes she'd pick out something they'd like. Jed said he had other errands and he'd be back in an hour. From the Mercantile he got the few things Emily couldn't grow or make herself and then had a meal in a restaurant on Main Street.

He thought, with all the money he was going to make, he might buy Emily a pickup truck. The only worry he had was that Bill seemed so much in charge. Jed liked to control any situation he was in but right now all the feeling of control he could muster was nothing compared to the suffocating nausea he felt about the whole situation. Bill would never finish on the short end of any financial deal. What was he missing? The horses looked good. He wouldn't have to pay for any that died, free vet service, almost three tons of sweet feed, no payments until he had a cash buyer, ten free horses. Interest? They hadn't discussed interest. Bill was going to have them sign a contract with an interest rate so high Bill would end with all their profits. Well, they wouldn't sign until they knew what the interest rate was and if there was an early payback penalty.

On the way home, Jed was wrapped in his thoughts. At every sound Traveller shied. Jed responded with, "Easy boy," or "Calm down, Traveller. Why you so fidgety?"

Traveller didn't know what or when so every deviation from what was normal made him think this was it, this was Jed getting back. What he hadn't figured out was that it wasn't Jed; it was Bill who was retaliating. Bill had set a plan in motion that would pay Jed back for all the misery he'd caused. Bill was the adversary and he wasn't playing.

The next day Jed talked it over with Emily. She thought it was a good idea. Emily could only see the good in people. Bill wouldn't try to harm her or Jed. He was a fine man—just not the man for her. She looked forward to seeing Bill again and finally meeting his daughter.

That afternoon Jed hitched his two mules to a sod-busting "grasshopper" plow. He planned on adding another plot to Emily's garden. Normally he used only one mule and a smaller moldboard plow but today he was breaking new ground and wanted to dig as deep as possible. The mules were stubborn though and would only work if they wanted to, a work ethic not unlike Jed's. Quite often they just stood in their harnesses trying to wait Jed out. They knew Jed wouldn't harm them and, if he was all bluster, they had the upper hand. One time Jed dangled a carrot from the end of a stick. Mordichai wasn't interested but Melchizedek loved carrots better than anything and pulled the plow by himself, dragging Mordichai along as well. After two dozen carrots the novelty wore off and both mules balked again. This time Jed got off the plow and whispered something in each mule's ear. That got them listening but not moving. As a last resort, Jed built a small fire under Mordichai. It was only a few minutes before the kindling was giving a good account of itself, but Mordichai was a tall mule and in full harness so he simply adjusted a bit. Jed added more kindling. He'd get something going now. When the flame got high enough to singe Mordichai's nether region, the mule jerked to the side and pulled forward four feet. This put the fire inches in front of the plow. Jed was standing astraddle the plow but turned backwards while he watered the ground. He didn't realize what had happened. It looked like the mules, or at least one mule, was starting to move, albeit a bit crooked. He kept from falling by reaching back and using his free hand to grab the plow handle. It was only a moment before he realized his situation. Damn, you can't even eat mule.

Emily watched from the back porch and came bustling over. "I smelled something burning. What's happening?" She appeared to look around then continued with, "I've brought a bucket of water. If there's not any fire, would you like a drink?"

Jed sat on the plow and said, "Woman, knowest thou not, these beasts of burden have caused me to burn my britches?"

Emily replied, "O Grand Sovereign, I do beseech thee, please to let me have the britches that I may relieve you of your pain and suffering."

Jed removed his trousers with great solemnity and said, "Let it be done."

Emily sat the bucket down, snatched up the trousers, and hurried back to the house.

Jed started to drink the water and thought he might offer some to the mules. They probably were as thirsty as he. Jedidiah held the bucket first to Mordichai then to Melchezidek. Both mules drank long and hard. In fact, when the mules were finished the bucket was finished. Jed went back to plowing and the mules moved off, but at a slow pace.

"That's why I love plowing with you guys. You know just how much effort to put out."

"Quite right you are, Jedidiah." Jed looked up to see his neighbor, Mrs. Miller. She said, "In my dealings with mules I've found they only work hard in the mornings and in the evenings. Mules, you see, are smarter than horses. They know it's too hot to work in the middle of the day." She paused, and then said, "I'll bet if you wait until an hour or so before sunset the mules will pull you and that big plow all over this field. Not necessarily in a straight line, mind you. They'll be under the inaccurate assumption you can't see as good as they and, without their keen eyesight, you won't know if you're going in a straight line or not. They retain the upper hand that way and, once again, prove the mule is the superior animal.

"Jedidiah, do you really think it's too hot to wear pants? Your pretty little wife told me you think it's too hot for pants but not too hot to plow."

On Friday afternoon, Bill and Rose drove their shiny new silver and grey Pierce Arrow roadster to see Emily—and Jedidiah, of course. Bill had made inquiries and found exactly where they lived. He had no problem negotiating the rural dirt roads until he got to the winding road up Lee Mountain. A spring shower earlier in the day left the road slippery with ruts where the runoff, from years of rain, had eaten away part of the road base. Rose was frightened when the road got near a steep drop-off. Bill was an experienced driver and wasn't in the least bit worried. He just hated to get mud on what he thought was something that would impress Emily.

At the front gate Bill made Rose get out and open it. She was mumbling something unintelligible when she accidentally stepped into a pile of something wet that completely sucked in a black patent leather shoe. She got back into the car wearing one shoe and holding the other. She didn't say anything to her dad. Bill sniffed the air, figured out what had happened, and decided not to pursue the matter. They simply ignored the earthy odor.

When they arrived at Jed and Emily's house, Rose removed the remaining shoe and left both on the porch. She put her socks inside a pocket. After introducing Rose, Bill pulled out a sheaf of papers and asked if they could get the paperwork out of the way so they could talk about where life had taken them since the last time they had been together.

"Bill, we never did discuss the interest rate."

"What would you be comfortable with, Jed?"

"Two percent."

"Jed, the prime interest rate is now at four. That's the lowest the bank goes to its very best customers—those we've had extensive dealings with and the same ones with sizable collateral. But, I'll agree to charge you the prime rate, simple? I want to sell the horses. I'm not all that interested in profiting the bank."

"What's the term of the loan?"

"Let's make it for four years. That way if you only sell a few head the first year you'll be able to pay $1,000 on the principal and $160 in interest. The next year you would need to sell a few more head, pay $1,000 on the principal and $120 interest. The third and fourth years would be a similar principal payment of $1,000 and the interest would decline to $80 and $40. If you decided to sell more head there wouldn't be any penalty if you used the extra money to make an early payoff."

Bill pulled out several legal-sized documents and pointed to where he had included the changes they had discussed in his office.

It was at this moment that David Blaine entered the house and said Balder had dragged something dead onto the porch.

"What do you think it was?" Jed asked.

"I couldn't tell. I just got a stick and heaved it into the woods."

"Was it right by the front door?" asked Rose.

"As a matter of fact, it was."

"Would you be so kind as to show me where you threw it? I think it might have been one of my shoes. I stepped in something by the gate and didn't want to bring the smell into your mother's house."

David said, "Oh no! I saw Balder get it and carry it toward the barn."

"David Blaine, you better fetch it for Rose. Clean it up and then bring it inside the house."

"Yes, sir."

After David left, Bill asked Jed, "Do you have any questions? We can pencil in anything you want added to the contract."

"No. I think you've been more than fair about the entire thing. Just show me and Emily where to sign."

"Jed, you and Emily will have to come into the bank sometime this week and sign so we can get your signatures notarized. However, we can shake hands on the deal."

Emily and Jed shook Bill's hand as he congratulated them on their purchase. He told them they were now the biggest horse traders in the entire county.

During the meal, Emily asked Rose if she had planned on auditioning with the drama department for the upcoming school play. She and Jed had been putting up with David Blaine reciting different soliloquies from *Hamlet* for days.

In a resonating voice Jed boomed, "A thought, which quartered, hath but one part wisdom and ever three parts coward—I do not know why yet I live to say, 'This thing's to do.'"

Emily looked at Jed, "I think we've had quite enough fun at David's expense." She added, "He's serious about getting the part and we've been pretty childish in our kidding."

"Oh, I agree," replied Jed. "But he's taking it well. I did promise to listen to his lines. Lately, he's been reciting to Balder."

Rose said, "I've been thinking about auditioning but haven't found a piece to recite."

Bill put his arm around Rose's shoulder, "Honey, you never told me about any play. Where can I get you one of those speeches? Will you need a tutor?" asked Bill.

Emily said, "There are several parts for female leads in the books David got from the library. After we finish the meal I'll help you pick one. I don't think you have enough time to have something sent."

There were not enough chairs for everyone to eat at the same time so David, Charlotte, and their two sisters ate earlier and now the girls waited in the living room for the adults to finish. They would then clean off the table and do the dishes. Charlotte had homework and was planning on retiring to their bedroom just as soon as the dishes were done, but the other two girls wanted to stay and listen to the grownups talk.

David Blaine came in holding two shiny black shoes. "Balder had the one he hauled off in his bed but he hadn't chewed on it. He likes collecting things that smell bad. I'll set them beside the front door."

Rose noticed he was holding them at a distance from his nose. Everyone traded places. The girls in the front room went to the eating area and the grownups went to the front room, including David Blaine and Rose. With so many women in the family, David never had to do anything in the kitchen. Emily and Rose got down on the living room rug and scanned David Blaine's books. Rose picked a reply Ophelia had made to her father's inquiry about her tears. The audition piece in question happened moments after Hamlet had left a chance meeting with Ophelia and her father had appeared. *Hamlet* suggested, while faking insanity, that Ophelia get herself to a nunnery.

Rose silently read the speech a couple of times then asked, "Dad, may I read it aloud?"

Before Bill could respond Emily said, "Please, Rose, we'd love to hear it."

David Blaine listened and, when Rose finished, was about to give his critical appraisal when his mother gave him a stare that made him steer clear. Soon after, Bill and Rose left and Jedidiah's life was fast approaching a bend in the road.

The following Monday Emily and Jed signed the contract and on Tuesday and Wednesday the horses were delivered. On Monday morning of the following week Stanley Muldaur, the Marsden County Agricultural Extension Agent, came by to look at the horses. He walked from the gate straight to the barn, looked at Traveller, and then found the large stall with attached paddock where the black stallion was kept. The stallion was in his paddock, soaking up the sun. Stanley sat his satchel on the ground and softly whistled. The big black strolled into his stall. Stanley looked toward the barn opening then gave the stallion a lump of sugar coated with a green substance. The horse ate it and nuzzled Stanley for more. Stanley patted the horse's forehead and said, "There isn't any more, big fella. I think one will be plenty."

In a few minutes the stallion started getting drowsy. He leaned against the fence panel that made up his front stall wall and felt a pin prick but was too sleepy to do anything about it. Stanley squatted to put away the syringe. He heard a low growl and looked nose to nose into the snarling face of a big black dog. Startled, Stanley lost his balance, dropped the syringe, and fell backward against the stall wall. Grabbing the medicine satchel and holding it between him and the monster dog, he slowly got to his feet. He talked softly hoping the ugly brute wouldn't attack. Stanley held the medicine satchel in front, much like a lion trainer would use a chair, and cursed the dog under his breath while backing out of the barn. Balder followed, keeping Muldaur within striking distance. With his head low to the ground Balder emitted a guttural growl that made the hair on Stanley's neck stand on end. When

Stanley reached the house, Balder turned and went back to the barn. After sniffing the syringe he pawed at it until the cylindrical tube rolled under a large work table.

Stanley knocked on the door and asked Emily if he could speak with Jed. She went to a back window and yelled to a man plowing with a team of mules. In a minute, Jed came in and he and Stanley Muldaur headed to the barn. Jed had been told to keep the delivered horses penned up until Stanley could make it out, so Jed put them in the big riding arena attached to, and just behind, the barn. He filled their galvanized water tank twice a day and once a day spread two dozen bales of hay. A large portion of his day was spent raking up their droppings.

Stanley looked them over and said they probably needed worming, but otherwise, they looked healthy to him. Jed agreed and was glad the worming was going to be covered by the contract. For the next two hours, Stanley gave each a shot and a dollop of something from a tube he inserted halfway down each horse's throat. Then, as he was putting his equipment away, he said, "I have enough worming medicine to do a few more horses. It'll just go to waste now that the packaging's been opened. Do you have any of your other horses you'd like wormed free of charge?"

Jed said, "My stallion and riding horse are in the barn. I have others but they're out to pasture."

Both men looked down as Balder came racing up growling at Stanley. Jed grabbed Balder by the nap of his neck and scolded him. Stanley followed Jed and an agitated Balder into the barn. The stallion was down. When Jed saw the black mass in a heap on the stall floor he let loose of Balder and broke out in a full run. He was in the stall with his prize stallion in seconds. Stanley followed, swinging his satchel to keep Balder at bay. At his first opportunity Stanley looked around for the lost syringe. It wasn't in sight. He'd look again in a few days.

Stanley reached the stall, leaned down, and said, "Here, let me have a look."

"He's only been a recent purchase. He was in perfect health until today."

"I'm sorry, sir. I'm not a vet. I mainly just worm and treat minor sores and abrasions. Do you have a regular vet?"

Jed nodded and gave him the name.

Stanley said, "I'll go see him as soon as I get into town. I'll tell him to come out this afternoon."

Jed thanked Stanley. He and Balder stayed with the stallion all day. During that time the big horse rallied and was standing when the vet arrived. He looked dazed but Jed was sure it was only temporary. The big black horse would be as good as new in a day or two.

The vet took a blood sample and the horse's temperature. He examined his mouth and tongue, his hooves, and a stool sample. He said he didn't know what happened to the horse but he'd send the blood off for analysis. He'd know something by next week. He suggested Jed keep the new horses penned up until the blood analysis came back.

On the following Monday morning, Emily heard a knock on the front screen door. It was the Marsden County Sheriff. Inside, Emily asked if he'd like a cup of coffee. The sheriff plopped his large frame down at the kitchen table, took the coffee, and handed her a sheet of paper. It was a legal document from the county judge.

"Mrs. Calhoun, the blood sample from your husband's stallion tested positive for hoof and mouth disease. A state health inspector, a bulldozer, and a team of national guardsmen are right behind me. We've got to slaughter your livestock." He took a sip of coffee. "That there's a court order. I'm sorry Mrs. Calhoun. Is your husband around? I'd like to take you somewhere while they do what's necessary."

"I can't believe this. You have to kill our animals because one horse has a disease?"

"Yes, ma'am. It's highly contagious. Yours is the first case we've had in Marsden County. The health guy said it's almost been eradicated. I didn't see your husband outside. Is he in town?"

"No. He's tending his orchard down by the creek. Here, I've got some biscuits and pear preserves from breakfast. Oh, and a few strips of bacon. Why don't you eat a bite while I go get him."

Jed baited his hook with a juicy night crawler. "Balder, you're supposed to wake me up when the bobber goes under. We've already talked about this." He tossed the line back into the slow moving creek and stuck the end of the cane pole into the soft dirt on the bank. "All right, now pay attention this time."

Emily found them. Jed lay on the grassy bank with his straw hat covering his face and Balder sat on the edge of the creek staring at a round cork bobber with a red painted stick extending into the air from its middle. "Jed, get up. You've got to go find Traveller. You don't have much time."

"Be quiet, woman. Balder and I are fishing. You want to scare off supper?"

"Jed, get up. That black stallion has hoof and mouth and the county sheriff says our stock has to be killed."

"What?"

"He's at the house right now with a court order. He says some national guardsmen will be here any minute and they're going to kill all the animals. You've got to find Traveller and hide him. We can live without the rest, but Traveller's different."

Jed was up. "They're not going to kill our horses."

"Darling, I don't think you can stop him. He has a court order. Just save Traveller."

Jed paced back and forth. "This is terrible. Of course you're right, as always." He thought for a moment then said, "I'll bet he's over on that meadow I just sprigged. But the only outside gate we got's up to the house. Exactly where is the sheriff?"

"I left him sitting in the kitchen eating the rest of your breakfast."

"Well, go back and keep him company, and away from the windows, while I take Traveller out the gate and down the road to Mrs. Miller's."

Jed and Balder were off like orphans after a found toy. They located Traveller in the pasture eating what Jed had just planted. "Traveller, boy, I'm going to ride you bareback without a bridle. We got to get you hid."

Jed grabbed hold of Traveller's mane and jumped. However, he couldn't get high enough for his foot to clear Traveller's back. On his second effort, he jumped head first and, when he had crawled up half way, he dragged his leg up and over, and then sat up. Holding on to

Traveller's mane, Jed gave him a jab in his flank and off they flew. When they were within sight of the house, Jed spied the sheriff's car in front and another car pulling up to the gate.

"Traveller we're going to have to go over the fence. Think you're up to it?" Jed kicked Traveller again. Soon he was leaning forward whispering to his best friend, both fists holding tight to the flying silver mane. When they reached the fence, instead of going over, Traveller turned and headed alongside. Jed pulled back to slow Traveller. When they came to a complete stop, Jed made Traveller look at the fence.

"We've got to jump right here. Come on, boy. You can do it." Jed made Traveller back off for a second try. This time when they came to the fence they were traveling at a slow lope. Traveller gauged his approach and gracefully cleared the fence with inches to spare. When he came down on the other side, he landed in the ditch beside the road and stumbled. Jed fell off. He landed hard, half in the ditch and half on the road.

Dazed, Jed sat up as the sheriff approached. "Nice try. I thought you might do some fool stunt like that. Now get up and get in the squad car."

The sheriff walked alongside Jed, with Traveller and Balder following close behind. Emily held her skirt and walked as fast as she could toward the front gate.

Beside the gate, Jed asked the sheriff if he could talk to his horse for a minute. The sheriff looked askance at Jed and then said, "Oh, why not."

Jed stroked Traveller's head between his ears and walked over a piece. The two animals followed. Emily got to the gate out of breath and saw Jed a few paces toward the barn talking to Traveller, his head inches from Traveller's. Balder was at Jed's feet with his head tilted at an angle. Moments later Jed turned and, with tears streaming down his face, walked toward the sheriff. To the amazement of the sheriff, Traveller turned and slowly walked in the direction of the barn.

The sheriff put Jed in the back seat of his cruiser and Balder on the front passenger's floorboard. He told Emily to go pack enough clothes for her and her family to spend a couple of days away. He said a man shouldn't have to watch his horse being put down.

"What's going to happen to them?" asked Jed.

"The guardsmen are going to shoot 'em—each with one bullet to the head. It'll be done as humanely as possible. Then the bulldozer operator will find a depression in the pasture and increase its breadth, width, and depth. Their carcasses will be moved to the hole dug by the big machine, diesel fuel will be poured over them, and they'll be burned, then covered over and packed down with lime and then dirt."

When Emily returned with a sack of clothes, the sheriff asked where he should take them. Jed's family lived down the mountain and up the road a few miles so that's where they headed. The car at the front gate was waiting for them to leave and, when they passed, Jed noticed it had a driver up front and two men in the back seat. One of the men in the back seat was Stanley Muldaur. Jed wondered why he was there but let it pass. Down the road, Jed looked back at his farm. He thought of the day his father walked over to him trying to pull a spirited silver gelding. The horse was prancing around with his head held high pulling back on the reins. He hadn't been broke to ride and didn't much care to be led anywhere. He snorted with displeasure and reared onto his hind legs. Yanking on the reins, Jed's father said the horse was a little wild but was still young and not yet trained. They'd have to learn the art of horsemanship together. After Jed had calmly retrieved the reins and talked in a low voice, the gelding's ears perked up. The horse sensed that nothing bad was going to happen and let Jed run a hand down his neck and chest. He kept a wary eye. After a few minutes, the gelding calmed down and was easily led around the front yard. Jed and his silver gelding formed a mutual trust that first day. Now, Jed had betrayed that trust. He'd let Traveller down. Jed had never felt so distraught. Things could never be the same.

Halfway down the mountain they met a truck pulling a flat bed trailer carrying a bulldozer. The truck driver flicked his cigarette as he moved to the edge of the road to let the sheriff's car pass. Behind the dozer came a second truck carrying five soldiers under a canvas cover. The guardsmen had rifles.

Balder had never ridden in an automobile. He hunkered down, shaking. By the time they got to the bottom of the mountain, Balder appeared sick. The sheriff suggested they leave Balder tied to a tree. Jed could come back later with a pail of water and a bowl of food. He'd be okay for a day or so.

Jed tied Balder under a shade tree with a length of rope supplied by the sheriff. He told Balder to lie down. He'd be back in a couple of hours.

As soon as the car drove out of sight, Balder got to his feet. He pulled on the rope with his teeth until it came loose. He then started back up the mountain at a fast trot.

The stallion was shot in his stall. The murderer gave a cursory look around but Traveller had walked out of his stall when he heard the man first approach. He was a few steps into his paddock. When the man left, Traveller walked back into his stall. He lowered his head and grabbed the leather strap on the stall gate and slid it to the right. He walked into the grooming area. All the new horses were still penned at the back of the barn in the big riding arena. Jed's remaining horses were led from the largest of Jed's pastures and placed in the riding arena. Traveller heard a shot, then another shot, and another. He stood beside the only stall that opened to the riding arena and saw the horses in a mass state of confusion. On the far back edge of the fence, assassins had climbed and were killing one horse at a time. The horses reared up, then ran in a big circle, not knowing what to do. The assassins sat on the fence shooting them, especially the ones who, in their confusion ran near the fence. It wasn't long before the horses started tripping over the carcasses of those shot.

Balder heard the shooting in the distance. He increased his speed and ran as swiftly as he had ever run, barely slowing down to slide under the gate. He charged for the barn.

Stanley Muldaur had come to make sure Jed was out of business and to find his lost syringe. While the health inspector helped gather Jed's other horses and shove them into the riding arena, Stanley thought he had the rest of the day, so he combed through the house first. He was looking for anything that could be used in a criminal trial against Jed if the occasion should arise. Of course, if he found anything of value he'd have to confiscate it. He thought he'd found a treasure when he spied a hidden wooden box. It was small and well crafted. It took him over a minute to figure out how to get it open. Except for an old piece of yellowed lace, it was empty. He threw the box across the room and went looking for the syringe.

He had almost reached the barn when Balder jumped him from the back. The dog hadn't barked or growled—just viciously attacked. Stanley fought back, but it was a losing battle. The dog was at his throat. Stanley got his arms around the big dog's neck but that was a mistake. Balder then attacked his face. Stanley screamed. The dog tore off his large bulbous nose and was working on an ear when a National Guardsman heard Stanley and shot Balder. The soldier jumped down from astraddle the fence and ran to Stanley. Kicking the dog away, he helped Stanley to his feet. Balder heard the soldier talking but was too weak to move. The state health inspector cleaned the wound and suggested they take Stanley to the hospital in town. The driver and the state health inspector loaded Stanley into the car.

Two other soldiers walked over and looked at the dog. One soldier said, "Would you look at that? He doesn't have any hair on his backside. This hoof and mouth disease is some serious business. We better get these horses killed and get out of here."

Traveller opened the gate to the only stall linked to the riding arena. At the back of the stall, another gate separated the two areas. As Traveller looked out over this last gate, he saw the carnage. Two mules stood in the middle of the arena with horses running counter-clockwise around them. Dead horses everywhere and still the arena was full of frenzied wild animals. Just outside the gate lay three dead horses. Traveller opened the last gate and walked into the maelstrom. He turned and shoved the gate closed before stepping over the carcasses of the three dead horses. He was now in the midst of the crazed madness. The mules saw him. Traveller blocked the frantic running of a small Welsh mare and nosed her toward the gate. A horse next to Traveller was shot. She fell at Traveller's feet. Traveller shoved the Welsh mare hard at the dead horses. She stumbled, stopped, then jumped over. Without drawing attention, Traveller stepped over the dead horses. The mare stood still as Traveller grabbed the leather strap and pulled the gate open. He stepped around and inside. The little mare followed. In another moment, the two mules stood at the gate. Traveller pushed it open. He stuck his head over the gate to hold it so it wouldn't swing wide. When the two mules made it inside, Traveller grabbed the leather strap, pulled the gate to, and slid the board into the locked position.

Traveller walked through the stall into the grooming area. The other three animals followed. He continued to the front of the barn and stood still in the middle of its opening. The gate was a hundred yards away with no cover along the way. The mules couldn't jump the fence and the mare was too short to even try. Traveller saw Balder's body and smelled the blood.

He walked around the grooming area until he found an old oiled tarp. Grabbing it with his teeth, he pulled it from the shelf above the work table. The tarp unfolded as it fell to the ground. Traveller dragged the tarp to Balder and nudged the dog with his nose. Balder slowly wagged his tail. Traveller pushed Balder onto the tarp. He then picked up one corner in his teeth and walked backwards, dragging it to the front gate. The Welsh mare and the two mules followed.

The Health Inspector and his driver were in town getting Stanley's face doctored. The assassins were slaughtering animals and the truck driver stood watching. The bulldozer operator had found a suitable spot for the burial and was digging. Nobody was guarding against escaping animals.

The health inspector had left the front gate open and when Traveller and his group reached it they walked through. Traveller dropped the end of the tarp and pulled the gate shut. He then slid the board into the locked position.

Melchezidek reached down and grabbed a corner of the tarp in his teeth. Deftly he tucked his head under and turned so that he had the tarp draped over his head and along the length of his body. In this manner Melchezidek walked forward, dragging Balder, and following his companions as they descended the mountain.

When they reached the bottom, Traveller turned left, away from town and toward his last home. Along the way, Mordichai took over for a tired Melchezidek. The procession continued single file with Traveller in the lead, followed by the little Welsh mare, and then the two mules. The last mule was Mordichai dragging Balder. They trudged down the dirt road. Every now and then a car approached. Without fail, each car stopped while its passengers watched the strange procession. One man said, "What do you think the dog's doing? I think he's in charge."

Balder was sitting up. His side hurt. But he still had his trophy. It was after midnight when Traveller and his entourage reached Jed's parent's house. They gathered around the water trough and nodded off into a well-earned, deep sleep.

CHAPTER 3—RESIGNATION
Dancing Deer - Spring 1933

When the sheriff took Jed and Emily to Jed's parent's home, Jed's dad asked how the children were going to get there. The sheriff said that he and Emily would retrieve them in his squad car before they got onto the school bus. Emily appraised her situation then said that Jed's parent's house was too small. It wasn't right for such a large family to just move in. She suggested they be taken to her parent's house in Possum Point. The sheriff looked at the small house and told Jed to get back in the car. They'd go get the children and then he'd take everyone to Possum Point.

Later that evening, Jed had Mr. Sinclair drive him back to get Balder. They found the rope, but no Balder. Jed reasoned that Balder had untied himself and went to a nearby spring. Balder knew the mountain and surrounding forest better than anybody. He'd be okay.

That night, Emily and Jed tried to figure out what they'd do. She said, "Jed, you've got to talk with Bill. The contract was for 110 live horses. He should make an adjustment. Without the horses, we can't pay off the loan."

Jed shrugged his shoulders. He was still in a daze. Emily said, "Darling, we've got three hundred dollars."

"I'll talk to Bill in the morning and then I've got to look for a job."

The next day Mr. Sinclair drove the children to school. Mrs. Sinclair fixed Emily and Jed breakfast and then went through the closets looking for suitable play clothing for her grandkids. When Mr. Sinclair returned and after he'd wolfed down his breakfast and two cups of coffee, he told Emily and Jed he was at their disposal. Emily told him they needed to go to Dancing Deer.

Stanley Muldaur sat in Bill's office with his head bandaged from ear to nose to second ear. The bandage was flat where his nose had been. He said, "I never knew how important the nose was for properly sounding out words. I guess I'll sound funny for the rest of my life. The doctor said, in the most inoffensive terms he could manage, that there was some surgery available but I'll forever have a face other people will find apprehensive." Stanley thought the doctor should have said grotesque.

With his lips tightly pinched, Bill shook his head. "Were all the livestock killed?"

"Yes, sir. Mr. Calhoun is now pretty much bankrupt unless he has some cash stowed away."

Bill asked, "How did you convince the authorities the stallion had hoof and mouth?"

"Aw, that was easy. The vaccine's made from the dead virus so when they check the blood sample of a horse that's been inoculated, he also shows positive for the virus."

Bill asked again, "And you're sure all the animals are dead?"

"Absolutely. It took them a while because each had to be shot in the head so it wouldn't suffer. But I think they suffered plenty. All the animals were burned and buried. Yes, sir. No animal survived."

Bill took out a blank deposit slip from his desk drawer and began filling it in. He said, "Five thousand dollars will be deposited to your account today. Send me your doctor's bills. I'll take care of them as well."

Both men stood, shook hands, and walked out the door. Bill put the deposit slip on his secretary's desk and said, "Take care of this today."

Stanley walked past Jed and out the door.

Jed said, "What happened to him?"

Bill was surprised to see Jed and stammered a little before he said, "Some wild dog tore off his nose. Come on in. I guess we've got some things to talk about."

Bill turned and walked into his office. Jed walked slowly past the secretary's desk and cocked his head in an effort to read the paper Bill had laid down, but the secretary was too swift. She quickly snatched it away.

"Bill, that contract's null and void. I never did get possession of those horses."

"Oh, I think you did. What do you think you were signing when the truck driver delivered them?"

"So, old friend, you're going to enforce the contract even though the collateral is dead and I have no way of paying you back?"

"Jed, you have one year to get me $1,160. Next year you'll have to get me $1,120, and so on. I think it'll soon be apparent to Emily that she married the wrong man. Your quick wits and ability to bamboozle those less sophisticated will get you just so far. Now, when the chips are down, everyone will find what kind of charlatan you are. Why don't you go beg someone for the money?"

"Why don't I just default on the loan and let you have possession of the collateral?"

"Jed, your farm is the collateral. That's why Emily had to sign with you. Grow up, you're in a man's world now."

Jed jumped out of the chair and charged around the desk. He grabbed Bill by his shirt collar and dragged him to his feet. Bill didn't resist. He simply said, "Jed, you don't want to compound your problems. Get a grip, man. You've been in scrapes before. Show everyone what you're made of. Now get out of my office before my secretary calls the police."

Jed paused, loosening his grip on Bill, he turned and walked out.

While Jed was hashing it out with Bill, Emily and her dad had gone to the mercantile. She looked up when Jed walked in. Holding a new dress she said, "Jed, look what Dad bought me."

"Put it back, Emily. These are too expensive for our budget."

"Jed, Dad paid for it, he bought some things for you too and for the kids."

Jed slumped into a seat and held his head.

Emily came over and put her hand on Jed's shoulder. "What's the matter, honey? Did you and Bill argue?"

Jed stood up, looked at his father-in-law, and said, "Silas, I'll pay you back. I swear." He then turned to Emily. "Honey, why do women solve their problems by shopping?"

"I don't know but chocolate also works."

Jed headed outside. Emily and her dad came out a few minutes later carrying several packages.

Mr. Sinclair said, "Jed, I don't want you to pay me back. I want to help."

"Silas, drive me around? I need to formulate a plan and somewhere in that plan is a job."

After a few minutes they had been over every street in the small town of Dancing Deer and stopped at several businesses for Jed to ask if they were hiring. At every one he heard the same answer: "No. Sorry." Then Jed told his father-in-law he needed to go to the vet's office.

In answer to Jed's questions the vet said, "Mr. Muldaur came by and said he thought your stallion had hoof and mouth disease. I asked why he thought that since there had not been any documented case in Marsden County. In all my years of practice, I've not actually seen a case first hand, only read about them in my trade journals. Mr. Muldaur shook his head, looked down, and muttered he'd like for me to check anyway."

Jed asked, "Did anything seem out of the ordinary?"

The vet thought a minute and said, "Yeah. The blood sample contained traces of a powerful anesthesia. And other than the blood sample, the horse exhibited no other symptoms. I thought the animal should have had blisters or lesions on his tongue or in his mouth and maybe on his hooves."

"I'd purchased the horse almost six months earlier and he'd received no medication whatever during that period."

"Well, somebody gave him a good dose less than two days before the blood sample was taken. Otherwise, it would have metabolized and been urinated out of his system."

The vet had already known from whom Jed bought the stallion. "None of Mr. Elliott's other horses tested positive."

Jed asked his father-in-law if he would drive him and Emily out to his dad's house. When they arrived, Jed's dad ran to the car. Too excited to get his words in any semblance of order, he hauled Jed off so he could talk with him privately.

"Jed, Traveller's here. He came in sometime during the night dragging Balder. He also brought a small mare and your two mules."

Jed was astonished. All he could do was grab his dad's arm and say, "Hallelujah!"

Jed's dad asked, "Are they going to infect my cattle? I can't afford to lose my cattle."

"Where are they?"

"Rupert and Claude took them down to the creek. They're going to build some sort of shelter where nobody will be able to see them—unless they go looking for 'em."

"Dad, let's get Emily and Silas and walk down there."

Emily and her dad were ecstatic, especially after Jed convinced them the hoof and mouth disease was a ruse.

When they got to the animals, Jed ran to Traveller and hugged his neck. He bent down to hug Balder but Rupert stopped him. "Jed, Balder's been shot. The bullet came from a high-powered rifle and went clean through. I couldn't tell what kind of internal damage's been done. There's not much bleeding. I cleaned the entry and exit wounds and treated them with a salve for infection." He reached out and patted Balder on his head. "He probably needs to remain lying down. I'd planned on taking him to a vet in Possum Point. Also, he's got something under his paw. Whatever it is, he won't let anyone look at it."

Jed bent down and stroked Balder's head. He got a pretty good look at what Balder had under his paw. Jed rose and said, "I think I know what it is." Everyone looked at him. He continued, "It's what's left of Stanley Muldaur's nose."

Jed went to Traveller and said, "What brave and noble warriors you and Balder are. I would've liked to have been witness to the heroics you must've performed."

Everyone there would like to have been such a witness and said as much. Jed looked at Mordichai and Melchezidek and then at the little Welsh mare. With a questioning look at Traveller he asked, "Why her?"

Emily said, "It's because she was David Blaine's childhood pony and now the girls think she's theirs."

Claude put his hand on Jed's shoulder. "Tomorrow we'll start fixing a proper barn. We'll even build the gates in it like you designed and with the same feeding system."

When Jed was satisfied with their accommodations, he gave each animal a parting caress. Back at the house, they decided no one knew the horses had escaped and none of the horses ever even had hoof and mouth disease. It was some sort of mean trick played on Jed by Bill.

The horses were dead and would not be replaced. The contract was legal and binding. Emily suggested Stanley Muldaur be castrated and stretched over an ant hill beside Bill Potter. At this new character revelation, Jed took a sideways glance at Mr. Sinclair. Silas shrugged his shoulders. They also decided Jed was going to have to repay the note or lose the farm.

Rupert eased Balder into a wheelbarrow. He and Claude gently placed the coon hound onto the back seat of Mr. Sinclair's car. Emily and her father drove Balder to the vet in Possum Point. He wouldn't know anything of the circumstances; they'd simply say the dog was accidentally shot. Jed and his father went outside and sat in the rocking chairs on the front porch.

"Dad, can you give me any advice I can use to get myself out of this situation?"

"Son, I can come up with $500. You're welcome to it. But you'll have to somehow get a job to pay the rest. Maybe Silas can help."

"I don't want to borrow from anyone. How can I take care of matters with just my own resources?"

His dad thought for a moment and then said, "Jedidiah, I don't see an easy answer to your problem. America is in a depression with lots of able-bodied men unemployed. You'll have to swallow your pride and take any job offered. And you'll have to be particular with how you spend the money you make. The only job I know of for sure is with one of my friends. Right after school's out, he and his family join a group of migrant workers. I think they head north to the Missouri border to pick spinach for a couple a' weeks, then a little farther north to pick strawberries. After they finish with the strawberries, they pick peaches. They end the harvesting season in the boot-hill area picking cotton. It's hard work but he usually comes home with enough money to get them through the winter. You might be able to make enough to go with my money to pay your note. Why don't you talk it over with Emily and I'll get in touch with my friend."

Eventually Emily and her dad returned to pick up Jed. She told Jed the vet wanted to keep Balder another day. He thought the dog was all right, but first he needed to make sure Balder didn't have any problems with a bowel movement. He also wanted to check for any passing of blood. He thinks the bullet passed through muscle and missed his organs.

That night Emily told Jed her dad offered to pay off the note in full. He didn't need to be repaid unless Jed wanted to pay him back. And, if he did, Jed could pick out whatever payment plan or repayment time period he thought appropriate.

Jed said marrying Emily, and being a part of her family, was the best thing he had ever done. He didn't know how he deserved such a wife. He told her he appreciated her dad's generous offer but it was time for him to be a responsible person. He needed to use his own abilities and his own means to take care of his own problems. He didn't want her dad's money, he wanted her dad's respect, and that was something he had to earn.

Jed told her about the migrant family who spent all summer, up through harvest-time, working for anyone who had a crop and needing help. His dad thought he could make seven to eight hundred dollars but he planned on making the entire $1,160. He and David Blaine would be back in time for school to start in the fall.

Emily cried. She said they were a family. If he went with the migrant workers, she and the girls were going too.

CHAPTER 4—EMILY
Possum Point - Spring 1933

Emily unfolded the note. It was always with her. Tucked into a corner of her purse, it was always there, the most precious thing she possessed.

I met the most wonderful woman yesterday. She offered water to quench my thirst. A beauty beyond compare, she was solace for a searching spirit. I have but a piece of lace and an aching in my heart. I must find her. I will travel to the ends of the earth. I will slay dragons. I will move mountains. Might you have seen her? I have naught but her fragrance to guide me. Tell me true, does she live here?

Emily's father found it. When they came home from church he put the car in the shed behind the house and they entered through the kitchen door. As soon as her father hung up his coat he retreated to his favorite room, the study. Through supper the note remained attached to the front door. After supper, he'd normally go onto the front porch and smoke a cigar. He was a methodical man; he had routines. When the dinner dishes were washed and put away Emily would often join him. Sometimes they talked on important topics, at other times she read to him from one of his fine books.

Emily relaxed into the swing. Her father asked how her day had been at the barn-raising. Emily said she had a wonderful time. She met several interesting people. He asked if there was anyone in particular.

Emily replied, "Actually, Dad, there were two gentlemen that stand out."

"Tell me about them."

"One comes from a wealthy family. He was polite and strolled around the building site sure of himself. He commented on people's work, suggested ways they could improve their efficiency, or pointed out deficiencies he had found. He compared their work to that of another doing a similar job. He never did any work himself, he was too busy tasting the food, trying to be some sort of supervisor, or following me around as I delivered water."

"What did he look like?"

"He was a handsome man, about six feet tall and muscular, pale skin with brooding features. And dark hair—almost black really. He carried himself . . . well, like he was used to being waited on and quite put out if his opinions weren't listened to or his instructions weren't followed. You should have heard the women when he told them how their dishes should have been seasoned."

"And the other?"

"He was completely different. His looks. His demeanor. His style. I mean . . . he was also handsome, but his features were fair. You know: blond hair and blue eyes—very expressive blue eyes. And he was tall. He was well over six feet and skinny as a rail. He was also clumsy. I heard several people say they had to find another place to work. When he hit a nail with his hammer the nail would sometimes go shooting across the floor. They compared working with him to dodging bullets during the war. He's left-handed and I imagine his thumb and index finger on his right hand are much larger today than normal. I didn't hear him use any foul language, though there were plenty of times he could have justified it.

"This second man has two older brothers. They looked out for him and kept moving him from one job to another. I think they were afraid he'd either get bored and quit or completely tear something up. So they kept moving him along to keep him interested and not have enough time to botch something up so bad they couldn't sneak over behind and repair the damage. They must've been in charge. The other men kept asking for their opinion and what should be done next. No one seemed to take offence if he was told to redo the work he'd just completed."

"Tell me more about this second young man."

"Oh, I don't know, Dad. He was very nice and well-mannered. I don't think he had much experience with working. And he drank so much water he spent a lot of time behind a convenient tree."

Mr. Sinclair chuckled. "Honey, not to know very much about him, it seems to me you know quite a bit." He handed Emily the note and said, "I found it on the front door. Which of the two do you think left it?"

Emily unfolded the note. Her face contorted from a grimace when she realized her father had read her note to one of sheer pleasure, when she realized someone had sent her a love note. She knew who sent it but told her dad, "I don't know. I'll have to think about it."

The next week Bill paid a visit to Mr. Sinclair's office and asked if he might call on Emily. Mr. Sinclair said, "Mr. Potter, why aren't you in school?"

Bill replied, "I've taken the day off to talk with you. My father owns the bank in Dancing Deer and loaned me his car. While I'm out I'm supposed to observe the prosperity of a couple of his clients."

Mr. Sinclair didn't give his permission, just said he'd think about it, and suggested the young man join them for supper and light conversation on Friday evening. When Mr. Sinclair told Emily of Bill's visit, she gave no visible sign to indicate if she was pleased or not. Emily, Mr. Sinclair thought, help me out here.

The meal had been pleasant enough. It was quite apparent Bill was in his element in social settings. He was properly attired, knew the important people, ate with the proper implements, conversed on interesting topics, and was a likable fellow. But it wasn't Mr. Sinclair who Bill needed to impress and to that other person he was performing dismally.

It appeared to Mr. Sinclair that Emily thought Bill Potter a bore. His attitude toward women played a large part. He directed most of his comments to Mr. Sinclair and not one time did Bill ask for Emily's opinion on anything of substance. He was extremely polite. But it looked like, to Mr. Sinclair, that Emily considered his politeness condescending when directed toward her.

Mr. Sinclair thought he was wasting his time on Bill when Emily, unexpectedly, said, "Bill, would you join us this Sunday for church. Afterwards, we can eat in the garden on the church grounds."

By the latter stages of the meal Bill had seemed down-trodden but now he was elated. Mr. Sinclair thought Emily was playing with Bill's emotions. Bill would have to pay. His crime was his attitude regarding the mental acuity of women and for treating Emily like an object to be admired rather than one to be reckoned with. Mr. Sinclair gave Emily an exasperated look. She had a mischievous grin. Mr. Sinclair thought Emily was actually causing him consternation for reading her note. Well, so be it. He probably shouldn't have read it, so now he had to suffer as well as Bill. He'd just go along and enjoy the young man's company. After all, it wasn't he who thought Bill Potter a bore.

On a Friday evening, one week after the first family meal with Bill and five days after the Sunday picnic, both men came for supper. It was an interesting evening. Bill arrived early. Emily was polite and very proper but when Jed arrived, in that sporty straw hat, her countenance dramatically improved. She became more animated. She smiled more. She joked and kidded and seemed to enjoy life. If it was that apparent to her father, he wondered, would it not be even more apparent to Bill? When Emily played the piano she played with so much emotion and bravado she had all three sitting on the edge of their seats. Emily, thought Mr. Sinclair, was in control—as it should be.

Emily re-read the note. When Jed sat beside her at church she had been expecting Bill. But Jed appeared and grabbed the empty seat. She almost laughed at the possibilities. One Prince Charming is not enough for every princess. The two men occupied opposite ends of the spectrum. Bill, the strategist, contrived elaborate schemes to achieve his goals. He knew what life had in store for him and was grabbing everything he needed along the way. Emily felt flattered he'd decided she had a part to play. Emily thought Jed was more easy-going. He had a carefree attitude. Whatever happened would happen. He didn't have a clue what he'd be doing ten years from now, or even one year from now—not yet anyway.

At church, Emily noticed Jed did not so much sing as listen. She knew listeners were the best people to talk to. They're not always butting in. However, he did appear somewhat out of kilter. His clothes didn't fit. They were, maybe, a size too small—at least in the length of the shirt sleeves and pant legs. He probably didn't have a lot of nice clothes, just an odd assortment for work. She would have liked for him to have arrived in polished boots. They looked like he walked all the way to Possum Point kicking rocks. Whatever Jedidiah's fashion statement lacked, he more than made up for in manners. And he was most pleasant to look at. Jed's mother probably played a large part in his deportment. That's a good sign. A man should always pay heed to a mother's advice.

Emily disliked Bill's attitude toward women. And she didn't much like him trying to usher her out to the church grounds for the Sunday picnic after the sermon. She considered that he probably didn't want Jed around but that didn't give him cause to take charge without considering other people's wishes.

The afternoon of the picnic the conversation started and ended with Bill. Seldom did it meander to the happenings in Jed's or Emily's lives. Why do men think they are the center of the universe? She didn't think Jed fit that mold, but possibly it was because Bill didn't give him a chance. Bill was so authoritative. And that was another thing. What woman wants to be told what to do?

So there we have it, she thought. On the one hand, we have a good-looking man with money. He's bossy, possessive, and self-centered. Being married to him would bring a woman all the good things in life, as long as she did what she was told.

On the other hand, we have another good looking man who is a gentleman without prospects. The woman he married would have to be a take-charge woman or they'd starve. But he'd been under a woman's influence before and fared the better for it. A woman, one like herself, could take this raw material and mold it into just the man she'd always hoped would come along.

Then, the next Friday evening, she smiled every time Jed looked her way but was only polite to Bill. She'd made her choice and tried to communicate it to Bill in the least offensive manner possible.

On Tuesday, November 11th, school was out as Possum Point, and the rest of the United States celebrated Armistice Day. At the eleventh hour, on the eleventh day, of the eleventh month it was exactly one year after an agreement had brought a close to the war that would end all wars. After the parade and town celebration, Mr. Sinclair decided to visit his properties. It was time to make sure his tenant farmers had what they needed to get in the last of their crops.

Sometimes Mr. Sinclair would advance a good tenant extra funds for additional harvest help. Emily went with him when she could and afterward she was usually treated to a meal in town. This time, both of Possum Point's cafes were closed.

When they returned, Mrs. Sinclair told Emily that Bill came by just after she and her dad had left. She said she noticed Bill walking by twice more. She then asked Emily if she'd walk to a neighbor's house for baking soda as the mercantile was closed and she needed to watch the oven.

Emily hadn't gotten very far when Bill intercepted her. Emily thought Bill was probably upset over her obvious preference for Jed. Emily also knew she and Bill should talk about it. She didn't want any lingering resentment.

"Hello, Emily. Beautiful day, isn't it?"

"Bill, did you just happen to be in the area?"

"No, I came specifically to talk with you. I need to know why you are so smitten with Jed? Why you could care less about me? It isn't right. Woman, what are you thinking?"

Emily stopped, turned, and said, "Bill, I like you and Jed both. I am certainly pleased that both of you have shown an interest in me. I think any girl in Possum Point or Dancing Deer would be ecstatic. But Jed actually listens to what I have to say. He seems genuinely interested in my opinions. And when we talk I have his undivided attention. You, on the other hand, spend most of the time talking about yourself."

"That's not true. I listen to you as well as he does. And what's more, you don't even know Jed. He's really a conniving blowhard . . . a bamboozler. He's also a liar and a drunkard. Emily, you shouldn't even be in the same room with someone like him. He doesn't have your best interests at heart. He hasn't any prospects. His family's poor. If you were to marry him your life would be one of work and tedium. You'd have to live in a barn and cook your meals over a wood-burning stove. You wouldn't get to travel anywhere. Jed would be in jail right now if he hadn't trained his dog to let him know when the revenue agents were prowling about."

Emily had had enough. "Bill, Jed doesn't say bad things about you. Do you think you're increasing your stature in my eyes by wildly exaggerating his faults?"

"No. I just thought you should know. He hadn't planned on working on that old man's barn, he never worked at the saw mill, and what's more, there isn't any cabinet maker going to take him as an apprentice."

Emily replied, "I know all that. I also know the people in Dancing Deer are marveling about the change that's come over him. I think whoever marries Jed will have a full and abundant life. She might not have money lavished at her feet or get to travel to exotic places but she would find she was on equal terms with her partner and together they would have a happy marriage, one of laughter and love."

Bill felt the anger seep in. This wasn't going the way he'd intended. Whatever he'd ever wanted his father had supplied. All he ever had to do was whine. When he was younger he'd get down on the floor and throw a temper tantrum. With Emily, he shouldn't expect to get what he wanted with those tactics. He shouldn't have to resort to tactics. Most of the girls in town would be impressed with his good looks, his connections, his prospects, his social skills—with his money. They'd come running with just the slightest bit of encouragement, just the bending of his index finger. Emily seemed immune to the advantages he had. That just made him the more determined. She'd eventually come to see Jed as he really was and then she'd be sorry. He might give her another chance. But then again, he might not. There were other women who might help him see things differently.

Bill spun around on his heel and started to walk away. He stopped. Turning back toward Emily he said, "Emily, you've made the wrong choice." He then turned around and continued on without looking back or waiting for her final reply or goodbye.

Emily refolded the note. She put it away in its little corner of her purse. She knew she had made the right choice. And now she had to step up and help her husband solve their recently surfaced problem.

CHAPTER 5—PHILIPPE
France - 1940

Philippe burst in on his father's afternoon nap. Shaking the old man, he blurted, "Oh Papa. Have you heard? Have you heard?"

"Calm down, Philippe. I'm certainly glad to see you. I've been worried. Now, what is it I should have heard?"

"The Germans have defeated us and are entering Paris. I barely made it out. The roads south are clogged with people. Some have autos, some bicycles, others donkeys pulling wooden-wheeled carts. I even saw three children pushing an old woman in a child's perambulator. They're all leaving Paris however they can with whatever they can."

"Yes, I've heard. The marshal thinks we should sue for peace. The Brits and what's left of our Army are on the shores of Dunkerque waiting to be rescued or annihilated. For some reason the Germans are dallying, probably waiting for reinforcements. Where's your car?"

"Out front. Why?"

"You should hide it. We don't want the Germans confiscating it. You can get around on that old motorcycle. It doesn't look like much and that's all the better. Just be thankful I made you drain the gas before you shoved it into the corner of the barn. And when gasoline gets scarce you'll have to travel on foot or by bicycle."

Philippe walked to the window. He looked across his family's vineyards. Maybe he should have joined the Army instead of going to the university. But how could he have made a difference? His dad was probably right; everything in its own time. "Where shall I hide it?"

"Put it inside the shed at the back of the new field. Make sure the top's up and cover it with a tarp. Stack hay around and over it then take a leaf rake and cover any tire marks you made getting it back there. Better prepare it like you did your cycle. Someday we may have to escape in it. While you're at it, take off the distributor cap and hide it high on the shelf on the back wall."

Pepe was an elder statesman but still had a keen intellect and the respect of both his children. Genevieve had gone to market with a neighbor. She wouldn't be back for another hour. Boy, was Pepe glad to know his son was safe. His children were adults but he felt it was his duty to look after them. He'd protect them as he always had.

"I understand General de Gaulle will be speaking on the radio again this evening. Let's not miss it. These other pantywaists want us to appease the invaders but de Gaulle wants us to resist. However, he wants us to do it while he watches. We'll just have to see how it plays out. On last night's broadcast he called on all French officers to get in touch with him."

Pepe looked around. He'd been talking but no one was listening. Philippe had already left to hide his prized Italian roadster. He might as well finish his nap.

Pepe awoke to the sound of clanging pots. Genevieve didn't like doing the cooking but they lost their cook when the Germans invaded. Being Roma the cook left taking the silver. It might be some time before another could be found. Next time he was going to ask for references.

He got up and turned on the radio. Two days before, Marshal Petain told the people of France he was forming a new government. He said the fighting must stop. He went on to say he was planning to ask for an armistice and for the terms of surrender. Pepe lit a cigar. Philippe was probably in the kitchen with Genevieve.

"Frenchmen must now be aware that all ordinary forms of authority have disappeared."

Pepe sprang from his chair and ran into the kitchen, yelling as he went for them to come into the sitting room and listen to this French general in London. Back, huddled around the radio, the three Martels listened as de Gaulle said, *"I, General de Gaulle, a French soldier and military leader, realize that I now speak for France.*

"In the name of France, I make the following solemn declaration: It is the bounden duty of all Frenchmen who still bear arms to continue the struggle. For them to lay down their arms, to evacuate any position of military importance, or to agree to hand over any part of French territory, however small, to enemy control would be a crime against our country."

A flash and black smoke came from the kitchen. All three were out of their chairs and into the kitchen like sailors after a loose cannon. The grease Genevieve had been heating had caught fire. Genevieve put her hands to both sides of her face. Philippe raced after a bucket of water. Pepe reached over and turned off the gas supply valve. Philippe came rushing back, water sloshing with each step. Pepe slid a lid over the burning grease, suffocating it. Philippe set the bucket down. They headed back into the sitting room in time to hear the last few words of de Gaulle's speech.

"Soldiers of France, wherever you may be, arise!"

Philippe got up from his chair and started pacing the room. "I can't just stay out of the fight. I've got to do something. I think I'll go to London and make myself useful."

"Now listen, Philippe. How would going to London help France? The fighting's here. If you really want to be of use, send information."

Genevieve walked into the kitchen immersed in her own cloud of disgust. Everything was spiraling down as Philippe becomes the spy and she becomes the cook. Life wasn't fair.

Philippe turned toward his father and asked, "What kind of information?"

"If the British are able to continue the fight they'll need to know the location of the German troops, what ports have been mined, locations of important bridges, buildings the Germans have requisitioned as offices, and railway schedules. There are any number of things they need to know."

"Okay, Papa. How would I get the information to them? I don't have a short-wave radio and dropping it in the mail's not gonna work."

"Philippe, don't worry. I'll figure a way. All you have to do is get the information." Pepe paused. "If we do this, we need to be smart. Let me think and we'll talk about it again tomorrow."

During the next few days they listened to radio broadcasts from Paris, from Berlin, and from London. The BBC seemed to have the most reliable information. Certain times of the day they broadcast in French and Pepe was a regular listener. He learned most of the British troops evacuated from Dunkerque, France surrendered with deaths estimated in excess of a hundred thousand, a million French soldiers were carted off to prison in Germany, and Marshal Petain would be allowed to continue the French government with jurisdiction over the southeast portion of France. He had only to agree not to hamper the German ability to wage war and to help Germany when asked. Petain was planning on setting up his new government in Vichy, a resort town a few miles south with plenty of housing. Pepe thought his own small hamlet was in this unoccupied zone. Philippe would need papers to come home from the university, as check points would probably be set to scrutinize the traffic crossing the line separating the two zones.

Pepe brought out a small leather pouch. From inside he retrieved a tiny Minox camera, a fistful of film cartridges, and several detailed road maps. He handed everything to Philippe, saying they were now his. With the camera and a new roll of film, Pepe took several pictures of Philippe, then he had Genevieve use her make-up and some old clothes to make Philippe look like an old man. More pictures. Then it was his and Genevieve's turn to have their pictures taken. In the wine cellar Pepe developed the film.

Soon he was ready to travel to Vichy. He called for a taxi. After arriving in the quaint little resort town he walked to the train station where he stored his luggage in a locked compartment. He spent the day wandering around with his head down and listening. He picked up bits of gossip and information. Eventually, he went to the Hotel du Parc, where the government had set up headquarters. Looking as shabby as he could, he asked if there might be a job for a maintenance worker. No luck.

That night, after retrieving his luggage, he went to an out-of-the-way hotel to check in for the night. There was a bustle of activity in the reception area where the woman in charge said, "We've only a few rooms left. The politicians have taken most of the upscale hotel rooms, causing everyone else to find lodging in places like ours." Pepe looked around. It was clean enough, the grounds outside were well maintained.

The woman understood what he was thinking and said, "The only problem I've got attracting guests is that we're in a fairly hidden spot and not well-known except to locals."

Pepe winked and took his room key. The woman gave an appraising look as he sprightly ascended the stairs.

The next morning he came down to the hotel café, sat in a corner away from most of the other tables, and ordered coffee. The same woman came over to his table and said, "We'll soon be out of coffee and I don't think we'll be getting any more delivered." She poured him a cup. "If you're real nice, I might have a small cache hidden for you the next time you're in town." She gave a big smile and went to another table clamoring for service.

Pepe drank the dark brew and started reading a book he had in his pocket. From what he could determine, most of the people in the café knew each other and were talking in muffled voices at each table and from table to table. When the woman came back with more coffee, Pepe asked in hushed tones if she knew anyone who worked for the new government. Just as quietly she replied that her daughter had just been hired as a clerk. What was it he needed?

"I need papers to allow me to occasionally go across the border into the occupied zone."

"Honey, why would you need to do something like that? We've got everything you need right here."

Pepe closed his book and looked up at the woman. She wore too much make-up but was pretty to look at. She was a good twenty years younger than he and still had an attractive girlish figure. Her dark brown hair was pulled to one side with a bright green barrette. Pepe returned her winning smile. He mused there must not be enough French men left to go around. "Madam, I have important business to attend to and I don't think the new government will be very accommodating."

She paused for a moment and then said, "Can you pay?"

"Within reason."

"How long will you be staying?"

"I don't know. I might move in. I don't have anything pressing at the moment. I'm too old for the military and too lazy for work."

The woman set the coffee pot down and held out her hand. "I'm Odette—the owner."

Pepe held her hand and said, "My name's Henri and you should be proud to have such a beautiful place to own."

Odette let him hold her hand. She thought, what a handsome gentleman: silver hair worn long and swept back, arched eyebrows, a fashionable mustache. His hand was warm and firm. It gave her a secure feeling. She stared at him. Such a dignified man. Leaning forward she whispered, "See me later."

Three weeks went by. Pepe crawled out of a luxurious feather bed and stretched. He had moved into Odette's room his second night there and yesterday she gave him four sets of papers for crossing the border: one for him as Henri Simeon, one for Genevieve, and two for Philippe, one as an old man. He told Odette, after putting the papers in his valise, he needed to be on his way the following morning. He said he would be back by the end of the month. He left through the rear exit.

That night he and Philippe decided that Philippe should go back to the university and ask for a reduced schedule. He would tell them his father was ill and he would be spending a large portion of his time away. They'd understand.

A week later, after hearing nothing from Philippe, Pepe went to see his old friend, Father Dominique, at the parish church. With a note testifying to his trustworthiness he left for Paris. He needed to find how the resistance was getting the shot-down fighter pilots they rescued back to England. His border check went smoothly.

Philippe's apartment was in the fashionable Latin Quarter. However, Pepe was not impressed with Philippe's fashionable furnishings. Clothes were strewn around the floor and stacked cardboard boxes were used as tables and for storage. Two ragged chairs and a broken-down bed made up the remainder of the furniture.

The rest of the day, until early afternoon, Pepe cleaned and discarded. When he thought he'd done sufficient damage, he left to buy his son replacement furniture. At a used furniture store he purchased an entire apartment's requirement. At another store he paid exorbitant prices for a slightly used refrigerator and stove—apartment size. Everything purchased was scheduled for delivery the following day. That night Pepe slept on dirty sheets strapped to a bed sagging in the middle. Pepe wondered how in the world his son managed without him.

The next morning, he couldn't find soap for bathing and there was nothing edible in the entire apartment. Pepe headed out the apartment door and down the interior hallway for breakfast. On the way, he looked in all open doors and asked everyone he saw if they might need two ragged chairs, a filthy refrigerator and stove, a bed in bad shape, or cardboard boxes. By the time he reached the front door of the apartment building he had found homes for all the wayward items. He pushed open a wrought iron security door and stepped out. Coming face-to-face with a woman, he almost knocked her off the front stoop. Surprised she dropped the sack of groceries she was carrying into the flower bed. Pepe apologized and ran down the few steps to retrieve her things. She started crying. The milk had spilled, the eggs were broken, and the other few items were scattered throughout the bushes.

Walking back up the steps with only a loaf of bread Pepe said, "I'm so sorry. Please, allow me to replace your purchases. I was heading to the market myself and if you would give me a list I'd be happy to replace every item."

"Thank you. Will you be very long? I was planning on fixing my breakfast but now . . . well, most of it's strewn throughout the flowers."

"Then, you must permit me to take you to breakfast. Afterwards we'll go to the market and buy them out. Whatever you want." Pepe paid an excited street urchin to clean up the flower bed. The woman tossed the bread to the boy and took Pepe's arm as he helped her down the steps. They strolled along the street in search of a sidewalk cafe. The furniture was not to be delivered until later that afternoon so Pepe had most of the day to do whatever he pleased and right now he pleased to have the company of a good-looking woman for breakfast.

"My name is Claudette." She added, "I teach philosophy at the university."

"I am very pleased to meet you, Claudette. You may call me Henri."

The rest of the day the two discussed all the important matters that dominated intellectual thinking. Pepe couldn't believe his good fortune: a good-looking woman and smart.

They paid horrendously inflated prices for groceries, linens, and the myriad other things Pepe thought his son needed. Pepe reasoned that the high prices were because of the uncertain times and the fact that everything was in such short supply. With the purchases made, the couple headed back. The rest of the day, Pepe helped the other students in the apartment building remove the ragtag items he had pushed into half of the front room. No sooner had this been accomplished than the new furniture arrived.

After the delivery men left, Pepe sat down in a leather chair and took a big breath. There was a knock on the door.

"I thought you might need some help putting everything in order. I'm a whirlwind at making a bed." Claudette stepped inside with a broom and started pushing the furniture into likely places. The delivery people had already hooked up the refrigerator and stove and even assembled the bed frame. Two hours later Claudette had the apartment looking spiffy. Pepe had hardly moved from his chair.

He got up, walked to Claudette, took her hand, and asked how he could ever repay her. She said, "It's been a while since I've been to the Moulin Rouge."

The next day Pepe went to a local Catholic church. He found the priest in his study. "Father, may I have a moment of your time?"

"Yes. I have some free time. Please, have a seat. Have you had coffee this morning? I'm afraid my supply is meager. Shortages, you know." He reached for a china carafe and poured black espresso into a tiny cup. Handing the cup to Pepe he said, "Now, how might I be of assistance?"

Pepe smelled the luxuriant aroma. It was yet too hot to drink so he paused to let the fumes intoxicate him with their rich bouquet. He looked over the top of his cup. "I have a packet to get to General de Gaulle. I thought I might give it to a downed fighter pilot being smuggled back to Britain."

"Oh my, I don't have any information about smuggled fighter pilots. Why have you sought such information from me? Has someone intimated that I was associated with that kind of endeavor?"

"Yes, your friend, Father Dominique, from my parish church. I have a letter from him attesting to my honesty." Pepe handed the priest the note.

For the next hour the Father and Pepe talked about the French people, the new government set up in the south, the German invaders, the Gestapo, and the attitude the French have about kowtowing to the militaristic Germans. Eventually, the priest said, "Let me ask around. Why don't you check back at the end of the week?"

Pepe and Claudette got along famously. On the morning of the day Pepe was to return to the church, the front door opened and in walked Philippe.

"Whoa, what's this? Where's my stuff?" Philippe walked into the bedroom and saw his father sitting up in bed.

"Philippe, I bought you new furnishings. Have you got anything?"

"Yes, Papa, I have." Philippe dropped his baggage and entered the bathroom. Pepe lowered his face into his hands. Philippe staggered out of the bathroom and said, "Papa, there's a naked woman in there."

"Yes, I know. Why don't we go into the front room and give her a little privacy while she gets dressed."

Philippe picked up his suitcase and looked around at all the new furniture. "I hope you found the gun I hid in the mattress."

"Oh, good God. No, I didn't."

"Well then, what about the sketches I had pinned to the wall in the kitchen? They were of the prison at Drancy."

"I threw them away. I thought they were trash."

The bedroom door opened and Claudette walked out.

"Hello, Doctor Spivey. Have you met my father?"

Pepe jumped up from his chair, gave his son a disapproving look, and took Claudette by the arm. He helped her to the door. "Claudette, honey, I'll have to talk to you later." He opened the door and then decided to follow her outside. "I'm so sorry."

Claudette said, "It's okay. I enjoyed our time together. Do you think he'll be staying long?"

"Could be. It's his apartment."

"When you can, come down. We need to talk. I think I'm pregnant."

Back inside, Pepe was visibly shaken. He plopped down on one of Philippe's new chairs. Philippe came over and put his hand on his father's shoulder. "Papa, I didn't have a gun and those sketches were my first drafts. I have better ones in my baggage. I was just fooling with you."

Pepe gave his son a mournful look and said, "Claudette . . . I mean Doctor Spivey thinks she's pregnant."

"Damn. How long have you been seeing her?"

"We've had sexual relations several times but only for the last two days."

"You've only known her for two days? And the two of you stayed in bed the entire time?"

"Pretty much."

"Well, Casanova, there's no way she would know so soon. Did she say how she'd determined she was pregnant?"

"Hell, no! She must also be fooling with me. I feel better already."

Philippe and Pepe went through the information Philippe had accumulated. They took snapshots of the sketches and another of a written list describing the pictures. At the bottom of the list Pepe suggested Philippe give de Gaulle some code name to call him by. Philippe scratched his head. "Have you got a suggestion? I'm not very clever with nicknames and a man's *nom de plume* should say something about him."

"How about 'the Seeker?'"

Philippe thought it was as good as any and indicative of his service. Philippe took all the sketches and the picture list and put them in a cast iron pot he found in a kitchen cabinet. With a match he lit them, then emptied the ashes into a dustbin.

That afternoon Pepe went to see the priest. He was given an address on a small scrap of paper. The location on the paper turned out to be a park. Pepe sat on a bench and waited. After a short while a young man approached and sat beside him. The man started to read a newspaper. Soon he struck up a conversation with Pepe, then left. Thirty minutes later a couple came and sat down.

The woman asked Pepe, "Have you lately visited a Catholic church a few blocks south?"

"I have. Are you connected with the escape route for downed aircraft pilots?"

"That depends. Are you connected with the Gestapo?"

Pepe said, "Good heavens, no. Here, let me show you my medals from the last war. I want to do what I can in this one—just short of donning a uniform. I need to get something to de Gaulle."

"We might be of assistance. Your medals are impressive. Did you fight at Verdun?"

"No."

They told Pepe they trusted the priest and agreed to take his packet. Several signals were then determined to be used when future shipments needed transport. A separate signal was decided upon if de Gaulle, himself, had a communication to be delivered. Pepe handed over the three film packets, shook their hands, and spent the rest of the day using the metro to criss-cross the city from one arrondissement to another, back to his son's apartment.

Pepe told Philippe about the signals and how he could make delivery from Paris or receive a communication directly from de Gaulle. That night, Pepe slept with Claudette in her apartment. The next morning, Pepe left after telling Claudette he'd be back in a couple of weeks.

For the next four years, Pepe made lots of trips to Vichy and many more to Paris. Philippe became one of the best sources of information for General de Gaulle and when Jean Moulin parachuted into France on New Year's Day, 1942, one of the assignments given him by General de Gaulle was to find the Seeker. De Gaulle told Moulin to look for an elderly person because the Seeker had been a successful spy in World War I but without a face.

When the Allied Forces landed in North Africa, the authorities in charge did not notify de Gaulle beforehand. When he found out, he stomped around and shouted he hoped the Vichy military threw the Allied invaders into the sea. De Gaulle said you don't get France by burglary. After calming down, he sent word to the Seeker to go to North Africa and determine the attitude of the Vichy authorities to him and to the Allies. De Gaulle also wanted to know why he was constantly left out of the top-level decision making, but that was something he'd have to find out on his own.

Philippe arrived in Algiers a month after the Allies. He traveled in his disguise as an old man. He had perfected an unsteady walk, a slight limp, and hunched-over shoulders. He had a hat pulled low over his ears and kept his head down and his ears open. He credited his father with polishing his mannerisms and his craft. He had long ago determined his father did more in the Great War than work at a desk in a supply depot.

His instructions from de Gaulle included a rendezvous with another undercover agent who was being re-assigned to Vichy. The fellow agent was to give him a list of contacts in Algiers.

Philippe sat at a picnic table and asked a man already sitting there if he might like a chess match. The man arranged some pieces from his pocket on an inlaid board and asked Philippe if he were seeking someone. Philippe answered that he was but could not remember the name. The man asked if it might be Aziz and Philippe answered, no, it had five letters and started with a "D."

The man looked up and said, "Drago."

Philippe said, "Seeker."

They talked for a few minutes as they played, then the man held his hand suspended over the table. Philippe held his breath. The man said, "I thought I heard a camera shutter click. There, I heard it again. This game is over." He got up, grabbed his chess pieces, and ambled away.

Philippe slowly stood and surveyed the area. He didn't see anyone. Then he heard it. In the bushes to his left. Two shadowy figures. He turned right and walked briskly into traffic. Dodging cars he raced across the street and down the sidewalk. Behind him he heard car tires squeal as someone hit the brakes. He turned down a dark alley, ran a block, and emerged onto a busy street. He ducked into an upscale restaurant and tried to blend in with the crowd. He was ushered into a bar and told he would have to wait for a table. One American soldier was there and probably fifty locals. Almost all were smoking. The assailants couldn't possibly find him in this den of iniquity.

The only available spot was at the bar beside the soldier. After removing his hat and coat he walked over and asked in English if he might sit in the empty chair. The American said he could, that most of the locals shunned him and the chair had been vacant for a half hour.

Philippe said, "I might need some help. I'm being pursued by two Gestapo agents. If they try to take me away I'll need a diversionary action to give me that second I'll require to get out the door." He gave the American a stern look as he said this so the man would know he wasn't playing games. The American nodded.

Philippe ordered a draft beer and flung down a large coin. The American watched the door. Presently, two men in brown trench coats appeared. Philippe watched through a mirror on the back wall. One of the men stood at the door while the other made his way through the crowd.

The American said, "They're here."

Philippe reached into his pocket and grabbed a handful of coins. His beer came just as one of the two men walked up.

"Excuse me. May I order at the bar?"

The American said, "Here, you can have my seat. My friend and I have just been notified our table's ready. Coming, Fred?"

The man at the door now stood in front of the American. He said, "I think Fred will be coming with us."

CHAPTER 6—JESSE

Dancing Deer - September 1941

The Bells had lived in Dancing Deer for five years. Before arriving, Mr. Bell was diagnosed with chronic allergies and told to move west—away from the moist air and humidity of Galveston. Dancing Deer wasn't on the way west so nobody really knows how they came to call Dancing Deer their home. Maybe they headed west and Mrs. Bell, being the navigator, somehow got the map turned wrong getting them going north. It happens all the time. Of course Mr. Bell could have asked for directions along the way, but he didn't want to do that. Whatever the reason, when they drove into the little town of Dancing Deer, Mr. Bell said this was it. He wasn't going any farther. If his allergies wouldn't let him live in Dancing Deer, the Lord could come and take him away because he had already found paradise.

In Galveston, Mr. Bell had worked for the newspaper. It was the only business he knew, so when he and his wife arrived in Dancing Deer, he looked for the local paper. There was only a bulletin printed once a week in the office of the Church of the Living Word on a mimeograph machine. It was tacked on a glass-enclosed cork board outside the church's front door with copies hand-delivered earlier in the week to the members of the congregation. The church pastor thought it was a good idea to let everybody know that, although preaching salvation was his primary concern, there were other advantages to being a member of this particular congregation. The church's bulletin contained some church news and some community news.

The Bells brought a letter of credit from their bank in Galveston. They had sold their home and, with the proceeds added to their savings, were financially secure. Mr. Bell decided to gamble it all on a weekly paper he planned on naming the *Marsden County Meteor*. Dancing Deer was the county seat of Marsden County and its largest town. It was fertile ground for a newspaper. After buying a small homestead with a large house a few miles from the city limits the remainder of Mr. Bell's money went fast and additional financing had to be procured from the First Bank and Trust of Dancing Deer.

When the *Meteor* opened for business Mr. Bell had hired two reporters, one secretary, and one man to run a decrepit offset press. Not one of his employees had any experience publishing a newspaper. Mr. Bell trained the pressman and wrote most of the columns. The secretary was the only position where the employee could come close to accomplishing what the job required. Mr. Bell worked eighty hours a week and loved it.

The Bells had one child, a boy named Jesse. He was the same age as David Blaine. But where David Blaine's interest was in the great outdoors, Jesse's interest was mainly in activities done inside. David Blaine loved hunting, fishing, hiking, canoeing, spelunking, and all the other wonderful things available to kids growing up in Northwest Arkansas. Jesse, however, liked to spend his time solving chess problems, reading, debating, cross-word puzzles, mind games, and more reading. Jesse was smart. His reading opened up new worlds to him. From a book Jesse had even taught himself to speak French. He eventually found his pronunciation lacked authenticity. Jesse was far more accomplished as a reader of something written in French than of actually speaking it.

Jesse's reading exposed him to events, people, and ideas that shaped the world. He averaged reading two novels a week and had three non-fiction books he was gleaning for particular information going all the time. The library was his favorite place in the entire town and if they didn't start to expand soon Jesse was going to have all their books read before he reached adulthood. If you wanted to know how far it was to the moon, Jesse would know. If you wanted to know how a light bulb worked, Jesse could make a diagram and explain all its many intricacies. Jesse was a straight-A student. Where the parents of other students had to beg or threaten their kids to do the assigned homework, Jesse looked forward to his and worked way ahead in his books. In math classes he would do every problem at the end of every chapter. When the teacher said she wanted them to do every odd numbered problem, Jesse handed in his paper with every problem done. He had done the assignment weeks before and was now six chapters ahead and pulling away.

However, Jesse was not very popular. His activities were primarily solitary so he lacked the social skills necessary to be, say, Senior Class President.

Bill Potter's daughter, Rose, on the other hand, was popular. Some girls have the innate ability to socialize. Rose had it. Her dad lavished money on her. She wore the latest fashions. What wasn't purchased on their numerous trips to Little Rock was ordered from catalogs. Rose would wander into the local dry-goods stores to see what types of clothing were available. From catalogs she ordered similarly designed dresses, blouses, and skirts but made of much more expensive fabrics. Her shoes and coats came directly from New York. Her underwear was imported from France or from New York stores carrying French merchandise. Rose was the envy of her girlfriends but she had one problem. Her dad wouldn't let her date. He treated her one of two ways, sometimes both: either the young man was not good enough or he thought she was still too young for a boyfriend. Rose was allowed to attend social events where lots of people came but she had to arrive and leave with her girl friends. Rose adjusted. She knew her dad loved her and it would only be a short time before she went away to college. Rose knew what college she went to would depend on her grades, her father's ability to pay, and her extra-curricular activities. Rose decided to run for Senior Class President.

The Dancing Deer High School had never had a female Senior Class President. They had never had a female who wanted to be Senior Class President. When she turned in her application several people took notice. The Principal asked his secretary for a list of applicants. The secretary said the only other one so far was Jesse Bell.

When the deadline passed they were the only applicants. The Principal thought it would be evenly split: the boys voting for Jesse and the girls for Rose. He wondered if his school was ready for women politicians. He could remember back when women were yet to be given the right to vote. The consensus of opinion was a woman was too emotional. She didn't have the rational ability necessary to select the best man for the job. His mother had been one of the original suffragettes. Things were going to get interesting.

There was one month between the application deadline and the election. This was the time each participant campaigned. Rose had a whole coalition of girls on her team. They were ready for a fight. Jesse didn't have anyone with him. The boys were apathetic. They didn't care who was Senior Class President. They had other things on their mind. More important things—the impending war, for example.

President Roosevelt was elected largely because he promised the American mothers he would keep their sons out of the war. Most Americans thought, after the Great War, there wouldn't be another similar conflict for many years. They certainly weren't ready for another this soon. In addition, they reasoned the war wasn't fought on American soil, for American land, so we ought to keep American boys out of it. However, we were being pressured by Churchill and Stalin. They needed help; they needed a second front. The Nazis had already defeated France, overrun most of Europe, and this last June invaded Russia. Italy and Germany were formidable opponents for anybody, especially the tiny island nation of Great Britain and the backward and undeveloped, sprawling nation of Russia. Everyone was talking about it. Would we be sucked in to make it a global conflict? Would the unlikely duo of the British and the Bolsheviks prevail? Would the militaristic Germans kick their butts? The young men in the town of Dancing Deer knew if war was declared they would be drafted. Who cared if a girl was elected Senior Class President?

David Blaine cared. He was brought up hating the banker. His whole family hated the banker—except for his mom who professed she didn't hate anybody. Rose received a share of David's rancor simply through her close proximity to the despicable ogre. David went to Jesse and asked what was his strategy to defeat the most popular girl in school? Jesse said he didn't have a clue.

David became Jesse's campaign manager. He convinced Jesse they needed posters printed at his dad's newspaper. Jesse's dad should start running articles about the contest with pictures of Jesse for better public recognition. David told Jesse to start making public appearances at all the sporting events, pep rallies, meetings of any and all clubs, and to start attracting popular kids around him. Jesse asked how would he be able to accomplish that.

David suggested they have a contest and give a trip as a prize. Jesse was all ears as David Blaine explained that they could have some sort of contest where the winner would receive something like a free bus trip to the University of Arkansas to check out the campus. Jesse could talk his dad into sponsoring the contest through the newspaper. Jesse's popularity would rise as he would be the one who decided which students got to go along as chaperones and guests of the paper. Jesse asked, what kind of contest? David Blaine asked what segment of the student population was he needing the most help with. Jesse answered, it was the girls of course. David Blaine said it would have to be something the girls would excel at—maybe a spelling bee. As it happens with all large projects, some items prevail and others fall by the wayside. The contest and newspaper stories didn't fly, but the posters and Jesse's increased presence at school athletic events did.

Early in the campaign David Blaine went to the Principal's office and said, "Sir, we'd like an office to set up campaign headquarters."

"I don't have any office space available." The Principal put down the paper he was reading. "I can't imagine why you need one."

"Well, the girls are more organized than we. Every girl in the school is going to vote for Rose and, if we're going to make a show of it, Jesse needs to look like a serious contender. An office would be a big boost."

"The best I can do is have a janitor clean out a supply closet."

David Blaine was a popular young man so when he asked two cute girls if they would help decorate Jesse's new headquarters they switched sides without blinking. Showing Rose their perfidious nature, they spent an entire afternoon hanging posters supplied by the newspaper. They also cut out and painted black cardboard letters for the closet door saying, "Jesse Bell, Campaign Headquarters."

David and Jesse put a table and a few chairs inside the closet and with them they stored their paints, poster paper, extra pre-printed posters, and other miscellaneous supplies. They held strategy sessions inside and even let the two female recruits have an occasional say in how the strategies should be perpetrated. Their suggestions, however, were not actually listened to or put into play.

David placed a desk and chair in the hallway beside the closet door. On the desk he stuck an old typewriter, a calendar, a couple of pads of paper, and a non-working telephone. He told the girls he would appreciate it if they could make sure someone sat at the desk between classes scribbling something on one of the pads of paper or faking a telephone call.

Water jugs were located in various places along the hallways. David Blaine got his two new recruits to draw signs saying, "Free Water! Courtesy of Jesse Bell, your candidate for Class President."

David started rumors that Jesse was negotiating with the principal for a longer lunch break, more travel time between classes, and more days off during the Christmas holidays. He also started a rumor that Rose was trying to get a Manifesto of Student Conduct instituted and, if approved by the principal, their scholastic lives would be as regimented as the French Foreign Legion.

David told the Principal that Friday was Arm Band Day, to commemorate the soldiers who had died in the ongoing European conflict. He presented the principal with enough red arm bands for not only the administrative employees, but also the kitchen staff, the nurse, and the janitors. David Blaine spent the rest of the week, through Thursday, telling everyone Friday was Arm Band Day. He didn't explain what the arm bands were to signify until early Friday morning when he, Jesse, and their two female helpers hung posters throughout the halls telling the students, "Today is Arm Band Day! Show your solidarity for the candidate of your choice for Senior Class President. Wear your arm band proud; pick up one today from your candidate's headquarters. Red for Jesse and Blue for Rose."

David, Jesse, and one of their two recruits began to circulate giving out bright red arm bands. Jesse and David mingled throughout the crowd, shaking hands and kissing babies—well, not exactly kissing babies. David did make sure all his friends, and especially the popular ones, wore red arm bands. The second recruit manned the desk in front of their campaign headquarters and proceeded to give out arm bands to everyone who walked by.

When Rose's supporters asked for an arm band, Rose had to admit she didn't have any. Shortly after the posters were hung and the students given enough time to see them, and before they were noticed by the Principal or one of his staff, they were hastily taken down by the two female recruits.

When the students saw the principal sporting a red arm band they thought he was supporting Jesse. Quite a few fence-hangers landed on Jesse's side and asked for their own arm bands. The principal, his assistants, secretaries, clerks, janitors, and all the kitchen staff proudly wore their red arm bands to signify their empathy for the fallen soldiers. The students caught the fever and Jesse's popularity had never been so high.

Rose cried foul. She accused the entire administration of showing favoritism. The principal, realizing he'd been duped, had his staff, in fact anyone who was not a student, remove their arm bands. He didn't explain why. He didn't want it known he'd been hoodwinked. Quite a few elected to keep theirs on in defiance, thinking they were supporting the memory of fallen soldiers.

Rose went home crying to her dad. She told him David Blaine was the campaign chairman of her adversary and he wasn't playing fair. The newspaper was printing his posters and they looked so good her helpers were reluctant to hang any posters whatsoever for her. That's all it took. Bill wasn't going to let any of the Calhoun clan best his little girl. Bill poured money into Rose's campaign. He told the principal things had to be made fair. With the principal's approval, he hired a band to entertain the students during their lunches. He wrote speeches for Rose to recite between musical sets. Bill even traveled to Little Rock and had an ad agency design and produce new posters. He arranged for Rose, and the main members of her coalition, to plan their strategy sessions in the meeting room of the largest restaurant in town and paid for their meals.

Jesse threw down the gauntlet and challenged Rose to debate him in the auditorium. He received the approval of the government teacher and the debate coach. The principal even agreed and told the debate coach to come up with an equitable format. He went looking for an open time slot for the auditorium.

No one was having a better time of this than the principal. He knew he was being pressured from both sides, each candidate was acting unfairly, and money was being injected improperly into each campaign. He also knew the voters were being duped, fleeced, coddled, and bribed. He had been heard to say this was how democracy worked. David

Blaine thought so too. He also became of the opinion that money and power talk.

Everyone was disappointed, and Rose lost a few votes, when she declined to debate. Although she was talented, she knew she was not of the same caliber as Jesse and thought declining to be in her best interest.

When the election came and ended three things had come to fruition: Rose was elected the first female Senior Class President at Dancing Deer High School, Rose hated David Blaine as much as he hated her, and Jesse and David Blaine were the very best of friends.

CHAPTER 7—ROSE
Dancing Deer - April 1942

David Blaine Calhoun was an extremely good-looking young man. He was tall and muscular, with blond hair and blue eyes. Most girls watched as he walked down the school corridors. Rose Potter was an extremely good-looking young woman. Of average height, she was poised, articulate, and curvy in all the right places. All the boys watched—even David—as she walked down the school corridors. Both were popular among their classmates, made good grades, and shared classes, but they seldom talked unless it was absolutely necessary. None of the students or teachers knew why. Just for their own amusement, and to keep the waters stirred, the teachers paired them on assignments. They were lab partners in biology, chief combatants on the debate team, and always placed together on whatever committee the teachers and students could dream up.

David Blaine and Rose added fuel to the fire themselves. They seemed to habitually take opposite sides on any controversial issue. Once Rose, at a Student Council meeting, suggested they cut the lunch break from an hour to thirty minutes and get dismissed in the afternoon thirty minutes earlier. David Blaine countered that would just give them time to get more chores done. David Blaine once suggested they play intramural basketball in the gym during the lunch break and Rose countered that the girls preferred volleyball and before school was a better time. Everyone knew these two didn't see eye-to-eye and it was pretty much a school effort to keep them at each other's throat.

The school play their senior year was Shakespeare's *Romeo and Juliet*. It would be performed just before graduation. The consensus of opinion was that the only two people to play the parts of the star-crossed lovers should be David Blaine and Rose. No one else was considered. Had someone had the audacity to suggest another pairing he would have been pummeled by one and all. David Blaine and Rose didn't have any say in the matter. It was a done deal.

Although David Blaine and Rose did not much care for the pairing, their parents abhorred the arrangement. Jed had to be restrained by Emily from driving over to the bank the first moment he heard about it and throttling Bill. Emily finally persuaded her distraught husband that Bill didn't have anything to do with it. Rose and David were the only two people in the drama class with the talent to play those parts. She said they were both adults and it was nothing more than play-acting.

Jed calmed down but said, "I'll be sitting on the front row and there had better not be any hanky-panky."

Bill was aware of David Blaine's ability to somehow persuade people to see things his way. He told Rose he got that from his dad. Jed had always been a cretin of the worst sort and with just that same ability. He was also aware that Rose despised David Blaine so decided to let things roll along for the present.

Each practiced their part separately and got proficient with the wording, phrasing, and gesturing. When they worked together things did not go so smoothly. David looked at Rose and forgot half his lines. Rose looked at David and started reciting lines from an entirely different scene. The students thought it was hilarious. The teachers shook their heads and concentrated on the remaining actors and their lines.

A guitar player who spent most of his time gazing at stars and writing music appropriate for his passion was hired by the school to play short chamber pieces between scenes. To increase the volume of sound emitted from his guitar he even rigged up a separate sound system with a microphone stuck inside the guitar suspended directly under the strings.

The musical composer was given *carte blanche* to develop his own score with the condition that during the performance he was to play something *pianissimo* and moving during special dramatic scenes and something *fortissimo* and forceful during ones deemed more climatic. He became adept at cutting and pasting as he tried to match his compositions to the play. He ended up using significant portions of his entire collection of sheet music. It was a *tour de force* and he was saturated with the juice of creation.

During one rehearsal, after Romeo had taken poison, and the grief-stricken Juliet was standing over the body of her dead lover—

about to kiss him on his cold lips—David opened one eye and stuck out his tongue. With closed eyes Rose lowered her head and kissed—or tried to kiss her Romeo. Thinking she had missed her mark she opened her eyes and proceeded to bite the tip of the offending appendage. David yelled in pain.

The students jabbed at each other as if to say, "See, I told ya."

The teachers groaned. Lately, their opinion had become that David and Rose should be performing *The Taming of the Shrew*.

When the Saturday came for the only performance slated, every seat in the auditorium had been sold. This was the cultural event of the year for Dancing Deer and even people from neighboring towns would be arriving for the eight p.m. curtain. David and Rose worked hard to memorize their entrances, exits, and all the other things that make a performer polished in his craft. Every performer had his lines down pat. They were ready. From the entire cast, but especially from David Blaine and Rose, the townspeople were expecting stellar performances. The students were expecting a melee of mishaps. The teachers didn't know what to expect.

On Saturday morning, they had the last rehearsal—in dress. David Blaine performed flawlessly until he set eyes on Rose, then stammered, forgot a line or two, made up a line or two, directed his conversation to the wrong cohort, then tripped over the lowest step of a staircase stage prop.

Jane Winters, the teacher in charge was about to yell, "Stop," but thought better of it and decided David needed to play through.

Rose did a better job at first but at the ball she was taking a drink when the masked Romeo entered. Her hand froze and let her metal cup slip. It clanged around on the wooden floor. The play continued.

Later, she was on a balcony reciting how much she loved Romeo. She could see him in the fake orchard trees below and said her lines out of the proper sequence. When she turned to go inside, at the beckoning of her maid, she stepped on the hem of her gown and tore out a section of the lining. The play went on.

There were more mishaps. Romeo dropped his sword during a battle with Tybalt, picked it up, and stabbed a *papier-mâché* pineapple. Juliet spilled the potion given her by the friar and still the play went on. Just before the final scene David Blaine got in a sneezing fit. And in the final scene as Juliet bent to kiss the dead Romeo, again she closed her eyes, Romeo moved just a bit, and she planted a kiss on his top lip and the side of his nose. When the curtain came down Rose ran off the stage and David Blaine slowly made his way to Miss Winters. He apologized and said he'd go back over his lines until the very last minute. When he walked away shaking his head, someone slipped him a deftly folded note with no corners or edges. He worked on getting the thing opened. He looked at it this way and that way and even held it up to a light bulb. He didn't have a clue of how to get into it. He wondered how in the devil anyone could have made such a contrivance then Rose walked up, snatched the note, and said they needed to talk.

David followed her to the deserted teacher's lounge where they sat opposite each other in arm chairs. Rose looked at David Blaine and said, "David, we can't continue this way. I need to know why you hate me."

David Blaine was afraid this was the reason for her sudden desire for communication and didn't have a good answer. He decided he should probably tell her the truth. "Rose, I've fallen in love with you but can't do anything about it because our fathers hate each other."

Rose turned her face so David couldn't see the tears forming in her eyes and managed to squeak out, "David, do you really love me?"

"Rose, you make me weak in the knees. When I see you I lose control of my senses. My train of thought escapes me. I don't know where I am or what I'm doing. Somehow, I'm lost in space and then something happens to bring me back into focus and I find I've stepped in something or sat down where there wasn't a chair. It's all very disconcerting. Rose, you've got me under some sort of spell. I don't know whether to run to you or from you."

Rose got up and walked to where David was sitting. She sat down on his knee, put one hand against the side of his face, the other hand behind his head, and kissed him hard on the lips.

David had never been kissed like that. When the kiss was over he put his arms around her waist and as she demurely looked down, he lightly kissed her eyelid. Rose murmured. The door sprung open and an excited Jesse ran in and said Rose's dad was right behind him. Rose jumped up. Jesse grabbed David by the arm and they ran into the adjacent room—the Principal's office. Hiding behind the door they heard Mr. Potter storm into the room and interrogate Rose.

"Where is he, Rose?'

"Who are you talking about, Daddy?"

"Don't give me that innocent, little girl look. They told me you and that Calhoun kid were headed to the teacher's lounge."

"Did they say why we were heading here?"

"No—no, they didn't."

"Well, David was just being nice. He was getting me a wet wash cloth to get dust from one of the stage props out of my eyes."

"Let me see."

Rose started to wipe the tears from her eyes then stopped and turned her face up toward her father. She said, "He came in here looking and came back outside. He said he'd have to go to the cafeteria, he'd be back in a minute. So I came in to wait. That was just a minute or so ago and he hasn't returned."

Rose's father then started edging his way toward one of the remaining two doors exiting the room. He turned the doorknob. It was locked. Rose was horrified. Bill quietly slipped to the Principal's office door and slowly turned the doorknob. He abruptly opened the door and rushed inside the darkened room. After looking around he went through to another door leading to the Principal's secretary's office. It was locked. Bill went back into the teacher's lounge, grabbed Rose by the elbow, and herded her out the door to his car.

Jesse wiped the sweat from his forehead and whispered to David Blaine that he should try to be more discrete. They both emerged from under the principal's big desk and gave a sigh of relief.

On the way home Rose asked, "Dad, why do you and David's father dislike each other so much?"

Bill thought a moment then said, "Jed stole something from me, I couldn't get over it, and I ended up retaliating in a brutal and unbecoming way. Jed can't forgive me for what I did so we're at an impasse."

"Couldn't you be the better man and offer some sort of reconciliation?"

"No, Rose. I couldn't. What's more, I still think of him as a thief-in-the-night. I haven't forgiven him and, I know for certain, he hasn't forgiven me. I do regret, however, the judgment I exercised in exacting my revenge. If I was given the opportunity of doing it again I probably wouldn't. As it was, I hurt not only Jed, but dear Emily as well."

"And David—did you hurt David?"

"Yes, I suppose I did."

"Are you still trying to hurt David, Daddy?"

"Rose, I thought you and David Blaine didn't like each other. Am I wrong . . . is there something between the two of you I'm not privy to?"

"Dad, you didn't answer my question. Are you still trying to hurt David?"

"Well, I certainly won't let him steal something from me like his father did. You are not to see him or to have any dealings with him whatsoever. I absolutely forbid it! And that's final! As far as hurting David, I do not wish the young man any ill will—as long as he stays the hell away from my daughter. Now, I don't want to talk about it any more."

That night people were queued in a long line at the box office to pick up their tickets. In addition to the permanent seats the school had added as many folding seats as the aisles and the fire marshal would allow and even placed some down front on both sides of the guitar player. Everywhere there was a place, there was a seat. Some people had waited to get their ticket at the door only to find the performance sold out with standing room only at the far back. Jed dropped Emily at the front door, parked his pickup truck, and walked back to escort her in. On the way a well-dressed man asked if Jed had a ticket.

"Yeah. I've got a ticket."

"I'll give you twenty for it."

"I don't think you want to be in the seat my ticket's for."

"Is it behind a post or something?"

"No. It's on the front row. The problem would be with the hostility of the crazy woman in the next seat."

With the man perplexed and scratching his head, Jed walked to the waiting arm of Emily and they sauntered into the auditorium. Jed's seat was indeed on the front row. He had expressly requested it from the very beginning.

Emily was amazed at the number of people in the audience. She said the school needed to provide more performances and Jed said limiting it to just the one made it all the more special. If they kept it to fewer performances than the demand called for they would always play to a full house.

Emily pinched his arm and said, "Mr. Calhoun, you are so smart."

A full hour before the play was set to start the fans started filing in and jostled around to find their seats with the help of the members of the drama class who had been assigned to build the props and stage sets and other volunteers working for a free seat. The crowd was becoming noisy as neighbors greeted each other, relatives wildly waved their arms to let others of their families know they had found the lost seats, and refreshments were purchased—then consumed at the refreshment stand when they were informed no refreshments would be allowed in the auditorium.

To quell the cacophony the guitar player tuned his instrument and adjusted his microphone and amplifier. Then he started playing a piece he had composed to quiet prison rebellions. One man folded his hands across his stomach and interlocked his thumbs. After ten minutes of listening he told his wife that whoever was playing the gee-tar could make bears hibernate early or rouse them from a deep slumber depending on what he wanted to accomplish.

Backstage, Rose and David Blaine were putting on their costumes in separate dressing rooms. Each was wondering what the other was thinking and how this would play out—not just tonight's play, but their lives as well.

Rose thought the play *apropos*. Her family was like the Capulets and David's family the Montagues. She knew if ever there was to be a reconciliation it would be up to her and David. A knock on the girls' dressing room door.

"Curtain call. Ten minutes."

In the other dressing room, David Blaine had a lot on his mind. The play was nothing. A few months earlier Japan attacked our Pacific Fleet while they were snoozing at Ford Island in Pearl Harbor. The

United States immediately declared war on Japan. Germany and Italy then declared war on the United States. The next few months the United States started readying herself for the impending effort. The Selective Service Act had already passed in 1940. Originally, the act was written only to draft men who were twenty-one years of age up to somewhere in their forties but the talk was now that they were going to widen the age limits.

David thought, soon after he graduated, he would be receiving his congratulatory letter. Jesse would be working at his dad's paper but that job would not be considered necessary for the war effort. Jesse would be just like him. He and Jesse decided to enlist, hoping they could serve together.

David wondered what would happen to Rose. She had already decided she would not be going away to college. She was determined to be of benefit to the war effort in Dancing Deer. Rose's dad told her she could have any job she wanted at the bank and Mr. Bell offered her a job at the paper. One of his reporters had been drafted—the other being too old. There was a knock on the boys' dressing room door.

"Curtain call. Five minutes."

Jesse stuck his head in. "Hey, man, break a leg."

David made the last adjustment to his costume and walked out of the dressing room to the area from which he would first enter the stage. Looking across the open stage floor to the opposite side where other actors were congregated, he spotted Rose. They made eye contact. David winked. Rose flashed a big smile. Everything was going to be all right.

That night everything went perfect. Neither Rose nor David missed a cue. They were so convincing in their lines the audience could actually believe the two were in love, really in love. Both Jed and Bill spent the evening squirming in their seats as the guitar player passionately reinforced the love radiating between the two actors.

In the last scene Juliet approached the dead body of Romeo laid before her on a bier. She rushed to his side. With tears flowing down her cheeks she said, "What's here? A cup closed in my true love's hand. Poison, I see hath been his timeless end. O churl! Drink all . . . and left no friendly drop to help me after."

"I will kiss thy lips. Haply some poison yet doth hang on them, to make me die with a restorative."

As Rose bent to kiss Romeo the guitar played the saddest melody anyone had ever heard. People in the audience were openly crying. David and Rose had made the story come alive. There were a lot of wet sleeves as there were not enough handkerchiefs in the crowd to go around. Juliet kissed the dead Romeo. It was a lingering kiss, tender, passionate, filled with emotion. The audience's crying became outright bawling. Juliet raised herself upright. She said, "Thy lips are warm."

A watchman approaches.

"Yea, noise? Then I'll be brief. Oh, happy dagger." Juliet clutches Romeo's dagger and says, "This is thy sheaf."

Juliet plunges the dagger into her heart. The audience gasps. Juliet says, "There, rust, and let me die." Juliet falls to the floor and the audience comes unglued. They'd never been so overtaken by a performance.

There were several curtain calls where the standing audience wouldn't quit clapping until the curtain opened and the actors came back onstage and bowed. Bill walked to the stage during the first curtain call and handed Rose a bouquet of long-stemmed red roses. The audience knew they had witnessed something special and they wanted the actors to know how much they appreciated it. They kept clapping. Another curtain call and then another. Eventually the audience pushed the guitarist to the stage to join the bowing with the troupe. He was so happy he was already making plans on taking his guitar and musical score to Hollywood.

Backstage, the teachers gushed with pride. Happy fathers and mothers pushed on the stage door to get in to congratulate their students. Both Jed and Bill were among the throng. Emily tarried and got caught by several well-wishers. Bill was on the first step to the stage door. He looked back, saw Jed, and said, "Jed, your boy did a fine job."

One of the teachers opened the door and let in the clamoring parents. Bill went straight to the girl's dressing room but wasn't allowed in. The teacher at the door said the young ladies were changing clothes and the parents would have to wait. One by one, and sometimes in groups, the young ladies emerged. Bill stood waiting, holding and wringing his hands. In a few minutes the girls quit coming out. He asked

Miss Winters if she would see if he had somehow missed Rose. The teacher opened the door and walked to the dressing area Rose had been using. Rose was sitting on a stool in front of a make-up table with a three-paneled mirror, crying.

The teacher said, "This has been some night. I don't think there's a dry eye in the house. Rose, you and David Blaine did such a wonderful job. I'm proud to have been a part of it with you. Honey, your dad's waiting outside the door. Now wipe away those tears and go greet your fans. There must be fifty people waiting by the stage door to tell you what they thought of your performance."

The drama teacher was a special friend to Rose and only a few years older. Rose looked up to her teacher and said as she slowly got up from her stool, "Miss Winters, I'm so tired. I'm emotionally exhausted."

The crowd that streamed into the boy's dressing room received a greater value for their admission price. At least it appeared so to the mothers—and especially to the sisters and girlfriends. The young men in the boy's dressing room had no one guarding their door. When the parents, siblings, and girlfriends came charging in what they saw were dozens of young men in various stages of undress. A similar circumstance in the girl's dressing room would have been met with shrieks as the young ladies covered themselves with whatever was handy. The young men didn't much care. They were elated with their performance. Everyone had done exceedingly well. They had adoring fans. Life was great. The feeling would only last for a short time however, until the boys thought about graduating in a few weeks and then being drafted soon after that.

Jed walked over to David Blaine and sat down on a bench beside him. He said, "Son that was the most romantic acting I've ever seen. Not that I've been to many plays but you and Rose were just outstanding. Your mother says it's play-acting. For your sake, I hope she's right. But if what I saw was what I think I saw, you have a long and difficult row to hoe. Bill's a devious man. He'll stop at nothing to exact justice. If he thinks he's been wronged, he'll make it his life's goal to set things straight. Nothing, or nobody, is too mean or too ruthless for him to use. And stealing his daughter—well, you'll be his enemy forever."

David Blaine nodded and quietly said, "Dad, I love Rose. But I'll be going to war soon and I don't want her to be tied to me. I don't know what lies ahead and it wouldn't be right to handcuff her to someone who might not make it back."

"Son, I know you'll do what's right. By the time you get back things may have changed. At least you and Rose will have time to formulate a plan. If I, or your mother, can help, you have but to ask. I also know you'll make it back. We Calhouns have always been a sturdy and resourceful breed of people. You'll make it back just fine or I'll go over there myself and whip every butt I come across."

David Blaine came out of his reverie and laughed. He knew his dad would do just that.

"Come on. Get dressed. Your mother's waiting. Also, there are a bunch of people outside who want to slap you on the back and throw rose petals on the ground in front of you as we walk to my old truck."

The next Monday, David Blaine and Rose were the talk of the school. During their English literature class Rose smuggled a note to David. It was folded just like the one he couldn't open the previous Saturday. On the outside of this one she had scribbled "Squeeze here—to here." When he did, a neat little flap appeared and from there he was able to get into the thing.

> *Romeo,*
>
> *I think we need to continue our little charade for awhile. I don't want to have to explain anything to anybody. If you agree, I think we should continue with the hostility until we can decide a better course of action. I never did get to tell you my feelings. We should meet after school. Will you make a suggestion about where? Dispose of this note after you have read it.*
>
> *Love,*
> *Juliet*

David carefully refolded the note and stuffed it into his pants pocket. Somehow he had to break this off. It would be no life for Rose waiting by the telephone for word that he'd been shot. What was he going to do?

The next day, he got another note from Juliet. It was simple and to the point.

> *Romeo,*
> *I want to see you. Down by the Little Creek water crossing. After school!*
> *Juliet*

When David got there Rose was sitting on the edge of the concrete with her socks and shoes off and her feet dangling in the flowing water. She didn't get up or even look up as David approached. He took off his shoes and socks, rolled up his pants legs, and sat down beside her. "I used to fish in this creek when I was eight or nine. Caught lots of little perch and a few brilliantly marked bream."

"David, why didn't you answer my note?"

"Rose, I'll be going off to war in a few weeks. That's no life for a beautiful woman. You don't want to spend your time waiting on me to return. Waiting for some officer to knock on your door to tell you I'm missing in action—or possibly I've been shot, or even killed."

At that Rose threw her arms around David and said, "David, I'll be here waiting for you no matter what you say or what you do. You don't have control over that. If you love me like I love you this will just be a trial for us. We'll come through this and everything will be okay. I just know it will."

A car came up slowly on the crossing and ran over one of David's shoes as it crept across. David said, "Rose, if I do make it back, what then? Our dads hate each other."

Rose said, "Why is that? I don't know what started it all in the first place."

David told her the story as he knew it. Rose was wide-eyed. Her father would not do such a thing. She got up, put her socks and shoes on, and walked to her dad's car. She told David, "You must be mistaken. I've got to think about this. I'll see you at school tomorrow."

It was just a few more days until graduation and Bill began keeping closer tabs on Rose. She couldn't sneak off anymore. Every so often she sent David a note. It usually said the same thing.

I'll be here when you get back. I love you, David.

Two weeks after graduation David and Jesse showed up at the Army Recruiting Office in Russellville with Jed and Mr. Bell. Being only eighteen they needed their parents to sign a permission slip. When they walked in, the recruiting officer jumped up, shook hands all around, slapped the two boys on their backs, and said they'd make their parents proud. He said the Army needed men just like them, the Army took care of its own. They would eat well, have the best medical care, and they would be able to serve together. Jesse thought the recruiting officer was just spouting off what he thought they wanted to hear and it might be true but, most likely, was not and the recruiting officer hoped to have an assignment somewhere else when the people he had signed up started returning from their tours of duty.

They were both slated to take physicals a couple of days later. At the appointed time the doctor said David was as healthy as a horse—which didn't sit well with David, knowing what he did about horses. The doctor told Jesse he had an irregularly beating heart and would be put in a deferred status. Jesse asked what that meant.

The doctor said, "Son, you're not going to war."

Jesse was both relieved and upset at the same time. He didn't feel it was sane to kill another human being and was scared to death of being shot himself but he also wanted to do what was right. Right now he thought his country needed him and he had come up lacking.

That night Mr. Bell had a heart attack. The doctor told Jesse and his mother that Mr. Bell needed bed rest. He had had a mild heart attack and was now doing better but it was the doctor's experience that if Mr. Bell's lifestyle wasn't altered another would soon occur, and another, and another until his system couldn't recover and he'd die. If they wanted to prolong Mr. Bell's life they needed to help him make certain changes. He couldn't work at the paper anymore, he needed to walk, eat healthier foods, and get plenty of rest.

Jesse took over running the newspaper and hired Rose as a reporter. The paper had prospered under his father's reign. A couple of years earlier he had retired the antiquated press and mortgaged everything, with Potter's bank, for a new offset press he had seen in a trade journal. It had been shipped from Chicago. The *Marsden County Meteor* was upscale now. Sharp clear pictures, distinct print, and a multitude of types. Their readership increased and other businesses needing quality printing started bringing rough drafts to be typeset and printed when the paper's employees weren't printing the newspaper.

Jesse told David, "You've got to promise to journal your activities and send me weekly updates."

"You planning on publishing them in the newspaper?"

"I won't if you object, but the people in town will want to keep up with their boys. It's news. Other men I've talked to have agreed and I plan on devoting a regular part of the paper to showing where each Dancing Deer soldier is stationed and what he's doing. I'd like your permission to print what's newsworthy."

"Okay, but leave out anything that might embarrass my family."

Jesse laughed and said, "Discretion is the greater part of valor."

A week and a half later, on a Saturday morning, David Blaine was scheduled to leave on a bus for an induction center in Little Rock. His soldiering career was about to commence. The night before he was to ship out, David Blaine stole over to Rose's house.

Rose was in the kitchen with most of the lights turned out when David tapped on the window above the sink. She peeked through the shears and saw David standing there about to tap again. She motioned for him to have a seat. She'd be right out. After running to her bedroom she spent a few minutes locating a terrycloth robe to wrap around her silk nightgown and, shoeless, hurried out the back door. She found David sitting on the porch swing.

"David, what are you doing here? It's after midnight."

"Rose, I leave tomorrow. I just wanted to come by and talk with you before I left."

"Oh, David, it's the day we've been dreading. You know though I think I can handle it. I'll write to you every day."

"Rose, if we get married when I get back, how can we get your dad and mine to reconcile their feud?"

"I don't know, darling. We'll just have to convince them it's childish to continue when they could be enjoying their grandchildren. You'd be surprised how unifying children can be."

Rose threw her arms around David and they kissed. David ended up staying the rest of the night. As things would have it, their love for each other got the better of their judgment. Rose knew David would come back but it would be a long, cold, hard period for her to wait. It was only a small sacrifice. Although she would not be able to yield herself for the first time on their wedding night, she was happy to have had the intimacy and knew, if it was not for the war, things would have played out more to her liking.

David had not intended for things to get out of hand. He had not meant for the evening to end this way and afterwards was remorseful. He apologized to Rose more than once. Rose appreciated his concern. She told him his apologies were sweet but it was her need as well as his and, for her, it had been very special, something she was not ashamed of. They fell asleep in each other's arms.

As the sun started to show itself on the horizon, David removed Rose's hand from his chest and tried to sit up. He ached all over. A wooden porch swing is no place to spend the night. He'd file that away in his mental drawer of useless information. Rose stirred and David whispered to her, "Rose, honey you have to get up. Your dad might be stepping out that back door soon and I want to be long gone when that happens."

"You don't have to worry. Dad goes into town on Friday nights and stays with a lady friend of his. He won't be back until lunch or after."

David said, "You mean we could've been in the house all this time?"

"I think a porch swing's more romantic, don't you?"

David sighed, "Dad told me women couldn't be understood or dealt with. They can only be admired and catered to."

"Your dad's one smart Calhoun."

David grabbed his things and said he had to go home. He'd packed before he'd come over. His bus left around noon and he wanted to say good-bye to Rose now—there. She understood. Rose said she had something for him and rushed into the house. She came back with a small oblong package wrapped in gaudy wine colored paper and matching ribbon. She said, "Don't open it until Sunday night at 7:15 p.m."

They kissed one last time. He left Rose with tears streaming down her face.

At exactly 7:15 on Sunday night in an old World War I Army barracks in Little Rock, David opened the package. In it he found a beautiful silver filigreed fountain pen and a small bottle of blue-black ink. There was a note that said:

> *Write to me David.*
>
> *I'm in church as you read this. I am praying right now that God will look out for you and keep you from harm. Don't worry about things here. I'll take care of everything.*
>
> *I'll pray for you every night at exactly seven fifteen. I love you David Blaine Calhoun—don't you ever forget it.*
>
> *Rose*

CHAPTER 8—BASIC TRAINING
Little Rock - June 1942

David sat in a sweltering railway car. The train was full but David was one of the first aboard and had a seat by the window. He needed the air. The Army ran on cigarette fumes. If he didn't sit by the window he'd be spending the entire trip wiping watery eyes. He did, however, get stung occasionally by a coal cinder blown from one of the engine stacks through the open window.

The heat made him think about those summers a few years back. David had gone for four straight summers to harvest other people's crops. He dreaded it the first time but soon learned he was important, each member of his family was important, and what work each provided was important. Charlotte worked as hard as David. She was lean and strong for a girl of eight. Amanda, seven, was the next and it was her responsibility to take care of her little sister, April, who was three and into more trouble than anyone anticipated. It was a steady job for Amanda, but she preferred playing with her little sister to the field work of her older siblings.

When the time came for them to leave, Mr. Turner arrived in an old pickup truck. He had his family in the cab and their traveling baggage in a corner of the bed. The Calhouns had the use of the remaining cargo area. Their first work was a hundred miles north so they had to endure the windy space for only one day.

Arriving at the migrant work camp, Mr. Turner helped his father find a suitable spot to pitch their tent. David's father looked at the other campsites and made theirs look similar but a bit more organized. He determined what their daily routine would be and arranged everything according to how and when it would be used.

His father quickly picked up on the methods yielding the most output with the least effort. He was constantly suggesting ways to improve their performance. It soon became apparent the Calhouns were on a mission. They produced more than any other similar group of workers and seemed to enjoy it.

That's when it hit David Blaine. His dad was an inventor. No, he was a production engineer. Everything he did was an effort to make a difficult task easier. He heard stories of the still his dad had made and how he mounted it on a platform beneath a giant oak tree. He attached some sort of block and tackle arrangement of pulleys and levers and in just a few seconds he could have the whole contraption hauled high in the tree. If anyone actually looked up they would think it was a kid's tree house but without a ladder to get to it. His dad never owned up to having a still, but the people in town seemed to think he had and, in their opinion, his shine was the best.

When they picked spinach his dad supplied them with special knives he purchased at the hardware store. Someone, pointing to the hook on the end, said they were for cutting linoleum. His dad sharpened that hook and, with a simple flick, the hook would effortlessly sever the spinach leaves. When they picked strawberries, his dad helped the owner of the field build a grader that would separate the fruit into different sizes. When they picked peaches, he got a basket weaver to split a bushel basket into two halves. The basket weaver curved the inside edges and re-wove them into two new half-bushel baskets. His dad then intertwined a big leather belt through the inside curves and wore them around his waist. When he climbed a ladder to pick peaches he had both hands free and didn't have to come down until the bushel basket halves were full. For the rest of the family he put a sack on the end of a pole just below a nail he'd bent into a half circle. Everyone in David's family, other than his dad, stood on the ground and reached up into the tree with their sticks. Each family member got as many as could be handled, sometimes a whole sack, without even getting on a ladder.

When hoeing cotton, David remembered the hours his dad worked filing to keep their hoes sharp. When it was time to pick each hand dragged a sack between the cotton rows. The sack would hold a hundred pounds. His dad's sack would hold more than twice that much. It was longer than everyone else's and bigger around with a hoop sewn in the end to keep it open. His father fashioned two shoulder straps in a criss-cross pattern so the sack dragged directly behind instead of over to one side and, since it was bigger around, he could toss in handfuls of cotton with his left or his right. He picked his cotton two rows at a time.

Since his sack was so much bigger than everyone else's, and would hold much more cotton, he had to fix it so it rolled along on a wooden platform with pneumatic tires. Sometimes, April would ride up and down the rows on top of the bag. She thought it was a hoot.

They worked each summer until they had earned enough money to make that year's payment to the bank. The first summer it was a close call. The next summer they had earned more than enough when it was time to travel back with the Turners. The third year the family had become so productive the Turners weren't ready when the Calhouns had earned their payment so they hitched a ride back with another returning family. Then the last summer it was just him and his dad and they had become so proficient in their work the other workers stood in awe and then tried to imitate their efforts.

The first two years, when they returned, neighbors brought over extra food they had canned or smoked. Two or three families said they planted extra rows and talked with each other about weeding the Calhoun beans or checking the Calhoun corn for insects or watering the Calhoun okra. The old man whose barn Jed's brothers re-built delivered two sides of beef and one dressed hog to their smokehouse. It was one neighbor helping another. The old man said he was glad to be able to repay their kindness and it was just an old Arkansas custom anyway. If he hadn't done it any number of other neighbors would have stepped up. That winter his dad killed a deer and gave the old man half of the dressed carcass.

David was feeling good. He had gone through the Induction Center, received his inoculations and a few vaccinations, been given two duffel bags of clothing and other essentials, and had his hair shorn. He was now heading to Branch Immaterial Training—better known as Basic. He made a high score on the Army General Classification Test and was told he qualified for Officer Candidate School or, if he chose, he could be in either Military Intelligence or the Army Air Corps. He couldn't decide and asked if he could have a few days to write his dad for advice. They told him he could have until half-way through. Basic Training was the same for everyone.

He received quite a bit of mail. His stint at the Induction Center lasted for two weeks and during that time he received a *Marsden County Meteor* and a stack of letters. Rose typed hers at the newspaper office.

She said she didn't want her father peering over her shoulder and finding she was writing to David. Jesse had bought her a new Underwood typewriter and she now typed everything she could. Jesse gave her a book on learning to touch type. She had a hard time not looking at the keys as she typed so Jesse bought, and installed, blank key caps. At first they exacerbated her slowness because she was constantly stopping to look at a chart Jesse had hung on the wall. It didn't take long to get to know where the keys were though and now she could type almost as fast as Jesse. She then wrote, "No. That was an exaggeration. No one types as fast as Jesse. And no one can put a story together as fast as Jesse." She said she really enjoyed her job. She ended by signing, "Love, Juliet," and kissing the paper with brilliant red lipstick. David saved her letters.

Jesse put a map of Europe and the Mediterranean on the left and the Pacific Rim on the right of the center section of the paper. He placed numbers showing the locations of each Dancing Deer soldier. The number matched up with a name at the bottom of the page and the soldier's mailing address. The next page included bits of news Jesse excerpted from the letters he received from each soldier. Most of the soldiers were still stateside. A few were training in England or Scotland, some were aboard ships, and one or two were with the marines already fighting the Japanese. There were forty-five Dancing Deer soldiers at the end of June 1942.

David received two letters from girls he went to school with. Both told him how proud they were of him and what was happening in their lives. They asked what was happening in his and hoped he would write them back. David wondered if writing them back would be proper. He loved Rose but reasoned if he were still in Dancing Deer and happened to see either on the street and they talked to him, it would just be polite to respond. He wrote to Rose and asked her what he should do. Rose replied that the girls didn't know about their relationship and they probably wrote to all the Dancing Deer soldiers. She said he might as well reply, that she was comfortable in their relationship, and not a jealous woman. But David need not go out of his way to test her. He should write them a short letter saying how hard he was training and how little sleep he was getting. When he got letters it was usually a month's worth at a time and not to count on him for regular return letters. David thought how smart Rose was and put the two letters away for another day.

Jed replied to David's letter and told him an officer directed other people's work . . . much like a supervisor. With David's intelligence, his supervising of subordinates would be a good way to make that intelligence more useful to the Army, especially if he got to sit behind a desk and supervise from afar. Sometimes a spoonful of sugar will sweeten the entire barrel. David wrote back saying his dad was just thinking of the fermentation process and a spoonful of sugar sounded like blarney from an Irishman.

David wrote Jesse and asked him for his advice. Both Military Intelligence and the Army Air Corps were enticing alternatives to Officer Candidate School. He also wondered if he should be considering a military career. David knew Jesse would have an informed opinion worth listening to. Jesse wrote back that he thought Military Intelligence was the way to go. David wouldn't do any actual fighting and he would be privy to the most interesting things going on in the entire war. He might be involved in decoding secret messages, clandestine rendezvous with the French Resistance, planning attacks or counter attacks. He'd be doing so many interesting things the war would whiz past and David would be headed home before he knew what had happened. He also said David should not plan on a military career as when the war did end the politicians would reduce the standing Army and the funds needed to operate it. David wrote Jesse and suggested Jesse was just looking for a better source of informative fodder for his paper's editorials. David said if he did pick Military Intelligence he would not be able to communicate with Jesse except on mundane issues.

Jesse printed most of David's letter about his choices. Jesse thought how proud the citizens of Dancing Deer would be when they found out what the Army thought of one of their own.

Bill Potter read David's letter in the paper one evening at dinner. He asked Rose if she had seen it. Rose's color reddened and she swallowed before she said Jesse had shown her the letter when it arrived. Bill told her the military must be lowering its standards. He watched to see what her response would be.

Rose stammered as she said, "No, I don't think that at all. David was one of the smartest students in school. If it had not been for Jesse he might have been Valedictorian."

"Rose, you were Salutatorian. If it had not been for Jesse you would have been Valedictorian!"

"Well, then David would have been Salutatorian."

"Which of his three choices do you think he ought to take?"

Rose thought for a moment then said in a squeaky voice, "Whatever brings him back alive."

The next day Bill Potter called the ROTC instructor at the eastern university he'd attended. Bill said a young friend of his was being pressured to go into Officer Candidate School but the boy really wanted to go to the front as soon as possible and asked Bill for a little help. The instructor replied that just about anything could be arranged but usually it was the other way around. Lately, when someone called for help they wanted a stateside desk job for their boy. After a little more wrangling, Bill got the name and telephone number of a classmate who was now a high-ranking official in Washington D. C.

Bill spent the rest of the morning trying to convince his old classmate what a good service he would be doing, as well as a favor for a buddy, if he could get this young man transferred as a rifleman to some infantry regiment heading out soon. All he got was a promise to look into it.

David's train traveled through the night and sometime during the early morning hours, two days later, arrived at Fort Benning, Georgia. The new recruits were greeted by two patient sergeants and marched off single file into the darkness. They didn't have to go far before they entered the main camp. This was a regular Army post and the new recruits were impressed. However, they marched right past those pristine barracks, manicured lawns, square blocks of asphalt tarmac, somber administrative buildings, and on into the night. Eventually, they came to tent city. Here the sergeants separated the men into small groups and herded each group into a tent.

The next morning the men awoke to a loud and obnoxious sergeant walking through yelling they had slept through first call. He hit their metal bed posts with a stick as he strode through. It was 5:40 a.m.

After a long train ride and only a few hours sleep, David and the other recruits were in no mood to be hollered at. They would soon learn they were in the Army now and the Army didn't care what they thought. An actual bugle played Reveille at 6:00 a.m. and they marched to breakfast at 6:30.

  The next thirteen weeks the men learned not only how to fire an M-1 Garand rifle, but also how to un-assemble, clean, and re-assemble it in the dark. They learned military courtesy, the chain of command, the elements of close order drill, how to read a map, and how to use a compass to fix a position. They learned hand-to-hand combat, how to fight with bayonets attached to their rifles, and how to fight at night when you couldn't even see the person you were fighting with. They learned how to slip on a gas mask, the graphic consequences of contracting venereal diseases, and why we were in the war in the first place. They watched films, did calisthenics, were yelled at, prodded with sticks, regularly checked for anything that might be contagious, and wished they could just go back home. They gradually increased the distance of their forced marches and the amount of weight they could carry. Twenty-mile marches with a full pack became commonplace. Fat recruits slimmed down, skinny recruits beefed up, strong recruits became stronger, and weak recruits were sorry they had ever been born. No one got babied, no one got special treatment, no one's grumbling made a damn bit of difference.

  The tent had to be kept spotless. The bunks had to be made regulation-style with the corners tucked in at exactly forty-five degree angles, hospital-style, with no wrinkles. If the sergeant wanted to toss a half dollar on the bunk, that coin had better bounce back into his hand.

  The recruits learned to wash and iron their clothes, polish their boots, belt buckles, and brass buttons, and to clean and to re-clean their rifles. They also learned how to pull guard duty in the middle of the night, peel potatoes, slop the mess-hall floor, and scrub the latrines. Somehow along the way they learned to depend on one another and what it felt like to be an integral part of a squad and a platoon.

  At the beginning of the second month of training David asked permission to speak with his commanding officer. When permission was granted he presented himself on time in a clean and pressed uniform and spit-shined boots. He told the captain he scored a grade on the Army

General Classification Test high enough to allow him to attend Officer Candidate School, Military Intelligence, or the Army Air Corps after Basic. He said he had been told he had until half-way through to decide which and he now wanted his choice entered in his personnel file.

The captain looked at David. With a big grin he said, "Private, that decision's already been made."

David was floored. He asked, "Sir, may I inquire which was chosen?"

The captain located a folder and opened it up. He said, "This is somewhat irregular but the Forty-fifth Division has asked for you to be assigned to it. That's quite an honor, soldier. It looks like they're putting you in one of their infantry regiments . . . uh, the 180th"

David didn't know what to say. The infantry wasn't even one of his three choices. Before he could voice an opinion or ask for a clarification the captain said, "That will be all, Private Calhoun."

David saluted, did an about-face, and retreated from the room.

That night he wrote letters home to say the Army was not very good about living up to its promises. He wanted to whine but decided he was a grown man and should look at it as an opportunity. After all, he was a crack shot with a rifle. He could track game in a rain storm, live off the land, read maps, and use a compass. Maybe being in the infantry was where he needed to be. He still hadn't quite convinced himself when he received an avalanche of return mail decrying his ill treatment at the hands of the Army.

After Basic was completed the Army gave him a train ticket to Fort Devens, Massachusetts. With almost three months' pay in his pocket and a two-week pass, David lit out for the railway station and exchanged his ticket and a little extra money for one heading home and another from home on to his next duty station.

David arrived in Russellville on Wednesday morning, October 28, 1942. He caught a bus to Dancing Deer, thirty more miles into the Ozark Mountains. He was there by mid-afternoon.

No one knew he was coming so when he stepped off the bus people looked him over before they recognized him. When they did recognize him he was slapped on the back, prodded for information, offered meals, a ride to his parent's house, and housing for the night.

People wanted to carry his duffel bags and one man offered him the latest edition of the *Marsden County Meteor*. David looked at that man, grabbed him, and put his arm around his shoulder. David said, "Jesse, I'm so glad to see you."

"Man, if you'd told me you were coming I would have had the town put up red, white, and blue bunting. We'd have a big banner across Main Street saying 'Welcome home, David.' I'd have the mayor present you with the keys to the city. Then you'd have to kiss all the pretty girls. This isn't fair for you to slip into town unannounced."

"Why don't we save all that until I return from actually doing some fighting? It'll take me a year or two to whip all those Germans and Italians."

After David said that, there was another round of back slapping and more offers of hospitality. Jesse finally was able to extricate David from the well-wishers and the two of them ran into the offices of Jesse's paper. Jesse gave David a good-natured shove and said, "That's Rose's office." The door opened and Rose came out holding a page of paper asking what all the commotion was about. She took one look at David, dropped the paper, reached out and grabbed him by his tie, and backed into her office pulling David with her. She shut the door with her foot. She then reached up and put her hands on both sides of David's face and kissed him with all the pent-up passion she had been harboring for these last four months. In a second David was struggling for air. Rose loosened her grip and sat David down into an overstuffed chair. Planning on staking her claim, she hastily applied bright red lipstick. With David looking around, she put her mirror and lipstick into her purse and sat on his lap. She then started lavishing more kisses. She kissed his mouth, his chin, his neck, his nose, his forehead, and his eyelids. She loosened his tie, unbuttoned his shirt, and stuck her hand inside to feel his taut muscles and his hairy chest. David was out of breath when the door swung open and every employee of the paper crashed in with two bottles of chilled champagne and paper cups for everyone.

Jesse said, "Sorry, bud. I couldn't keep 'em out."

David stood up, tried to compose himself, and, while the females giggled, he buttoned his shirt, and was in the process of adjusting his tie when the throng separated and in walked Bill Potter.

"Welcome home, Mr. Calhoun."

"Uh, thank you, sir."

Bill stared. Everyone in the room held their breath. "I see the town has already been showing its hospitality." He paused a moment then said, "Let me just say how proud we are of you. It's men like you who are going to save democracy and win the fight against the evil aggressor."

Bill held out his hand and, after a moment's hesitation, David clasped hands with him and they shook. Someone saw an opportune moment and shot the picture. Rose was astonished at her father's congeniality and had to sit down in her swivel chair.

Bill asked David, "Do your parents know you're back?"

"No, sir. I've not told anyone."

"Then will you allow Rose and me to drive you up Lee Mountain? That is after we've drunk all of Jesse's champagne. Has anyone got a cup for me?"

Jesse poured Bill a cup and handed it to him. An hour later Rose sat in the back seat of her dad's big black Packard touring sedan, allowing the men to occupy the front. She fervently hoped they could find some mutual ground upon which to start building a friendship.

Bill started off with a comment on what a quality outfit he'd been assigned. David said he was a little disappointed he'd not been allowed to make his own choice but he thought everything would turn out okay. The rest of their conversation was small talk of little substance.

When they reached the front gate Rose opened her door so David and her dad could continue their conversation, but David insisted he'd get it so she wouldn't step in something like she did the last time she'd been there. As David slid the wooden latch to one side he heard a soft padded footstep and looked down to see Balder nudge under his free hand. He motioned for them to pull on through, and then closed the gate. David walked to Bill's window and told him to drive on to the house, he wanted to walk with Balder. He said Balder was old; the dog could just barely hobble along. Bill agreed and drove toward the house before Rose had a chance to ask if she might walk with David and Balder.

David loved Balder. He had heard stories his whole life of things his dad and Balder had done. Traveller died the year before and, for months, it looked like Balder was going to will himself to die as well. But something got hold of Balder and he came out of his depression. It was as if he had decided there was unfinished business he had to attend to.

The ground was wet and Bill pulled his car all the way up to Jed's front porch so Rose could step out and not get her feet muddy. They waited on David and Balder before going to the front door.

Balder was almost blind, couldn't hear anymore, and smelled bad. He wasn't allowed in the house. As they approached the car and the house, Balder started a low growl. Almost all of his teeth were gone. For months, his dad had made a paste of Balder's feed, so even if he could growl, there was no need for anyone to fear him. David stopped short of the house and told Balder to go to the barn. He'd see him again before he went to bed. Balder sat down. David thought it was a wonder that Balder could even hear him, much less understand what he was saying. As he marveled on this he walked to the front door, knocked, opened and held the door for Rose and Bill, and then walked inside.

Jed and Emily were in the kitchen and when David appeared in the doorway Emily started crying. He walked on in and Jed rushed and grabbed him around the shoulders. He gave David a hearty hug that lifted him completely off the floor.

Bill said, "I thought I'd better deliver him before the town got together and put him up in the Presidential Suite at the Ritz."

Jed turned toward Bill, took a couple of steps forward, and was blocked when Emily adroitly stepped between them. She held out her hand to Bill as she was wiping her eyes with her other. She said, "Oh thank you so much, Bill. Our old truck isn't running that good. In fact, it's not running at all. It's just sitting out by the barn rusting."

Rose wanted desperately to say something but was afraid with the tears welling up in her own eyes that whatever she said would give her and David's situation away.

Bill took Rose's hand and said they had to get back into town. He turned toward David and said, "After you've had time to get re-acquainted, why don't you drop by the bank. I'd like to take you to lunch." With that, they said their goodbyes and headed out the door.

There was still a bit of daylight left when Bill opened the door for Rose and walked around to the driver's side. Jed, Emily, and David were on the front porch when Bill opened his door, paused, and walked around the car door to the front of the Packard. "What's this?" he said as he used his hand to brush off something from the hood. Whatever it was had been placed directly in front of the steering wheel. "My God, it's dog shit!"

He wiped his hand on his trouser leg and, getting into the car, slammed the door shut. He slid to a stop just before crashing into the front gate. Rose jumped out and unlatched the gate. She didn't know whether to laugh or cry—to be deliriously happy or upset. Things were so confusing.

On the porch Jed, Emily, and David looked at each other and began laughing. Charlotte, Amanda, and April came up from the barn carrying a bucket of freshly churned butter. They hugged David's neck and told their dad he needed to go see about Balder. He was acting funny. Jed and David ran to the barn. Balder was in Traveller's old stall curled up in a ball and snoring.

On the way back to the house Jed said, "Son, how'd you get that lipstick all over your face?"

CHAPTER 9—BALDER
Lee Mountain - Late October 1942

David woke early the next morning and went to check on his dad's truck. Sure enough it wouldn't start. The battery was weak so before he tried to start the truck again, after that short first effort, he checked the oil and then the water in the radiator and siphoned out the old gas. Balder hobbled over. David added water to the battery, changed the oil and oil filter, cleaned the air filter, cleaned the fuel filter, disassembled and cleaned the carburetor, and lubricated the throttle and choke cables.

Balder spent the entire morning beside David as he worked. David was looking for fresh gas when Jesse drove up. David wiped his hands on a rag he used to clean the dipstick. "I've done what I could but I can't find any gas to see if I've done any good."

Jesse said, "Why don't we siphon gas from my car?"

With the new gas David turned the key and the starter turned the motor over a couple of times, then quit. Jesse said, "I've also got jumper cables."

When they were attached, the old truck roared into life. For the next ten minutes David fiddled with the air and fuel mixture screws until, what started off as an engine running with a bad case of asthma, got its wind back and began purring like Emily's treadle sewing machine.

David Blaine said, "I have to spend time with my grandparent's this afternoon but before I head that way I'd like to show you my hideout."

Jesse said he had only one important item on his agenda. He had to deliver a message from Rose and once he did that he had the afternoon free. Jesse said, "That is some girlfriend you've got there, buddy. She told me to tell you she'd cook you dinner this Friday evening. She said for you to come to her house about dark and see if the red flag on the mailbox was up. She'd raise the flag when her dad left.

David, I don't want to tell you what to do but you're walking a narrow line. Hitler doesn't have a thing on Bill Potter. All right, that's hyperbole, but you should realize you're in dangerous territory."

David shook his head and said, "I think it's the same the world over. We want those things we can't have and the more obstacles placed before us the harder we strive to overcome. But I love Rose and together we've got to figure something out."

David turned and headed to the front door calling back over his shoulder, "Come on, I'm going to fix sandwiches, cause where I'm planning on taking you is food depleted."

Emily said she'd prepare the sandwiches and wondered if they needed anything to drink. David said no while Jesse said yes. David told his mom they'd drink from the spring and for her to include two cups. She also put in two pieces of apple pie.

Jesse was wearing dress slacks, a silk shirt, and Italian leather loafers. David gave him a pair of jeans, a chambray work shirt, and Red Wing work boots to change into. Everything was too big. Jesse was short, at five foot eight, and slight of build compared to David's whopping six feet plus and muscular torso. In fact, David looked like he would make two of Jesse. David weighed over two hundred pounds and was physically fit. He had no trouble in Basic Training and was looking forward to the more intensive training he'd be receiving when he reached the Forty-fifth. Jesse cinched up the belt and said he'd manage if he could borrow another pair of thick socks. They headed off with Balder tagging along.

David told Jesse about Balder making a small deposit with the local banker. Balder was twenty-four years old and, since Traveller had died, they got up every morning wondering if he had passed in the night. Balder was the oldest dog in the county and, according to all the Calhouns, the smartest as well.

David grabbed the sack of sandwiches and led Jesse out the back of the house, through his mother's garden, past his dad's orchard, and used stepping stones peeking uneven surfaces above the glassy water's surface to cross a small meandering creek. When they reached the woods there was a make-shift gate that looked like it had been built by a child. David grabbed hold of the closest fence post and leaped over the gate. He turned around and opened the gate for Jesse, who was trying to figure out the latch.

David said they were still on his dad's land but he'd decided not to clear it. They had sixty acres of good fertile land divided into several pastures. His dad had decided to make his comeback raising cattle instead of horses. The county agricultural extension agent gave him advice on the types of grasses to plant and how to cross-fence so his stock could be rotated. His dad figured out, on his own, how to use a homemade windmill to let the wind deliver water into a trough from a hand-dug well on high ground and let it flow through buried pipe to lower troughs in other pastures. He had another ten acres for the house, barns, outbuildings, orchard, and garden. The rest of the level area was about thirty more acres and his dad left it as he'd found it—deep woods with a meandering creek. In addition to the hundred acres of reasonably level land, David said his family owned two hundred acres on the backside of the mountain and that was where he was taking Jesse now. Balder was slowing them down but it looked like he was trying his best to keep up. David adjusted their pace to what Balder could handle.

The first place David went was the ridgeback. The backside of Lee Mountain was made of black shale and at the ridgeback, millions of years ago, diastrophism had pushed up and broke a ridge of shale so that it jutted up, looking like the back of a razorback hog. There were gigantic sheets of black shale sticking out of the ground at a low angle to a fault line and then, on the other side another slab, sloping back into the earth. David said he'd found lots of arrowheads, pieces of flint, and one tomahawk—complete with rawhide whipping. Jesse was impressed. He'd heard stories of Indians in the area but, until now, didn't have any idea where they might have lived.

The second place David took Jesse and Balder was the waterfall. After a decent rain the water would run off the back side of the mountain. Several small rivulets of water coalesced at the top of a rock wall and gushed water down the side of the cliff face twenty feet into a rock pool. The pool overflowed and dropped more water from several low points on down the cliff to a shallow basin and from there the water flowed in a turbulent stream off the mountain toward the Big Piney River. David located a narrow ledge and with his back facing a dangerously deep chasm and his hands grabbing worn-down rock edges he sidestepped to a wet area on the cliff face covered with moss. Jesse was worried sick. He wished he'd just given the message and headed back to town. But he kept a game face and tried his best to keep his friend from knowing he was scared out of his mind. Balder didn't follow. He sat down on his haunches and watched. He wasn't steady enough nor could he see well enough to traverse the difficult terrain.

When David and Jesse reached the mossy area the ledge widened. David said he was also afraid of heights and it took quite a few efforts when he first found it before actually making his way to the spring. David reached a hand to a small hollowed-out pocket in the side of the cliff. He brushed out water and little pieces of dirt and bracken leaving the purifying moss. The pocket quickly refilled from a rivulet of spring water coming right out of the rock. He bent and drank. David told Jesse it was the best-tasting water to be found anywhere and, after Jesse drank from his cupped hand, David filled the two cups his mother had packed. David said they should go back to where Balder was waiting; it was too wet at the spring to be comfortable.

Jesse said, "You know this is about the prettiest place I've ever seen. May I come back with the paper's camera and take pictures? With the arrowheads and waterfall I could write a nice piece."

"No, I don't want anyone to know about this. I used to come here to solve all those difficult problems children seem to be obsessed with while growing up. Other people knowing about it would be an invasion of privacy."

David took one of the sandwiches apart and broke the bits of meat into small portions and held them out to Balder. The big gray dog sniffed the food but just nuzzled against the backside of David's hand, declining to eat. A few minutes later they were ready to go but now Balder was in the lead and he turned from their entering path and started back in a new direction. David said they might as well follow; the property was not so big they would get lost.

David told Jesse how Balder walked down the mountainside every morning with him and his sisters to catch the school bus. When they got home in the afternoon he was there to walk them back. He said, when Balder was just a pup, his dad taught him the normal dog tricks of shaking hands, sitting, rolling over, and playing dead but his dad became of the opinion that Balder was too noble a dog for such trivialities and started giving him more important duties. He told Jesse about the stories he'd heard, telling of when his dad worked a still and Balder kept the lookout. They were a formidable team.

When the old elementary school was torn down, his two uncles had been hired to do some of the carpentry work. One day they came home with the playground bell saying the school was doing away with it. David said his dad mounted it on top of a tall pole and trained Balder to jump and grab the hanging rope whenever someone come visiting. Balder would swing in circles ringing the bell. If anyone heard the bell ring they knew to come to the house. His dad also knew to hide the still.

They walked quite a ways until the rocks turned from black shale to whiter limestone. Balder stopped beside a large bushy cedar. David looked the tree over. It was growing up tight against a rock wall. David said, "Balder, you wanted to show me this tree?"

Jesse said, "Here, look at this." He pulled a low-hanging branch away from the rock and exposed a small opening about two feet in diameter.

David got down on his knees and peered inside. He said "Hello" in a loud voice. The word bounced around a large cavern and returned a second later.

Jesse said, "Balder has taken us to his hideout. I'm amazed." They looked at Balder but he was slowly walking farther down the trail. They decided to follow him to see if there was anything else he had to show. They also wanted to go to the house and bring back a lantern and pickax. The opening needed to be enlarged and the tree needed to be cut back so they could see what was inside. Soon they could see David's house and realized Balder was leading them home. David easily caught up with Balder, patted him on his head, and said good things about him.

David and Jesse ran into the house and asked Emily if they could have the lantern. Jesse said, "Mrs. Calhoun, Balder's shown us the most wonderful cave."

Emily looked at David. She said, "Did you forget you promised to go over to your grandparent's house this afternoon?"

"You're right, Mom. The cave will always be there but I only have one more day before I have to leave." He turned to Jesse, "We'll have to put this off until I get another furlough. But I promise not to explore the cave without you."

"I completely understand. None of my grandparents are still alive but when they were they were a big part of my life."

Balder went to the barn. He was not feeling well. The day's activities had completely tuckered him out. He could barely walk. His whole body ached. Four times he crawled under Jed's big working table and backed out clutching something in his mouth. Most of his teeth were gone so he gummed the items.

He picked up one item and slowly walked out of the barn. He made it to the gate and carefully crawled under the fence. Slowly he made his way down the mountain. When he reached the bottom he lay exhausted next to a row of mailboxes and waited for the school bus. Balder slept.

When the bus arrived, David's three sisters got off and started up the road. It was Amanda who first spotted Balder. She walked over to the mailboxes and peered down at the great dog. She said, "Balder, what are you doing here? It's been years since you've come down to walk us back."

April reached down to stroke Balder's gray coat and said, "Looky here, Balder's found Bottom Buster."

Charlotte bent down to have a better look. Bottom Buster was the name given to a family heirloom. Their great-grandfather had lovingly whittled the paddle from the yellow resinous wood of a *Bois d' Arc* tree. He hand-rubbed in a salve-like substance, honed the blade, and whipped the handle with rawhide. They heard stories about their grandfather getting paddled with it and, they understood, their dad had his attitude adjusted on several occasions. When April was just a baby their grandpa made a big deal of turning over Bottom Buster to their dad. But the first time he had an occasion to use it he couldn't find it. Over the years he would good-naturedly make a remark about getting out Bottom Buster when he thought someone's attitude needed adjusting but everyone knew the paddle was lost and he was only making a point.

Charlotte said, "Balder, wake up. It's time to go home."

Balder slowly awakened and lovingly gazed at the three girls he had watched over since they were first born. He dragged himself to his feet and the four of them started up the mountain. It was dark when they arrived.

Emily greeted the girls and asked why they were so late. She said she had already fixed supper and was just about to send their dad looking for them. Amanda promptly held up Bottom Buster. She told her mother, "Balder brought it down the mountain and it took a long time for us to walk back up. Every few feet we had to stop to let Balder rest."

Jed said Balder was acting funny. David Blaine told everyone how Balder had shown Jesse and him a cave. Jed questioned David about its location and shook his head in bewilderment. "I'm still wondering about the mess he left on Bill's windshield. It must have been difficult for him to climb up there, even with Bill parking his car against the porch. Balder must've thought he had accomplished a great feat and now he's tidying up what's left. He's an amazing dog."

That night, Jed lay in bed reminiscing about the wonderful times he had spent with Traveller and Balder. He thought about the time his mother had told him she needed an opossum to cook for Thanksgiving dinner.

The spring of that year his aunt and her family arrived from Oklahoma with everything they owned stuffed into and strapped onto the top of their car, their farm laid waste under a thick layer of dust. After years of poor soil management, a drought, and howling winds, a large portion of Oklahoma, Kansas, and the panhandle of Texas were suffering through the dust bowl. Lots of farmers found they couldn't continue and, loading up what they could, headed to California. There was an old joke that asked how a person could tell a wealthy Oklahoman from a poor one. The answer was determined by counting the number of mattresses tied to the roof of his car.

Aunt Sadie, Uncle Ben, and their three kids decided to check out their relatives in Arkansas before heading west. At first, Jed's mother and father were thrilled and went overboard to make their new guests feel at home. However, their relatives were lazy and didn't do any work to help. All they did was lay about the house and eat. As the short stay lengthened into months it became apparent the Calhouns, with the extra mouths to feed, didn't have enough food in their pantry to make it through the winter. Jed's mother talked to Aunt Sadie about when they would be leaving for California and didn't get any kind of commitment. Jed's dad told Uncle Ben he might be able to get a job at the sawmill but was told they really wouldn't be staying that long and Uncle Ben said he was afraid of the machinery anyway.

The kids were worthless. They wouldn't work in a candy store. Evidently, the children didn't have to do chores back on their own farm and now they just wanted to play.

Jed's father asked Jed if he'd help. With Claude and Rupert, the four of them sat down and tried to cook up a plan to get rid of the invading in-laws. First, Jed took his uncle and the children gar fishing. Late one afternoon Jed stood in the front of a punt with a short stout bow. He attached a heavy waxed twine to an arrow and they drifted along the slow-moving Illinois Bayou. When he spotted a large gar floating on top of the water he shot it with the arrow, tied off the twine, and sat down in the punt beside Balder while the big fish thrashed about in the water. It pulled the punt from one side of the river to the other. Jed thought his relatives would be scared but they likened it to a carnival ride and squealed with delight. When the big fish finally tired, Jed hauled the monster aboard and beaned it with a paddle.

That night for supper his father deep-fried big chunks of the rather fishy-tasting gar. Effort number one was a flop and Jed's mother was appalled at the lengths her family would go to get rid of Sadie and her mooching family.

The second was a meal of frog legs. Jed took his uncle and the kids out in the punt again—this time to a large stagnant pond after dark. He told his uncle to shine a flashlight along the bank. When they picked up the squinting eyes of a bullfrog the children slowly paddled the punt in their direction. Jed was in the bow with a long pole having a three-pronged metal trident attached to its end. When the kids maneuvered the boat within range, Jed reached out and skewered the unsuspecting prey. That night Jed's father cut off and skinned the large back legs leaving the muscle tendon intact. As everyone watched, Claude heated grease in a huge cast iron skillet. Rupert stood close by wearing two oven mitts. When Claude dropped a handful of battered frog legs into the crackling grease, they immediately started moving around in the skillet.

Since the muscle connecting the lower part of the leg to the upper part had not been severed, the legs feverously contracted and some popped completely out of the skillet. That's where Rupert came in. It was his job to catch the flying legs before they hit the floor—much like an outfielder shagging fly balls, except sometimes there were more than one pair of legs in the air at a time. Rupert decided he needed help so gave the children paper sacks and positioned them in various places around the stove. There were a lot of legs hitting the floor but Claude and Rupert just placed them back in the skillet like it was nothing unusual. This second effort was also a dismal failure as the food was rather tasty and their guests thoroughly enjoyed the show.

Jed, his father, and his two brothers gave up. They were beat. For the next few weeks they simply endured the situation. When Thanksgiving came, Aunt Sadie informed Jed's mother she would be making the dressing and gave Jed's mother a list of needed ingredients. That was the last straw. For some reason women consider the making of dressing a sacred rite. It was her kitchen and no one but she was going to make the dressing. It was time for Aunt Sadie and her bunch of ungratefuls to be moving on. His mother told Aunt Sadie she had the meal all planned, thank you.

That evening Jed's mother and dad came over to Lee Mountain. Jed's mother asked Jed if he would get her a fat opossum. The next evening Jed and Balder went hunting. Balder figured out what Jed wanted and spent an hour or so rounding up a particularly large specimen, which he herded to Jed squatting behind a bush with his gun ready. Jed couldn't just shoot the animal from three feet so instead he took a length of rope and made a loop in one end. When he threatened the opossum with a stick the animal sulled and fell down, playing dead. Jed quickly looped the rope around the animal's four feet and tied it off. He stuck a stout pole through the knot and hefted it up over his shoulder.

Back at his parent's house, Claude fashioned a cage of intertwined grapevines and chicken wire. The kids' mouths were agape over the hideous looking creature. Jed's mother told Aunt Sadie how good opossum meat was—albeit a might greasy. Jed's dad shook his head. He wasn't going to like this Thanksgiving dinner.

The next day the meat had to be prepared because the following day was Thanksgiving. It would be just one meal. They could do anything for one day if it meant getting rid of the freeloaders. Jed's father killed and dressed the animal under the watchful eyes of his guests. They were squeamish during the evisceration of the entrails. Rupert brushed the long incisor teeth with baking soda and salt. He told the kids it was their family custom to cook a opossum for Thanksgiving dinner and it had always been his job to make the carcass look presentable. He asked the kids if they wanted to help while he removed the eyes. He said sometimes he would replace them with cranberries but this year he was going to use two red marbles.

Jed's mother said, with having such a magnificent animal there would not be any need for much else. In fact, he was such a huge opossum they would be eating leftovers for a week. She told Jed's father to separate the liver, kidneys, heart, and brains. She would cook those the day after Thanksgiving.

The next morning Jed's mother fired her wood-burning stove and, under the close supervision of loathsome relatives, she prepared the beast. She started to scrape off the remnants of hair Jed's father had missed then quit, deciding to leave it. With wooden clothes pins she forced the animal's upper lips back making the monster look like he was emitting a nasty snarl.

Finishing the preparation, she salted the carcass before inserting it into the oven. Several times she noticed Aunt Sadie and her clan huddled at the far edge of the room discussing something she could not quite make out.

She spent a couple of hours making a decent stuffing, but not her favorite recipe. Every so often she opened the oven door, pulled out the sizzling corpse, and dipped a wooden spoon into the liquefied fat accumulating in the bottom of the pan. She used this greasy residue to baste the animal's body. When it was about half cooked she stuffed it with dressing.

Mrs. Calhoun fixed turnip greens and beets to accompany their main course and said she had prepared a special herbal tea for everyone to drink. She poured glasses of tea from two pitchers and placed the glasses on the table, making special note of where everyone normally sat and which glass went by which plate. His mother was so accomplished no one realized the two pitchers contained different types of tea.

Jed came for the meal but he'd not been able to talk any of his family into attending. They'd decided to eat Thanksgiving that year with Emily's parents. Jed could smell the senna tea and almost gagged. He was relieved when he discovered his mother poured regular tea in his glass.

Jed's dad got up to carry in his wife's magnificent main dish. She'd stuffed a crabapple in the animal's mouth to go with Rupert's red marbles in its eye sockets. The beast sat on a large platter surrounded by salty boiled potatoes, carrots, and onions. His tail hung limp over the side of the platter almost to Jed's father's waist. Jed's mother said the blessing. Jed's father took a huge knife and fork and began cutting the meat away from the bone. When he finished he invited his guests to dig in.

Everyone sat quietly, not wanting to partake of anything. Rupert finally said, if no one minded, he wanted the tail. He looked around the table. It was apparent no one objected and everyone was waiting to see how he was planning on doing it. Mr. Calhoun came down on the tail with the big knife severing it cleanly. He handed it to Rupert.

The Calhouns looked like they relished the portion of meat they ate, getting grease all over their faces. A little meat was eaten by their sponging relatives, hardly any turnip greens or beets, and most of the salty carrots, potatoes, and onions. When refills of tea were needed Mrs. Calhoun immediately brought two pitchers of tea to the table. She talked about insignificant things as she refilled each person's glass. To Sadie and her family she poured from the pitcher containing the senna tea and for herself and her family she poured from the one containing regular tea. No one noticed.

That night, all night long, there was a steady stream of Aunt Sadie and her family to the outhouse. Senna tea is a natural laxative anyway and Jed's mother had made it rather strong. The next morning Aunt Sadie and Uncle Ben started packing their belongings. They said it was time to go to California and they were sorry they wouldn't be able to eat any more of Mrs. Calhoun's fine cooking. Jed's mother suggested she make them opossum sandwiches for the trip. Uncle Ben said, as much as he liked opossum, he'd eaten so much the day before he wouldn't be able to eat another bite for at least a week.

At that moment Claude came in and told his mother she needed to break open another box of toilet paper for the outhouse. Mrs. Calhoun said she'd run out the day before and had taken the Sears and Roebuck catalog out to use until she could get into town to buy more. Claude said the catalog didn't work so well now that they had gone to the slick pages and there was no catalog out there anyway. It must have gotten used the night before. At this bit of news the Calhouns looked at their relatives. Aunt Sadie and Uncle Ben looked a little sheepish while shrugging their shoulders. They were gone in fifteen minutes.

Claude took the remnants of the opossum out behind the barn and buried it. Jed's dad said he was sure glad Jed's mother hadn't asked him to clean the opossum's intestines for frying. His mother carried three rolls of toilet paper to the outhouse.

Earlier that evening, around supper, Balder placed three collars and four leashes on the back porch underneath the kitchen window. Whenever Emily had taken him to get his shots, she could never find his collar or leash. Since the vet required them, Emily had to stop at the general store for a new collar and leash each trip. She didn't know what happened to all those collars and leashes, but figured they'd show up some day. On the front porch, beside Jed's rocking chair, Balder dropped the syringe Stanley Muldaur had used to inoculate the black stallion. He then went back to the barn one last time and found an old oiled tarp—the same one Mr. Sinclair covered the lumber Jed used to build the house. It was later used by Traveller and the two mules to haul him to Jed's parent's farm. He dragged it out to the grassy knoll where Traveller was buried. By taking one corner at a time he positioned it over the exact spot where his old buddy lay. He sat on one corner of the tarp and spent a few minutes surveying the farm.

After a short while, Balder raised his head toward the sky, lengthening his vocal cords. In the peaceful quiet of a crisp November evening he let out a low melodious howl. Jed listened, turned his head, and cried into his pillow.

CHAPTER 10—NADINE

Dancing Deer - November 1942

David couldn't wait later than the noon bus on Saturday to head to Massachusetts. After an early breakfast on Friday, he found his dad ambling toward a rocking chair on the front porch. "Dad, I'd like to borrow the truck to go into town."

Jed said, "Sure. For some reason it's started running again. The gas ration coupons are in the glove box and you can get a week's quota at Big John Lynch's Automotive. He'll put it on our account."

David's first stop was the library. It had just opened so the only person there was Nadine, the librarian. When David walked in, Nadine was hanging up her coat. She was surprised to see the town celebrity everyone had been talking about. "Hello, David. It looks like the Army's been treating you well."

David smiled. "I've been getting a lot of exercise."

"Do you need some good books to help you pass the time?"

"Nadine, I could use a few books but I've really come to talk to you about Uncle Rupert."

Nadine's face flushed. Rupert was the man she dreamed about. She had fallen in love with him the first time she saw him. Like all the Calhoun men, he was tall and skinny. Rupert had a rugged, weather-beaten face begging to be caressed and kissed. He was also shy, quiet, and unassuming. Nadine knew he didn't have much of an education; he'd had to work to help support his family.

After she helped him find a book with pictures of wooden bridges he started coming in on Saturdays. At first, he visited the magazine area. From the magazines he progressed to the newspapers. One day, Rupert asked Nadine for a book on travel. She asked him where he'd like to go. He answered her question with one of his own by asking where she'd like to go. She told him anywhere. He read several of the travel books she'd recommended and after that, for the next ten years, Rupert would occasionally ask Nadine to a church social.

Sometimes they'd even go to a live show now that Bill Potter had opened the Ritz Grand Hotel and Ballroom with a stage.

Sometime during that long period their relationship snagged on a sand bar. Neither knew how to get it back into the current. They had not yet held hands, much less kissed. He had not once given her any indication she meant anything more to him than his carpenter's apron.

To Jed, Nadine said, "Does Ru know you've come to talk to me?"

"No, ma'am. I decided you two needed a shove in the right direction on my own."

Nadine took a handkerchief and dabbed at her eyes. She sat down in her swivel chair, put her elbows on the desk, and leaned her head forward into her hands. She tried to compose herself. Presently she said, "David, I'm forty-five years old. If you looked up 'plain Jane' in Webster's you'd see my picture. Besides Rupert, no one has shown any interest in me in my entire life. I was never asked to any of the school dances, to drink a soda at Eudy's Drug and Fountain, or even what my opinion on the war might be. Your uncle came in one day and wanted to know if there were any books showing pictures of wooden bridges. From that day to this, I have a good week if he comes in one day for a chat and a bad week if he doesn't. If he were to hold my hand I think I would . . . well, I'd probably faint."

David was floored by her honesty. "Nadine, I have a plan. You'll need to be open to any suggestion, to any change, to any irrelevant and unbelievable opportunity. If you can agree to that I can promise you, within a year, your relationship with Uncle Rupert will be whatever you want it to be."

Nadine looked at David. Was he serious? She turned away and stared into space. How could that be? How would that feel? What right did she have to dream of such an event? To kiss Rupert? To hold him in her arms? For him to want to touch her?

"Well? Nadine, what do you say?"

"David, you're off your rocker."

"Nadine, be open-minded. Take a chance. What have you got to lose?"

David had a point there. In the last ten years she'd not been able to accomplish anything on her own. Maybe another perspective, especially from David, someone related to Rupert, someone the entire town adored. He might be the catalyst Rupert needed.

"Oh, indeed. Why not! But . . . wait. What do you have in mind?"

"Give me some time to get things started and you'll know opportunity when it comes calling."

David climbed into his father's truck to go to his next stop. Rupert pulled up in an old decrepit Hudson and excitedly waved David down. Rupert jumped out of the Hudson and ran to Jed's truck. He was out of breath as he yelled into the rolled down window. "David, don't take the truck home for a while. Balder's dead and your dad says he going after Stanley Muldaur."

"What? Balder's dead and Dad blames Muldaur?"

"No. Balder gave everyone a present and then passed away. It was the present he gave your dad that's caused the ruckus. This morning after you left, your dad took his coffee to his rocking chair on the front porch. Your mother went out the back door to toss the dishwater where she found several leashes and collars. You know how Balder hated to wear a collar. I guess he stashed them away. Anyway, she carried them to the front porch to show your dad. Right beside his rocker she found a syringe. Your dad swears it looks exactly like the one Stanley Muldaur used on those horses that had the disease. He says he watched Stanley put the one he used in his medicine case and thinks this is the one he must have used to infect the stallion. You need to wait. Let him cool off first."

"What about Balder?"

"Your dad went looking for Balder and found him on an old tarp he'd stretched over Traveller's grave."

David shook his head and bit his lip before looking up. "Balder took me to a cave I'd never seen before."

"Yes. I know. It was your present."

"Uncle Rupert, Balder really was a smart dog wasn't he?"

"Yes, David, he was a dog of a lifetime."

"When I take the car back I'll siphon the gas out and give Mom the ration coupons. That ought to keep Dad home for a while. Do you think Muldaur lives in Dancing Deer? Dad said there's a new agent who replaced him."

"I don't know. I could ask Nadine. She knows just about everybody in town. You might check with your friend at the paper. I'd like to see your dad get a hold of Muldaur—that is if he actually did what your dad thinks he did. I just don't want your dad doing anything foolish while he's upset. Muldaur had no reason to hurt your family so he had to be doing it for someone else and the one everyone thinks is really responsible is so sneaky he probably has all his bases covered."

David drove to the paper and went into Jesse's office carrying his military uniform on a hanger. After carefully laying his clothing across a second chair he told Jesse about Balder and about the syringe. Then he asked about Stanley Muldaur. With Jesse shaking his head, David asked if Jesse would take his picture.

"Sure. That'll be fantastic. It'll be the official photo of our town hero."

While Jesse was making preparations, David walked down the hall to Rose's office. She wasn't in. David looked around. It was a clean and organized office. On the wall behind her desk was a cork bulletin board with Jesse's war maps tacked to it.

Back in Jesse's office David changed into his military uniform while Jesse adjusted the lights and stretched a piece of fabric to be used as a backdrop. Jesse walked from the tripod holding the camera. "Stand on this mark, David, and look this direction." Jesse took several pictures using different angles, poses, distances, and depths of field. It was an hour before lunch when Jesse was through shooting.

David told Jesse, "Pick out the best one and develop it into a size that'll fit inside a locket. I'd like to pick it up this afternoon." David started to change back into his civilian clothes but Jesse stopped him.

"Man, if you're going to be in town for a while you should keep on your uniform. The town needs to see you dressed like a soldier so they can remember what you look like when they're reading about you in my articles."

"Okay, but the civvies are more comfortable."

"Maybe, but your uniform is more impressive and more memorable. Now I better get to work on developing these pictures. Rose should be back in a few minutes. She went to the post office to pick up the newspaper's mail."

"Jesse, are you dating anyone these days? With so many men gone there should be several lonely hearts needing their hands held."

"You're so funny. I have my standards. She's got to be smart to hold my interest. And good-looking is always a plus. Maybe long legs." Jesse checked the lighting with a meter. "You know, David, you're a lucky man. Rose is the only attractive girl I know who can carry on an intelligent conversation. I think I'm going to order one just like her from the Monkey Ward catalog." Jesse paused a moment. "I wonder how much extra I'll have to pay for the long legs."

It was time for David's next stop. He left the truck parked in front of the paper and walked the two blocks to the bank. Jennifer, Bill's secretary, said she was glad to see David. Mr. Potter had been asking if he had come by or called. "Have a seat, Mr. Calhoun. I'll tell him you're here."

Moments later, Bill burst through the door with his hand outstretched. "Let's walk over to the new hotel and eat in their restaurant. It's construction is finally complete."

David remembered when Bill announced in the paper he was going to build a hotel and restaurant. That was in the summer prior to his senior year in school. It had supplied badly needed jobs until Roosevelt started building war implements and materiel necessary for the taking of lives. As they walked down the street David could see the building in the distance. It was the tallest building in town at four stories and easily the most impressive with almond colored marble decorating the front entrance. David had not yet been inside but like most of the town's residents had often walked by to marvel at its impressive grandeur. He said, "Mr. Potter, isn't that your hotel?"

"Yes, it is. I named it after one that's famous in Paris. There it is," Bill pointed with his finger, "about five or six blocks down Main Street, where the Livery Feed and Seed once stood."

They walked the few blocks and along the way people stopped to shake hands with David Blaine. Bill tipped his hat to the women they met. He seemed to know just about everyone. Some people though, when they saw Potter walking their way, looked down, turned away, or even crossed the street. David wondered what Bill Potter could have done to make so many people dislike him.

When they walked into the glitzy Ritz Hotel Bistro they were promptly shown to a table separated from the others and in front of a bay window looking out onto Main Street. David decided it must be Bill's regular table. He said, "Quite a remodel job from once being a livery stable."

"I opened a new Livery Feed and Seed down the road a piece and demolished the old building and feed lot. It gave me the space I needed to build this and I had enough room left over for a parking lot. I'm now trying to get the city council to do away with parking on the street, and if they do, I'll expand the parking lot and charge people to leave their cars when they come into town to do their shopping."

The waiter arrived with menus and two glasses of water. He asked what they would like to drink. Bill asked for coffee, David for a tall glass of milk. David began reading the menu. He didn't want to make the appearance of being too much a hick and was certainly glad that beside each listed entrée was an elaborate description. He picked a skewer of braised beef, mushrooms, and bell peppers with a side of new potatoes swimming in melted butter and a cup of cheese-broccoli soup. Bill ordered a small prime rib with horseradish sauce and a caesar salad.

David glanced around the restaurant. It was multi-level and further divided into several smaller seating areas by short railings. At one end, on the lowest level, was a dance floor with a stage directly behind. At the back of the stage and extending forward a few feet were heavy curtains. David squared himself to the table and saw over Bill's shoulder that the front walls were covered with expansive amounts of glass looking out over busy streets. All the other walls were decorated with floor-to-ceiling mirrors. A number of crystal chandeliers hung from the tall ceiling. Along the back right wall was a long lacquered wooden bar curving around a corner and out of sight. It had a brass foot rail and empty barstools.

David asked, "Do you serve alcohol?"

"Not yet. Marsden County is still dry but I'm trying to get that changed. In fact, that's one of the things I wanted to talk with you about."

David didn't know what to say. He wasn't much of a drinker, only a beer every once in a while with his Army buddies. No one else in his family drank. His dad stopped when he met his mother. David wondered what Bill Potter was leading up to.

Bill continued, "David, have you ever thought of running for political office? You're extremely popular with the residents of Dancing Deer. Everyone in town looks forward to the Wednesday paper to see what's happening to their boys. I think Jesse gives you more press than me. You're a local hero. I think you'd be a shoo-in for the City Council. A couple of terms there and you'd be ready to move on up to the county or even the state level." Bill paused a moment trying to read David's reaction and continued with, "David, have you even thought what you'd like to do when you return from the war?"

"No, sir. All I know is that I don't want to farm. I finally made up my mind to join the Army Air Corps and learn to be a pilot before the Army made my choice for me and put me in an infantry regiment. Now, I'm wondering what kind of job might be available for a gunslinger."

"David, you're a real comedian. Maybe you should shuck this country venue and head to California. Get into show business or radio broadcasting." Bill paused a moment then continued with, "But the first thing is to get through the war. And do give some thought to life as a public servant. I think I could be of benefit to you there. Of course, you'd eventually have to live part of each year in Little Rock while still maintaining your residence in Dancing Deer. It would be a life of excitement, one of prestige, one where the decisions you help to make would drive the economy and affect the lives of all Arkansans."

David thought how good it would feel doing something important. For the rest of the meal they talked about baseball, the war, food rationing, and the town accepting or rejecting live burlesque at the Ritz Hotel Grand Hotel and Ballroom. They even talked about the problems with liquor-by-the-drink. Bill thought it was a great idea. David had a different opinion but was careful not to be argumentative.

After lunch, David said, "Thank you for the meal, Mr. Potter. I need to be about my business. Today's my last day in town and I have a few errands still to take care of."

Bill said, "You leaving tomorrow on the bus to Russellville or on the one to Little Rock?"

"To Little Rock. I'd have too much of a layover in Russellville as the bus and train schedules don't match up well going that direction."

"I see. Maybe one day you'll be instrumental in getting the train to run a connecting line to Dancing Deer. That's what politicians do . . . look out for the welfare of their constituents. It's called pork—as in 'pork barreled politics.'"

"I've never given much thought of going into politics but I'm sure it would be an interesting vocation."

When Rose got back with the paper's mail she saw David's truck parked in front and ran inside as fast as she could. She was disappointed David wasn't there and went to find Jesse. The door of the dark-room came open and Jesse strode out with a big smile on his face.

"Where is he?"

"Rose, I don't know who you're talking about."

"Jesse, don't be smart with me. You know I haven't seen David since he's been back. You did give him my message didn't you? Didn't you?"

"Yes, I did. But you probably should know his dog died last night. He might not be in the best of spirits."

"Oh, I'm sorry to hear that. David really loved that old dog. You know every time he had to write a paper in English and was allowed to pick his own topic he'd write about something he or his dad did with Balder. At first, everyone thought he was making up those stories, then one day he came to a pep rally and brought Balder. The dog was wearing a straw hat and had a red bandanna tied around his neck. David introduced everyone to Balder and right on cue the dog held out his paw to shake hands. When people talked to him he cocked his head, lifted one of his ears, or arched an eyebrow. He acted like he actually knew what they were saying. I remember someone made a funny remark. Everyone laughed. Balder took one of his paws and wiped at the side of his face like it was so funny it made him cry. After that, the students clamored until the teacher would read David's paper in class."

Jesse nodded his head. "I remember. You know Balder gave everyone a present before he died. Something he gave Mr. Calhoun helped him figure out how his horses got infected with the hoof and mouth."

Rose gave Jesse a look that begged him to continue. She just knew her dad didn't have any part to play in the sorry event and this might be the start of mending the fences she and David needed.

"Balder placed a syringe beside Mr. Calhoun's chair. David's dad said it looked like the one the Agricultural Extension Agent used when he came to doctor the horses, but Mr. Calhoun was pretty sure he had put that one away. He remembered that Balder growled at . . ." Jesse paused a moment, "I think his name was Muldaur. Yes . . . let me think. It's Stanley Muldaur. David asked me if he might still be living in Dancing Deer but I don't think I've ever met the man. He wasn't listed as one of our subscribers. Do you know where he might be? David's father wants to talk with him."

Rose looked down and said the man's name under her breath. She thought about it for a moment and shook her head while biting her bottom lip. She said, "The county might have some records. I'll talk it over with David tonight." She went into her office and called her dad.

"Hello, honey. I'm glad you called. I thought, since it's Friday, you might like going to a movie."

"But, Dad, it's Friday night and you always stay overnight in town on Friday night."

"I know, dear, but I thought tonight I might spend some time with someone I really love."

Rose paused then said, "Actually, Daddy, I have work I'm bringing home from the office and if I can get it done tonight I thought tomorrow morning we might make a shopping trip to Little Rock. I need some new summer clothes—some new shoes."

Rose was already putting a plan together where her father would be exonerated from the hoof-and-mouth fiasco. Then they could offer David a ride to Little Rock so he and her dad could work on their new friendship.

"Dad, do you know a man by the name of Stanley Muldaur?"

Bill had not been expecting this and stammered a bit before he said, "Yeah, I think he was a customer here at the bank and, if I'm not mistaken, he was once the Agricultural Extension Agent for the county. Why do you ask?"

"Do you think you could get me his address and telephone number? I think David's father needs to talk with him."

"Sure, honey. I'll see what I can do."

"Good. I'll be over in a little while. I want to get it to Mr. Calhoun as soon as I can. Thanks, Dad."

Rose replaced the telephone and sat back in her chair. Things were working out so marvelously. She'd have all their problems solved in no time. Then they wouldn't have to see each other on the sly.

Bill sat at his desk and pondered the situation. In a few minutes he told Jennifer to get the obituary department at *The Memphis Globe* on the phone. Soon he was asking about the old folk's home that had been in the paper recently.

"Which one would that be, sir?"

Bill hesitated then said, "I think there was one where a patient died from an infection and your paper did an expose about the facility's cleanliness."

The voice on the telephone said, "I don't remember such an article. However, a while back we did rate a selection of that type of facility on hygiene and cleanliness. If I remember correctly, it raised quite a furor."

Bill said, "If you would be so kind as to look that up and give me the names, addresses, and telephone numbers of the worst offenders I'd be happy to reimburse you for your time. Give me your name and home address and I'll mail you a hundred dollars."

"Give me an hour. Is there a number I can call you at?"

Bill said, "No. I'll have my secretary call you back in an hour." Bill jotted down the man's name and address.

David's next stop was Creighton's Jewelers. Everywhere he went people opened doors for him, told him how proud they were, and said what a rotten deal the Army had handed him. They wished him well with the 180th Infantry Regiment of the Forty-fifth Division. David had achieved a slight notoriety. He wondered how people like Jack Benny and Edward R. Murrow handled themselves when out in public.

Mr. Creighton himself helped David. He wanted to look at a locket. Mr. Creighton showed him the ones in sterling silver but David was afraid silver would tarnish. He wanted to buy Rose one in gold. Mr. Creighton pulled out a velvet pad, placed it on the glass display case, and, from a safe in the back, he brought out a small padded leather case containing a dozen or so of the lockets David had in mind. Mr. Creighton opened the case and started removing and displaying them on the velvet pad.

David asked, "May I?" as he reached out to touch one that had caught his attention.

"Certainly. Young man, you do have good taste. That particular locket is 18-karat gold and overlaid with a splash of white enamel. It's hand-painted in the French impressionistic style with a picture of a French peasant and his lady friend. Have you ever been to France?"

"No, sir. But I plan to go some day. I'd like to travel everywhere but especially to Italy and France. How much is it?"

"It's my most expensive locket. Most of the others are stamped out by machine but this one is hand-made by an old-world master. There's not another one like it. And for that it's priced at one hundred and twenty-five dollars." Mr. Creighton observed David's reaction. He said, "I have others much cheaper. This one, for instance, is also gold and it's only thirty dollars."

David was floored by the exorbitant price of the first locket but also mesmerized by its beauty. He put the first locket down and picked up the thirty-dollar locket. He opened it to see how the mechanism worked and observed how flimsy the chain was. He quickly looked at the chain on the first locket.

The old man stroked his chin and asked, "Are you the David Calhoun I've been reading about in the paper; the one who came home a few days ago on leave?"

"Yes, sir. That would be me."

"Well, son, if you're agreeable I think we might be able to strike a deal. If you would consent to having your picture taken purchasing this locket and let me use it as advertising for the store I will sell you the hundred and twenty-five dollar locket for thirty dollars."

"Would you throw in a better quality gold chain than the one it's displayed with?"

"Yes. I'll even do that. You may choose any one you like and I'll give you a nice velvet presentation box as well."

"Then, Mr. Creighton, we have a deal."

Mr. Creighton rubbed his hands together, enthusiastically shook hands with David, and said he'd be right back. He went to the telephone and called the paper telling the receptionist to send their photographer straight away. He had an urgent picture that needed taking.

While they waited, Mr. Creighton got out a selection of gold chains and helped David pick one that was the proper length and weight and with a double-action clasp. In a moment the front door opened and Jesse and his photographer came bouncing in.

Jesse grinned at David and said his picture was ready. He then shook Mr. Creighton's hand and asked what could he do for him.

In a few minutes the picture was taken, a quote written down, and an advertising promotion planned. David walked out of the store with Jesse's arm around his shoulder telling him what a close call he'd side-stepped. Jesse said, "Normally, Rose would have been the one to come with the photographer. But she's out of the office on an errand. David, you are the luckiest man in Dancing Deer." Back at the newspaper office Jesse expertly cut out David's picture and placed it in the locket. David was now ready.

When Rose came into her dad's office, Bill handed his daughter a piece of paper with a woman's name and address. He said, "She lives in Cakebread. The bank's records show Stanley Muldaur listed her as his next of kin. Mr. Muldaur didn't live in Dancing Deer and the address he gave the bank as his home address was hers. Quite a number of years back Mr. Muldaur closed his account and hasn't been seen by anyone since." Bill waited on Rose to respond and when she didn't he asked, "Why do you think Mr. Calhoun wants to talk with Muldaur?"

Rose said, "I don't know for certain but I heard that something has shown up related to the loss of his horses."

She stuffed the paper in her purse. Now she had something she could use to get things rolling. She kissed her dad on the cheek and sailed out of the room in high spirits.

In a few more minutes Bill's secretary came into his office with the list of old folks homes in Memphis. She said the man had given her seven names. Six had ten to fifteen health code violations and one had chalked up twenty-seven. Bill asked her to get in touch with the worst offender. Fifteen minutes later he had made arrangements for the transfer of one Stanley Muldaur from a facility in Little Rock to a facility in Memphis. The facility in Little Rock was not to know the name of the facility Stanley was being transferred to or even the name of the person or company doing the transfer. Since Bill was the one who paid the nursing fee, the Little Rock facility agreed to whatever his demands were. Once a year there had been a rather large amount wired into their bank account and the payor remained anonymous.

Jennifer started writing her resignation. This was the last straw. Her Christian beliefs would not allow her to continue working for such a despicable man.

Rose headed home and did some fast house cleaning. On the table in the kitchen she had several stacks of papers and a partially typed article stuffed in her typewriter. Her dad usually grabbed a change of clothes and was gone ten minutes after he arrived. Evidently, his town sweetie kept regular hours, or at least required her dad to keep regular hours. He always left Friday evenings a few minutes before six. Saturdays he would return at various times but never early in the morning.

Tonight he took his time. He walked in and peered over his daughter's shoulder as she was working on the typewriter. He walked around the kitchen noticing how everything had been put away and the counter tops cleaned. When Rose stopped typing for a moment he asked, "How was your day? Were you able to give the information to Mr. Calhoun?"

Rose said, "No. I'm going to let Jesse have the honors. I have a deadline to meet. This article has to be finished and mailed by Saturday morning. Jesse will have to pick up the slack."

"What's the article about?"

Rose said, "We've made arrangements with *The Courier Democrat* in Russellville to write contributing stories. I'm writing about the people leaving the Dancing Deer area to work in the munitions factories in Fort Smith. Next week, Russellville will be sending us an article on something important happening in their area. Their last effort was an article about the inflationary selling prices the land on Skyline Drive had attained. The world's getting smaller all the time."

Rose went back to typing. She noticed her dad trying to read over her shoulder and she ripped the paper from the typewriter, and with a red pencil, started making corrections. Bill walked into the parlor, turned on the radio, and sat in his chair listening to *The Great Gildersleeve*.

Why didn't he get ready? Was he privy to her plans? Rose didn't say anything, she just kept working. In a few minutes she went to get a drink from the refrigerator. She asked her dad if he would like something. He said no, he'd better get a move on; Friday only came once a week. Rose let out a nervous sigh and thought about going in and packing his things for him. It was well after dark before Bill got in his car and left. Rose immediately went through the front door and raised the red flag on their mailbox. A few minutes later, while Rose was going around the house adjusting the lighting and finding some Ray Anthony music on the radio, Bill walked back in.

Rose was visually upset when she saw him. In as calm a voice as she could muster she asked, "Is there something the matter, Daddy?"

"No. I forgot a book I wanted to take with me." Bill looked around the house and picked up a book he found in his bathroom. He headed out again.

Rose sat down in his comfortable chair and decided she was not cut out to be so deceptive. Her system couldn't stand the strain. She had heard stories of traveling salesmen who positioned women in different towns—even more than one wife. She wondered how such a deceitful man could keep his lies straight and what happened when he got caught. Life was so complicated.

She turned on the oven and went to the refrigerator for her entree. She retrieved two round beef fillets which she seared in a skillet containing a small amount of cooking sherry before placing in the broiler of her oven to cook through. From her dad's wine stash she retrieved his most prized bottle. Then she heard a rattling on the back door and saw David Blaine leaning against the door casing. She opened the door, reached out, grabbed him by the arm, and yanked him inside.

"David, I'm a nervous wreck. The first thing we have to do is decide what to do if my dad comes back."

"Rose, honey. I'm so glad to see you. May I have a kiss first?"

"David Blaine Calhoun, you are worthless. My sanity is at stake here. But . . . well . . ." and with that she put both arms around his neck melting into his embrace. Rose knocked off his Army hat and run her fingers through what the Army had left of his hair.

In a moment she shoved him toward the kitchen and said how she had planned the entire evening. She said everything had its time and its place and right now it was time to cook their meal and the place was in the kitchen. She asked David to set the table. She retrieved two tossed salads from the refrigerator. Before long they were seated at a candlelit table drinking an aged bottle of cabernet sauvignon her dad had been saving for a special occasion and eating a tasty filet mignon, complete with baked potato liberally saturated with melted sweet butter and covered with broken bits of bacon and smashed black peppercorns.

David looked across the table at Rose. She had changed into some flimsy little red number that clung to her body in all the right places. His heart raced. This must be what heaven's like.

"Rose, have you met either of my two uncles?"

"No. But I've heard about them. Aren't they the two carpenters who are so quiet?"

David shrugged. He loved his two uncles but both were introverted. "Uncle Rupert has been seeing Nadine, the librarian, every once in a while for the last ten years."

Rose's interest was piqued. She asked, "Ten years? Is it serious?"

"I know. That's a long time. I think both parties would like for it to be, but here's the conundrum: she lacks the self esteem to take matters into her own hands and push the romance forward and my uncle is too shy. If I don't figure a way to help them they're gonna grow old and never realize what could have been."

"Wow. What have you got in mind?"

David answered, "I thought I'd ask for your help and together we could make a project of fixing things for them. If you could figure some way to bolster Nadine's self esteem she might take charge and get the ball rolling by herself. She thinks she's so unattractive she's lucky Uncle Rupert occasionally comes around. She says they've never even held hands."

"And you want me to help them jump into bed?"

"Rose, you're taking the romance out of it. No, I think nature will take its course if we could get it started. Maybe you could show Nadine how to fix her hair or how to put on make-up. She really is plain but I don't think she's a lost cause."

"I know the woman all right. She has a hard time looking at you while talking, her hair is a mousy brown with lots of gray, and she always wears it up in a bun. And those clothes she wears. They were probably out of style when her mother was young."

"Then you'll help me?"

Rose looked at David's face reflecting the shimmering light of the candles. When he smiled at her like that there was not a thing he could ask that she would not do. She continued to gaze at David wondering how their children would look. Would they have his blond hair? His blue eyes?

"Well, Rose. What do you say?"

Rose broke out of her reverie. She nodded her head and said, "David, just go win the war and come back as quick as you can. I'll take care of things here."

"I told Nadine I had a plan and for her to be on the lookout for any opportunity. I guess my plan was to turn everything over to my one true love."

"Oh, David. You have such a way with words. My dad says you Calhoun men can talk your way out of quicksand; you bamboozle women with beguiling words." Rose took a sip of wine. "By the way I've located the name and address of Stanley Muldaur's next of kin. She's probably his sister since they have different last names. Here, give this to your dad." Rose handed David the piece of paper her dad had given her earlier. "Jesse told me all about it."

"Did he also tell you about Balder?"

"Yes, and I'm so sorry. Balder was a wonderful dog. Even though it didn't look like it, I loved to hear you, or the teacher, read your papers about him in class. Did he really do all those things you said?"

"Well, I might have taken a little artistic license but most of the stories had some grains of truth. I'm pretty upset."

After they finished their meal David helped Rose carry the dishes to the kitchen. She helped him remove his jacket then tied an apron around his waist to keep his pants from getting wet. He dried while she washed. They put everything away and Rose redecorated the table with her papers and typewriter. She told David about the ruse she had used on her father. They both laughed.

David said, "Rose, I have a present for you." He reached into his pocket and pulled out a blue velvet jewelry box and handed it to Rose.

Rose let out a gasp of air as she fondled the small box. "David, you shouldn't have. You need all the money they pay you just to survive. I love you, David."

She opened the box and let out a squeal of delight as she lifted the locket and studied its painting. She deftly opened it and, with tears welling up in her eyes, looked at David's handsome face in the picture. She closed the locket, unfastened the clasp on its chain, and turned her body at an angle while David refastened the necklace clasp after placing it around her lovely neck.

"I'll never take it off."

David asked, "What are your plans for the rest of the evening. It seems like you've taken charge?"

Rose said, "Let's go to the parlor."

It was dark with the fire throwing flickers of orange and yellow tongues throughout the room. She tuned the radio to a station playing Jo Stafford, sat David in her dad's big chair facing the fireplace, and crawled in on top of him. It wasn't but a few seconds before they were passionately kissing. One thing led to another and before long most of their clothes were strewn around the big chair.

Later, after their passions abated, Rose and David talked about their life together when he returned from the war. For the next hour or so they discussed what kind of work David could do, where they might live, and how they would solve life's problems. David finally said he had to go home and he walked around the chair picking up and putting on his clothes. Rose went into her bedroom and came out wrapped in a sumptuous bathrobe. She would just mention to her dad that David was going to Little Rock and leave it up to him. There was no need to say anything to David unless it actually worked out.

David kissed her again at the back door and left across the back yard. He walked through the houses to the street behind where he had parked the truck. Rose went into the bathroom and started a hot bath. She felt like soaking in a thick bubble bath while she figured out the best way to build up Nadine's self esteem. She also imagined what life would be like married to David Blaine Calhoun. She then slowly slid deep into a sea of liquid pearls.

The next morning Emily was up before daylight. She pressed David's washed clothes, the wrinkled uniform he had worn the day before, and prepared his favorite breakfast. Jed sniffed the aroma of coffee brewing and crackling bacon cooking in the skillet. He went quietly into the kitchen, crept up behind Emily stirring the chocolate gravy and pinched her bottom. She jumped, then slowly turned holding out a big spoon dripping chocolate gravy on the rug under her bare feet. She told Jed how often he was in a vulnerable state and that retaliation from her could be swift and lethal. Jed said he knew the possible consequences but the temptation was so great and he was so weak, that even though he wanted to resist, he just couldn't. Emily laughed. She was glad to see Jed was back in good spirits.

Before long she sent Jed to wake up David and the girls. Emily thought breakfast was her favorite meal and she had her whole family for this one so she made it special. She opened the oven door and removed the biscuits. From the icebox she brought forth home-churned, sweet butter and pear preserves. Everything was ready but before she let anyone eat she gave thanks for her family, for all their blessings, and prayed that God would look out for David and return him to them unhurt. Everyone said, "Amen."

Jed looked at David and asked, "Son, have you heard about Balder?"

"Yes, I have. He was a wonderful dog but it was time. I think he had arthritis in a bad way. All his joints must've hurt terribly. I think he was in a lot of pain. I'm just glad he had been our dog."

Emily turned toward David. "Your dad buried him beside Traveller. Your grandparents and two uncles were here and we had a little ceremony. Everyone told episodes they had been in with Balder. We all cried. I was not aware of how one dog's life could impact a family in so many ways. We are all glad he had been our dog, but maybe instead we were his family."

David wiped a tear from his eye. He understood the difference. In a moment he held out a piece of paper to his dad. "I think this is Stanley Muldaur's sister. She might know where he is. Rose got it from her dad."

Jed took the piece of paper, looked at the name, and put it in his pocket. After breakfast David and Jed walked outside to the front porch. David sat in his mother's rocking chair and drank a cup of coffee with a smidgen of cream. He had started drinking coffee these past few months but was still pretty much a neophyte.

They didn't say anything for a while then David said, "What are you going to do when you find Muldaur?"

"I'm going to ask him why he did it."

"Is there any way you could bring him to justice? I mean is the syringe enough proof to get him convicted?"

"I doubt it. There's no way to prove it was his. I could probably beat it out of him but what would that get me? He'd recant if I hauled him before a magistrate and then I'd have to spend a few nights in jail for assault. Besides, he was put up to it by someone else. I would really like to determine who that person was and why."

"Do you think it was Mr. Potter? Muldaur was in the bank the next day talking with Bill."

"I've thought about that. I think Muldaur was either arranging a loan to pay for his medical bills or giving Bill a statement for the worming medicine. Bill didn't sell me the black stallion and he was the only one that tested positive. So at this point all we know is that Bill Potter is the type of person who could have done it. However, I had other people who hated me as much as Bill and they also were of the type who could've done it. Before I met your mother I led a pretty rough life. Let's talk about you though. Do you know anything about the 180th Regiment or the Forty-fifth Division?"

"Only that other people have said they are among the best."

David and his father talked for over an hour before Emily and the girls emerged and said it was time to head into town. If David missed his bus he'd never make it to Massachusetts by the appointed time and he'd be considered AWOL. David said he didn't want that as it was customary to spend three days in confinement for each day of AWOL and it would go in his personnel file.

At noon his family, both sets of grandparents, two uncles, and quite a number of friends sent David off to war again. Rose and her dad had left two hours earlier.

The following Monday Rose walked into the library and asked Nadine if she might have a few minutes to spare after work. They met at the Ritz Hotel Bistro. Nadine wondered if this was the opportunity David had told her about.

Nadine was a little apprehensive at first but Rose was such a pretty young lady and so poised. She was all the things Nadine was not, but wanted to be. Rose said Nadine needed to make some small changes. Nadine informed Rose she had a small amount of discretionary funds at her disposal. She said her parents left her a house and a savings account. Also, she seldom spent any money. She kept putting what she earned away for a rainy day. Rose told her it was time to dip into those funds and she would be forever glad she did. They looked through the catalogues of new clothes sent to Rose, at new hair fashions in magazines, and talked about the new role women were playing in commerce, in politics, in the community, and in their own families. Nadine got caught in the excitement and couldn't wait to start fulfilling her new destiny.

Rose said, "Let's start with a handshake."

"Okay. What are we agreeing on?"

"We're not agreeing on anything in particular, I'm talking about the social convention of actually shaking hands."

Rose then showed Nadine how you held your wrist firm, held the other person's hand tight with a slight pressure exerted from the palm and thumb, and shook in an up and down motion from the elbow. She told Nadine to always look someone in their eyes when talking to them. She explained how eye contact sealed out external distractions, made both people feel they had the other person's complete attention, and both parties would know that whatever was being said was important.

She gave Nadine examples of how a woman could steer the conversation from one topic to another that was more appropriate to the occasion or more to the liking of the woman who was now in charge.

Nadine was beginning to understand why Rose seemed so poised. She was a take charge woman. Nadine wanted to be just like her.

Rose took Nadine's measurements. They ordered silk underwear from New York City because Rose said a woman needed the luxuriant feeling of silk sliding against bare skin to really understand the power she controlled. Rose talked of how men relied so much on their senses of smell, touch, and sight that women had come to understand how they could use that to control their men. A woman could sway a man's behavior with a whiff of a captivating fragrance, the touch of a slinky piece of fabric, or exposing the curvature of some body part.

Rose and Nadine sampled expensive perfumes, shopped for fine merino cotton dresses and cashmere sweaters, bought short skirts to show off Nadine's long legs, and started hiking to build up her calves and to firm her derrière. They also discussed, for hours, what made men tick.

Nadine threw out everything in her closet. Rose helped her pick fabrics and colors that would mix and match. At the beauty shop Gina cropped Nadine's long tresses to shoulder length and colored away the gray. She was shown several different styles her hair could be worn depending on what she wanted to achieve. Up in a French bun with curled strands hanging down in the front framing her oval face when she wanted to appear smart and sophisticated. Down in a soft wavy roll with the tips tucked under when she wanted to appear sultry and seductive. And the use of a barrette to keep her hair pulled to one side and almost covering one eye when she wanted to appear mysterious. She was told this last hairstyle should be used sparingly and only when she wanted to arouse the curiosity of someone normally ambivalent.

Nadine's eyebrows were plucked and reshaped. Rose told Nadine about her natural skin tone and how to use that color to pick the shades of eye shadow, mascara, blush, and lipstick that would best enhance her natural beauty. Rose educated Nadine in the intricacies of applying the make-up using different brushes, pads, and pencils.

Nadine was becoming a woman of the times. People started noticing. Nadine walked to work every morning and, where she had always before had her head down, now she kept her head up looking straight ahead. If someone spoke, as was happening more and more often, she locked eyes with them until they flushed and muttered something incoherent. Men tipped their hats, offered an arm when she had to cross the street, and offered to share their umbrellas when it was raining or might start raining. Business was even picking up at the library. Nadine blossomed.

Rupert came into the library and saw Nadine. He stopped. He could go no farther and sat down. He didn't know what to say. Was this the same woman he'd taken to the church social just a few weeks before? He did notice she had become more talkative, more assertive, more comfortable but now she looked like . . . like someone off the cover of a fashion magazine.

"Hello, Ru."

"Hello, Nadine."

"Ru, would you like to see this month's *Woodworking Gazette*?"

"Thank you, Nadine." For the next ten minutes Rupert held but did not look at the magazine. Instead, he spent the time peeking over the cover at Nadine.

"Ru, they have a traveling vaudeville troupe coming to the Ritz this weekend. Would you like to go?"

"Nadine, is that really you? You look so pretty I thought I might be dreaming and had become an actor in a movie."

Nadine gazed intently at the only man she had ever loved. She got up from her chair, glided around the corner of her desk, and gracefully sat down beside him. She placed a hand on his knee, leaned forward close to his face, and cooed, "Yes Ru, it's really me."

CHAPTER 11—HMS *QUEEN ELIZABETH*
Fort Devens, Massachusetts - November 1942

It took David seven days to complete his journey to Fort Devens, Massachusetts. He arrived in a wrinkled uniform, unshaved, and sleep deprived. With two days furlough left he departed the train and set out to find a hotel, a laundry, and a good restaurant. A street vendor headed him to the Palace Hotel where a freckled girl in pigtails asked David to sign the register. She took his clothes needing to be laundered and headed him to a room at the end of the hall on the second floor.

Earlier, when walking to the hotel, he passed the USO. Later in the evening, after he had bathed and eaten supper, he thought he might see what was cooking at every serviceman's favorite social gathering.

The bathroom was down the hall, but at three in the afternoon, he felt safe he'd be the only one using it. He inserted a new blade in his safety razor, lathered up, and scraped off a three-day growth. Next, he ran a tub of steaming hot water and climbed in with a bar of Octagon soap. He scrubbed until his hide began turning bright pink. He then lounged in the water for at least twenty minutes—every so often letting out a little water and replacing it with new, hot water. As he was lounging in the water, he thought he might eat a big steak and come back to his room to write Rose a letter and forget the USO until a later time. Periodically he'd receive a whole passel of letters from her. So far the situation had been lop-sided.

David left the bathroom wrapped in a towel. He didn't get but a few steps before the hotel desk clerk came out of his room with an empty water pitcher. "I thought you might like some fresh water," she said as she lowered her head and quickly slipped past. She looked back over her shoulder before descending the stairs.

Later, dressed in the only uniform he hadn't given the girl and with his short hair neatly combed, David sauntered into the hotel lobby.

"Where would a hungry soldier get a huge steak at a reasonable price?"

"There's a steakhouse a few blocks north. Turn right from the front door. The owner has a son in the Army and gives a discount to anyone wearing a uniform." She pierced David through with green eyes. "Will you be going to the USO after your dinner?"

There were not many servicemen in the USO. In fact, there were more women than men. The young lady from the hotel met him at the door and said she and her friends had saved him a seat. There were seats all over the room but he followed her to a table brimming-full of young ladies. David asked why there were not more servicemen.

"The Forty-fifth shipped out to upstate New York," said a pretty brunette. "Normally it's quite lively. Would you care to play a game of pool?"

"Annette, you're not going to hog him that way. Here, have a seat, soldier-boy. We've been waiting for you. My name's Ellen."

David sat down like he was told. Each girl in turn offered her name but David wasn't listening. He asked, "When did they leave?"

No one seemed to know. All they knew for certain was that, for the last two nights, the USO had been devoid of much activity. David shrugged his shoulders. He'd find out everything in the morning. He spent the evening drinking lemonade and entertaining the girls with his homespun yarns. He even danced a few times but with so many potential partners he became good at offering lame excuses.

At ten he started yawning and told the young ladies he'd better go back to his room before he fell asleep at the table.

"Stay just a little while longer—we'll carry you back to your room and tuck you in if you go to sleep." They all seemed of a like mind.

He thought about that for a moment then politely declined.

The next morning David arose before daybreak. He quickly emerged from the bathroom cleanly shaven and bathed and went downstairs to check on his laundry. The girl at the desk said they would be delivering it around ten. He had plenty of time to eat breakfast. David paid for his room then ate breakfast in the coffee shop. Afterwards he came back into the reception area and spent the remaining two hours writing letters and getting his shoes shined. He ended up stuffing his cleaned clothes, less the one set he changed into, in his duffel bag. He then purchased a newspaper and hailed a taxi. The headlines said the Forty-fifth Division moved to Pine Camp, New York, that very morning. David groaned. He arrived on post just before noon on the eighth of November, in a pressed uniform and shined shoes.

A young sergeant was leafing through a number of cards attached to a circular spindle when David arrived. He barely looked up as David approached and stood at attention in front of his desk. "Sir," the young sergeant said to a nearby colonel, "that's the last of the hospitals. I'll try the hotels next." The colonel looked David's way and returned David's smart salute.

"Good morning, sir." David turned from the colonel and to the sergeant said, "Private David Calhoun reporting for duty."

The sergeant took David's papers and put them in a wire basket. "Have a seat, Calhoun. I've got some important telephone calls to make then I'll get you taken care of."

"I'm in no hurry, Sergeant." David turned and walked to a chair out of the way.

The colonel started pacing the floor. "When I find that young man, he'll be peeling potatoes for a month." He then walked into an adjoining office and plopped down in a big chair.

Five telephone calls later the sergeant slammed down the telephone and picked up David's papers from the basket. Soon he was up and heading to the colonel with the papers stuffed under his arm. In a few minutes the sergeant came back and the colonel asked David from his doorway if David would join him. The colonel shut the door, told David his name was Colonel Fulbright, to make himself at ease, and pointed to a straight-backed, wooden chair.

"Private Calhoun, are you aware the 180th Infantry Regiment re-billeted to New York this morning along with other components of the Forty-fifth?"

"Yes, sir. I found out from today's newspaper. I still have one day left on my chit but thought I might better get here to see if there were any stragglers I could hitch a ride with."

The colonel fumbled through the papers. "Calhoun, I'm the Second Battalion Commander of the 180th. I have orders to travel to the

Allied Command Headquarters in Algiers. It seems General Montgomery has Rommel, lately referred to as the Desert Fox, on the run and they want me, and several other battalion commanders, to observe. To get a little battle experience, you might say. I'm scheduled to leave on the *Queen Elizabeth* Monday morning. I'll be traveling with my sergeant-major and with you. We need someone to carry our dispatches between the field and headquarters, to drive the jeep, and to coordinate our schedules. The soldier who was going with us is AWOL. We'll be gone three months, returning in early February. Are you ready to see some action?"

"Sir, I've just gotten out of Basic Training. I haven't been on maneuvers, through any of the schools, or received the specialized tactical training most men get before being deployed."

"Well, soldier, you'll not actually be in any action. You'll just be observing it. We'll get you all that training when you get back in February."

"Sir, I belong to the Army. Wherever the Army needs me, that's where I want to be."

The colonel looked through David's papers. Presently he looked up and said, "It says here you achieved an exceptionally high score on the General Classification Test, you're an expert marksman, had no demerits assigned, and didn't volunteer for anything. Am I missing something? Are you planning a career in the military?"

"No, sir. I just stay out of trouble."

"Also, that some hotshot in Washington had you assigned to us."

"Sir, does it say who that hotshot was?"

"No. It says that the request was made by the Bureau of Military Personnel. Private Calhoun, I am hereby promoting you to private first class. See the sergeant outside about getting your stripes and insignia. Have them sewed on to your uniform as soon as you can. I assume you can drive a jeep?"

"Yes, sir."

"Good. That will be all, Private First Class Calhoun. The sergeant will show you where the mess hall is. We leave at 1600 hours."

The sergeant told David he could leave his two duffel bags where they lay. For the next few hours the sergeant took David from the headquarters building to the quartermaster where he got his new stripe sewed on and enough additional insignias for him to make similar adjustments to his packed uniforms. At sickbay he was given additional shots. They ate in the mess and on the way back to headquarters the sergeant allowed David a few minutes in the base PX. David purchased a black leather attaché, a set of maps that folded and snapped shut, and more writing paper. They got back to headquarters just as someone started to heft David's duffle bags into the back of a waiting jeep.

The sergeant said, "You'll be traveling aboard the *Queen Elizabeth*. Usually the trip takes three weeks but she's swift. She makes the trip in six days." He handed David an updated set of papers and waved to the colonel. David and a driver in one jeep followed the sergeant-major, the colonel, and another driver in the first jeep now ten car lengths ahead.

At the train station David retrieved his writing tablet, a book, and his letters from Rose. He stuffed these in the attaché and sat looking over his new atlas. In a few minutes he had located Dancing Deer on the Arkansas map, Columbus on the Georgia map, Fort Devens on the Massachusetts map, and traced with his finger his travels so far and then on to New York City on the USA map. On the world map he traced from New York City across the Atlantic to England. It took him a few minutes to find Algiers. He wondered what lay in store for him there.

The colonel sat in a privileged section and David didn't see him again until they were unloading at their destination. That night David was overawed by the sights and sounds of New York City. His neck hurt from looking up at the skyscrapers. Glitzy lights illuminated the sidewalks. Hawkers stood outside nightclubs with bills describing the gorgeous ladies inside. There were people of every description, nationality, and ethnicity. They walked fast and talked fast like they were in a hurry to get somewhere and had something to say. David soaked up the intensity and the energy emanating from the people and the city.

The next morning Colonel Fulbright came into the lobby of their hotel. "Gentlemen, we'll be leaving to board ship at ten hundred hours. Sergeant, you and Private Calhoun have time to eat breakfast but be outside with your bags at ten sharp."

The sergeant-major asked David, "Son, would you care to join me for a Belgian waffle?"

"Sure. Sounds good to me."

The concierge said their bags would be safe in a corner of the lobby and off they went.

The sergeant said, "I'm glad you're a big, strong-looking man. The private you're replacing was a wimp. He didn't make the right impression for the colonel. Besides, you never know what kind of circumstance we might find ourselves in. And you look like you could handle yourself if matters get out of hand."

David waited for the sergeant to order then ordered the same thing for himself. In a few minutes the waitress brought gigantic crispy pancakes with ridges. David watched the sergeant slather on two heaping spoons of butter and pour on enough maple syrup to cover the waffle and fill the platter. David followed suit. The two of them ate, drank coffee, talked about the war, and what they would do after the war. They became the best of friends.

The sergeant told David the history of the outfit to which he'd been assigned. He'd fit right in. The sergeant had been in the military for twenty years and had seen a lot and been a lot of places. He never regretted giving up the civilian life. The Army supplied him with everything he needed and gave him good pay to boot.

"After the war I plan on retiring to Wisconsin and spending my days with my children and with their children."

During the meal he told David he liked to ice fish and listen to baseball games on the radio. His favorite team was the Milwaukee Brewers.

That afternoon, aboard the *Queen Elizabeth*, the soldiers hung over the rails as thousands of people waved goodbye. A band played. The only song David recognized was "Over There." As they were leaving port, orderlies handed out life-saver vests and told the soldiers if the ship was torpedoed all people without life-saver vests would perish. David thought, also those with life-saver vests, but dutifully put his on just like everyone else. He was given a sheet and a blanket for his bed and assigned to a numbered swinging berth. There was a time to be in it and a time to be out of it. Evidently someone else would have it before him and a third soldier would be in it after David. The ship was crowded. She was designed to carry 3,000 passengers and a few hundred members of the crew comfortably. She was now carrying 16,000 soldiers elbow to elbow. When David made it to the berthing deck he saw hammocks strung six high on each side of narrow aisles. Each hammock was separated from the one below and the one above by a two foot clearance. People were already getting seasick and you could still see the city in the distance.

David wondered what would happen if the person in the top hammock, at twelve feet up, vomited before he managed to get out. And, if he did get sick, how would he be able to navigate the distance to the floor on weak legs while holding his stomach. David quickly realized the bottom hammock was not the place to be and asked if anyone on the top would prefer a more convenient one closer to the bottom. David thought he could manage the climb easier than sleeping under a soiled blanket. A heavyset man said he'd change. David and the man exchanged berthing tickets. David then went topside to figure the location and hours of mess.

"We're damn lucky to be sailing in November." The sergeant-major leaned against the railing. "It's unbearable in summer. We got fans of course, but they only stir up the smell making it that much worse. The Atlantic is a rough sea and, in such tight quarters, when one man gets sick he makes everyone around him nauseated."

David thought how nice this would be if it was a pleasure cruise he and Rose were taking to some distant shore.

"It's six days. A body can stand just about anything for six days." The sergeant-major stretched, looked around at the soldiers already getting sick. "David, when you feel the least bit nauseated make it to an outside deck and breathe in fresh air. Also keep something on your stomach. The dry heaves is a sickness unto itself."

David thanked him for his advice and returned to his thoughts of Rose and the pleasures of her company and when they had money and would be traveling like this for pleasure. That evening David ate some weird-tasting concoction a fellow soldier called a kidney pie. The Brits have strange culinary tastes. He remembered what the sergeant-major had said and pushed the food around, taking tiny bites until he actually had finished the distasteful entrée. He didn't much care for it, but he did believe he needed to keep something on his stomach.

When his time for the berth came, the ship had made it out to open sea and the wind and waves had picked up. It was just as he had assumed. People were sick everywhere. Some made it out of their hammocks and some didn't. The air was thick with the smell of sickness. David climbed into his hammock two feet below the ceiling bulkhead and tried to fall asleep as fast as he could. Between the gagging of the already sick and the snoring of the ones not, David thought six days would be an interminable period of time.

Four days out matters escalated. They encountered turbulent weather and the ship pitched and yawed. Soldiers swung in their hammocks too sick to relinquish them to their rightful occupants. Stench filled the berthing areas. David, and a lot of others, went to the outside deck and sequestered corners in which to curl up. If you were lucky enough to have a clean blanket you kept it with you all day. Other than the belt holding up your trousers, it was your most valuable possession. The salt sea spray, the unrelenting wind, the occasional rain, the cold, and the ever-present stench of vomit combined to make the voyage a very unpleasant experience.

David overheard one man say, "I have no doubt we'll win this damn war, but I'll not be making the trip home unless they cut a tunnel under the sea and pack it with a fast train."

Although there were plenty of drills for fire and being under enemy attack, none of these two situations actually occurred. They steamed into a fortified harbor just outside London proper on the 15th of November 1942. Their duffel bags were taken to the pier and sorted according to the regiment, battalion, and company each soldier belonged to. It didn't take long for David to locate his two duffel bags and make it to where the colonel and the sergeant-major were waiting.

That night they stayed in a hotel in downtown London. David thought it was a large hotel for his room to be so small. He was taking a cold shower when sirens started blaring. People were running through the hallways yelling for everybody to get out, to get into the subway tunnels. David hastily dressed and followed the throng. As he huddled in a dark, cavernous expanse he could hear bombers overhead and loud explosions.

There weren't any children. David remembered hearing someone say the children had been sent into the countryside. The people left had a somber look that somehow conveyed to David that they were a people who could take anything the Germans could throw. They were a resourceful and defiant people. He was glad they were on his side.

The next day they loaded onto a long-range bomber and headed for Algiers. It was the first time David had been on an airplane. Of course, the trip over on the *Queen Elizabeth* was the first time he'd been on an ocean-liner.

The sergeant-major said, "We'll be traveling over Allied occupied territory. We should be arriving in Algiers early this evening."

The plane wasn't pressurized so everyone had to breathe through facial cups attached to breathing tubes suspended from the bulkhead. David was sitting on a bench along the starboard fuselage with a parachute strapped to his back. The colonel was up front with the pilot and co-pilot and the sergeant was sitting in a chair bolted to the floor. There were other passengers, all pretty much in the same situation as he. The plane had a crew of six. David didn't have a window to look out so he took out his world atlas and memorized the town names, the desert areas, and the topographical defiles throughout northern Algeria. He wondered where the action would be taking place. In a few minutes he became bored with his atlas and started to write a letter to his dad. He had so many things to tell him since the last letter and now they needed to find out about this hotshot in Washington.

When the plane landed in Gibraltar David found where headquarters had been until the commencement of the North African invasion. General Eisenhower's office had been deep inside the rock with radio communication to every major force under his command. They changed to a smaller bomber and, with about half of the former passengers, they continued to Algiers.

CHAPTER 12—ALGIERS

The Southern Shores of the Mediterranean - November 1942

Algiers was not like any city David had ever been to. It was foreign—real foreign. There were French men sporting pencil-thin mustaches and swarthy Algerians wearing flowing robes of cotton or linen. Some wore a funny-looking hat a fellow GI called a fez; others wore turbans. They carried themselves like they were important in some way and all had haughty attitudes toward anyone they thought might be British.

It was fairly easy to tell the British from the Americans. The British were professional soldiers. You could tell by the smart way they walked, their precise mannerisms, and their strict adherence to any kind of rule or order. Americans, by comparison, slouched when they walked, didn't shave all that often, and tried to circumvent the rules whenever possible. The locals hissed under their breath when a Tommy walked by and snickered when they might happen on a Yank.

David Blaine's duties consisted of driving Colonel Fulbright's jeep and running oddball errands. Usually the day started, after a substantial breakfast, with carrying the colonel and the sergeant-major to headquarters. During the day he had their clothes washed and pressed and, sometimes, the jeep washed and waxed. He also accomplished whatever errands they gave him. There was a lot of time for goofing off. He was supposed to be back at headquarters to pick them up at five every afternoon but they were never ready. He sat around twiddling his thumbs until, usually late in the evening, an exhausted colonel and sergeant stumbled out needing delivery to their quarters. David had a lot of time on his hands.

From what he understood of the fighting, Fieldmarshal Rommel was giving the American forces a lesson in humility. At the battle of Kesserine Pass the vaunted American forces were routed. He had heard that General Bradley told General Eisenhower, "Basically, our boys threw down their guns and ran."

It was right after this embarrassing event that General Patton was brought up and put in charge of the intimidated men. David wrote to Nadine and asked if Rommel had ever written a book.

One day, at mail call, a large package was given to David containing the book *Infantry Attacks* by Erwin Rommel. He looked under the front cover and found the date due had been left blank. And it was listed as belonging to the Library at West Point.

That day, on the way to headquarters, the colonel noticed the book, thumbed through, and asked if David thought he might like to replace General Patton. He and the sergeant thought the comment extremely funny and laughed all the way through the front door. David found a shady spot to park the jeep and spent the rest of the day reading his new treasure. Several times during the day the sergeant came outside looking for the jeep. At five that afternoon the colonel came sauntering out the front door expecting to see David and the jeep. He stopped, looked around, and then saw David a good ways from his normal spot under a shade tree. He marched over and politely asked if David had enjoyed the day. David snapped to attention. He put the book down and saluted. "Yes, sir."

"Private Calhoun, give me that book."

David handed the colonel the book, "Yes, sir."

As the colonel walked toward headquarters he yelled over his shoulder. "Calhoun, take the evening off. The sergeant and I can make it back okay. In fact, why don't you take tomorrow off as well. Go into town and get a good local meal. See a show."

"Yes, sir."

David drove around until he found a fashionable restaurant, flipped a half dollar to an attendant to park the jeep close to the door and strode inside. Even though it was still early for the evening meal the place was booming. The maître d' told David there were no tables available but if he would go into the adjoining saloon someone would come and get him when his turn came.

David stepped through hanging beads into a room full of smoke. Just like in the dining room, there weren't any tables open in the saloon so he took an empty seat at the bar. He was into his second beer when an elderly gentleman holding his hat and coat and looking a little disheveled asked if he could sit on the empty barstool next to David. David told him he could, that most locals shunned him, and the seat had been vacant for thirty minutes or longer.

The man stared at David. In a low serious voice, he said, "I might need some help. I'm being pursued by two Gestapo agents. If they try to take me away I'll need a diversionary action to give me that second I'll need to get out the door."

David believed him. Something about the man made David think he better stay alert and help if he could. He shoved the beer away and turned to watch the door. In a few minutes two tall slender men wearing long saddle-brown leather coats opened the entry door. They gave a look around. One stood at the door while the other started making his way through the crowd. David said, "They're here."

The old man had his back to the door. He took a big swig of beer as one of his pursuers asked, "Excuse me. May I order at the bar?"

David said, "Here, you can have my seat. My friend and I have just been notified our table's ready. Coming, Fred?"

David kept his seat as the first man was more interested in the old man than in ordering. The man at the door was now in front of David. He said, "I think Fred will be coming with us." The old man swiveled his seat around until he was facing his adversary. Suddenly, coins hit the tiled floor and everyone stopped talking. Several people seated close by began picking up the coins. The first man turned to see what was going on and the old man jumped off his seat. David took the cue and jumped off his seat, landing heel first on the second man's front foot. David grabbed him by his lapels and they fell into the first man as David's new friend scrambled out the door. People were all over the three of them, grabbing at the coins. The man who had been standing at the door, the same one David had landed on when jumping off his barstool, got up, dusted himself off, and said, "*Dummkopf.*"

David paid for his two drinks. The first man now up from the floor said in perfect English, "We'll meet again, Joe."

David walked outside carrying the old man's hat and coat. No need letting the Gestapo go through his pockets. He wondered why the old man was running in the first place. He decided to walk up the street to another restaurant and left the jeep where it was. He still had not eaten supper.

"Psst." The sound came whistled through pursed lips.

David stopped in his tracks. The old man was standing in the shadows. "I just want to thank you. Do you feel up to an adventure?"

"Yeah. Why not?"

"Those two goons have taken my picture. I've got to get their camera and destroy the film. Otherwise, they'll figure out who I am and my family's security won't be worth a damn."

"Okay. How're we going to do it? I'm not allowed to carry a gun in town and I'll bet both of them are armed."

The old man pondered a moment. "How would my father handle it?"

"I know what my dad would do. He'd fashion some contraption that caught them like a bear trap and then punch their lights out if they struggled."

"Well, we don't have a bear trap and I don't have any sort of weapon."

David said, "We've got weapons. Does anyone live close by?"

"Yeah. These are all apartments along this side of the street."

A few minutes later David had scrambled up a fire escape and retrieved several lengths of rope the tenants had been using to hang drying laundry between apartments.

"I can make a lasso, lay a trap, or do rope tricks while you sneak up from behind and hit them over the head with a brick."

"Those are all good options but the margin of error's too great."

"You think they have a car?" David looked up and down the street as he said this.

"I think that black Citroen would probably be their car. I've got it," said the stranger. "They'll have other weapons hid in their car. Let's hope they decided to eat, giving us enough time to shake it down."

"You go check it out and I'll loiter by the front door in case they do come out. By the way, my name's David Calhoun."

Extending his hand the old man said, "I'm sorry, I can't tell you my name but you can call me the Seeker. It's an alias I use sometimes."

Philippe ran to the Citroen and David went toward the door leading into the saloon. He soon realized if they were eating they would be emerging from another door further up the street. He had not quite reached the second door when it opened and out came the two agents. One had a toothpick in his mouth and the other stretched like he had put in a hard day. David crouched in an alcove behind clay pots holding small tropical trees. He reached down and tested the weight of one of the pots. It moved under his touch and when the two agents walked by he picked up a pot, stepped out, and brought it down on the closest man's head. The struck agent staggered into the other before falling to the ground. David grabbed the standing agent's arm pinning it behind his back.

He whispered into the man's ear, "You're right, we do meet again." With that said, David jerked the man's shoulder out of socket and threw him head first into the brick façade of the restaurant. Both agents were now sprawled on the sidewalk. David reached into the first man's pocket and retrieved a Lugar. He then searched through the pockets of the second man. Nothing but a camera. Under the second man's coat, David found a P-38 in a shoulder holster. When pedestrians walked by, they acted like nothing unusual was going on as David reset the separated shoulder. Both captured men were groggy and afraid to move. When Philippe arrived David had them sitting up against the building wall.

Philippe said, "Mr. Calhoun, are you a cowboy?"

"No. A hillbilly." He handed Philippe a Leica 35mm camera with a telephoto lens. "Quite a setup. They probably have a close-up of you. However, I suggest you don't ruin the film. Intelligence might find other pictures on the roll to be of value."

"You're right but I don't want anyone to have my particular picture. I'll take the film and have my father develop it then add the pictures in my next pouch. They'll eventually reach the proper authorities with an explanation."

"What should we do with these gents? We can't just let them go and I'd feel mighty uncomfortable shooting them in cold blood."

"I've already secured lodging. Why don't we go there for the night? It's not far. We can tie them up. Then I'll go through their clothes and their papers. Tomorrow we'll give their auto a good going over and you can take them in to the authorities. You'll be a hero."

They threw both Germans into the back of David's jeep and drove to the hotel where Philippe was staying. In German Philippe told the two captives that if they behaved themselves they would not be hurt and tomorrow they would be given to the Allied authorities. They would spend the remainder of the war in luxurious accommodations somewhere in the United States or Britain.

They entered the hotel through the back entrance and ascended the stairs to Philippe's two-room suite. Philippe went into the bathroom and retrieved two washcloths, which he used to securely blindfold the agents. Philippe told them to take off their jackets. One man couldn't move his arm very well so David helped him while Philippe kept them covered with the stolen Lugar. He had one man completely undress. He then went through every bit of his clothing looking for hidden needles or other similar items. What he found was a pair of handcuffs and a cyanide capsule sewed inside the German's shirt sleeve cuff. He threw back the man's underwear, pants and shirt. After Philippe followed the same procedure with the second agent, he had David sit them in two chairs back to back. David then handcuffed them together with one man clearly in pain.

"What's with him? You mistreating the prisoners?"

"No, sir. He's probably suffering from cramps. I'm going to tie their feet together, then I'll go out and bring us back something to eat."

"Take your time, I've got their coats, hats, shoes, and quite a bit of papers to still look through." With the two Gestapo agents blindfolded and properly secured, Philippe removed his hat and coat, fake mustache, and eyebrows. David realized the Seeker was actually an actor in his middle to late twenties.

An hour later, David returned with several sacks and a bottle of wine. He gave each of the two captives a healthy drink of water from a cup. Then he and Philippe ate their meal and quietly talked about what they would do after the war.

Philippe told David about his family's vineyard, how it sat on the side of a hill, and about a shallow stream he played in as a child. David talked about Balder and Traveller. They divided the night, with

Philippe sleeping the first half and David the second. Several times during the night water was given to the two Gestapo agents, and the next morning David and Philippe had to let their captives have the bathroom first—leaving the door open. With their hands cuffed behind their backs and their pants and shorts around their ankles, they raced to the toilet. The slowest had to wait and ended up urinating in the tub. It took Philippe and David two hours to clean up the mess and to get bathed while keeping a wary eye for any trouble.

The Gestapo agents had not been driving the Citroen but a Horch convertible parked a few streets over. They found three packs of film and a folio on the agent Philippe had played chess with. There were other papers stacked neatly in the back seat alongside a short-wave direction finder. In the glove box was a length of piano wire with two "D" clips attached, a spring-loaded knife, and some bomb-making apparatus. Philippe kept the folio and film. He gave David the papers and other items. When they were finished searching the auto David gave Philippe his stateside address, and made Philippe agree to get in touch with him after the war. David then, with his two prisoners stowed in the back of the jeep, headed to Allied Headquarters. At the front gate David showed his ID papers and told the guard he had two German Gestapo prisoners. The guard went to a telephone and moments later two more guards arrived to escort David and his two prisoners inside. David had to leave the jeep as they all marched in formation to a holding cell, with David carrying his found loot. Colonel Fulbright and the sergeant-major were called and David was given a piece of paper and told to write down everything just as it happened. The Seeker had said for him to tell it just like it happened as well.

There were a lot of excited soldiers hustling about, snatching papers, and looking at the direction-finder, wondering what it was. All were wearing massive numbers of assorted cloth stripes or brass bars. There were others wearing stars on their lapels.

The first week in February they headed home. David now considered himself a veteran. He'd been promoted to corporal and spent quite a long while composing a letter to Jesse that would make it pass the censor. Colonel Fulbright couldn't wait to tell everyone how he'd been able to stand up and tell his superiors what he thought Rommel's next moves were going to be. He was right more often than not. He also was proud of David capturing two Gestapo agents and making him look good. The sergeant-major was just glad to be getting back before David got himself in a situation he couldn't get out of and before the colonel embarrassed the entire 180th.

CHAPTER 13—STATESIDE
Virginia – February 1943

David was glad to be on native soil. He had never traveled much before joining the Army and, now that he had a taste of it, he longed to be back on familiar turf. The piney woods of Virginia, where Camp Pickett was located, was pretty close to northern Arkansas as far as climate and scenery, but without his family and Rose it was as foreign as North Africa. He'd travel later—for pleasure. Right now he wanted to do something to get this war moving so he could go home. He and Rose had so much to do.

David located the barracks he was assigned and wandered in carrying both duffel bags. No one offered to help but that was all right. One of the first things you learn in the military is to take care of yourself. As he made his way down the corridor between bunks he felt like a new initiate walking a gauntlet. One man, a boy really, was shining shoes. David wondered how many pairs of shoes a soldier was supposed to have. He had a pair of dress shoes and a pair of boots but the young soldier shining shoes had six pairs of assorted boots and shoes shined, standing in a neat row, and working on a seventh.

At the end of the aisle he found an empty pair of bunk beds and dropped his duffel bags on the floor and the linens he had been given on the lower bunk of two beds. A man in the next bunk asked if he was a draftee replacement or if he had transferred in from another outfit. David replied that he enlisted and this was his first permanent assignment after basic training. The man held out his hand saying he was Boyd.

"Hey, newbie." Three burley characters walked up beside David's bunk. The one standing in the middle held out a rifle. "This piece needs cleaning."

David looked at the three men and continued unloading his first duffel bag. "You looking for a gun cleaning service?"

"Something like that. I'd rather have someone else do it than have to mess with it myself." He laughed as he ribbed the man to his right and poked the gun at David again. Several more people joined the group. Evidently they were waiting for something to happen.

David put the shirt he was holding down, straightened up, and took the proffered weapon. He expertly pulled back the bolt and looked inside, then turned the piece around and looked down the barrel. "Yep, she needs cleaning all right." David handed the gun back to the man.

"Damnit, moron. I want you to clean it."

David paused then reached out and took the gun a second time. With a good grip on the stock, he walked to the center aisle and whopped the end of the barrel hard against the cast iron stove making it slide a few inches on the concrete floor. He then tossed it back to an astonished soldier. "If I was you I'd get that checked before I fired it." He reached down and picked up his shirt from the bunk.

The man handed the gun to one of his friends and took a step closer to David. As quick as David had ever seen, the man landed an overhand right against David's jaw. He now had David's full attention. David looked at the man through squinted eyes and put down the shirt.

The man sniggered and took a boxer's stance on the balls of his feet. With his knees slightly bent and both fists clinched he was ready; he fully expected David to take a swing. When David didn't, the man came back with another overhand right. This time David was ready and reached up, just as fast, catching the man's fist inches in front of his face. He twisted the fist, locking the man's bent elbow. The man winced in pain. David then ducked his head and stepped under the man's caught arm giving it a slight jerk. The man's body flipped in a somersault, landing horizontal at David's feet. Changing grips to his right hand, David continued to hold the man's arm. David took his boot and put it on the man's face, pulling it back, and letting the ridges of his sole turn the man's face down onto the floor.

David asked, "And what might your name be?"

The man managed to get out a word or two but with his lips smashed up against his nose and both his nose and lips against the floor David couldn't make out anything he said. David looked at the man's two buddies. One had an indignant look and refused to answer, the other said it was Gino. David motioned for the first of the two to come forward. A little reluctantly he took a couple of steps toward David and, after the second step, was greeted by the back of David's open left hand across the face. He went flying and landed in the aisle. The second man shifted his weight from foot to foot while wringing his hands like they needed warming.

David relaxed his hold on Gino, reached down, and grabbing him by the waistband of his trousers and the unbuttoned collar of his shirt, hefted him up to the bunk above the one David had chosen for himself.

"Gino, if you get off that bunk tonight someone will be taking you to the infirmary."

Gino nodded and the party broke up with the second of Gino's friends helping the first to his feet. He suffered a bloody nose and a serious loss of respect. The young man shining shoes tossed every pair into the center hallway and put his polish and cloths up. Everyone else went back to doing what they had been doing. In a few minutes David had everything put away and his bed ready. He opened a tied bundle of letters. He had been gone for over three months and some of his early letters, written before he had been able to get out his North African address, accumulated at the 180th Infantry Regiment mail-call awaiting his arrival. Taps sounded and the men made ready for bed.

Gino leaned over the side of his bunk. "I'd like to go to the latrine."

During the next week, David got adjusted to his new billet and Gino apologized for his ungentlemanly behavior. David asked, "How's your weapon shooting?"

Gino shrugged his shoulders and said, "I haven't fired it yet. If I have it checked, and it needs to be replaced, they'll take it out of my pay."

"Well, you'd better think of something fast. We go to the range tomorrow."

The next day at the range, while everyone was firing, Gino was fumbling with his rifle. The gunnery sergeant walked by and asked, "What's the matter, Private?"

Gino squirmed and said, "Can't get this thing to fire, Sergeant."

"What the hell! Give me that piece."

Everyone close moved a few steps distant. The sergeant grabbed the weapon, opened the bolt, and slid it back and forth looking for restriction. He inserted a clip, slammed the bolt shut and, without aiming at anything in particular, fired down range. The sergeant handed the weapon back to a relieved Gino.

"Sorry, Sergeant. I must've had a dud round."

The rest of the morning Gino tried to figure out how to shoot with a mangled front sight. It was an insignificant problem when compared to a bent barrel. "If I can't figure out how to hit something with this thing I might as well learn some new off-color language. Yelling at the enemy will be just as effective as shooting."

During the second half of February a rumor started making it around that Colonel Wilson had made a wager with Colonel Fulbright over the fighting capability of the men under their commands. A mini-maneuver was being talked about and both colonels were working out the rules of the engagement.

On the first day of March David found himself hiking in the middle of the New England woods with thirty-four other men and a strutting little sergeant who had recently transferred in. That afternoon they were transported to a wooded area and told to make camp.

The next morning they were issued blue arm bands and assigned to take and hold a small hill in the enemy sector. Besides having a weapon, David was assigned a length of rope. Each soldier had some form of survival equipment as well as his weapon with the sergeant having a compass and a topographical map. The red forces, under Colonel Wilson, were separated from the blue forces, under Colonel Fulbright, by a free-flowing mountain stream.

The new sergeant had them lost in the woods and, for most of the morning, they wandered in circles. The sergeant was sitting on a tree stump peering over his map trying to sight his compass when a blue-force jeep rolled up containing an umpire and a second lieutenant with a field phone.

"You the second platoon of Fox Company?"

"Yes, sir." answered the sergeant.

"Good. The colonel wants to talk with Corporal Calhoun."

David could tell the sergeant was miffed but, as David walked to the jeep, the little guy went back to solving his most pressing problem and asked the umpire if he would show him where on the map his second platoon might be.

Into the field phone the second lieutenant said, "This is Corporal Calhoun, sir." And promptly handed David the phone.

"Good morning, Calhoun, we seem to have a slight problem. It appears most of the blue forces have been captured. The only ones left are lost. I think that might be your predicament. Is that right, Calhoun?"

"Yes, sir."

"Calhoun, I want you to make up a squad from your platoon and see if you can salvage the operation. You've got to go straight for the red headquarters. Leave the remaining men with the sergeant to take and hold his hill. If he can find the hill. Has he found the stream yet?"

"Yes, sir. We've encountered the stream several times."

"Calhoun, put the sergeant on the phone."

"Yes, sir."

The sergeant was on the phone with the colonel for several minutes and then walked over to David, holding out the map and compass. "I'm supposed to let you look at this and let you have whoever you want from the platoon—up to half. The colonel said he's given you a secret assignment and you're to leave as soon as you're ready."

It was apparent the sergeant was fuming. But David had to obey orders and what the sergeant thought was of little concern. Among the men David chose was Gino, Boyd, and Little Billy Jenks—the shoeshine boy. David and Gino walked away from the others with the map and compass. They looked over the map trying to determine where they were, where the red force headquarters might be, and where would be a good spot to cross the stream. After they had made their decisions they headed out, leaving a choleric sergeant muttering to himself. Several other men were left wondering why they hadn't been asked to go as well.

David told Little Billy to walk point with the next six walking two abreast fifty yards apart and the remaining two at the rear on the right and left flanks.

Before taking his assigned placement Gino asked, "Bro, what plan have you come up with?"

"Most of the other blue forces have already been captured so before long the woods on our side of the stream will contain a large number of red forces trying to find and capture the remaining lost blue platoons. I imagine the red forces studied the map closely and picked out the few wide, shallow areas of the stream. All they had to do was hide in the bushes and wait on the blue forces to come across. Once the blue forces stepped out of the water onto the bank and regrouped, the red forces would come out from their cover and have the blue forces surrounded. Now, it's a game of cat and mouse with the reds being a herd of hungry cats."

"Then we need to get across that stream as soon as possible, before this area becomes saturated with enemy." Gino slapped David on the back. "We're with you all the way. Just tell us what to do."

Less than an hour later, Little Billy held up his hand signaling he'd spotted the reference point David had told him look for. From there they made a ninety-degree turn and soon came to the stream. Here it was deep and narrow and straight. The men wondered how they would get across without drowning. David found a tall lodge pole pine close to the bank and had the two men with hatchets hew it down. He had to show them how to make their cuts so that when the tree fell it would topple in the direction where it would bridge the stream. In an hour the tall tree came crashing to the ground, spanning the chasm. The first man across took out the branches sticking straight up blocking his way. They were just ten feet or so above the water; still, two of the men had to be helped across. Both professed an inability to swim.

Once across David told his men, "We need to sneak up on one of the red teams just as they capture one of our blue teams wading across a shallow area. That way they'll all be pretty much grouped together and a lot easier for a smaller force to encircle."

Little Billy led them in a hundred yards from the stream and then back up-river to a place where, according to the map, there was a big looping bend. David said the bends were where the stream would be the widest and slowest. The water generated more force on the outside edges of a bend, eating away the bank, and shooting everything it dislodged to the inside of the curve. Rocks moved to the other bank slower than sand, causing the water to be shallower with a wide expanse of accumulated rocks gradually decreasing in size and ending as a sand bar. David's men were mightily impressed and began to think they had a chance of succeeding if David had a few more tricks up his sleeve.

Sure enough, when they got close to the bend they heard voices. Creeping up in a circular line surrounding the voices, the men kept deathly quiet. The red forces had just captured the remainder of their old platoon and their new sergeant. Overhearing the enemies' conversation, David and his men learned the red team thought they now had all the blue forces captured and would march them back to their prisoner detainee camp and get some lunch.

David motioned to his men to remain concealed and let them pass. With their hands on their heads the sergeant and his depleted platoon were marched single file down a pathway between David's men hidden in tall grass. The capturing red forces swaggered when they walked and chatted among themselves about how easy it had been. David and his squad followed at a safe distance.

An hour later they reached a fenced area containing the captured blue forces. The weapons confiscated from the blue prisoners were stacked in a pile a few yards away. The fenced area had only one gate manned by two guards: one standing at attention and the other sitting at a table. Each of the remaining three sides of the fenced perimeter was patrolled by two sentries. They walked from one end of their section of fence to the other end. At the half-way mark they crossed each other. At each end they did an about-face and retraced their steps. David watched as his platoon was deposited, their weapons added to the pile, and their numbers and unit designation entered on a tablet by the man at the table. The capturing red team then left, with everyone but one heading down a worn wide path. The remaining soldier went by himself down a different path.

David grouped his men together and asked if anyone had anything red they could use as a counterfeit arm band. One man said he had a white handkerchief. Another man offered to cut his finger. David nixed that idea and said they'd wing it. Gino stuffed a knife in his shirt and put his hands above his head. Little Billy walked behind him with his weapon held at the ready. They timed it so the sentries on both adjoining sides were a few steps shy of the half-way mark walking away, before they walked up to confront the guard sitting at the table and the guard manning the front gate.

Little Billy said, "Here's one more. There any chow left?"

One guard reached down to open the gate and when he swung it open Gino had his knife pulled out. With his other hand he gripped the guard's arm and said, "You're dead."

The man writing on the tally sheets looked up. Little Billy had his rifle pointed at the man's forehead. Both were disarmed, relieved of their arm bands, and shoved inside to eight hundred happy blue prisoners.

Gino made a motion with his hands—palms down—meaning to stay calm as he and Billy donned the red arm bands and took the guards' positions. The sentries approached, turned, and started walking back. In a few moments Gino opened the gate and let David and the remaining platoon inside. Two went to the back, two to the left, and two to the right. The blue prisoners were amazed at their proficiency and helped their rescuers stay concealed. The prisoners carried on like nothing was happening.

Each pair of David's men grouped where their two sentries would cross and when they did cross, David's men stuck their weapons through the fence simultaneously and said something like, "Soldier, you are my prisoner. Don't move."

With the prisoners loosed and the guards and sentries imprisoned, David took the confiscated red arm bands and told two loosed prisoners now armed, to guard the guards. To the highest ranking prisoners David suggested they go capture the red forces eating chow down the wide path. With his men he headed down the narrow path hoping it didn't go to the latrine.

Ten minutes later they came upon an opening and a big tent with six guards standing at attention. David decided to march right up, in a tight formation, wearing the red arm bands, and capture the guards. There would be more inside. The plan worked as choreographed and the six perplexed guards were moved under a tree and relieved of their weapons. David and his men replaced their red arm bands with blue ones and, leaving two men to guard their prisoners, David surrounded the tent with his remaining soldiers. When David raised his hand his men started pulling up every other tent peg. Pretty soon the tent was coming down and the occupants were looking for a way out. When they emerged they were surrounded by armed blue forces with David standing directly in front of their tent-opening brandishing his weapon.

Calmly David said, "Gentlemen, the game is finished, you are my prisoners."

Colonel Wilson was flabbergasted. He cried foul but the umpire, who was within the tent, said, "I think, Colonel Wilson, we've learned some valuable lessons here. I declare this game over."

On the ride back to camp, David Blaine was hailed as a hero, or labeled a miscreant, depending on which bus a listener was riding. That weekend David and his men were issued three-day passes to be added to their weekend by an enthusiastic Colonel Fulbright.

A weekend and a three-day pass was not enough time for David to make the round trip home so he and Gino decided to check out New York City. Gino called his family in Syracuse and they were so glad to hear from him they decided to meet him in New York City. Gino said he and his parents went to the Big Apple every so often. He said he would show David the sights.

They caught a bus after the Saturday morning muster and were in the city by dark. On the bus ride David asked where they should stay and Gino said he had relatives there. He and David could save their money and stay with them. David was all for that.

That night at dinner David was introduced to Gino's family and to Gino's uncle and his family. It was just one Donatello after another.

To David, Gino said, "We're all Sicilians. My parents and uncle emigrated to America when they were in their twenties. Now they both have restaurants, big families, and are as happy as bears in a honey tree."

David said, "I once read that the happiest time in any man's life is when he is in red-hot pursuit of the dollar, with a reasonable prospect of overtaking it."

"That's funny. I think it appropriately applies to both families. New York City and Syracuse have large Sicilian populations and we've easily continued our traditional customs, retained our ethnicity, and made plenty of money. And the food, David, you have never eaten so well as what you have now to look forward to."

It did look like everyone was well-fed. Gino's mother piled huge portions of food on David's plate. He was also given a goblet of red wine poured from a fat bottle wrapped in straw. David paid attention to how the others ate and tried to duplicate their efforts. He opened his napkin and stuffed a corner under his shirt collar. He lifted his wine and drank to all the toasts. He ate prodigious quantities of bread covered with cheese and diced garlic. He found hairy little fish in his salad. They tasted salty—but not bad if you followed with a big swig of wine. He also found little green peas that had sifted down to the bottom and were now soaking in a vinegar based liquid. When he ate one he realized they were most certainly not green peas but what someone called a caper. He had a difficult time with the pasta until Gino's sister, Gabriela, showed him how to use a spoon to hold the noodles while twining them around a fork. For dessert they had a sweet and wet cake. It was drenched all the way through with a milky sweet icing.

Mr. Donatello asked David, "What kind of work does your father do?"

"He's a production engineer. He figures out easy ways to accomplish difficult tasks."

"Is he promoting the new assembly-line methods pioneered by the meat-packing industry and perfected by Henry Ford?"

"I don't know, there's not much manufacturing in Northern Arkansas."

Gino got everyone's attention when he told them how David had led eight men to free hundreds of prisoners in a concentration camp and ended the maneuvers by capturing the opposing colonel right under the nose of the head official. Heads leaned forward, forks were put down, and private conversations ceased. Gino was asked to tell the complete story and not to leave anything out.

Gino's ability to keep everyone in suspense while he explained how David planned the strategy amazed even David. They laughed at the strutting little sergeant, were proud of David when the colonel called, were impressed at how David figured out the strategy used by the red forces to easily capture most of the blue forces, and how he knew so much about streams and sand bars. They howled with delight when David had his men go around pulling up tent pegs. Gino finished with the bus ride back and the little sergeant having to hand them three-day passes. Everyone thought David was too clever by far.

Mr. Donatello raised his glass and toasted David. Gabriela leaned toward David and whispered, "Gino thinks you walk on water."

David whispered back, "I am but a mere cock. Yet this morning I crowed and the dawn broke."

The remainder of their time in New York City was one big party. Gabriela, Gino, and David saw the Empire State Building, the Statue of Liberty, and Central Park. They ate at fine restaurants and street vendors, they shopped Fifth Avenue, and they heard stories of men jumping from buildings on Wall Street during the stock market crash. At night they saw a vaudeville act, a Broadway play, and the Rockettes kick their legs high in the air at Radio City Music Hall. It was a magical time and Gino's dad provided all the tickets. He also gave Gino ample cash to pay for the meals, taxi fare, and whatever incidentals they wanted.

When David complained that he should be paying his share. Gino said his family would take it as an insult if they were not allowed to show their gratitude this way. David shrugged his shoulders and enjoyed being treated to a very special time.

When it was the hour for Gino's family to say goodbye Gino's dad took David's arm. With tears in his eyes, he said, "David, you look after my Gino."

David felt the warmth and solemnly said, "I will. You have my word on it."

David felt like he had a second family, Gino's family felt like they had a second son, and Gabriela felt like she had a boyfriend who didn't know it yet.

Handsome Harry joined the Army right out of high school. He had always been a scrawny kid and was constantly overcompensating for any shortcomings he thought he might have or others might accuse him of having. He was short so, naturally, he played basketball in high school. Not able to jump with the taller boys, he learned to dribble. His quick feet more than made up for his lack of height. Added to his talent of working-the-floor came good shooting ability from long distances.

At football though, the bigger boys ran over him. His best position was defensive end and the best he could do was second string. So he quit football and joined the wrestling team where he was in his element. Always a scrapper and not averse to underhanded tactics—if it meant winning his match—Harry Fallon made the all-state wrestling team at the 115-pound weight class.

He was given the nickname of "Handsome" by the jocks because he had difficulty getting dates. True he was short, and a little underweight, but the real reason for his lack of social charisma was his attitude. He didn't take lip from anyone.

In the Army, Handsome Harry Fallon made sergeant and made life tough on anyone who commented on him being short, or scrawny, or having an attitude. It didn't matter that these accusations were all true. What did matter was that Handsome Harry didn't take lip. He also didn't like being shown up and Corporal Calhoun had shown him up. He didn't understand why the colonel wanted Calhoun for a secret mission. He could have done it just as well—even better. It made him look bad and he didn't like looking bad. Then he had to hand over the three-day passes. Well, that just infuriated the hell out of him. At his first opportunity Handsome Harry made everyone pay. For the last three days he'd punished what was left of his platoon. They went for fifteen-mile hikes in the mornings. In the afternoons he had them marching on the tarmac the first day, running the obstacle course the second day, and climbing 40 foot mockups using cargo nets the third day. Today was the fourth day and those damn three-day passes were up. He had something special planned for the returning goldbricks.

"Gentlemen, what we're going to work on today is physical combat. Say you've been captured and your weapon has been taken. You're being escorted back to enemy headquarters for interrogation. Everybody get around the mat. I need a volunteer. Private Jenks, front and center."

Harry picked up a rifle and inspected it to make sure it wasn't loaded. He took out the clip. He checked and reinserted it, then pulled back the bolt to make sure there wasn't a round in the chamber. He didn't want anybody accidentally, or intentionally, getting shot. He handed the weapon to Little Billy.

"Private, act like you're escorting me somewhere." Handsome Harry put his hands on his head and stood with his back to Little Billy. The sergeant's fingers intertwined, then one hand griped the other wrist, then he changed to just having his hands lay flat on his head. The sergeant suddenly turned clockwise, grabbed Billy's weapon, wrenched it from his grip, and smashed Little Billy in the side of the face with it. Little Billy stumbled and fell to the mat.

"What happened here was that Private Jenks was watching my hands. I positioned us so I could see his shadow. From the shadow I could see how he was holding his weapon: with which hand, over which shoulder, and in what direction. With that distraction and those bits of information, I had all I needed to turn the tables and be in control of the situation."

Billy got up and rubbed his ear. He scrambled off the mat with a searing pain emanating outward from his temple in all directions. As soon as he could, he'd show up at sick bay and get something for a headache. He'd also strap on an icepack.

"Now let's work with a knife. Private Donatello! We got a Private Donatello here?" Gino slinked to the center of the mat. The sergeant handed him a bayonet and informed the worried audience that a soldier can overcome any disparity in weaponry. He handily disarmed Gino, kicked him in the shins, and body slammed him to the mat for good measure. Gino scrambled off the mat to where David was standing and said, "It's your turn, amigo."

"Okay, enough with the props. What happens when you come face to face with the enemy and neither of you have a weapon? If you fight, it might be to the death so how do you deal with that? I think for this exercise we need someone big. Someone strong. Someone like . . . like Corporal Calhoun."

A rumbling started among the men as they belatedly figured out what was going on. David dutifully walked onto the mat. He noticed the sergeant had removed his boots and socks. Not a good sign.

"Now for this exercise . . . Corporal Calhoun, would you stand over here?" As David walked to the new position, the sergeant let fly a lethal foot that caught David in his solar plexus, knocking out his wind. David sank to his knees. A hush descended over the watching men.

"Gentlemen, always be prepared. You can't expect the enemy to play by the Marquis of Queensberry's rules."

Can't let the bastard show me up like that. He's not going to get the best of me. In the long run this will do him good. He's got to learn. Got to pay his dues. Walk around. Pick my spot.

"Now when you have a man hurting, you can't let up. This is the time when he needs to be put out of his misery, before he can recoup and inflict damage on you."

On his knees and clutching his stomach, David gasped for air. The sergeant smashed a stiff palm into the side of David's face. He fell sideways from his knees to the mat, blood trickled from his ear. Laying face down on the mat, David cringed in pain. The sergeant walked behind the crumpled body, bent down, and punched David in his lower back with a doubled up fist. David's left kidney started pulsating. He shuddered then groaned through clinched teeth. Pain surged throughout his body. The sergeant stood up and, nonchalantly put one foot on David's back striking a pose you might see a hunter do after he'd killed a defenseless animal and wanted someone to congratulate him. David rolled over and grabbed at the sergeant's leg but missed.

"See what I mean? Once you have your opponent down you have to finish him off. It's no time to be lenient. It's a game all right and the stakes are as high as they come."

The sergeant let David stagger to his feet. A low murmur started building. The sergeant walked around his teetering opponent with David having a hard time standing on the cushiony surface. His adversary circling around was making David even more unsteady. The sergeant shot out with his leg and, with his body in an exaggerated "Y," landed a solid foot to David's sternum. David convulsed and fell to the mat with a thud that sounded like a wet towel being hurled against a wall.

He needs to stay down. I don't want to hit him in the face. Not like last time. No telltale marks. Can't do any permanent damage. Just stay down, dammit.

David struggled to his feet.

"Well, Corporal Calhoun thinks this is fun. We're through, Calhoun. What are you mumbling? I can't hear you, soldier."

"I said, we're not done yet." David swung his fist, but was holding his side and was woefully slow. The sergeant deftly stepped back and the fist sailed by several inches in front of his face.

"Now, we've taken his wind with the first kick to the stomach, he's dizzy from the palm to the temple, a punch to a kidney is always good, and a hard kick to his sternum just over the heart. Well, gentlemen, what's left? That's right. You guessed it. The groin."

The sergeant let out his most potent kick yet—straight to the groin. However, when David heard the word he shifted his weight and was in the process of turning. So when the kick landed it hit him in the pelvic area and spun David around like a top.

David staggered, drool oozed from the corner of his mouth. He was standing directly in front of Handsome Harry, his arms hanging limp at his sides. David jerked his head. He looked over the left shoulder of the sergeant, his eyes grew wide, his jaw dropped, he whimpered, "Nooo."

"What?" The sergeant looked over his left shoulder. He looked back just in time to see David's left fist come crashing into his jaw. He didn't see anything else.

Gino ran to help David sit up. David had stepped forward to throw the punch and, after it landed, he sank to his knees and then toppled over on his side. Boyd checked to see if the sergeant was still alive. David said to roll him over face down so he wouldn't drown in his spit. One of the men attending the sergeant said he wouldn't be drowning from his spit but he might from all the blood. They sent for a medic with a stretcher.

Gino propped David up and, with his arm around David's shoulder asked, "Dave, my boy, what did you see just before you knocked the snot out of him?"

David was trying to get his breathing under control and let the pain subside. He held his head in his hands. "Nothing, I just needed that extra second."

At sick bay they used smelling salts to arouse Handsome Harry, who didn't look so handsome laying on the table. His face was becoming puffy on his right side. Three teeth had been knocked out—one embedded in his cheek. The tip of his tongue had been bitten off and his jaw was broken in two places.

"Good lord. Someone get me a ambulance. This man's got to go to a hospital." Using a small flashlight the medic probed inside Handsome Harry's mouth then, with slender tongs he removed the embedded tooth, and said, "They'll have to do surgery. The jaw will be wired shut for months. Hell, it might be bad enough to get the poor boy completely out of the Army."

Gino and David tried to figure what repercussions might come of the episode but they both decided the sergeant was due and probably nothing would happen. It was just the hazards of the job.

The next morning they found differently. At the morning muster two MPs carted David to the brig. That afternoon he was summarily court-marshaled, knocked back in rank to buck private, and sentenced to a month in solitary confinement. The first week he would be fed only bread and water.

The presiding official looked at David over the top of his table and said, "A 230-pound man, who is well over 6 feet tall, and physically fit like you should know better than to hit someone eighty pounds lighter and a foot shorter. It just isn't right. It doesn't matter that it was an exercise to learn physical combat. A corporal should know better than to maul a sergeant and one that much smaller just makes the offense that much more offensive."

Gino came to see David and walked beside him as the MPs escorted him to solitary confinement.

David said, "Do you think you could get me some books on martial arts? I would not have believed such a little guy could have manhandled me that way."

"Sorry, bub. There's only four books that fit that description on the entire base and every one's been checked out by someone in our platoon. And the waiting list is long. I'm on it myself."

"What happened to Sergeant Fallon?"

"They've taken him off-base somewhere. I heard someone say his locker's been cleaned out. They think he's going back to civilian life. A friend of his said he'd been thinking about leaving the Army and working for the police department in some small town out west."

"Gino, would you consider Arkansas out west? I mean, I sure wouldn't want to get a traffic ticket from Sergeant Fallon and him carrying a gun."

The first few days were tough on David. Solitary confinement is pretty bad in itself but eating only bread and water soon wore thin. However, rumors started flying and on the third night a cook brought a sack of food which was slipped under David's door. The sack contained two sandwiches, an apple, a piece of cherry pie wrapped in wax paper, and a small thermos of steaming coffee. David thought he might give the cook a hug when he got out. But then again that might look a little strange.

The next night someone slipped in another sack of food and a bundle of letters the guy from the mail room had smuggled over. David spent the night and most of the next day reading and re-reading his mail.

He received a letter from his dad saying he went to talk to Stanley Muldaur's sister. She said Stanley sent a Christmas card last year with his address on the envelope. She's looking for it.

His dad talked about his small herd of cattle and how they were easier to take care of than horses but he had purchased a new buckskin gelding so he could herd them properly. He said they'll follow you anywhere if you have a bucket of feed but that's not the cowboy way of doing things. He closed by saying how proud he was of David and for David to keep up the good work.

He received letters from his sisters. They talked about school and about each other. April told him about Amanda's new boyfriend sneaking up Lee Mountain in his dad's car to take Amanda for a joyride but got them stuck going down. In his effort to get unstuck he almost lost the car over the side. Amanda walked home and told their dad who went looking for the young man. David's dad got there just after the boy's own father had shown up and was giving the young man a thrashing. It took the three of them over an hour with a car and a truck trying to pull the stolen automobile onto the road.

Charlotte said Jesse had published a short story of hers in the paper. She now wanted to be a newspaper reporter and work for *The Kansas City Star*. She said April wasn't very good about doing her chores; she would take a book and go hide somewhere. Amanda said in her letter she was going to marry Skip. He was such a gentleman, always doing nice things for her. He told her that after he graduated from high school he was going to learn to be an automobile mechanic. He had a friend who worked in one of the car assembly plants in Detroit but now was building tanks for the war and making tons of money.

David also got a letter from his mother. She was already harvesting from an early garden. She said she and his dad had planted an entire acre in cucumbers. They had such pretty flowers. There were honeybees everywhere. This spring there was plenty of rain and now the wildflowers were painting Lee Mountain in reds, yellows, and oranges, with a sprinkling here and there of blue and purple. This was going to be a good year for the farmer.

She said some old momma dog straggled up and crawled under their front porch. No one could coax her out so his dad had started taking food from the dinner table and sliding it under the edge of the porch. He talked to the dog in that slow drawl of his but she growled when he tried to get close. He said he thought she was pregnant and started giving her a bowl of milk every night.

In a letter from his Grandpa and Grandma Calhoun David learned Rupert's trying to work up enough courage to propose to Nadine. Nadine had already suggested Rupert turn a shed she had in the back of her house into a cabinetry shop. Nadine said she'd give him enough money to buy the tools and the wood he'd need to get started. Claude was so upset he went to join the Army. Of course, he was too old so he'd gone to Fort Smith to work in an ammunition factory. Rupert was planning on going after him. He said he wouldn't even consider opening a cabinetry shop without Claude. Everyone thought Claude was upset because he didn't have any money to contribute.

Jesse sent a letter and a *Marsden County Meteor* newspaper with an ad circled. It was a picture of David purchasing the hand-painted locket under the store name.

In his letter Jesse said, "Mr. Creighton claims his business picked up after he started running the ad but now he wants more pictures or something in one of David's letters referring to his store. He said he'll pay for anything I can put in print." David thought about saying how helpful Mr. Creighton had been; how he had known the particulars of lockets in general and how he knew the artistry involved in this particular locket's creation. Maybe a couple of sentences like that would supply Mr. Creighton with what he wanted. It would be easy money and entirely true, probably get him a discount on a wedding ring to boot.

Jesse continued with, "Also, Rose wears the locket on the inside of her clothes because it showed up so distinctly in the picture that anyone who sees it would instantly recognize it.

"The entire town's trying to determine who you bought it for. More than one woman says she has it. I think they're going to sell raffle tickets at the fair this year. For a dollar, a person will get to put his name and the name of the girl he thinks was the lucky recipient on an entry. David, when you come home the town will want to know who you gave it to. They're going to give the person with the winning entry some sort of prize, with the dollars raised donated to the war effort.

"Man, do you know the women call you 'Baby Cakes?' You've got to tell me how the nickname came about. When I asked, all I could get was a few giggles in reply."

David also got a letter from Gabriela. This was not entirely unexpected. David could tell early on she was attracted to him. He told her he already had a girlfriend but when she asked if he was married he had to answer no. She retorted she'd just have to change his mind. The entire time in New York City Gabriela spent trying to get close to David and David spent the entire time trying to keep Gino between the two of them. Gino thought it was funny and commented on the obstinacy of Sicilian women. In her letter she included a stunning picture of herself in a bathing suit at Coney Island. She asked for one of David. She rambled on about trivial matters and then asked about Arkansas. She'd been to the library and got picture books showing the beautiful scenery—including the Buffalo River. He folded her letter and wondered how he got himself into these scrapes.

David saved the letter from Rose to read last. She talked about her job at the paper and how she was now writing pieces Jesse was printing on the front page. She said he only wanted to write the editorial page and answer the letters to the editor. They had started purchasing two separate syndicated columns and one political cartoon for each edition.

"Jesse says it gives the paper a more cosmopolitan look. Our subscription base has increased so much we've gone to publishing twice a week—on Wednesday and again on Saturday.

"Things are booming in Dancing Deer. Dad has opened a new farmer's market and rents stalls to the local producers so they can display their fresh fruits and vegetables. A pickle company, out of Atkins, came by looking for cucumbers last year and this year every farmer has planted entire fields. No one from the pickle company has shown up yet, so it looks like there's going to be a lot of home-canned pickles."

She went on to say how much she loved David and didn't know how she would manage until he returned. She also told him about the locket and how much trouble she was having not wearing it where everyone could see and marvel on her good fortune. A lump raised in David's throat as he thought about Rose. He felt warm just remembering how she looked at him.

That night David asked the guard through his door, "Might I be allowed some paper and a pencil?"

"Soldier, you're in solitary confinement. You're not supposed to have anything, and this first week just bread and water. Deal with it." An hour later someone slipped a sack of food, a tablet, and a pencil under his door.

After the first week of confinement, David was allowed into an exercise area for a couple of hours in the morning and again in the afternoon. No one else was in the brig so he didn't have anyone to talk to or to play games with. He shot hoops, lifted weights, and jogged around the perimeter. Every other day he was allowed a shower. There was a toilet and a sink in his cell. Both were bolted to the floor. One day after he returned from the exercise area he found someone had left a comfortable chair.

Gino came by regularly and the guard let him talk to David through the door. On one occasion Gino mentioned they were moving out to Arnold Valley to do some mountain training exercises. He'd heard they might be scaling cliff faces. David didn't hear from Gino during the last two weeks of his incarceration.

During the final week David received his last letter from Rose.

Dearest David:

This letter is hard for me to write. Bear with me as I try to explain. My dad and I had a big argument and I left to go live with my mother in Boston. I thought about getting a job but was finally convinced I should go to college. College isn't like High School. The teachers don't care if you show up for class or not. However, if you don't go to class there is no way you can pass the course. The teachers also don't care if you pass or not. They are there to give you the information but, unlike high school, they won't try and beat it in.

In my English class we had to write a short essay about someone emotionally important to us. I wrote about you. Each person had to read their essay in class and we discussed how well the person wrote the essay and if she properly communicated the emotion she had for the person chosen.

After listening to the other papers, I think maybe we dove into our relationship too soon. Actually, our differences are greater and more important than what we have in common. I probably will continue to live in Boston after I graduate and expect to have a career. Would you be happy living in a city where you have to walk to a park if you want to sit on a patch of grass? Where you can't have a dog because your landlord prohibits pets? The differences don't stop there. I want to live in a big house with servants and wear expensive clothes. Will you have a job that makes enough money to provide me with those things? I've met a man who can and have been seeing him for the past couple of weeks.

David, I know we had plans, but I don't think it would have worked out. My life is different here and I like it.

Please don't write. I want to get over the heartache of a breakup as soon as possible. If you want

to see me, and I'm not married, you can come to Boston after the war.
Stay safe,
Rose

When David was released there was no one there to greet him. He walked to his barracks. His bed, locker, and all of his possessions were just like he had left them but there was no sign of his buddies. The next morning he found they were still in Arnold Valley and wouldn't be getting back until the end of the week. David moped around. He had suffered through setbacks in the past. Coming to grips with losing Rose would take time but he would somehow get through it. She was probably better off with a college graduate. He would never be able to provide for her in the manner she wanted.

David spent most of those next few days at the camp library or at the rifle range. A gunnery sergeant took special interest in David and showed him how a mortar and a rocket launcher—called a bazooka—worked. David lost his appetite. When he did eat he'd had to make excuses.

Everyone finally made it back from Arnold Valley. Gino was glad to see David but couldn't understand why he had such a downtrodden look. David told Gino about the letter. Gino said it sounded like the standard "Dear John letter" men in every army had dreaded receiving since Alexander the Great invaded Persia. Gino asked if he could tell Gabriela.

Two days later they went to Norfolk, Virginia, where they boarded a ship and sailed to Chesapeake Bay. There they practiced amphibious operations. For ten days they drilled and everything went smoothly except for the work of the coxswains of the LCVs—Landing Craft Vehicles. The coxswains had a difficult time determining where to deliver their passengers and then getting them close enough to shore to safely jump overboard. On more than one occasion the men jumped into water over their heads with full back-packs strapped on. Several men came close to drowning.

The middle of May they returned to Camp Pickett where they received a "Warning Order" to be ready to ship out. On May 25th they moved to a staging area at Camp Patrick Henry and on June 4th shipped out on the USS *Neville* from Hampton Roads Port of Embarkation, Newport News, Virginia. This is the same place where the great battle between the *Merrimack* and the *Monitor* was staged during the Civil War.

The trip over was fairly uneventful. However, most of the men became deathly ill, including Gino. David had his sea legs and stayed topside for most of the trip. The smell in the hold was overpowering of vomit. The *Neville* tossed and bobbed a lot worse than the *Queen Elizabeth* even though the *Neville* was traveling over calmer seas, encountered no turbulent storms, and had warm weather. She was also slower. David spent his time topside enjoying a pleasant trip.

On June 21st they passed the Straits of Gibraltar into the Mediterranean. On June 22nd the *Neville* dropped anchor at Mers el Kebir—the same harbor where the British Royal Navy ordered the French Navy to sail to a neutral port or be blown up where they lay.

The French had the largest standing Army in Europe and was defeated in five weeks by a smaller but vastly more modern and mobilized German Army. France was forced to sign an armistice allowing the Germans to occupy the northern and eastern half of France. They also required the new French government to relocate and to assist the victorious Germans in their fight against the Allied Forces. The British wanted to be reasonably sure the French Navy, now headquartered in North Africa, would not eventually be pitted against them on the high seas so they gave the French their ultimatum. The French would not agree so the British Royal Navy destroyed a large part of the French fleet and killed 1,300 French seamen. The French never forgave the Brits.

For the next two weeks they practiced more ship-to-shore exercises—never actually getting it right. On July 4th David and his friends celebrated Independence Day aboard ship in Oran Harbor proper. On July 9th, late at night, they dropped anchor just off the southern coast of Sicily. Operation Husky was to commence early the next morning.

CHAPTER 14—LEAVING TOWN
Dancing Deer – March 1943

Rose wanted to look at David's picture. She wore the locket constantly. The only times it was not adorning her neck was when she had it off to look at David's handsome smiling face and his blue eyes. She went to Creighton's Jewelers right after she saw the advertisement in the paper and bought a matinee-length necklace so she could wear it inside her clothes close to her heart. Actually, it dangled between her breasts but that was all right as long as it didn't accidentally fall out while bending over.

The latest rumor going around town was that it must have been purchased for a girlfriend living in another town, although no one could come up with another town David frequented. What other explanation could there be? David could have gone out with any girl in the school and, even though there were no serious relationships, he had dated several.

Rose wanted to speak out. She wanted to say, "David Blaine Calhoun is mine. We are to be wed. Here . . . here's proof . . . I've got the locket." And, if that was not enough, she would say, "I'm carrying his child."

It happened on the rug in front of the fireplace. She relived those moments whenever she was alone, whenever it was raining, whenever she saw couples holding hands. David was hers and hers alone. She knew it from the depths of her soul. He would come back from this war and they would be married and he would love her and their baby and everything would be okay. But if, for whatever purpose the Lord saw fit, David did not return from this war. Rose shuddered at the thought. Of course he's going to return. But if he didn't return how would she take care of their baby? Would she tell everyone he was David's, tarnishing David's name with the town? What would David's parents say? What would her dad say? Should she go somewhere, have the baby, and come back when David came home? If he didn't come home, would she then come back and say they were wedded all along and let the town think whatever it wanted? How could she live if David didn't come home?

Rose's emotions about being pregnant were confused. She knew the townspeople would gossip and say petty things when they found out. It wasn't done. It wasn't right. A young Christian lady waited to be married to taste the intimacies that came with matrimony. Had she messed up? Had she ruined her chance at happiness? Would David want a child? It was a big responsibility. Of course, she'd be the one to take care of him—or her. She'd be the one to sing her to sleep, to nurse her through the baby illnesses, through the colic, through teething. She'd be the one to get up when she cried in the night, when her diaper needed changing, when she was afraid of the thunder or the monster living under the bed.

Would David feel like she had betrayed him? It was expensive to have a family, the extra food, the clothing, the doctoring, and a myriad other things. David didn't even know where he would work. She had been saving her money, keeping it in the top drawer of her dresser. Jesse paid her forty dollars a week. The only expenses she had were her daily meals. Her dad was still buying her clothing and giving her incidental money. If she told him, would he stand by her? Would he yell and scream and throw one of his celebrated temper fits? Would he make her go to another town and have an abortion? Could she let that happen to David's baby? Should she even tell David? Would that interfere with his ability to perform as a soldier? Would he then take fewer chances, be more conservative in his decisions, spend his time planning ahead instead of taking care of the job at hand? Or would he feel cheated? He'd always wanted to travel, to do big things. A baby ties you down, even when the mother takes care of all its needs. What if it was born blind or with some horrible defect? Would anyone be with her, stand by her, console her, hold her hand? David would.

She looked at his picture, rubbed a smudge from the curved glass where a tear had landed, and set it down on the table beside her father's chair. She sank down into its cushiony leather and just wanted to sleep. She'd wake up and, somehow, all her troubles would be resolved.

When she awoke her dad was standing in front of her holding the open locket. His face cold. His jaw set. His brow furrowed. Through clinched teeth he snapped, "Young lady, what have you done?"

"Don't be mad at me, Daddy. I was going to tell you—honest. David and I love each other. We're going to get married when he returns from the war."

"The hell you are. You're going to pack your things, quit that miserable little job, and get into college. I won't have you marrying any Calhoun riff-raff. You need to broaden your horizons. See the bigger picture. Plan for the future. There are lots of eligible young men for you to meet in one of those big universities back east."

"But, Daddy, this is my life. I love David. I'm not interested in anyone else."

"Now listen to me, young lady. I'm still your father. I know what's best. You'll see. I wouldn't have you do something not in your best interest. Right now, all I'm saying is you have your entire life ahead of you. This Calhoun kid's a dead-end. He doesn't have any prospects. He'll never amount to anything. He's just like his dad. You'll see."

With tears running down her cheeks, Rose had an important question answered. Her dad would not stand by her. If she told him about the child he would have her sequestered away until she had an abortion or had given birth and then he'd give the baby to some other woman who wanted to be a mother.

"I think I see all right. It's not what I expected. It's not what I wanted." Rose took the locket from her father's grasp. "I'm a grown woman and I think I'll be making the decisions for my life from now on. You'll be the one to see. David's a wonderful man and if you can't perceive that then you'll just have to live with it."

At these words the resentment, the grief, the hatred took over Bill Potter's body. Before he could stop himself he reached out and slapped Rose. He was instantly sorry. He didn't want to hurt Rose. He loved Rose. She was all he had. Sure he had material things—even a woman. But she didn't love him, she loved his money—his power. In the morning he'd talk with Rose in a more sensible manner. He'd apologize. He'd talk her into going away to college. He'd appeal to her fine sense of judgment.

Bill thought Rose needed to be prepared. Even if she and David were to be married she'd still need a college education. That kid would never be able to provide for her in the manner she was accustomed. She'd have to supplement his paltry income. Nowadays women were not just adornments, they were an integral part of the union. She'd need to be educated so she would have ideas, thoughts, and opinions worth listening to. She'd have to help manage her family, not just be along for the ride. And along the way, achieving the goals she and her father decided were best for her she'd meet another man, someone more suited. David was just a passing fascination. He's not the man for her. She would eventually come to that conclusion herself. Bill decided that what he needed to do was to get her in a situation where an alternative possibility was available. To some big university. To an ivy-league university. Nothing was too good for his daughter.

Rose ran from the room bawling. Remorse set in. He sank deep into his chair. What had he done?

In her room, Rose tried to compose herself. What was she to do now? She was five months pregnant and showing. She wouldn't be able to keep it from her father another month. If he didn't notice, someone else would. He'd find out from them. She had to leave. Where would she go? Her mother lived in Boston. She had over a thousand dollars in her dresser. That's plenty to get her there and it wasn't like she was needing any of her mother's money, just a place to stay while she figured things out. If her mother wasn't receptive to receiving a pregnant daughter then she'd be able to figure that out and she'd continue on to somewhere else. What was it David had said? "Just one day at a time." No. That wasn't it, he said, "Break your big problem down into its component parts and solve each of those little problems one at a time." She loved him.

Rose was quiet as she got her things together. She had to pack clothes she could work in. Leave all the keep-sakes, hats, her hundred pairs of shoes, all the frilly-girlie things that would just take up room in the suitcase. She'd only pack the essentials. She could purchase anything she missed as she went along. One purse, one big coat—the weather had turned cold again. Sometimes Northern Arkansas did that.

Late March and one last batch of cold weather to let everyone know who was in charge.

She went into the bathroom and gathered her make-up, her mirror, her toothbrush, and all the other things she had to have. When she had everything packed, she sat down on the corner of her bed and pondered how, in just a few short minutes, the course of an entire life could change. Was she making the right decision? Actually, her dad had made her decision for her.

She heard rustling in the living room. A few minutes later she heard the water pipes gurgling. He was in his bathroom getting ready for bed. Another hour and she'd sneak out. She heard a light switch, waited a few more minutes, then tip-toed into the living room to call Jesse. She told him to pick her up in an hour, to turn off his headlights, and park in the street a couple of houses away.

When the time came Rose left her dad a note in his chair. She quietly opened the front door and trudged to Jesse's car dragging her suitcase, make-up bag, and purse. It was one o'clock in the morning on March 28, 1943. She was embarking on a part of her life that would be filled with pain, suffering, and grief but she didn't know it as she held her hair and helped Jesse stow the luggage in the trunk of his car. The wind had picked up. She shivered. It was cold. Such an ominous start to the next chapter in her life.

Jesse wanted to know what had happened. She agreed to go to the all-night diner on the main highway and tell him all about it. First, though, they had to go to the bus station and see what buses were leaving, when, and to where. The lady at the counter said the first bus going east would be arriving at five a.m., departing at five-fifteen. Rose bought a ticket to St. Louis. There she would have several choices. She didn't have to make the trip all in one night. After all, she had not been feeling good lately: morning sickness, nausea, mood swings, depression. Rose was already suffering.

Rain pelted down as she and Jesse made their way to his car. At the diner they both ordered coffee and sat in a back booth. Rose cradled her cup with both hands. She told Jesse about the baby, about her father finding the locket, his fit, her fears, and her decision to take all her troubles to her mother in Boston.

"Have you talked to your mother lately?"

"Oh, yeah. She calls on my birthday and on holidays. She's sent me pictures. She says she still loves Daddy. She just couldn't be tied down in our little, one-horse town." They both laughed at the urban perception of rural America. "The last time we talked she asked if there was a decent restaurant here yet. They're pretty snobbish but I think I'll be all right. Dad will come around once he's had a chance to appraise his situation. He doesn't want to lose the only one he really cares about. He'll take up with the baby too. Just wait and see."

"What about David? When are you going to tell him? Don't you think he has a right to know?"

"Jesse, don't say anything about this to David. I'll tell him myself."

"Rose, it's not my place to tell David. I was just asking you if you're going to tell him. In his last letter to me he had just come back from a trip to New York City. In another month or two he'll be heading to England or Norway. Before this war's over he'll have been all over Europe, to Germany, to the Balkan states, maybe even to Russia. When he gets back he'll be ready to stay put for a while. You'll have to take care of yourself and your baby and be ready. Be there when he steps off the bus. You two were meant for each other."

Jesse reached into his pocket and pulled out a crisp hundred-dollar bill. "Here is some money to help cover your expenses."

"Thank you, Jesse. You're the most wonderful person. But I don't need the money. I've been saving most of my paychecks. I have quite enough money to get to Mother's."

"Take it just in case. Keep it for the baby. You'll need to write to me and give me your address so I can send you your last paycheck. And how do you want me to handle your letters from David?"

Rose thought about David, about their relationship, about what she had done, about what she was planning on doing. It was overwhelming. She started crying. At first it was a single tear wandering down her cheek in a haphazard way, then a torrent of tears collecting in rivulets seeking the shortest route to her chin. Jesse reached into his back pocket and pulled out a linen handkerchief. He handed it to Rose. A gentleman should always have a handkerchief. He must always be prepared to come to the aid of any woman in distress. Jesse was a gentleman in every sense of the word.

Sniffling, Rose suggested he let the letters accumulate in her mail slot and once a month, or whenever Jesse had a minute, he could package them together and send them to her.

"What do you think your dad will do?"

"I left a note saying I had decided to stay with Mom for a while. He'll be upset. After a few days he'll call and try to apologize. He'll make big plans for what I should be doing and try to persuade me to see everything from his point of view. However, if he throws a temper fit, he might head out in his car to find me—or worse yet, tell the police I've run away and have them issue a Missing Persons Bulletin. Maybe I should stop at the sheriff's office before I leave." Jesse thought that was a good idea. Cover all bases. Have a plan. Jesse paid the bill and left a generous tip. They headed to the sheriff's office.

Rose told Jesse to wait in the car while she went in. If he wasn't involved he wouldn't have to explain or answer questions from her dad. The only person in the office was the dispatcher. She told the man she was leaving to go live with her mother in Boston and her dad didn't want her to go. He might come in to get their help in locating her. But she was a woman of age who was capable of making her own decisions—of taking care of herself. She just wanted them to know she was leaving of her own accord and she was not running away, just moving to another parent's house.

The wind subsided but the rain and the cold decided to stay around for awhile. Jesse met her at the front door of the sheriff's office holding an umbrella. She had an hour before her bus left. They decided if she was early she might get a seat close to a heater vent. Maybe even a seat to herself. There was one other family waiting. When the bus arrived that other family met an arriving passenger and left after hugging and kissing and saying how well the arriving passenger looked. Rose was the only one waiting to board. Several other passengers got off long enough to stretch their legs and head to the bathroom.

The driver walked in and asked to see Rose's ticket. He then asked if she had any luggage she wanted him to stow. He carried it out, raised a clamshell door on the undercarriage, and shoved in her two bags. He then shut the door and headed for coffee. He said he'd be leaving in ten minutes.

Rose gave Jesse a hug and told him what a good friend he was. Jesse handed her a magazine he found in his car. She'd need something to read before she slipped into the deep sleep people find themselves in after climactic events.

The bus was about half full with most of the passengers congregated close to the front. Toward the back there were some vacant seats and she plopped down in one. Most of her fellow passengers were asleep. A few had gotten off and purchased coffee or sandwiches at the counter but the majority stayed onboard and continued to sleep. Each seat had a small reading light and she flicked hers on. She stared at Jesse's Look Magazine. On the cover it said, "The War in Pictures. See What Our Boys Are Doing." She put the magazine away and turned off the light. She looked out the window as the bus pulled away from the depot and away from her life as she knew it. She felt strange, upset, exhilarated, and more than a little tired. She retrieved a pillow from an overhead compartment, removed her shoes, raised her feet up under her, and pulled her jacket close around. It was a cocoon shielding her from the harmful things the world could throw. Rose slept.

The bus driver had started in Fort Smith. He was not yet halfway through his shift. He'd drive on through, eventually arriving in Springfield, where he'd be relieved by another driver. In Springfield, he'd sleep then head back to Fort Smith with a busload of passengers heading west. In Fort Smith, after a day off, he'd start it all over again.

Wide awake, plenty of coffee, a treacherous two-lane, twisting, mountainous road, and a boatload of people depending on him to get them to their destination. He had an important job. Tonight it was raining and cold. When the road veered close to the side of the mountain during the day, the passengers would be glued to the windows in awe of the beautiful, scenic vistas, while he fought with the wind. Tonight, if anyone was looking, they would be peering into a black void. However, the wind was still there. It was still trying to push and pull the big Scenic Cruiser off the mountain, to dash it to pieces on the rocks and pine trees below. He was constantly fighting to keep the big bus in its lane. He had it toasty warm, his passengers snoring peacefully. He took his job seriously. No drinking for him. They could count on him.

An hour out of Dancing Deer the rain turned to sleet. The bridges wore thin sheets of ice. The driver slowed to a speed he felt was safe. Damn the schedule. A late bus that made it was a lot better than one wrecked in a chasm or fallen into a river because she slid off an iced-over bridge. Got to keep the passengers safe.

An hour later, and twenty miles further down the road, the sleet stopped. It was now snowing. The bus slid all over the road and the driver made up his mind he was going to wait at his next stop until the highway department hauled sand out and made his hazardous journey safe again. He climbed a steep incline, his speed decreased even further as he lost traction, and the incline continued. He down-shifted, finally cleared the summit, and started descending the other side. A sigh of relief as he picked up speed. Tap the brakes, not too fast. The rear of the bus swerved, he compensated by turning into the slide, ran off the road, and plowed into a load of sand left by the highway department. The passengers were jostled. The bus was stopped. He tried to back up. The tires spun. He couldn't go forward over the embankment of sand. He slammed his hand against the steering wheel, stood up, and turned to the travelers in his bus.

"Sorry, folks. The bus slid on this icy highway into a pile of sand. We're not going anywhere until a wrecker comes to pull us out. If anyone needs their luggage, bring me your ticket and I'll get it for you. I'm sorry you're going to be late. It should be just a few hours. The sun is already up and help should be arriving shortly."

Rose slept through the entire ordeal. She didn't wake until being bumped by a passenger going to the bus driver with her ticket. Rose sat up, stretched, and looked out the window. They were stopped. They weren't even on the road. She looked at her watch. It was five minutes after eight. She looked around, people were talking, children were crying. What's going on? The passenger in the seat in front of her told her what happened.

Well, just relax, she thought. You don't have an itinerary. Go back to sleep. An hour later she awoke again and looked out the window. The bus driver had a shovel and was trying to manually extricate the goliath by himself. She might write a story about him someday—an American unsung hero.

Rose decided to put on her shoes and see if she could help. She emerged from the bus, shivered while taking in the marmoreal landscape, and walked to where the bus driver was bent over trying to shovel soft sand from behind the back tires. "Can I be of any assistance?"

"No, Missy. I only have the one shovel." The bus driver took his hand and wiped away the snow that had accumulated in his mustache.

He's been shoveling for a long time, Rose thought.

"As long as we've been here not one car has passed. I'm worried the sheriff's closed the road before inspecting to see if anyone was on it. If that's the case we won't get any help until the weather clears."

"What can we do?"

"Well, if you were to walk up the road a piece to the first house you come to and call the county sheriff he'd send someone out."

"I can do that. Do you think the closest house would be in front of us? Do you remember seeing any house before you run off the road?"

"No, Missy. I was fighting to stay on the road but I don't remember seeing a house for quite a spell. I think your best bet is to go forward. Surely someone lives in this beautiful countryside."

Was he being facetious? The countryside certainly was beautiful, but a man shoveling out a bus, thirty upset passengers, and his mustache frozen to his face should have difficulty appreciating it. He was just trying to address the situation with a wry sense of humor. Rose stuffed her hands into her pockets and started down the road. The snow was coming down so thick now, that when she had gone a hundred yards and turned to look, she couldn't see the bus in the distance. Her feet were cold. Her shoes were a pair of low heels she had brought because they were comfortable and dressy enough to work in. She hadn't brought any boots. The coat she had looked so stylish in was way too flimsy to withstand the rigors of a blizzard. Rose was freezing. No gloves, no socks. How did the saying go? "Cold hands, warm heart."

Well, what if you had cold feet, cold legs, and cold arms? Even her ears and nose were cold. She was cold all over.

As time dragged, Rose's body grew numb. Her pace decreased. Her mind wandered. She thought about David. She thought about hot chocolate, a steaming bowl of chicken noodle soup, hot oatmeal with a big scoop of melting butter, plenty of brown sugar, and a handful of raisins. Toast with orange marmalade—no make that muscadine jelly. She must be hungry as well as cold. Rose walked for hours. There wasn't any house. No little cabin with smoke curling from its chimney. No town with a café for sojourners in a foreign land. She came to a road sign. She was on a county road. Where was the state highway? Had she veered away at an intersection? Were they running together? Was she lost in this godforsaken "beautiful countryside?" She might have to slap that bus driver when she made it back.

What happens when your nose freezes? Does it break off? Does gangrene set in? If they had to surgically remove her nose to get rid of the gangrene could they give her another one? Would it be as pretty as the one she lost? Would it be just any old nose they happened to have laying around? Maybe a bulbous nose like W. C. Fields' or a long snout like Jimmy Durante's. Would David love her if she sported a snout?

Rose's situation was getting serious. She came to a sign saying her county road was ending in five hundred feet. She turned around and started walking back. Where was her shoe? Her feet were numb and somewhere she had lost one of her shoes. "This is tragic," she whimpered, "I guess I'm not really a big girl, someone who can take care of herself. Where's my daddy?"

Rose kept going. She would not give up. Eventually, she came to the intersection where she had made the wrong turn. If she went left it would be back toward the stranded bus and defeat. If she turned right she would be continuing her venture, looking for a house with a telephone. If she turned right she would be looking defeat in the eye and saying, "I can overcome you." She turned right.

In a few minutes a hulking beast creeping along the asphalt stopped beside her. A voice she remembered from her past called out. "Can I give you a lift, Missy?"

No one had come, no sheriff inspecting his county's highways, no wrecker looking for stranded busses. The driver just kept after it and four hours after first getting stuck had his bus backed onto the road and was trying to find the young lady he had sent looking for a telephone. After continuing down the road farther than she could have walked he turned around and retraced his steps. He had the passengers looking out the windows on both sides. She might be lying on the shoulder of the road or walking blindly in the middle. She'd been gone long enough to be suffering from hypothermia. He wasn't leaving until he found her.

He helped her to her seat, removed her wet and soiled coat, and replaced it with a blanket from his own luggage. When he had her as comfortable as possible, he ambled back up front and, sitting behind a large horizontal steering-wheel, he got the bus headed to Springfield.

Several hours later, just outside the city limits, a woman walked up behind the bus driver. "Sir, the girl's sick. I'm only a nurse's aide but I know when someone's in trouble. She's mumbling incoherently, and shivering. I can't wake her. There's a hospital only a few blocks from the highway. I work there. If you would make the detour and stop, I'll get off the bus and get her checked into the emergency room."

"Then, that's what we're gonna do."

When the morning dawned Bill was up. He decided to cook breakfast for his little girl. He'd apologize for his behavior and together they'd figure something out. He couldn't let her throw her life away, but then again, it would be a long while before anything had to be done. Maybe he'd let her get her way—or think she was getting her way. The war was going to be a long one. Germany was powerful—just ask the Poles, or the French for that matter. He quickly shaved and showered. This was going to be fun. It had been a long time since he'd cooked a meal. He'd show her how much he cared.

Bill tiptoed into the kitchen and started a pot of coffee. In the refrigerator he located a slab of bacon, a few eggs, and some bread. He didn't think he had the skills for biscuits—toast would have to do. He thought about it, then decided if he cooked the bacon first he could use the bacon grease to cook the eggs. He had talent. He could've been a chef. He went back into his bedroom and got a baseball cap he occasionally wore, turned it inside out, and plopped it on his head upside down with the bill facing backwards. It wasn't exactly a chef's hat but it's what he had. It would do. He cooked the bacon, eggs, and toast. He poured a cup of coffee and wondered if he should wake Rose or just let her sleep. He decided to open her bedroom door so she could smell the aroma of the bacon and the coffee and wait for her to wake of her own accord. He opened the door and went into the living room to sit and plan the day. In his chair he found the note.

CHAPTER 15—CLAUDE
Springfield, Missouri – March 1943

Rose's situation was serious. She had pneumonia in both lungs. The doctors put her in a semi-private room and proceeded to save her life, and the life of her baby, through advanced medicine and loving care. They dripped antibiotics and other liquids into her system, routinely gave her sedatives to help her sleep off the fever, and woke her periodically to make sure she was sleeping okay.

When the fever subsided and she was able to sit up, the nurse's aide who had brought her in came by for a visit. "Honey, the bus driver wouldn't give up until he found you. And then he detoured from his regular route to drop you here." She adjusted Rose's gown. "All your personal belongings are in the locker." She pointed to a metal cabinet beside the bed.

Rose gasped and felt to see if the locket was still there. She was relieved to feel its familiar oval shape beneath her fingers.

The woman said, "They got into your purse for identification but didn't bother anything else."

Rose thanked her profusely. If the bus driver had not been so determined she would have died in the cold of the snow. And if this woman had not been so attentive she would have died on the bus. She just knew it.

That afternoon, her doctor came to her bedside during his rounds. "You need to stay in the hospital for a few more days. It appears the baby's okay, but you'll not be able to do much for an extended period of time. Pneumonia weakens a person and has a long recovery. Have you got a place where someone can look after you?"

"No, but I'll find one."

"You also need to take better care of yourself. Your body needs a healthy assortment of vitamins to help the baby develop. Have you got a regular doctor?"

"No. I'd planned on getting one but this trip came up unexpected. Thank you so much for getting me through this."

Two days later, Rose emerged from the hospital with a sack of prescription drugs and vitamins and four hundred dollars left of her money. The doctor told her he wanted to see her again in a week and for her to get plenty of rest. She and her baby were lucky.

Rose looked around and determined Springfield was a nice town. It was a lot bigger than Dancing Deer. There was a daily newspaper, a bustling main street, and cars whizzing by everywhere. She resolved to find a furnished apartment and then a job. It looked like Springfield would be her new home. As soon as she found a place to live she'd write Jesse.

Bill received a call from his ex-wife. She told him Rose never arrived. It had now been a week and, without any word from Rose, he decided he better go see the sheriff. But first, he'd do a little police work of his own. He went into her bedroom and combed through her dresser, her closet, and the pockets of her clothing. The closet was brimming full. Had she not taken any clothes? Her suitcase was missing so she had to have packed something. She didn't leave any clue as to where she was going other than the note.

Bill needed to take the morning off to figure things out. His first stop was the paper. He told Jesse, "I'd like to look around Rose's office and see if she left any clue indicating where she was headed. According to her note, she was going to spend some time with her mother but never arrived and now we're worried sick."

Jesse said, "Nothing's been moved from her office except for one article she was writing and that's been turned over to another reporter to finish. I've kept her office locked. Make yourself comfortable while I go get the key."

Bill glanced around the reception area. There were mail cubby holes on the back wall. In the one marked R. P. were circulars and one letter. He quickly took the letter and placed it in his coat pocket. When Jesse came back they walked down the hall to Rose's office. Jesse unlocked the door and they stepped inside. Bill went through every drawer of her desk. He also made a mental note of the brand and model of her typewriter. Then he went through her filing cabinet. Nothing out of the ordinary. Just a well organized and meticulously cared for office—like his home when she had been there.

Bill asked, "May I talk to the reporter who finished Rose's last article?"

He was ushered into Miss Faye Spencer's office. She was a tall, delicious redhead, in her late thirties. Bill asked about the article she finished for Rose.

"No, Mr. Potter. I don't think there's any connection there. It was a straight-forward case of bickering neighbors. One neighbor's dog was keeping the other neighbor from sleeping so the second neighbor sued the first neighbor and won."

"Excuse me, Miss Spencer, is that news? Do you people report murders, rapes, or kidnapped children?"

"Mr. Potter, we don't have that sort of crime in Dancing Deer."

"What was Rose's angle? Surely something made the story interesting. And please call me Bill, I'm not that much older than your father."

"Mr. Potter . . . Bill. You're not that much older than me."

Bill leaned closer in his chair. He was liking this woman.

She continued, "According to Rose's notes the judge awarded the second neighbor fifty dollars and told the first neighbor to do something about the dog. Your daughter's article suggested the presiding judge should have recused himself."

"Aha. I knew she'd find some news in it. Please, Miss Spencer, tell me more."

"It seemed that the judge's grandson was a second-string outfielder on the school baseball team coached by the second neighbor. After the verdict, the kid started playing on the starting lineup."

There was a pause. Miss Spencer had finished and Bill was waiting for more. "Miss Spencer, you need to come by the bank, we have more interesting news than that happening every day in the commercial accounts section."

Bill left the paper and went to the Marsden County Sheriff's Office. There he was allowed to read the dispatcher's report of his interview with Rose. Bill told the sheriff that it didn't matter. She never showed up at her mother's and he wanted an investigation. Bill made a special mention that the sheriff was an elected official and it wouldn't be long before he'd need every vote and all the help he could get. The sheriff said he understood and it looked like he did need to open an investigation.

Back at his office Bill told Carla, his new secretary, to send a dozen red roses to Miss Faye Spencer at *The Marsden County Meteor* and to order an Underwood typewriter, model AS200.

Rose found a furnished room from a classified ad in the newspaper and fell exhausted on the bed. Maybe she could put off getting a job until she was feeling better. She was completely tuckered out and hadn't done anything. She checked out of the hospital, bought a paper, hailed a taxi, rented the first place she went to, climbed one flight of stairs, and now was too weak to get off the bed. Bed-rest—that's what the doctor said she needed.

The next day Rose sent a letter to Jesse. She tried to downplay the seriousness of her illness but confessed to being too weak to look for work. She gave him her address and said she would stay in touch.

There were four rented rooms on the second floor and, she guessed, the same number on the first floor. Also, there were two bathrooms on each floor, one at each end of the short hallway. Her room had a small stove, sink, and icebox stuck in a corner. If you weren't careful you'd bump into yourself while working there. All of the other tenants were women and the landlord said no men were allowed in the rooms. She said if you had a male guest there was a diner across the street with late hours.

It was ten in the morning and no one around. Rose guessed they worked. She trudged down the hall to the bathroom and took a long bath with the water as hot as she could stand and as full of water as the iron claw tub would hold. The warmth of the water wicked away the last of her energy. When the water cooled she struggled back to her room and collapsed on the bed. Rose had never been sick much and the weakness, the nausea, and the dizzy spells were disconcerting. However, it would soon pass and she'd get on with her life.

That afternoon, Rose managed to dress and left the boarding house to buy milk and groceries. She needed to eat if she expected to get better and the baby needed calcium from the milk. She remembered what the doctor said about taking better care of herself and swallowed a handful of vitamins on her way out the door.

Down the street, around a corner, and over to a busier street. Where were the taxis? Rose grew weary and had to sit on a park bench while she caught her breath. Two men were playing chess on a picnic table behind her. It must be a city park. So where were the grocery stores? All she wanted was a few things she could take to her room. Rose slowly got to her feet and headed back. She didn't want to get lost or get too far from her room. She might get sick again. When she found her boarding house, she was almost too weak to climb the stairs. That evening she went out again—this time to the diner. Someone else would have to cook.

"What'll you have, honey?"

"What?" Rose looked up, "Do you have a menu?"

"Sure thing. Here, I'll bring you some water and take your order in a minute. Honey, you don't look so good. You feeling okay?"

"I'm under the weather but I'll be back to normal in a few days."

Rose ordered and forced herself to eat. She wasn't hungry but knew that wasn't right. She hadn't eaten anything since leaving the hospital the morning before. Her brain must not be receiving news from her stomach. She ate what she could and had the waitress wrap up the remaining portion for later. On the way out Rose asked if there was a grocery store close by. The waitress said there was and it was within walking distance. She gave Rose the directions then headed to take another order.

Jedidiah hated the telephone. Emily made him have one installed when they brought the wire up the mountainside to Mrs. Miller's. It was a party-line. Two long rings and one short. When he heard it ring like that he knew it was for him—more likely for one of his three daughters. Of course anyone on the party line could pick it up and listen. They could hear the telephone ringing as well as he. When he heard the telephone ring his ring, and he was busy doing something and no one was close to pick it up, he'd just let it ring. His neighbors became accustomed to answering for him, then driving over to his house to tell him about the call he'd missed.

The telephone rang two long rings and one short, a pause, then again. Jed reluctantly got up from his chair and went to answer. He thought Emily was probably in the house. She was just waiting him out. Now if the girls were there it would not have rung twice. They could be in the front yard or in the barn doing chores and if the telephone rang they were there. It must be some bit of magic God gave young women—the ability to materialize whenever the telephone rang.

He picked it up. It was Stanley Muldaur's sister. She had been crying. She calmed herself enough to say that Stanley had died in an old folk's home in Memphis. He listed her as his next of kin and they called to give her the sad news. She said they wanted to send her his personal effects. Also, they wanted to know what she wanted done with the body. She told them she'd pick up his things there and asked if they could arrange for a funeral. She was leaving to take care of the details on this afternoon's bus. If there was anything related to Jed's horses she'd let him know. Jed told her how sorry he was and asked her to find out how Stanley died and why he got transferred there from the home in Little Rock.

The next day Faye Spencer got the flowers from Bill and a letter from her sister in Kansas City. Katy was a little older than Faye and married to an abusive husband. Faye vowed she'd never get herself in a similar situation. She was comfortable being single and, although she received the occasional offer, she did not date much. Unlike her troubled sister, Faye was totally immersed in a rewarding career.

From the break room Faye retrieved a large iced tea glass and displayed the glass of roses on a table under the window. She thought about the man who sent them. From her listening to him rant in the city council chambers she thought he was some sort of radical. Faye had heard stories of him foreclosing on family farms when the family living there had unforeseen setbacks and couldn't make their payments. Bill Potter was not a forgiving or a compassionate man. Not a man she wanted to spend time with. She mentally classified Bill Potter in the same folder as Galen, Katy's despicable husband.

Faye was going to talk with Jesse. Now that it was apparent Rose had not arrived at her mother's house in Boston she wanted to begin investigating and gathering the facts. Faye was currently working on an article about the misappropriation of school funds but that could be put on a back burner if something with foul play was available.

There was a knock on her door. Bill stuck his head in. "Hello, Miss Spencer. Would you join me for lunch?"

"Oh, I don't think so. Thank you for asking. I have something I'm working on and it has a deadline so I'll be eating lunch in the break room."

"That's too bad. The chef at the Ritz Hotel Bistro has a bacon-wrapped fillet covered with a creamy béarnaise sauce as his special today. It comes with asparagus tips and a cup of corn chowder."

"My, but you are tempting. I think, however, I'll have to pass."

"May I use your telephone, Miss Spencer?"

"Yes. Certainly."

Bill walked to her desk, picked up the telephone, and dialed. "Hello, this is Bill. Get me the kitchen please." Bill waited a few moments then said, "Hello, Andre. Prepare two of your specials—one medium and one medium-well. Have one of the busboys deliver them with a pitcher of raspberry tea to me at the newspaper's office. Oh, and add one of those wonderful chocolate desserts you have the women fighting over. Yes, right away. Thank you."

Bill had a mischievous grin. "We'll arm-wrestle for the dessert."

Rupert finally asked Nadine to marry. He didn't quite have it all said before Nadine accepted and proceeded to kiss him all over his face. They just had one—no, make that two—small problems. Rupert wanted Claude to be the best man and Nadine wanted Rose to be the maid of honor. Neither could be found. Claude had moved to Fort Smith and hadn't written in months. No one knew where Rose had gone. Rupert said he was going after his brother and for Nadine to find Rose. They'd get married when he got back.

Rupert caught a bus for Fort Smith. He carried a small suitcase and the two letters Claude had managed to write. The bus trip was three hours and, when Rupert got off, his body ached from sitting in too small a seat without enough room for his long legs. Like all the Calhoun men, Rupert was well over six feet. He once had been skinny but Nadine had been fixing his meals the past month and he had started to fill out. He was a little embarrassed when he had to go to the dry goods store and buy a larger pair of overalls. He decided to go ahead and buy three pair and three new plaid shirts. Get this embarrassment thing past him. He wouldn't need to go back there for a spell.

Rupert found a taxi and headed to the return address on the letters. The people there told him to check Jell's Café; Claude hadn't lived at their address for several months. Rupert wondered if Claude was cooking, washing dishes, or waiting on tables. When he arrived he sat at the counter and ordered lunch. He didn't see Claude. Rupert ate the meal then asked the waitress if she knew a Claude Calhoun.

The waitress stopped in her tracks. She looked at Rupert with a look that made Rupert look behind him. "You Rupert?"

"Yes, ma'am."

"Claude said you'd come looking for him. We got him put up at The Painted Lady. He's just fine. We're glad you made it."

"Would it be possible for me to see Claude? Is he in jail?"

"Are you kidding me? Claude's the king of the roost. We done took him in. He's the man."

Rupert thought she was pulling his leg. He cocked his head to one side, picked up a toothpick, and said, "Claude's got our parents worried sick. I'll at least have to see him so I can report back he's okay." Rupert reached for his billfold.

The waitress gave Rupert an address, then she said, "Sweetie, your money's no good in here. Your lunch is on me. And if you'll come back for supper I'll spring for that as well. Even make it myself. I've been known to cook for a man or two."

Rupert fled. Bolting through the door and shaking his head with each long stride, Rupert wondered what was going on. As far as he knew Claude was not much of a ladies' man. Well, shoot, neither was he. Claude just worked and read. He mostly though, just worked. They thought they would be old bachelors, never to marry. Neither had much opportunity for dating, but by the sounds of it, Claude had come into his own in Fort Smith.

When Rupert told the taxi driver he wanted to go to The Painted Lady, the driver pulled away from the curb and headed downtown. Rupert offered the scrap of paper with the address but the driver said he knew where it was. When they arrived, Rupert was amazed. It was a two-story Victorian a few blocks toward the river from Main Street. It was painted rose-pink and trimmed in white. He could see the river not more than two hundred yards beyond and at a lower elevation. The house looked fully restored, complete with white picket fence. Rupert paid the taxi driver, who snickered, took the money, and slowly pulled away wondering how many tricks a man would be buying if he was staying long enough to require a suitcase.

Rupert moved through the gate onto the front porch. The front door was open but a latched screen door blocked his way. He knocked and a woman walked by, stopped, and headed toward him.

"May I help you?"

"Yes, ma'am. Is there a Claude Calhoun here?"

"Well, there surely is. Are you Rupert?"

"Yes, ma'am."

"Come right on in. We were hoping you'd make it. Claude talks about you all the time. His favorite saying is, 'Boy, if Rupert could see me now.'"

"Is he here?"

Another lady walked up wearing a nightgown—in the middle of the afternoon! "Bea, honey, who's this?"

"Rupert."

"Rupert, really?" She looked at Rupert from top to bottom. "Sugar, would you turn around for me." She looked at Bea, "Arkansas sure turns out some fine-looking men."

Bea took Rupert by the arm. "Rupert, I think Claude's in the garden."

They walked down a long hall open to the ceiling of the second floor. A parlor was on the left. Rupert looked in and saw several chairs, a couple of couches, a Victrola, and an upright piano. On the right was a small office, a room with the door shut, and an open area followed by a wide staircase leading to a landing on the second floor. From the landing there was a walk over the hallway to a group of rooms ahead and behind. Back on the lower floor behind the parlor was a room with the door shut and then the kitchen on the left and a large dining room on the right. They walked straight through to another screen door. On the other side was a sumptuous garden. It was the middle of April so there was a profusion of flowers in bloom and plenty of insects flying from one to another. Rupert smelled a heady aroma of earth, perfume, and river. They walked down a curving path, sometimes pushing back small leafy tree branches or flowering plant stalks. Rounding a curve they almost bumped into a woman wearing a servant's uniform and carrying a tray. Behind the woman was a round, wrought-iron table with a slender man sitting, reading a paper, and sipping a cup of coffee. When he saw them walk up, he spilled coffee on his dark green sport coat with satin lapels. Bea rushed up, took his napkin, and started dabbing at the droplets of coffee.

"Oh, Claude, honey. Let Bea get that for you."

Claude was up out of the chair. He hugged Rupert. "I'm so glad to see you, Rupert. Would you like coffee? Bea, have Wanda bring Rupert a cup of coffee and cream."

Rupert sat down. "Claude, what's going on? I thought you worked at the ammunitions factory."

"I got fired from there. I was spending my days working and my nights drinking and playing pool with the local hustlers. The next day I would show up at work looking terrible and smelling worse. Finally, they had all they could take and told me to find gainful employment elsewhere.

"One day I lost every bit of my money and couldn't pay the rent. A waitress told me to come out here. She said some ladies were looking for a man to do chores and a room was part of his pay. I've been here ever since."

Rupert leaned close to Claude. "What kind of chores do you do?"

Claude laughed. "Well, first I did some repairs. I had to get heavy-duty jacks under the house to level it. The doors weren't shutting properly. Then, I put in an alarm with a ringer and lights. After the first couple of days the girls started treating me like royalty."

Rupert leaned closer still and whispered, "What kind of work do the girls do?"

"They do just what you think they do."

Rupert let out a gasp of air that whistled when it rolled over his tongue and escaped between spaces in his teeth.

"It's almost legal here." Claude drank the last of his coffee. "Once a month the girls have to be checked by a local doctor. If he says they're okay the house is issued a month's license to operate as a gentleman's social club. It's my job to see the rowdies are thrown out. I hooked up a ringer and a panel of lights. When one of the girls has a problem she flips a switch and a bulb comes on in my bedroom. If I'm working on something or want to sleep I can also make it ring. When I hear it ring I look to see what room's light has come on and head up with a baseball bat. Some weeks go by and I don't have any problems, then I'll have two, one right after the other. I just ask them to leave and if they give me any lip I march them out the front door—in front of their neighbors—with them trying desperately to get their pants pulled up. But usually they apologize and I let them go out the back. However, they can never come back. There are other houses they can go to."

Wanda appeared with a tray. She placed a lace cloth on the table and set down a small lidded cup of cream. A china saucer and cup were placed in front of Rupert. From about ten inches she poured a long stream of steaming coffee into Rupert's cup and refilled Claude's cup. She then placed the insulated coffee pot and a plate of sweets in the center of the tablecloth.

"Thank you, Wanda. That'll be all."

Wanda curtsied and glided away. Rupert thought there were lots of changes in Claude. He asked, "How long you been here?"

"About three months, maybe four. Once a week we march as a troop into town so they can do their shopping. The first time almost everything the girls bought was for me. They said I needed to dress to the nines—whatever that means. They even had me change my hairstyle and grow this thin mustache. See how dark red it came in."

"Claude, I can't get over the change that's come over you. Nadine's the same way. She comes right out and says what's on her mind. No more the timid creature I could barely get to notice I was there. I thought, of the three of us, I was the most worldly and outgoing. Now I'm the one most cursed by always wanting to blend in, not to stand out, afraid to speak up—even when I think I've got something important to say. I guess that just goes to show how everything changes."

Rupert sipped his coffee. "How much do they pay you?"

"That's something else. Besides a small weekly paycheck, I make so much per client. Every morning each girl brings me down a dollar for every two men she entertained the night before. I make more in one good day than I did working at the ammunitions factory all week. What's more I've been finding money stuffed in the oddest places in my bedroom. When I asked the girls about it they said it was mine."

"You find money?"

"Yep, and presents. Sometimes, under a corner of the bedside lamp. Also, in the top drawer of my dresser, stuffed between my books, in my cigar humidor, or even down in one of my shoes. It's the damnedest thing."

"It's probably the girls thanking you for looking out for them."

"No. I told them what they pay me was plenty and they said it wasn't them leaving the money." He paused, looked down, and mumbled, "I guess it could be the cooks."

"You have more cooks than Wanda?"

"Wanda isn't a cook. Our cook is a older and more rotund woman—but light on her feet. But, I'm not even talking about her. Once or twice a week a lady will call to see if she can cook me dinner. The girls let them in the back door. Our cook gets off early in the afternoons leaving us a plate of sandwiches and tidbits of things stuck on toothpicks. So when some woman says she wants to cook me supper I let her. Occasionally we'll dance in the kitchen when someone in the parlor is playing the piano or the Victrola. If she's going to all that trouble how could I refuse? Sometimes we go into my bedroom. I've got it fixed up like it's a sitting room on one end with the bed completely out of the way on the other. They just want to talk. To tell me how their day went. I listen, nod sometimes, and have been known to hold their hand if what they're telling me upsets them in some way. They'll get me a cigar, clip off the end, light it, and hold it out for me to smoke—sometimes smudged with lipstick."

"Claude, you need to write, we got all worried when you quit sending letters. The ones we sent to you were returned so I come to check on you and to ask if you'd come home for my marriage to Nadine. I want you to be the best man."

The rest of the afternoon Claude and Rupert talked about what had happened to them in the six months they had been apart. They finally agreed it was the cooks leaving the money. That evening they ate sandwiches and little round sausage links stuck on toothpicks. Claude said he liked to dip the sausages in spicy hot mustard. He warned Rupert he better have plenty of iced tea handy. They sat in the dining room eating while the girls were busy getting ready for the evening. They were applying and re-applying their make-up, curling their long tresses with some sort of hot poker, and getting Claude or Rupert to give an opinion as to how they looked. Bea was a little older than the others and when the first man came in she went into the office with the client. He soon came out holding high over his head and rubbing together two wooden tokens. He went into the parlor and the women went in after him, giggling.

Claude and Rupert retired to Claude's bedroom where they sat around a small table in two comfortable wing-back chairs. Claude smoked a fancy, white, carved meerschaum pipe and filled the room with the sweet smell of a moist tobacco laced with vanilla and latakia. Rupert read the paper while Claude took out a novel he was working on about a woman who had to wear the letter "A" embroidered on her clothing. Claude said he was not expecting any cook so they passed the time like they used to when they lived at their parent's home.

Around midnight a light came on and Claude was up and out of the room with a baseball bat. Soon he was leading a man to the back door while the man was apologizing and asking if he could come back. He said it was only a garter snake. Rupert listened as Claude said he would see what the girl said. He'd let the man know.

They listened to the Victrola play. Claude said they had a big collection of disks. During one of the lulls, someone started plinking on the keys of the piano. Rupert could barely hear the voices singing to it. Claude said it was because the house had thick walls. The builder layered over the studs with rough planks then covered each side with two layers of a thin gypsum board. Claude said they had to get pretty loud before it was annoying. He then turned on an Emerson bakelite radio and they listened to Rochester take Jack Benny to the race track.

The next morning, having secured a promise that Claude would be arriving by the weekend, Rupert had a taxi pick him up for delivery to the bus station. The girls were sorry to see him go. Rupert took a last look at The Painted Lady through the taxi's back window. He was glad one of Claude's cooks had not stopped by for a quickie—maybe just whipping up *hors d'oeuvres*.

Mr. Muldaur's sister called after returning home from her brother's funeral and informed Jed the substance of what she had discovered. Stanley died of a staphylococcus infection. His nose had never healed properly. Everyone knew it was just a matter of time. There wasn't anything in his personal effects, just a few medical papers relating to the treatments he'd received, a crumpled application to run for public office in Arkansas, and a life insurance policy. It was for five thousand dollars. She was listed as a beneficiary for twenty-five hundred and Jed was listed as the beneficiary for the remainder. She said she had given the insurance company Jed's address and telephone number. They should be calling soon.

Jed was floored. After a moment, while he collected himself, he asked why Stanley had been moved from Little Rock. She said no one knew. Someone had called and made the arrangements. He arrived by ambulance with nothing but a ramshackle suitcase and a name tag around his wrist. They said someone anonymously wired payment of their monthly charges but there was no account or name on the wire. And Stanley didn't have money of his own to buy incidentals. They said the wire included twenty dollars to be parceled to Stanley throughout the month. Jed thanked her and sat down to figure out this new revelation.

Emily and Jed decided that Stanley had gotten the stallion to where he would test positive for the disease. But with his health issues he couldn't continue to work and, with the person behind the entire escapade paying the bill, he went to live in an old folk's home. He must have been moved about the time the syringe showed up. Someone was trying to keep Stanley from being found.

Jedidiah said, "I don't want the money."

"I think Stanley was sorry for the part he played and accepting the money is just another way of forgiving him."

"Well, I'm not a forgiving man," said Jed.

"I've forgiven him and I'll keep the money, unless you'd like to buy a tractor."

Jed paused, and then said, "I'll have to think about it. Emily, you're a lot more devious than I've given you credit for."

The day before the wedding, Bill walked into the newspaper office and, when no one was looking, stuffed a letter into the mail slot for R. P.

He then strode into Faye Spencer's office and told her he'd reserved a table for Saturday night's performance by the Big Band of Baxter Black. He also told her they received a load of the biggest crawdads anyone in Northern Arkansas had ever seen and his chef was busting the buttons off his shirt telling everyone that the taste of these behemoths would make them think they were sinning.

Miss Spencer said, "I'm sorry, Bill. I already have a date for Saturday night." Bill fell into her visitor's chair. Shaken he asked, "Who's the lucky fellow?"

"Bill, I don't think you're my type. I'm a quiet person who never makes waves. You, on the other hand, are the one out there stirring up the waters. I'm too much a conservative and you're too much a liberal. I watch and you do. We're completely opposite of each other." And, she thought, you remind me of my sister's husband—Galen, the despot.

"What if I said I could change?"

"What if I said I wouldn't believe it?" She had heard that before.

"Well, where is he taking you?"

"We have tickets to the Baxter Black performance. Are there enough of those giant crawdads to go around?"

"Save me a dance and I'll make sure there are."

"I don't think one dance would hurt his feelings. It's not like he and I are romantically involved."

Bill's attitude improved immensely. "What color dress will you be wearing? I want to make sure my tie coordinates."

"Bill Potter, you are too much." She took out an envelope of papers and started reading. The meeting was over, she had work to do.

On the way out Bill slipped the paper's young photographer a twenty-dollar bill and said he'd like to know who Faye was going out with Saturday night.

Back at his office Bill got out a new Underwood typewriter and started typing a letter to David. This was his second letter. He had already composed the first letter, had it written in a counterfeit hand, stuffed it in David's envelope, and placed it in Rose's mail slot at the newspaper office earlier in the day. That first scheme involved taking the pilfered letter to a handwriting expert in Little Rock.

This greasy little man came by his office one day and suggested Bill should buy a check writing machine that entered the numbers, in numerical form and written out, as a series of punched holes. Supposedly this would stop people from altering the amount in any way. Just before Bill had him ejected from the building the man challenged that if he could duplicate Bill's signature to where Bill couldn't tell the real one from his counterfeit would Bill then be persuaded that, in the proper hands, a check could be altered in a similar manner. Bill hesitated. The man went on to say he'd do it left-handed and backwards. Bill agreed to the demonstration and ended up purchasing the machine. He never used it but thought the show well worth its cost. The man had duplicated his signature close enough that the representation would most likely fool the clerks trained to find such counterfeits.

The grifter hadn't written it in a flourish like someone would when signing their name. No, he drew it. He put his right hand down and his left hand on top, steadied by the right hand, and drew the name backwards. Doing it backwards was probably easier than forwards. Later Bill noticed the man was left-handed anyway.

Bill composed his letter, supposedly to Rose from David, and located the man in Little Rock. For a small fortune the man wrote the letter in David's hand. It was now in Rose's mail box at the paper. One of Rose's girlfriends was probably sneaking them to her without anyone at the paper even noticing.

The letter to David would be written on Rose's typewriter and only the signature had to be forged. With enough practice he thought he could do it. He would simply imitate the most devious man in Little Rock.

"Sheriff Sherman Shodtoe." The boy telephoned and said Faye Spencer was going to the Ritz with the county's sleazy sheriff. Shodtoe was overweight and a degenerate. Faye Spencer had lost her mind. What could she possibly get from him? Information. That's it. She's working on some story and would be prying information out of the sheriff. Hot dog!

That evening Bill ate at the Ritz Hotel Bistro, as he had been doing every night except Friday since Rose left. He started having misgivings about sending David the counterfeit letter and even talked himself into going back to the newspaper's office and retrieving Rose's letter from David, maybe even breaking in later that night.

To the *maitre d' hotel* he said, "Tomorrow night I want you to set the sheriff and his date behind one of those big pillars. Move the tables around so they don't have a good view of the band or dance floor."

He walked to the newspaper's office after his meal but couldn't get the counterfeit letter. There were lots of people working. Bill had never thought about the long hours it takes to get a newspaper out. He probably still had a day or so. He'd just slip in and remove it like he did the first time.

On the day of the wedding Claude arrived at two in the afternoon. The wedding was for six with a reception afterwards at the Ritz Grand Hotel and Ballroom. Baxter Black and his big band were slated to perform and Nadine had reserved a large table just to the left of the stage for her new family and their closest friends.

She had not been able to find Rose. She even talked with Bill's new secretary, Carla. She was no help. Jennifer, his old secretary, was a regular visitor to the library and told Nadine Bill had been searching everywhere, but so far with no luck. Nadine already knew he had talked Sheriff Sherman Shodtoe into putting out an APB on her with a picture and hired a detective agency in Little Rock to see what they could come up with. The detectives posted bulletins saying they would appreciate the town's cooperation as they planned on questioning everybody.

Nadine was an only child and her parents had passed away years before so she and Rupert decided on an intimate wedding with just a few friends and Rupert's family. Claude was the best man and Emily was asked to replace Rose. She was the matron of honor. Nadine was one happy camper. She was not only getting a husband but he came with a nice family. Jed and Emily's daughters were regular visitors to the library and—well, everyone knew what a fine man David was.

She was so ecstatic over the whole thing she was having a hard time keeping her make-up on. Tears of joy kept washing it away. She had already soiled two handkerchiefs with running mascara. It didn't matter, this was her day. The day she had dreamed about. And it was all because David Blaine had come by and offered it to her. Then Rose came by and changed her life. Before long she had a new view on things and things had a new view on her.

At the wedding Ru looked so handsome in his navy blue suit. Emily had tied his tie. Mrs. Calhoun, Ru's mother, brought flowers from her garden and made a bouquet for her to carry and boutonnières for Ru and Claude.

The ceremony took place in a small conference room with Pastor Townsend from Possum Point officiating. He was the same minister who had married Jed and Emily. Amanda sang a song, several people cried, the vows were recited, and her veil lifted. They kissed and were presented as Mr. and Mrs. Rupert T Calhoun. Rupert told her the T didn't stand for anything. It wasn't even an initial, just a one letter word. After the ceremony everyone walked down the hall to the ballroom where the members of the band could be heard tuning their instruments.

Bill got to the ballroom early. The *maitre d'* had put a reserved sign on the best table in the house for him. It was down front in the center. Bill was wearing a sharp-looking English tweed sport coat over light-weight wool slacks. He spent an hour polishing his shoes. Earlier that day he had his hair cut and his fingernails manicured. He was putting his best foot forward for the tall, good-looking red-head from the newspaper, Miss Faye Spencer.

People started arriving. A sign out front said a coat and tie were required for all gentlemen. At the hat and coat check-in counter he had an assortment of men's coats and ties for those who hadn't taken him seriously. He'd bring this backwater town into respectability if he had to drag it like a mule to water. Bill went around welcoming everyone and saying how pleased he was to see them. He could hear the sound of crystal glasses chinking together. Crisp linen tablecloths and napkins adorned the tables with a single red rose rising out of wisps of baby's breath in the center of each. The chandeliers were shining brightly. They'd be turned down when the band started performing. Right now people were appraising their seating arrangements and wondering why they weren't sitting down front. The place was filling up fast. The sheriff and the stunning Miss Spencer came in and were led to their table. Bill went to his table and ordered a bottle of French Riesling. Soon, there was a commotion in the back of the room and Bill got up and walked back to see what was going on.

The sheriff had the *maitre d'* by his lapels and was telling him he wanted a different table. The *maitre d'* said all of the tables were spoken for and he couldn't very well tell someone to get up and move—not with the election just weeks away. There'd probably be a scene and with all the cameras present it'd surely make the next newspaper. The sheriff was red under the collar but had just about reconciled himself when Bill spoke.

"Sheriff, why don't you and your beautiful lady-friend join me? My table is the best in the house—down front in the center. It's plenty big enough for three and I won't be there very much of the time. It's part of my job to mingle and make sure everyone is having a good time."

The sheriff agreed and started dragging Miss Spencer in her green strapless evening gown until she pulled loose and told him to keep his hands to himself. Bill thought how he had always liked tall women. They made such a presence; always made the guy they were with look good. This particular tall redhead was way out of the toady sheriff's league. Bill smiled as he led them down front. The band finished tuning and started softly playing the same background music they had recorded for movies years before. Rupert and Nadine's wedding party came in and took a huge table just to the left of the dance floor. Bill and Faye ordered lobster thermador with a caesar salad and a baked potato. They drank Bill's bottle of Riesling and piled large spoonfuls of butter, sour cream, chives, and crumpled bits of bacon onto their baked potatoes. The sheriff had a Texas T-bone, fries, and bottled beer. Faye was enjoying the evening considering she was sandwiched between one loathsome cretin and one urbane scoundrel. However, the music was great and the food even better. She was determined to have a good time.

After everyone had been given enough time to eat, Baxter Black walked to the microphone and said how much the band members appreciated their fans. He told the audience how they got started, how they had been playing musical scores in Hollywood and only recently started going on tour. He told everyone to relax, to enjoy the music, and to dance till their feet hurt. He said if anyone had a special request, to bring it up front. Also, there were some special people in the audience and went on to introduce a federal judge, a state representative, William Carrington Potter, the owner of the Ritz Grand Hotel and Ballroom, and Rupert T and Nadine Calhoun who had just gotten married and wanted to spend their wedding night with him. That got a round of laughter. He announced the first dance would be dedicated to the lovely bride and her groom. The lights dimmed with a spotlight on the dance floor and the band started playing a slow, melodic waltz. No one got up to dance.

Bill asked Miss Spencer if she would like to take a twirl. She glowered at him. She said that the bride and groom should dance first and just as she said this they did proceed to the floor.

Rupert was petrified. He'd never danced in his life. Nadine told him to move his feet to the rhythm of the beat and she'd do the rest. They sashayed around the floor for a few minutes and then Claude came out and tapped his brother on the shoulder. Rupert was relieved and sat down with perspiration dripping from his brow. Claude took Nadine's hand and, with everyone in the room watching, they glided and turned in perfect rhythm with the music. To the audience it looked like they were floating on air. Claude's footwork was so fluid, his back so straight, his demeanor so polished that most of the women thought he was a professional. Miss Spencer asked the sheriff who he was but the sheriff had his head down in the steak and was not even watching. She turned to Bill.

"I think he's one of those introverted carpenters. He's probably the brother to the groom."

Sweetly, Faye said, "Bill, how do you keep your bank from going broke? You are such a poor judge of character. Anyone can tell he must have come with the band or, maybe, he's planning on opening a dance studio. If you want us to dance tonight you better see if you can introduce me. There's a story here."

"I'm telling you he's a carpenter. He's never been married. I don't think he's ever even dated anyone. He just builds stuff. He and his brother work with their hands. Neither one can carry on a decent conversation."

"I don't believe you."

"Okay, I'll see if he'll join us for a few minutes." Reluctantly, Bill walked toward their table as Claude and Nadine retired from the dance floor and new couples entered. When he arrived he took Nadine's hand and told her how pleased he was that she brought her group to his ballroom. She was such a lovely bride and how lucky Rupert was. He looked closely at Nadine and thought to himself, and he is too—the lucky bastard.

Bill turned to Emily and took her hand. "Emily, would you introduce me to the other guests?" As she stood, he held out his hand to Jed and said, "I already know this Calhoun. How are you doing, Jed?"

"Everything's just hunky-dory. I was going to call on you next week. I'm thinking about buying a tractor with the money Stanley Muldaur left me in his will."

Bill was shaken but regained his composure in quick fashion. He asked, "Is he the same Muldaur who was the County Extension Agent some years back? The same one who lost his nose to a wild dog?"

Jed said, "A courageous dog. But yes, he's the one."

Bill turned to Emily. She introduced him to the others at the table. After all the hands were shaken and pleasantries exchanged, Bill asked Claude, "Mr. Calhoun, would you mind meeting someone at my table. She thinks she might know you."

When the music stopped and the members of the band were turning to a new page, Bill and Claude crossed over a corner of the dance floor to Bill's table about twenty feet away. Bill introduced Claude to Faye and to Sheriff Shodtoe. Claude faced Faye Spencer. He stood straight and, with his feet close together, he bowed from the waist, gently held, and kissed the back of Faye's hand. The color rose in her cheeks. She asked Claude to join them.

"I'm a member of the wedding party and can only be gone for a few minutes." Claude shook the sheriff's hand and sat in the fourth chair.

Bill had a perplexed look on his face. Who the hell is this?

Claude only had eyes for Faye, who only had eyes for Claude. She asked, "What kind of work do you do, Mr. Calhoun?"

"At present, I manage an investment for a group of ladies in Fort Smith, but I hope to return soon to Dancing Deer. Rupert and I will be opening a cabinetry shop. I love to work with my hands, to create fine pieces of furniture future generations will cherish. Rupert and I are a good team. We've repaired or remodeled quite a few churches in the area. We've also built the wooden bridge that's photographed and displayed on postcards sold to the tourists."

Claude looked closely at Faye for several long moments. "I'm sorry for staring at your lovely face, Miss Spencer, but I think I recognize you. You look like a person described in a book I've read."

She reached out, put her hand on his, and said, "Really, Mr. Calhoun? What book would that be?"

"It's the *Iliad*. You have a face that could launch a thousand ships."

The sheriff leaned behind Faye's back toward Bill and whispered, "You think I should run his scrawny ass in?"

Faye said, "Mr. Calhoun, would you dance with me?"

"Nothing would please me more."

She led him out as a song was ending. "Can you tango?"

"Barely," he replied. "But for you, I'll do my best."

Faye walked up to the stage and asked Baxter Black, "Could you play something we can tango to?"

"I can, but in some areas the tango's outlawed. It's so suggestive."

"It's not outlawed in Arkansas."

"No, I don't believe it is. Give me a minute while we locate appropriate music."

Meanwhile the dancers who had been waiting for the next piece to be played went back to their tables thinking it must be break time.

When the band had located their music the floor was empty except for Claude and Faye. A spotlight located the couple. Claude struck a contemptuous pose. A camera flashed. The music started a haunting lyrical beat. Faye slinked over and ran her hand through Claude's hair. He roughly reached out, grabbed Faye's hand and slung her around in a circle—perfect timing to the beat. A second camera flashed. The music speeded up. They glided around the floor in fluid languid movements, both looking the same direction over outstretched arms. No one joined them on the dance floor. They had it to themselves: the two dancers, the music, and the spotlight.

The music slowed, became softer. Faye ran one hand up her side, high into the air, palm down parallel to the floor. Claude pulled it down and twirled her about. The beat accelerated. The volume reached a crescendo as Claude yanked her to him. With one hand around her waist he raised the other and they glided a few pulsating steps. They turned. Claude let her loose and circled. He grabbed her waist and pulled her close. They turned and glided, doing figure eights across the floor. More cameras flashed.

In unison they stepped. They turned. Faye tried to get away. Claude stepped to the side. She turned, moved her hands to her head, she turned again, and he's there right in her face. He roughly embraced her. The music reached a feverish pitch. Body pressed against body.

They turned, they stepped, and they glided, facing the same direction, in a straight line to the other end of the floor. Faye tried to get away. He lost his grip. She escaped. She went right, turned, and went left. Claude found her, grabbed her hand, and twirled her around.

The music began slowing. Deftly, in slow-motion, Claude twirled Faye in a circle one last time. He reached out and grabbed her again, pulling her close against him. Their two bodies pressed together. Faye broke free. She stood directly in front of him, looking up into his eyes. Her hand traced a pattern down his chest. The music followed her lead. It became slower and slower and slower as she slid lower and lower and lower to the floor like a rope retreating into a fakir's straw basket. Her arm curled around Claude's pants leg. She reached the floor as the music faded to silence and the spotlight faded to darkness.

Cameras flashed from everywhere piercing the black that bathed the dance floor. Moments later, the house lights came on to thunderous applause. The audience watched as Claude escorted the beautiful Miss Spencer to her seat, her shining red tresses disheveled in a voluptuous disarray. Bill thought she was a wild woman. His heart raced. He had to have her.

The band members were giving each other slaps on the back as Baxter Black walked to the microphone. He wiped the sweat from his brow and said, "Whew. That was amazing. Ladies and gentlemen the band will now take a short break. Don't forget these fine people bringing you food and drink."

After helping Miss Spencer to her seat Claude said he had to return to the wedding party and thanked Miss Spencer for the wonderful dance.

Ladies throughout the audience watched the tall, elegant man stroll in long strides to the wedding-party table. Jed leaned forward over his chocolate fudge dessert and asked Claude where he had learned to dance. Claude said his cook had been a dance instructor. She loved to dance as well as to cook. He had found that when he danced with her the quality of his meals improved. It became a matter of how well did he want to eat.

A woman in her late twenties walked over to their table and asked for Claude's autograph. Claude told her, "Miss, I'm no one important."

"You are tonight."

She held out her table reservation card and a pen. "My name is Meredith. Would you please write something on the back of the card?"

Claude scribbled something, leaned forward, and whispered in her ear. The woman blushed and took the piece of paper. After reading his inscription, she gushed her thanks and excitedly walked away holding it against her heart.

In a few minutes more women found their way to the wedding table and formed a line ending at Claude's chair. There was even one man who told the woman behind him he was sent to ask the man if he would dance with his daughter.

Miss Spencer asked Bill, "What else do you know about Mr. Calhoun?"

"Not much. He and his brother Rupert are such quiet men there isn't much to know. The reason they've remodeled so many churches is that they do the work in their spare time and don't charge for their labor—just for the materials. The churches would have used anybody if they were dumb enough to do the work *pro bono*. But, of course, the Calhoun's work is always magnificent. And the bridge was built because spring rains washed away the old bridge on the county road leading up to the Calhoun farm. The county had put off rebuilding it because it was lightly traveled. However, it is true that a man in an old beat-up truck came by one day looking for the bridge. He told Big John Lynch he was a photographer for *National Geographic* and was looking for the Calhoun Bridge."

To no one in particular, Faye said, "Someday I'm going to have that man build me a dining room table."

Bill thought of losing Emily to Jed Calhoun. If he wasn't able to intervene he would be losing Rose to David Calhoun, and now the beautiful Miss Faye Spencer was swooning over that tall gangling Claude Calhoun. What is it with these Calhoun men; what is it with the Dancing Deer women. Tomorrow he'd finish the letter to David—and start taking dance lessons.

CHAPTER 16—SICILY

An Island in the Mediterranean – July 1943

The Mediterranean is a fickle friend. It had been as calm as glass since they first slid into its waters at Gibraltar, but now that they were scheduled to invade Sicily, it had started churning. Forty mile-per-hour gales, rolling seas, and high waves made the Allied generals consider delaying the landing. The men were seasick when word came that the winds were dying down and the invasion was still a go. They were extremely happy—not so much for the actual action—but for the chance to get their feet on terra firma once again.

David and his platoon were scheduled for the first wave and climbed down the side of the ship clinging to a cargo net and finally jumping the last few feet into a waiting amphibious landing craft. It was five in the morning on July 10, 1943. Dawn was breaking. It was going to be a glorious day to be about their country's business.

The coxswain told them to get situated and not to be moving around. He said, even though the winds had died down, the sea was still choppy and they could easily capsize with the weight they were carrying.

This was their first taste of actual combat. Some of the men were eager to get started while others were shaking in their boots. David and Gino were among the latter group. They sat toward the back of the craft and made a pact to look out for each other. This was the way it was. Each man covered another. Each man knew he could count on other men in his unit to help him make it through. It was this camaraderie, this feeling of being part of a unified whole—one of the tribe—that enabled a lot of terrified young men to grit their teeth and bear it. Not much was said out loud. However, there was a lot of mumbling as prayer after prayer sifted heavenward.

After twenty minutes, the coxswain yelled out, "Get ready to go ashore. Red Neville Beach straight ahead." He slowed the craft and began lowering the ramp.

All night the naval batteries had been shelling the areas beyond the sand dunes at the far reaches of the beaches where the enemy was thought to be entrenched. None of David's friends believed anyone still alive would be close enough to the landing areas to offer any resistance. They were wrong.

When the landing ramp was three quarters of the way down they were strafed with machine-gun fire. Two men in the front of the craft were shot in the head and killed instantly. Some soldiers revolted at their first sight of the blood and gore that would soon become commonplace. The ones that could scrambled over the bodies of their fallen comrades. They intended to hit the beaches and either take out the opposing forces or hide behind something that would protect them from the whistling rounds currently striking the landing craft, riddling the bodies piling up behind the descended landing ramp, or plinking innocently into the water. David froze. Gino slapped him on the shoulder and yelled above the cacophony of war that they should jump over the side.

The water was chest high. Holding their weapons above their heads they waded through lukewarm surf. The soldiers ran to the sand dunes then hunkered down. The machine gun chatter, so prevalent when they first arrived, had died down and more and more of the landing party eased up and started getting organized.

There had only been a few machine-gun pillboxes. One brave soldier took out two by himself with some fancy footwork and an extraordinarily accurate throwing arm. He walked away leaving fourteen dead Italian soldiers and harboring one humble Italian prisoner. A few old salts tackled the other two machine-gun nests and were now in possession of three Italian prisoners.

"What outfit you with, soldier?"

David peered into the darting black eyes of a first lieutenant. "Forty-fifth Division, 180th Infantry Regiment, Second Battalion, Company F, sir."

"I thought you would be landing on Red Neville Beach, Private."

"Yes, sir. The coxswain unloaded us here saying it was Red Neville Beach."

"Well, it's not. This here beach is for the 179th. Red Neville's six miles west. Where's your platoon leader?"

"Killed when the ramp lowered, sir."

"That's too bad. Get your group together and try to rendezvous with the rest of your forces. You'll have to track the hypotenuse. Your comrades won't wait long enough for you to manage the six miles. They'll probably wait an hour for stragglers then head out to tackle their objective. Good luck, son."

David located Gino and relayed the bad news. "Gino, you're a corporal. With the second louie and first sarge both dead you're probably in charge. I suggest we start gathering our men and head north by northwest. Highway 115 should be only a few miles and we can skirt it to the bridge. If we hurry we might make it at the same time as the rest of F Company."

"Man, David. I don't want to be in charge. There's not one bone in my body that's not shaking and—well, hell, no one's even shooting at us."

David felt the same way but was too embarrassed to own up to it. "You go that way. Yell out for our company as you walk and meet me back here in thirty minutes. It looks like there's a path up ahead going in the right general direction. What time you got?"

"Five-thirty."

"Me too. Let's go."

At six in the morning on July 10, 1943 David, Gino, and twenty-three fellow soldiers of Fox Company headed into battle. They had survived yet another less than adequate amphibious landing and now had to find the rest of their company and accomplish their objective. Gino was relieved to find there were five other corporals and one staff sergeant. He didn't have to be in charge. He had some time to come to grips with the overwhelming fear that consumed his entire being. He just wanted to stay close to David and dart from one protective cover to another.

At eight that morning they reached Highway 115. There wasn't any traffic. None of the residents ventured outside their houses. No opposing forces came to rout them back to the sea. On the black-topped highway the men turned west toward the coastal town of Gela. They marched double-time for thirty minutes, then slowed to a fast walk for fifteen minutes, then it was back to double-time.

At noon they approached the bridge over the Acate River. Their company objective was to take and hold the bridge and to link up with the remainder of their battalion the next day. From there they would head north to the interior town of Biscari with the other two battalions.

They were late. The bridge had already been secured by the portion of F Company who had landed on the correct beach. A detachment of engineers was expected any minute to come and set charges in case the bridge needed to be blown before moving on.

The newly arrived troops were welcomed, then assigned to take out some pesky snipers located on two hill tops just past the bridge on either side of Highway 115. Beyond the hills the highway continued its serpentine course to the town of Gela. This would be their first battle. David and Gino were not looking forward to it. However, the Italians were not in the mood to fight and when David's group arrived and flanked them on the right and the left the Italians came out with their hands up.

With a commanding view of the road, the sergeant in charge decided to split up. Half of the men would stay on the two hills while the rest returned to the bridge with the prisoners. David and Gino stayed.

The engineers never made it to the bridge and the explosives were never set. At daylight David, Gino, and the older soldiers overlooking the road were greeted with cannon fire from four advancing German Mark VI tanks. A firefight broke out, but without artillery or anti-tank weaponry Fox Company was out-matched. The men fired their guns and fell back as the huge tanks came relentlessly forward. The tanks were quickly in control of the bridge and both hills. Fox Company was forced to retreat toward the beach and went looking for the remainder of their battalion and an anti-tank platoon. They traveled about fifteen miles through no-man's land before meeting friendly faces.

As they moved among the other members of the Second Battalion, Captain Jeremy Marcinko looked for battalion headquarters so he could report to his commander. First Sergeant Gerald Geiger looked for a place to park the company.

As they trudged along Gino said, "That was scary. I didn't know they made tanks that big, with that big a cannon, or that could move that fast. If they'd caught us it would have been lights out. You can't fight something like that with no stinking pellet gun."

"Gino, did you ever get that sight fixed?"

"Hell, no. I just learned to shoot it, mangled sight and all. I'll tell you this; no one had better ask to borrow it. I must've used four or five dozen clips before I started hitting the target. You know though, I'm now a better marksman with the crooked sight than I ever was when the damn thing sighted true."

"I'll bet with all that practice you started squeezing the trigger instead of jerking it. Also, I noticed you had a whole basketful of bad habits. You must've got those worked out without even realizing it."

"What kind of bad habits?"

"Oh, like blinking when you pulled the trigger. Your breathing was erratic and you had one eye closed when sighting."

"You're supposed to sight with both eyes open?"

"Yeah. Do you know which of your eyes is the dominant one?"

"Quit it, David. You're scaring me, man."

Sergeant Geiger assigned David and Gino to dig a latrine. They were among the first to get their tent halves buttoned together and set up, so other duties were found for them as the remainder of the company struggled to make camp. Their latrine was thirty feet long, a foot and a half wide, and two feet deep. It took three hours to dig in the rocky Sicilian soil. During that time Gino told David the wonderful things he had heard his family say about Sicily.

"My parents emigrated to America from the Sicilian city of Syracuse. That's a fairly large city a hundred and fifty miles due east of here."

"I thought they lived in Syracuse now."

"They do. When they went through processing at Ellis Island they found there was a Syracuse, New York and reasoned it would have a good-sized Sicilian population. So they took that as a lucky omen and told the processing clerk that was where they were headed. You know the Syracuse in Sicily is famous. It was founded by the Corinthians seven hundred years before Christ. The inhabitants have had to fight a lot of battles to keep it. They fought off the Carthaginians numerous times and once the Athenians. Then Rome came calling. The mighty power of Rome was held at bay by this comparatively small city for three years—mainly through the efforts of one man. He was a great inventor and most learned people think he was one of the three most important mathematicians of all time. You probably read about him in school. He was Archimedes. He discovered pi. He also discovered quite a number of mathematical truisms—not the least of which was a general concept of infinity.

"Archimedes was a good friend of the king. When the king ordered a golden crown he became suspicious of the goldsmith. He thought the craftsman might have alloyed the gold with silver and asked Archimedes to discover a way to determine if his suspicions were true without damaging the crown. About that time Archimedes figured out his law of water displacement while taking a bath. Realizing this would be a way to solve the king's dilemma he jumped up and ran through the streets stark naked crying 'Eureka! Eureka!—I have found it! I have found it!"

David leaned on his shovel, "How did he hold off the Romans?"

"Well, that same king asked Archimedes to design some offensive and defensive weaponry that could be used if they ever came under siege. One of his inventions was two giant lenses he positioned high on a platform. They were arranged in such a way that a focused ray of sunlight cast a burning beam out to sea. When the Roman ships entered the harbor he used the beam to catch their sails on fire and to burn holes in their hulls.

"He also had gigantic claws. When a ship got close to the high wall surrounding the city a claw would reach out and grab the ship by its prow. The claw would lift the ship completely out of the water. By swinging the arm, that held the claw, back and forth the city defenders shook off the men who were aboard. The claw would eventually dash the ship against the rocky shore or drop it stern first back into the sea.

"Those Roman ships were called quinqueremes. They were enormous. About a hundred feet long and fifteen feet wide they had over three hundred men on three decks."

"Well, what happened? Did Rome give up and go home?"

"No such luck. They were treacherous. They sent a party under a banner of truce to negotiate a settlement and when the citizens opened the gates they burst through and were followed by a marauding horde. Archimedes was killed during the sack.

"Someday, I'll visit his grave and pay him homage. That's one of my great ambitions. You know, he's buried in Syracuse. He asked to have a circle and a cylinder on his gravestone to signify what he considered his greatest achievement, determining the area of a circle inscribed in a cylinder.

"Cicero once described Syracuse as 'The greatest Greek city and the most beautiful of them all.'"

That night, after a meal of C-rations, a squadron of German Luftwaffe attacked the naval ships that had brought the Allied infantry to Sicily from North Africa. Sortie after sortie flew over with the naval guns answering. After a while the air raid was over and the night became quiet again. Then more planes. Several were shot down by land-based artillery and naval batteries. From others, paratroops were let out and floated down amid a maelstrom of flying lead. Then word came to stop shooting—they were our paratroopers. A lack of communication and poor navigating had led to our forces shooting down others of our forces. Gino sat down with a smoking gun lamenting how it was quite possible the first man he would kill was a fellow American.

The next morning the entire battalion set out to recapture the bridge but it had already been abandoned. Their next objective was to take the town of Biscari. The advance on the town was led by the Third Battalion. David, Gino, and the rest of the Second Battalion were deployed to the Third Battalion's right. They were to flank the opposing forces when they were encountered by the Third Battalion. However, no opposing forces were met. The Second Battalion did, however, start receiving artillery fire upon reaching the southern outskirts of town.

Battalion Commander Colonel Fulbright sent word to Captain Marcinko to take Fox Company around the town on the left. He was to cut off any retreating Germans who might want to escape using the main road going north. The rest of the Second Battalion joined the Third Battalion and cleared the town of any remaining German and Italian forces. Eighteen trucks, two tanks, an armored car, a large quantity of ammunition, machine guns, gasoline, and other supplies were found abandoned. Once the town was secured it started receiving artillery rounds from the retreating German forces.

The Third Battalion went through the town going east and eventually took up a position a mile out on that side of town. First Battalion came up and settled just south of town and the remainder of the Second Battalion joined Fox Company to the north of town.

That night Gino told David about other attractions in Syracuse. He told him about the Greek theater and about the famous tragedian, Aeschylus, putting his plays on there. He talked about the freshwater spring of Arethusa—where the Greek goddess, Artemis, changed Arethusa into a spring of fresh water to escape the river god Alpheus. He talked about the temple of Apollo, the extensive catacombs beneath the San Lucia Cathedral, the Euryalus Castle with its moats and immense walls, and the quarry prison known as the "Ear of Dionysius" because of its crystal-clear acoustics. Gino said he had heard stories about these places his entire life and here he was within a 150 miles and having to shoot his cousins instead of soaking up the island's ambiance and re-energizing his heritage.

The next morning all three battalions advanced on the Biscari airport. The order of battle was Second, Third, and then First. Company F led the Second Battalion with Captain Marcinko needing desperately to successfully complete an assignment. They had an observer from the 171st Artillery Battalion and an observer from the 189th Field Artillery Battalion. To reach the airport it was necessary for Sergeant Geiger to lead the company in a northwestern loop of six miles. With the prodding of Captain Marcinko, the sergeant soon had Company F almost a mile ahead of the remaining advancing forces. They had to traverse two wide valleys, each with little cover, and climb to a high and level plateau just beyond the second valley before assaulting the defending German and Italian forces. On reaching the plateau the airport was finally within sight and the two observers radioed the coordinates to their units. The 171st started firing its 105 millimeter howitzers and the 189th commenced firing its 155 millimeter howitzers. It sounded to David like all hell had broken loose. The howitzers were so accurate, with the coordinates given, that every building they could sight with their field glasses, soon became completely destroyed or severely damaged.

In retaliation, a battalion of German artillery began shelling the positions held by Captain Marcinko and his men. Soon an overwhelming number of German infantry forces were advancing. Captain Marcinko decided it was again time to withdraw and wait on reinforcements. Dodging bullets and mortar shells, Gino was not far behind the swiftest of the withdrawing Fox Company. He yelled over his shoulder to a slower David, "I've never done so much running in my life."

When reaching the edge of the plateau, Company F came upon the leading elements of the other companies of the Second Battalion. Machine-gun units started setting up and returning fire over the heads of their arriving comrades. Captain Marcinko reported to his commander about the terrain up ahead and of the strength of the defending forces.

That night the First and Third Battalions quietly moved across the plateau toward the Biscari Airport. The Second Battalion was held in reserve. The advancing soldiers met with light sniper fire and then, in the dark, with an avalanche of Italian soldiers ready to surrender. They were carrying suitcases. As the Italians were being marched to the rear, several German tanks approached and fired at anything they could see moving. The First and Third Battalions dug in and waited for daylight.

The next morning a fearsome attack took place. The Germans had a dozen tanks, an entire artillery battalion, and more than a full battalion of infantry. They fought with such tenacity that it took all morning for the First and Third Battalions to start seeing an improvement in their position. The First Battalion fought up the middle. The Third Battalion, on their left flank, emptied buildings and a series of caves hiding embedded snipers and machine-gun emplacements. Captain Marcinko almost lost control of his patience before the Germans consolidated their forces and counter attacked with every infantry soldier they had behind six Mark VI Tiger tanks and four lighter Mark IV tanks. Immediately, the Second Battalion was sent into action and Company F led the charge. Captain Marcinko would later say that it was his Fox Company that made the difference and, indeed, when they entered the battle, the overwhelming number of Allied soldiers and armament began decimating the German belligerents.

Gino and David got separated in the melee. At one point, while Gino was advancing, a Tiger tank was lying in ambush in an alleyway between two buildings. With its machine-guns ripping up the ground all around Gino, the tank started forward toward the flank of the charging Captain Marcinko and most of Company F. Gino threw himself behind a burned-out armored car and waited for the tank to pass. When it did, he fitted a grenade to the end of his Garand rifle, and shot it at the tank's vulnerable back side. His aim was wide of its mark and the exploding grenade did little damage. Gino ran forward to the next cover but the fast tank had traveled out of his effective range.

A soldier to Gino's left, in the doorway to one of the tin buildings, sat holding his stomach. He tried to stand and was shot in the head by sniper fire coming through an open second-floor window of the building across the street. Gino knew the dead soldier, but not so well as to recall his name. He decided he would take out the sniper.

Gino waited for his opportunity but the sniper was firing from the recesses of the room. Gino lowered his rifle, raced across the street, and entered the doorway of the building. It was some sort of office with scattered desks, overturned chairs, and strewn papers everywhere. Five Italian soldiers and one American GI lay dead among the mélange. Gino went to check out his fellow infantryman. After all, he reasoned, he might simply be in shock. The soldier was lying in a puddle of blood with a heavy canvas bag clutched in both hands. Under the canvas bag was a gaping hole in the man's chest. The poor guy was definitely dead.

Gino, get your head back to the here and now. Gino dropped the hands holding the bag and quietly climbed the stairs to the second-floor where the sniper waited. He didn't have to worry about being all that quiet. A noisy battle was raging outside and the tin building shook and rattled with each exploding shell. At the top of the stairs Gino saw the back of the sniper as the man looked down into the street for another victim. With only his head above floor level Gino raised his weapon. Three quick shots dispatched the German. Gino thought, God, I hope this gets easier. Back to the bottom floor Gino went to the dead GI and said, "I got him for you, bub."

On the floor not far from the fallen soldier lay a blood-stained piece of Italian currency. Gino picked it up and then quickly snatched the canvas bag from the dead soldier and peered inside. It was full of money. There were bills of different denominations. On closer inspection Gino determined most of the bills were the huge Italian thousand-lire notes. Soon, naked to the waist, Gino tied the bag with string across his chest and stomach. He put his shirt on and stuffed the tail into his trousers. He then walked outside into the midst of a firefight. As he hunkered down behind a burned-out armored car he looked back and saw the inscription over the door of the tin building. In Italian it read Army Finance Office.

Farther up the street, David raised his weapon and sighted a man carrying as many belts of machine-gun ammunition as he could manage and still run. David took a slight breath, let out a little air, and squeezed the trigger. The running German soldier was shot in the side of his face, just above the ear. David had his first kill. He retched.

When the fighting was over they had captured eighty airplanes, a cache of artillery pieces and automatic weapons, and an ammunition dump. Later that afternoon, long after the counter attack had been beaten off and everything was relatively quiet, one of the captured German aircraft suddenly lumbered down the runway and took off. An agitated voice yelled out, "Damnit, someone go check those planes."

The retreating remnants of the German force headed north toward the supply city of Caltagirone. Following in hot pursuit was Captain Marcinko leading his Fox Company with the rest of the Second Battalion trying to keep up and a tired Third Battalion quite a ways behind. From a reconnaissance report the Second Battalion was told to occupy an advantageous hill on the right side of the road a quarter mile shy of the town proper. That is, if they reached it before they encountered the retreating Germans. The Third Battalion would have a comparable hill on the opposite side of the road when they made it in sometime after dark. The First Battalion had the highest number of casualties and would limp toward a camp several miles farther south. That night sentries for the Second Battalion determined the area across the road was infested with Germans. Thinking they were the retreating forces from the Biscari airport, the Second Battalion entered into a lively local battle. Actually, the Second Battalion had stumbled onto a reinforced mobile company with additional armor and a considerable number of tiger tanks. They were well concealed in an olive orchard, making it difficult to place accurate fire.

The next morning a full-scale battle raged with all three of 180th's infantry battalions and two artillery battalions joining the fray. Allied against the formidable German forces was an antitank platoon firing their 37 millimeter guns, Company H with its heavy machine guns and 81 millimeter mortars, and the antitank weaponry of the 171st Artillery Battalion. When the tanks came directly at Company F this time they didn't fall back. With grenades and rocket launchers they blunted the German thrust and dropped most of the advancing German infantry with accurate small-weapons fire.

A second counter-offensive was stopped dead in its tracks by the precision firing of a dozen or more 57 millimeter antitank guns from the 189th Field Artillery Battalion.

By mid-morning most of the German forces were destroyed or fleeing to Caltagirone with Company F trying to catch them before they made the city residential area. Caltagirone was supposedly off-limits to the 45th, as General Montgomery and the British Eighth Army had their dibs on the city. The 45th could only enter Caltagirone should such entry become a matter of military necessity.

Captain Marcinko decided it was a military necessity and instructed Sergeant Geiger to get the Germans even if they entered the city. With the help of the rest of the Second Battalion, they spent the entire day rounding up every stray German soldier, every piece of armament, tank, antitank weapon, and cache of military supplies in the city.

That night they camped outside the city limits feeling pretty good about themselves and waiting on the thorough but slow-moving Brits to arrive. After the evening meal, Gino approached Captain Marcinko's tent and asked for permission to speak with the captain. He explained that Caltagirone was widely known for its fine Marsala wine and, since he spoke fluent Italian, he asked for permission to go into town to purchase a case or two of their magnificent wine so the company could properly celebrate their heroics. He was given a traveling chit and two dollars from every man in Fox Company to make the purchase. He asked to take along David to help carry the wine and any other delicacies he might be able to find. Everyone wanted to go but the captain told Gino he could take anyone he wanted as long as he would guarantee that he'd be successful with his venture.

David was impressed with their good fortune. He was also glad to have been promoted to private first class by the captain. He was now only one promotion away from being corporal again with its higher rate of pay. Gino gave David the money supplied to purchase the wine for safekeeping and they walked briskly into the waiting arms of a liberated town.

David asked, "Where do we go first?"

"Let's buy the wine, some cheese, and whatever else we can find and get that job over with. Then we can settle back and take a short vacation."

"Have we got enough money?"

"We've got more than enough. You don't know how much more than enough."

Kids played in the streets, women hung clothing, soon to be flapping, on lines strung from the window of one apartment to another across narrow alleyways, people swept the sidewalks in front of retail stores, café proprietors arranged chairs and small circular tables streetside, girls and boys pedaled bicycles, laughing on being free once again. Everywhere they looked, they saw smiling faces and a city dotted with beautiful tiles, terra cotta statues, grand boulevards, and ceramics of all descriptions. It was a wonderful time to be in Sicily, in Caltagirone, the city of ceramics, and to be carrying a canvas bag chock-full of money.

Gino asked an elderly man where they might find a store selling wine. After receiving animated directions they headed toward a cheery street lined with quaint little shops. They only stopped long enough to purchase a cup of extremely strong coffee served in tiny cups and some sort of sweet confection Gino said was a ricotta puffed pastry.

At the store the proprietor was in the process of bringing out his hidden cache of wines. Gino bought four cases of his best Marsala vino and four cases of a good table red. Much to the annoyance of David, he did only the minimum required haggling.

When Gino and the store owner reached an agreement—or what looked like an agreement—David started to pull the American Occupation Currency from his pocket. Gino stopped him, producing a rather large Italian bill. Not only was the dimensions large but the denomination was also large. It required more change than the proprietor had. Not to lose the sale he offered Gino and David a very old and dusty bottle of French red wine from his cellar. He then tallied the bill and left, soon returning with two bottles of his very best Chianti. Gino said if the boxed wine could be promptly delivered to Captain Marcinko just south of town they would have a deal. He said he and David would keep the bottle of French wine and the proprietor could keep the remaining change and the two bottles of Chianti for the delivery charges. An hour and two stores later a second arrangement had been made for a large order of sardines, cheeses, and dried meats attached with knotted strings.

"Whew, that was sure a whirlwind shopping spree."

"Davy, my boy, you ain't seen nothing yet." Gino then suggested they travel to the center of town where the oldest buildings and the financial district were. Most large Sicilian towns are also centers for local government and taxing authorities. These towns have courthouses, the required constituency of lawyers, and financial institutions. Caltagirone was such a town.

Gino and David waved to, greeted and were greeted by, shook hands with, received enthusiastic salutes from, and were shown gracious hospitality from the friendly and thankful inhabitants of Caltagirone. Everyone was in a good mood. When Gino found a bank he asked David if they might take a minute to step inside.

In Italian Gino said, "Good morning, Miss. I'd like to talk with your manager."

"May I tell him what it might regard?"

"Just tell him I would like to make some investments."

The young lady asked if they would have a seat and she withdrew saying she it would just be a minute. David and Gino sat on two overstuffed chairs and gazed around at the warmth of an old-world office not yet sanitized with modern furniture.

Soon the young lady came back bringing another woman a few years her senior and very striking. She held out a long slender hand saying in Italian her name was Cecilia something-or-other. Gino had a big smile on his face. He shook her hand and said in Italian he had some financial transactions to make and a very limited amount of time for their execution. David and Gino were then ushered into her private office with David showing Gino along the way that the name on her office door was the same name as the bank's.

In Italian Gino said, "Miss Tarintino, my parents are Sicilian. They emigrated to America before I was born and after this war is over I plan on moving back. I brought my savings because I thought I might have an opportunity to travel to Sicily on a furlough while I was fighting in Europe. Then was told I would actually be here helping to shove the Germans from your sacred soil. I had hoped that with all the turmoil, the lack of saleable commodities, and the German rape of your economy, I might be able to infuse my meager funds through the purchase of a business. I will be coming back after the fighting is over to manage whatever business I am able to procure. My currency is Italian lire. Might this be possible?"

"Yes, Mr. Donatello, it is possible. However, the local populace would frown on someone displacing a hard-working native simply because the war had brought him into hard times and a foreigner, with money to spare, wanted to take advantage of his plight."

"I completely understand, Miss Tarintino. I'm not looking to take undue advantage. I'm willing to pay a fair market price for value received. However, I want a business, and it's current work force, that can manage—with an influx of working capital—to stay in business, if not prosper, until I can return."

"I see. Well, what kind of business might you be interested in? What kind of work did you do before the war? Will you need living accommodations?"

"Mmm, let's see. Restaurant, restaurant, and yes."

"I know of only one restaurant for sale. There are many others closed because food supplies has been hard to come by. The owner of the one I have in mind tried to keep his open but had a difficult time of it. Now he says he's burned out. It seats sixty, is in an older area of the city, and has limited parking. I believe he's asking seventy-five thousand lire."

"Actually, I was thinking of a much larger, more elaborate establishment. My funds are not as meager as I might have led you to believe."

"I see. How about a 100-room hotel with a posh restaurant and sumptuous gardens overlooking the city?"

"That's the ticket. When can we see it?"

"Really, Mr. Donatello. Do you think we have a hotel like that? I was—as they say in your American movies—pulling your leg."

"Miss Tarintino. You are simply astounding. Are you married?"

"No, I'm not, nor do I wish to be. My father has my career planned for me. It does not include marriage until I have my education completed and I'm in firm control of our family bank."

"While I keep that in mind, let's talk about the hotel with the posh restaurant. Is there a villa overlooking the city that might be for sale?"

"We have several of those. Most are owned by wealthy people who want to divest themselves of their country estates in order to consolidate their holdings. Who knows what the economy will be like once the war has ended? We also have one hotel just a few blocks from here. The Germans used it as their headquarters until you gentlemen showed them the door. The Germans requisitioned the hotel and have not paid any money to the proprietor for its use—not even for his expenses. He lost most of his staff because of the abusive nature of the German officers and his lack of funds for payroll. It ended being run exclusively by him, his wife, and their children. We've tried to work with them but the bank has its own investors it must consider. We're in the process of helping the proprietor find a buyer. It needs some work to return it to its original beauty but, if you might be interested, I think it would be a wonderful opportunity."

"How much are we talking about?"

"Around five hundred thousand lire."

"That's a lot of lire. Will he negotiate? Might the bank be willing to work a payment plan if I could pay a sizable portion up front?"

"That might be arranged, especially if you can provide some assurance you will be profitable. I'll have to talk with my father. I do think you should actually see it before we consummate the deal. It's within walking distance." Cecilia Tarintino paused, leaned forward, and politely asked, "Does your friend not speak Italian? He hasn't said a word."

A few minutes later they were back on the street. David was uneasy with Gino's affable behavior. What's going on? He and Miss Bank seemed to be getting along like they were long lost family.

"Gino, I know this sounds strange but I was hoping on finding a restaurant, a bar, some loose women, maybe take a bath. What have you got up your sleeve? I can't for the life of me figure out what's going on."

"A restaurant, a bar, and a bath are all available in our beloved city but the loose women left with the Germans." The woman steered them across the street and watched David as he turned several shades of red.

"I'm sorry, ma'am. After listening to both of you speaking Italian I was not aware you were also fluent in English. I beg your pardon for my rude manner of speech."

"Think nothing of it. Mr. Donatello told me you were shy around women and a little slow."

"I did no such thing."

Cecilia looked at Gino with a sideways glance. A smirk stretched her grin higher on one side than the other. She laughed, slung her purse as she took a big step over a water puddle, and marveled at how interesting the day was turning out.

"I was just trying to save his masculinity from the ravages of a career-oriented Sicilian beauty. A spirited woman, much like his girlfriend back home, who prefers argumentative repartee to tranquil domesticity. I didn't want to subject him to such an ordeal after we've been without female companionship for these many months."

"Mr. Donatello, you are, indeed, Sicilian. I think Caltagirone would be pleased if you decided to make your home here with us."

David and Gino were shown the hotel. It was within a hundred yards of the base of a magnificent straight and wide staircase leading to a cathedral overlooking the city. Cecilia said it was called the Santa Maria del Monte Stairway. It had 142 steps and each year, during the feast day of San Giacomo, it would be illuminated with thousands of small lamps in a most romantic way.

The first floor of the hotel had a reception lobby, a ballroom, two offices, a restaurant and kitchen, and a bar. All the rooms had twelve foot ceilings, crystal chandeliers, antique furniture, Persian rugs, and plenty of ceramic tile-work. The next three floors were identical, each with sixteen rooms per floor, each room had a wrought-iron balcony. The top floor of the five story building had been the living quarters of the proprietor and his family with a large wrap-around wrought-iron balcony. The owner and his family were in the process of cleaning the top floor when the pretty banker and the two GIs arrived.

Before their unexpected sudden departure the German officers, who earlier had tossed the proprietor and his family so they could take up residence on the top floor, had thrown a tremendous party. The owners had been cleaning all morning and so far had collected a large box of discarded clothing. They had another box of empty liquor bottles, a sack of cigarette butts, and a second sack of broken condom packages. One interior door was barely hanging on its hinges and several holes had been punched in the walls.

The proprietor didn't want to sell the property but understood the glare he received from his banker's daughter and earnestly negotiated with the American soldier. He couldn't borrow additional funds and, without some capital improvements and repairs, he would not be able to bring back his regular customers. When the deal was finally made all parties were ecstatically happy.

The proprietor was to continue to manage the establishment. He would hire an adequate number of employees to operate the hotel, restaurant, and bar. He would contract out the building maintenance, landscaping, and gardening. A construction supervisor would be hired to oversee the modernizing of the electrical, plumbing, and elevator systems. The construction supervisor would also work with an interior decorator to add bathrooms to each room on the second and third floors, reducing the number as needed. The rooms on the fourth floor would be remodeled into suites with the fifth floor turned into two luxury penthouses. Two hundred thousand lire was to be in the construction account. Fifty thousand was to be placed in an operating account. A decent salary would be paid to the owner to continue to manage everything until Gino could take over after the war.

The proprietor would be absolved of the debt to the bank and would have one hundred and fifty thousand lire in his pocket, Gino would pay one hundred thousand lire on the proprietor's note and assume the balance. Gino would also have one hundred and fifty thousand on deposit with the bank to be converted into gold coin and safely stored in a secure vault as soon as the bank could make arrangements. The bank was to arrange for contracting the construction supervisor, the interior decorator, and the public accountant who would oversee the financial management of the hotel's currency and the separation of financial responsibilities and duties of anyone handling hotel funds. The bank was also responsible for procuring general liability insurance, surety bonds, and the city permits and licenses. The proprietor was totally responsible for the actual management, hiring employees, public relations, and the advertising. Gino gave Cecilia all but a fistful of bills from the canvas bag he had strapped to his chest. David was floored. He didn't know where Gino had gotten the money, how much money there was, or just exactly what Gino was doing. Cecilia gave Gino a receipt and asked if she might take them to dinner that evening after they had found suitable lodging and taken the baths they had been looking forward to.

That evening a couple of refreshed American GIs met their beautiful banker in the restaurant of their hotel. They were lavishly treated to a home-cooked meal of locally grown vegetables, fresh fish brought in that morning by truck from the coast, and hand-prepared pasta. They washed it down with a smooth and fruity red wine with a curious cinnamon aftertaste. The meal took most of the evening to consume. Cecilia looked beautiful in a stunning lavender evening dress. She wore pearls and had her hair up in some sort of twist with a few wild strands defying containment. A violin played in the background. David thought of Rose.

Gino and Cecilia plotted and planned how the hotel would look, how well it would be received, and how lucky everyone believed his position to be. Gino's future was set. Cecilia was the toast of her bank. The hotel owner was out from under a mountain of debt. He had a good job with all the authority and funds he needed for its administration. He also had a sizable amount of personal cash to do with as he pleased. And his family was happy to be over the drudgery of slaving for an unappreciative clientele. Everyone was happy except David. He thanked Cecilia for the meal and excused himself saying he wanted to go to the bar for a few drinks before calling it a night.

The rest of the evening Gino sank deeper and deeper in love with a woman who had no intentions of becoming romantically involved or with getting her career side-tracked. She did, however, agree to supervise the interior decorator and to try and understand the overall theme Gino envisioned. She also desperately tried to evade the languid charm oozing from every pore of Gino's body. The soothing melody from the violin was not helping. After dinner they ordered a bottle of Marsala. Gino told Cecilia about America and how the women in his country were able to balance the demands of being a housewife and a mother with the excitement of a career. He wasn't sure how it went over. He didn't believe it himself. It was just hogwash. After they finished the bottle of Marsala they ordered Napoleon cognac, which arrived in crystal glasses suspended in a wire contraption above small flickering candles.

Gino felt he was making inroads when Cecilia excused herself and walked a little crookedly toward the women's restroom. Gino started thinking about a new, more tempting, strategy when she abruptly returned saying she had better leave while she could still stand. No entreaty Gino could muster worked to sway her from her firm resolve. Gino stood as she told him the papers would be ready to sign at noon the next day and held out her hand saying what a wonderful time she'd had. Gino took her hand in his. He reached up with his free hand and caressed her face. He then bent forward and kissed her lips. She placed her arms around his neck and returned the kiss, knowing her determination was dissolving. Then suddenly she broke free and bolted from the room.

That night Gino told David how he came by the money. David said Gino was the luckiest man on the planet. It would be only a short time before Cecilia's willpower would be completely useless and after the war Gino could look forward to spending his life at ease arguing with a beautiful woman. David lay in bed. Sleep did not come easily. He spent most of his hours until midnight wondering how he had lost the only woman he had ever loved.

The next day Gino met Cecilia's father and signed the necessary papers in his presence. They were then notarized. He had his picture taken. When developed it would be placed in his file. He signed a letter of intent telling the bank who would own the hotel if he should die before assuming control. He wrote down his military address, his stateside address, both parents' names, his grandmother's name and address in Syracuse, his military ID, and two questions only he, or his family, would know the answers to. Afterwards, hands were shaken all around and everyone went to look one last time at the purchased property before Gino and David had to head back to their company.

As a last gesture Gino and Cecilia traded addresses and Cecilia placed her picture in Gino's envelope containing his important purchasing and bank transaction papers. Her father had his chauffeur drive Gino and David back to their camp just in time for them to jump on the back of one of the last trucks in a convoy taking their entire division on a bearing north and west to liberate Palermo.

CHAPTER 17—ITALY
The European Theater – July 1943

David and Gino never reached Palermo. Its liberation had been officially reserved for General Patton's triumphal entry with the Third Infantry Division. Instead, the men of the Forty-fifth were diverted toward Messina—on the northeast corner of Sicily, just two miles from the toe of Italy. The road they traveled was the narrow coastal Highway 113. It wound its way on a high ledge with cliffs on its left down to the sea. On its right was craggy and steep mountainous terrain. Machine-gun emplacements were liberally scattered in the higher reaches to their right, each with a commanding view of the road hugged by the American soldiers.

At Castel di Tusa they fought a battle that became known as the Battle of Bloody Ridge. The men of the different infantry regiments fought hard but the Axis Forces had a vastly superior vantage. The casualties sustained were soon lopsided against the Americans. However, they persevered and, with superior numbers, better weaponry, more ammunition, and a stronger will to fight, they got the upper hand and were given the opportunity to continue along the treacherous coastal road.

On 25 July 1943 Mussolini was removed from office by Italy's King, Victor Emmanuel, and arrested. On 31 July 1943 the dog-tired 45th Division was relieved by the Third Division and moved to a rest area. General Patton continued his race to Messina with the Third. He was adamant about reaching Messina before General Bernard Montgomery and the British Eighth Army. He did outrun Monty but was two days late stopping the Germans from escaping over the straits to Italy.

The 45th Division repaired and cleaned their weapons. They rested, took baths, washed clothes, received mail, and slapped each other on the back for a job well done. David was awarded two packages and nine letters from Gabriela. One of the packages contained a loaf of salami, the other an assortment of jams and jellies. Gabriela was a woman with much to gain and a determined attitude. David looked through his stack of letters for one from Rose. Not finding one, he was glad to have the ones from Gabriela.

Gino received a letter from Cecilia. Before opening it, he jumped up and ran around their tent holding the letter high in the air and giving a whoop that would have made any Native American proud should he be close by.

Before shipping out to Italy they were told the Germans had only been fighting a delaying action. The Italian portion of their opposing forces was not enthusiastic, was poorly supplied with ammunition, and their weaponry was old—mostly of World War I vintage. The Allied forces were militarily much stronger and should have easily taken Sicily. Thirty-eight days was nothing to boast about. Sixty-thousand Germans had managed to hold off eight times their number of Allied troops. They even orchestrated an effective evacuation against an ineffective Allied containment. The Allied forces would have another opportunity when they fought again in Italy. There, both the Germans and the American GIs would be more evenly matched.

On the ninth of September, General Eisenhower announced that Italy and the Allied forces had signed an armistice. Just hours after this announcement the British landed on Italy's lower east coast and started inland against sparse German opposition.

A day later, on the tenth of September, David, Gino, and the rest of the 180th Infantry Regiment landed on Italy's west coast, just south of Salerno and northeast of the ancient Grecian town of Paestum. They came ashore under smoke screens laid down by warships moved in close. They were well south of where an intense battle was being waged between the Germans and an earlier arriving portion of the 45th Division and the entire 36th Division. The Germans were intent on overrunning the Allied beachhead and throwing them back into the sea. Their drive was stopped just shy of that goal by accurate naval artillery effectively blasting the German positions. This battle lasted eight days, between September 9th and 16th. Before retreating the Germans had inflicted a staggering 8,659 casualties.

The 180th stayed in Paestum while their vehicles went through a de-waterproofing procedure. They were ordered to move forward at dawn on September 19 to an assembly area near Persano and to be prepared to relieve the 157th that had been slowly driving the Germans back. It was at about this time the British Eighth Army joined the fray and the Germans pulled back.

Through a captured soldier it was learned the Germans had a particular fear of the men in the 45th Division. David's division contained fifteen hundred Native American Indians from Oklahoma. The Germans had been told they were cannibals. The German soldiers thought they would have to fight to the finish—to surrender would be to become dinner.

For the next four months David and his buddies chased, fought, and pushed the retreating Germans. The Axis forces mined the roads, ditches, and stream-beds. They felled bridges and blew gigantic craters in the few roads available. Then they found easily defended positions on high ground overlooking flat valleys and dug in. The advancing Allied forces arrived in those valleys and had to fight, with little cover, up into the hills against well-entrenched fortified positions.

The Allied soldiers' dogged pursuit eventually caused the Germans to abandon their positions and to retreat closer to the Gustav Line and to other well-prepared positions along the way—leaving devastating obstacles in their wake. All the while the German infantry was buying time for the skill and ingenuity of several German engineer and construction battalions—as well as 44,000 Todt Organization workers—to strengthen and re-strengthen their choke-hold called the *Gustav Line*.

Spectacular snow-covered peaks and rocky escarpments jutted out both north and south of the ancient monastery of Monte Cassino. Highway 6 was the only road negotiable for mechanized vehicular traffic to reach Rome from southern Italy. It passed through a tight gap in those mountains just south and under the watchful eye of the perching lion that was this old monastery. The Germans were waiting.

General Fieldmarshal Kesselring, Commander in Chief Southwest, thought he might be able to hold the Allied Forces there indefinitely. Certainly he had favorable weather. It started raining in October and winter blustered in with an arctic blast in early November.

Trench foot was common as there were no dry clothes. Frost-bite cost the amputation of numerous toes with gangrene setting in when the men couldn't be evacuated to medical facilities. The Germans suffered as well and had even less medical supplies in the field. As the battle grew closer and closer to the *Gustav line* the encounters became fierce, small-scale actions in which opposing patrols encountered each other in the fog, the rain, the sleet, and the snow. Hand-to-hand combat was commonplace on the narrow ledges. Many men on both sides plunged to their deaths from the slippery slopes and rocky outcroppings. In tight quarters where there was little room to maneuver, those who could fought with detached bayonets, fists, or rocks in preference to their shouldered Garand M-1s or Mousers.

In the sixth century Saint Benedict founded his monastery, and the Benedictine order, on the crest of a 1,700 foot hill overlooking a Roman town called Cassino. Even earlier, the site he chose for his monastery had been a temple to the Greek god Apollo. It now held a vast library of rare and irreplaceable books, documents, and artifacts. It also contained numerous paintings, sculptures, frescoes, icons, stained glass, and six grizzled monks. The monks would not leave. The Germans let it be known that the monastery was clear of any of their soldiers. This was later verified as true but the Allied generals thought it a ruse and received permission from the Pope to bomb the medieval Catholic legacy. The Pope asked the monks to leave but again they refused.

At 9:30 on the morning of the 15th of February 1944, one hundred and thirty-five Flying Fortresses flew over the old building and enclosed grounds. They dropped their payload of 287 tons of 500 lb. general-purpose bombs and 66 tons of 100 lb. incendiaries. Forty-seven B-25 Mitchell and forty B-26 Marauder medium bombers followed and dropped a further 140 tons of 1,000 lb. bombs. That afternoon an octogenarian abbot led five disheveled monks out of the ruins. They were swiftly removed to a safe area by the Germans. The abbot announced there had never been any Germans within the confines of the monastery. He added, however, the Germans were now setting up their artillery and machine-guns amid the rubble.

Before all this had taken place, David and the 45th Division fought their way to the *Gustav line* but could go no farther. It was impregnable. On the 3rd of January 1944 they were relieved by the French Expeditionary Force commanded by General Alphonse Juin. David and his comrades then marched to an assembly area in the vicinity of Maestro Giovanni and Lagone.

For the next two weeks they cleaned and repaired their weaponry and recuperated from the fatigue of battle. They also opened Christmas presents sent from home. David received a monstrous Bowie knife in an oiled calfskin sheaf from his dad. Gino received a battery-operated shortwave radio from his. Gabriela sent Gino an autographed pin-up picture of Rita Hayworth. To David she sent an autographed pin-up picture of herself, striking the same pose, and wearing the same clothing as Rita Hayworth in Gino's picture. Gino told David his dad had made the arrangements with a photographer at Gabriela's insistence but that his mother thought the whole thing morally repugnant. The remaining presents were home-cooked pastries, dried beef, and other delicious items that would travel well. David also received a many-paged Christmas card signed by every citizen of Dancing Deer.

Gino promptly hooked up a dry-cell battery to his new radio. On "Jerry's Front" he picked up a propaganda broadcast called *Midge at the Mike*. Other soldiers came over and listened to her talk about the evil President Roosevelt and his Jew-loving advisors. She read names and military ID numbers of captured soldiers. She said some of them had given her notes to read on the air. Invariably they were along the line of how well-treated they were by their German captors. Then they criticized their Allied officers for sending them into battle without proper support or sufficient ammunition. After several minutes of this diatribe, Bruno and His Swinging Tigers played big-band swing. The Three Doves of Peace finished the program by singing songs in a peculiar variant of English that made everyone homesick. Gino eventually turned the dial and found "The Allied Forces Network." Here they listened to *The Voice of the Army*. Gino's radio was a big hit and the next day there were numerous letters mailed home with requests for similar contraptions.

On the 15th of January they were trucked to Faicchio and on January 26 they continued on to Casapuzzano. It was at this port city where they loaded onto amphibious landing craft. They were to be taken to Anzio—on the other side of the *Gustav line*. The landing craft David and Gino had been assigned was a new sort of funny-looking conveyance called a DUKW and pronounced "duck." It was a cross between a truck and a boat. It was large enough to carry a 36-man platoon and could negotiate rough waters.

While the 45th was in transit General Lucas ordered the British First Division to extend their area north of Anzio to include the town of Campoleone. He also ordered the U. S. Third Division to take over the southern town of Cisterna.

The British sent two infantry battalions, supported by tanks, on a night advance. They paid a dreadful price for "the thumb." The battalion that spearheaded the attack lost their battalion commander and every company commander. Of its 820 men, they suffered 560 casualties. All for a piece of land jutting out from the crescent like a thumb. The newly conquered territory included a new fascist farming community they called "the factory" because the British thought a bell tower looked like a smokestack. When the Germans counter attacked they retook the thumb, including the factory.

The U. S. Third faired even more poorly. They sent two battalions of lightly armed Darby's Rangers up a gully defile to within a half mile of their objective. When they arrived at dawn they jumped out of the gully into the middle of the Panzer Division Hermann Goering, who were gearing up an attack of their own. A tremendous melee broke loose but the Rangers were severely outgunned. And when they were successful in capturing a German tank and using it to retreat to their own lines they were blown up by artillery fire from their own forces.

Six men made it back. The remaining 761 Rangers were either killed or captured. Days later, Gino and David listened to the radio as Midge on the German radio program *Midge at the Mike* suggested her boys—the Allied soldiers listening in—join the Rangers and see Berlin. She referred to Colonel Darby as the Lone Ranger. Allied Intelligence had vastly underrated the strength of the German forces.

When the 45th arrived at Anzio on 30 January 1944 David and Gino's duck didn't stop in chest-high water expecting its cargo to jump off and wade ashore. No, it cruised right up on the shore and deposited them on dry ground. David and Gino thought it was a nifty improvement to their earlier rides.

When they reported they were told to march south along the coastline toward the town of Nettuno. The 45th Division was to protect the beachhead in case the Germans counter attacked. That night German fighter planes strafed the area. Additionally, artillery fire came in sporadically from the Alban hills to the east and kept everyone jumping. It was finally decided that most Allied activity would be accomplished after dark as the Germans held unobstructed views of everything happening from those hills.

In an ancient time Anzio was the home of Cicero, the Roman orator. In 445 AD the Vandals made their own amphibious landing at Anzio and proceeded north to sack Rome. Later, during medieval times, the Saracens sacked and destroyed Anzio. They then proceeded down the coastline and started a new town called Nettuno. It was in caves close to this second town that soldiers of the 45th Division located huge casks of a very good light wine. Before long someone had a still operating and was doctoring up the wine. Many canteens were filled with the result and it proved a valuable aid in the fight against the cold and wet environment. It did not improve their marksmanship however. Still, the American GIs were excellent at hitting what they were aiming at.

On February 1st the men of the Second Battalion were instructed to march north to an area just south of the little town of Padiglione. Their destination was near the junction of a road called Nero's Pike and a long-forgotten railroad track. They were told to dig in. The beachhead was to be made secure so they could repulse the inevitable German counter attack. There was a rumor they would eventually break out of the beachhead and attack the *Gustav line* from the rear.

When they reached the place they were assigned David looked around. "Gino, this is really flat. Look, there's not even any gullies for the water to drain off by. When it rains it must just stay right here until it soaks in . . . and there's no cover. There's trees way over there to the left but not a thing to hide behind right here."

Gino took out his shovel, snapped the blade into place, and thrust it into the sandy soil. He commented, "As they told us in basic, 'Dig in or die.'"

When they had their foxhole two feet deep they hit water. At first it was just a trickle but with the next spade the muddy water started seeping in from all sides.

David stopped shoveling and looked around. "Gino, we've got to find higher ground. Hell, it's February. We can't stay in a waterlogged foxhole. Let's find out exactly where our boundaries are."

Gino walked over to his platoon sergeant and suggested they move the platoon to another area where there was some elevation or even to where there was effective cover. He was told to dig in or die. David was sitting on his pack pondering the situation when Gino arrived with the bad news.

"Well, let's figure this out. We shoveled down two feet before we hit water. So if we dig a shallow slip trench less than two feet we can stay above the water table. But that's not a very safe foxhole. So let's take the dirt and build up the ground around it." With that David jumped up and started digging another hole in front of the one he and Gino had already dug. Gino watched as David dug a shallow pit. He threw the dirt in front. He then told Gino to separate the dirt from the sand and to use the dirt to build up the area around their new hole and to spread the sand farther out so that it looked like it was just a normal ground swelling. Other holes would have to be dug for the additional dirt needed.

David said, "We'll let any water that gets into our hole seep into this back hole that we'll make much deeper. With a little bit of effort we can have a decent hole that's only a foot below the original ground surface."

Gino surveyed his friend's handiwork and said, "And we'll have dug foxholes for all our friends, not to mention this wonderful swimming hole out our backdoor."

"Gino!"

"Okay. I'm working on it."

Other members of their platoon observed the work David and Gino were doing and when they hit water themselves they had to dig another and to decide to either imitate David and Gino's efforts or to make it very shallow. Most thought David's hole was too much work, they would only be there a couple of nights at most, and the fighting wouldn't be from the slip trenches anyway.

That night David and Gino lined their hole with their tent halves and fell into a tired slumber. At two in the morning David was awakened by the platoon sergeant. He said David needed to report for sentry duty. He would be relieved in four hours.

The next morning was overcast. David and Gino ate fast and went looking for corrugated tin to cover their new home. They not only had to fight the Germans but also the elements. Later that morning they were assigned to a work crew to store their battalion's excess weaponry and ammunition. In the afternoon it started raining at the same time as the German artillery fire intensified. David and Gino retreated to their fairly dry hole now covered with corrugated tin. Gino turned on his radio and they listened to the BBC and then to CBS where Walter Shirer was broadcasting. Until Germany declared war on the U. S. he had been assigned to the Berlin desk. Now he gave regular talks about what the prevailing attitude of the German citizenry had been, the staunch support the Nazi Party had, the hysteria that Hitler could instigate with his inflammatory speeches, and the work ethic of the German citizen. Every once in a while Gino located "Jerry's Front" and they listened to *Midge at the Mike*. The GIs started calling her "Axis Sally." Sometime during her program, a siren would start to wail and she would seductively articulate with her mouth close to the microphone, "Careful boys, there's danger ahead."

When the Luftwaffe flew over and dropped their payloads they started to include containers filled with hundreds of tiny anti-personnel explosives. Occasionally, David and Gino heard shrapnel from one striking their tin roof. When evening came and they emerged for a work detail they found quite a few of their friends had been injured. They had used their canvas tent halves as shelter. Where it might keep off the rain it didn't do a very good job against small bomb fragments from munitions designed to explode ten feet above the ground.

The next day David noticed most of the platoon had moved their foxholes to the distant reaches of their cordoned area. While eating a hearty breakfast at daybreak David suggested they find some way to take a shower. Gino thought that was funny. No one bathed in a firefight. After eating, David and Gino scurried back to their quarters to wait out the daily dressing-down they would receive from the Alban hills and from the Luftwaffe. Hours later several howitzer rounds landed close by. In fact, there were some long, some short, and a few wide of their foxhole but still fairly close. The firing continued off and on for most of the day. When they emerged for the evening meal and to continue their work of mining the roads and laying concertina wire David realized why the shells had been so close. Someone had painted a red bulls-eye on their corrugated tin roof. The Germans had been sitting in the Alban hills trying their damnedest to hit the bulls-eye. His buddies were a bunch of comedians.

It was at about this time that everyone noticed there were fewer ships providing naval artillery barrages. From headquarters a rumor started making the rounds that the Luftwaffe had begun using unmanned guided missiles and the ships were thinking of leaving altogether. The German bombers came in carrying two missiles each. When they got in a close enough range the bombers let them go. A pilot on the bomber guided the missiles to their target. The Allied Naval Forces had started slinking back to safer waters. Someone in authority came to the infantry's aid and stopped the departure of the ships. The Allied Air Forces then began concentrating their efforts on bombing the fields where the new weapons were flying in from. Later it was determined that the ships would stay close to shore and shell the enemy positions until 1600 hours when the cruisers and most of the destroyers were allowed to mosey out to sea.

It was at about this same time that the Allied fighter planes started sporting a new piece of equipment that let them have a superior advantage—especially at night. They were getting equipped with radar.

The next morning David and Gino heard the first of the thunderous incoming rounds from a railway gun. The men dubbed it the "Anzio Express." From intelligence, rumors started coming around that it was such a large gun the only way it could be moved was by a flat-bed train car. It had a 280 mm barrel and could fire a 500 lb. projectile 36 miles. From then on it fired a few rounds every day. The Germans were big on sound and this weapon made a loud sound and a big crater wherever it hit.

On the 10th of February the Second and Third Battalions were ordered north of Padiglione to relieve units of the First British Division. David and Gino took their new foxhole design and made some improvements. Their new foxhole included a sloping floor dug in the earth. They even floored it level with scraps of lumber leaving a gap underneath where any water seepage could collect and run to the back on the slope and out of the foxhole altogether into a deeper collection reservoir. They carried their corrugated tin with them to their new digs and placed it with the painted side down. A hard rain started that would last off and on into the spring. There was a rumor that the Germans were about ready to attack as a reconnaissance airplane reported new units had been steadily arriving and now the total of the Axis forces were considerably more than the total of the Allied forces.

The beachhead was shaped in a crescent with the middle about ten miles from the coast and the northern and southern ends tapering back to the sea. The northern third of the crescent was manned by the British First Army Division. The southern third was controlled by the US Third Infantry Division. The center was where the 45th called home.

Adolph Hitler told Fieldmarshal Kesselring he specifically wanted this amphibious landing repulsed. It would be good for the morale his eastern troops would need for the upcoming spring offensive on the Russian front. He would send secret weapons to help. Kesselring and his 14th Army Commander, Generaloberst Eberhard von Mackensen, started planning Operation Fischfang. They decided that to attack on the north or on the south would allow the Allied Forces the maximum utilization of their naval guns. So with their superior number of soldiers—9 divisions for the Axis, compared with 6 divisions for the Allies, a recently acquired battalion of Germany's brand new heavy Panther Tanks, and their new secret weapons they would go right down the Via Anziate into the middle of the beachhead. Their path of attack would be straight for the 45th. It was scheduled for February 16th.

At the evening meal on February 11 the Allied Forces were served a hot meal and Coca Cola to drink. This was the first bottled soda served at their mess since leaving the states and most of the men were grateful. As they were to soon learn, Coca Cola, the duck, the railway gun, fighter-equipped radar, and the Hs-293 missiles would not be the only innovations first used at Anzio. The new German secret weapons included remote-controlled demolition vehicles and Neger-manned torpedoes. The Allies countered with fake tanks.

Every day the Navy guns shelled the Alban hills in retaliation against the daily German artillery barrage. Every night the infantry forces mined the roads and fortified their positions. It rained. And it was cold.

On 16 February 1944 the skies cleared and the rain paused. However, the sandy marshy areas of the beachhead were saturated with water and, although the living conditions were terrible for David and his fellow soldiers, they were also no place for tanks, or any vehicle for that matter. The Germans came anyway. The main concentration of their forces charged right down the Via Anziate toward the six-mile sector containing the 45th Infantry Division. The Germans held a three-to-one manpower advantage and expected to easily overrun their objective. The Panzer tanks were augmented by a new weapon of small remote-controlled vehicles containing explosive charges. Both the tanks and these new weapons became stuck and inoperable when they left the hard surface of the Via Anziate. They were easy pickings for the Allied's lighter tank-destroyers. With the main attack against the 45th in the middle there were also diversionary attacks to the north against the British and to the south against the Third Infantry. By the end of the day the Allied Forces had held and the Germans suffered 1,531 casualties. They came back at midnight with lighter tanks and a larger number of infantry. By dawn they had opened a wide gap between the 157th Infantry and the 175th Infantry. The Luftwaffe attacked the center at dawn and was followed by three regiments of infantry and 60 tanks. They proceeded to push back the 45th Infantry along a front two miles wide and a mile deep. To support the overmatched 45th the Navy guns and shore-based artillery pieces blasted away at the advancing German troops. Three companies of tanks came over from the First Armored Division and Air Support flew 700 missions against the advancing Germans. In the afternoon Mackensen rotated his German units and these new troops continued the attack, trying to broaden their penetration. The 45th fought valiantly and as they fell back they concentrated their efforts and began pushing against the onslaught. The fight continued throughout the night and the next day in a seesaw battle with first one force getting the edge and then the other. During the night of the 18th Mackensen ordered all of his reserve troops to spearhead the advance specifically against the 180th in a last ditch effort to break the beachhead into two halves.

David and what was left of the 180th Regiment tried to hold their ground but, with almost constant fighting for three days and nights, their abilities were on their last bit of strength. Just when it looked like they would be overrun and every man killed or captured, the Germans stopped and pulled back. They had also suffered heavy losses and decided, even if successful, the advantages they gained would not hold in the long run and it was prudent to fall back and regroup for another attack at a later date.

Mackensen pulled back his main forces but allowed his forces that surrounded the Second Battalion of the 157th Infantry Regiment to continue. They had this hard-fighting group of the 45th Division trapped in a series of caves. Tanks pulled up to the openings and fired inside point-blank. Then the German infantry scooted into the pitch-black recesses for hand-to-hand combat. Mackensen also allowed limited attacks to the north and to the south but after another day he pulled back all his troops, leaving a whopping number of casualties and the remnants of the Allied 157th Second Battalion lost among the corpses of fallen comrades and adversaries.

During the ensuing months there were other attacks by the German forces. All were repulsed with the factory changing hands several times. By the first week in March the fighting had deteriorated to night-time raids on both sides. The Germans had suffered so many casualties they were not strong enough to man an offensive and the Allied Forces were not strong enough to break out of the beachhead.

David and Gino soon became adept at the procedure and every night they went out armed to the hilt. Usually they came back with at least one prisoner and sometimes many more. Gino led with the prisoners following, their hands on their heads, in single file. David walked in the rear now carrying a Browning Automatic Rifle. They would march into camp an hour or so before dawn, turn in their prisoners to battalion headquarters for questioning, and sack out fully clothed in their foxhole.

By the first of May the Allied Forces at Anzio had suffered 4,400 dead, 18,000 wounded, and 6,800 captured. They had non-combat casualties totaling 37,000 from trench-foot, malaria, and other diseases. These were mainly because of the soggy ground, water-logged foxholes, lack of dry clothing, and a plague of mosquitoes.

With the spring came reinforcements. The Allied brass on the beachhead started planning for a breakout. In the second week of May General Clark and his Fifth Army broke through the *Gustav line*. The British Eighth Army overran the town of Cassino and the Polish forces captured the rubble that was now the deserted and ruined Benedictine Monastery of Monte Cassino. They immediately headed after the retreating German 10th Army.

Mackensen was ordered to send most of his forces to cover the retreating 10th Army. When the Allied Forces on the beachhead were willing to make the effort they found it easy to break free. They quietly moved their forces to the eastern perimeter, leaving inflated fake tanks in their original positions. The illusion given was that everything was still normal. After the breakout they attacked and routed the forces Mackensen left behind. They captured the Alban hills and then divided up, sending a small force toward their assignment of blocking the retreating 10th Army and the remainder up Highway 6 toward Rome. Officially, Rome was liberated on the 4th of June 1944—two days before D-Day.

Prior to the breakout from the beachhead, on the first of May a jeep drove up to where Fox Company was dug in. A second lieutenant told Captain Marcinko that Corporal Calhoun was wanted at Battalion Headquarters immediately and for him to bring his gear.

CHAPTER 18—GENEVIEVE
Provence, France – Middle of May 1944

When David arrived at Battalion Headquarters everyone who was anyone in the 180th was there. They were all seated facing a stern, standing Colonel Fulbright, who said he did his best thinking on his feet. His chair was offered to David. After saluting everyone but the clerk taking notes, David sat in the proffered chair wondering what was going on. Maybe, he thought, they had figured out that almost everyone he shot was just wounded or that he had a definite fear of the monstrous German tanks. He also feared the numerous mines and their trip wires, machine gun nests, all forms of artillery, and especially the crazed lunatics running at him with their bayonets slicing the air. In fact, there wasn't much in this war he did not have a high regard for. He felt like he could hold his own fighting any man in a no-holds-barred contest but give the scrawniest misfit a weapon and the game was played on a different field with different rules.

The meeting was about something else. General de Gaulle wanted to get an urgent message to the Seeker and, since no one but David knew what he looked like, he was the logical choice for its delivery. De Gaulle even sent the name of a small village where it was thought the Seeker might be located. The message to be delivered was in code with instructions that it was to be memorized then destroyed. David was all for the secret mission until Colonel Fulbright mentioned he would be parachuted in on a moonless night. That's when David's knees began shaking. He couldn't say he wouldn't do it—that he was afraid. Somehow, he had to come to grips with his fear. Later, he met Paul Aragon who told him how easy parachute jumping was. David started to feel a bit better.

Colonel Fulbright impressed upon David's conscience the importance of the mission and the fact that General de Gaulle had specifically requested David be the man to get the job done. The colonel said someone would take care of his personal belongings and, until he left on the assignment, he would be reassigned to headquarters.

David Blaine had never received parachute training so Colonel Fulbright had requested and received permission to have another GI go along. That's where Paul came in. He was a career Army sergeant of French descent and spoke semi-fluent French—just well enough to get and give information. He told David he had five combat jumps under his belt and scads of training jumps. With a smile he added that this little foray into his family's native country was going to be nothing but a piece of cake. He spent an hour preparing both of their chutes and another hour acquainting David with several methods paratroopers' used to steel up their nerves before actually thrusting their bodies into the black of night from two miles up. Paul said they would need to land with their knees bent and roll to the ground on impact. Like most of the Calhoun men, David had a phobia of heights. He couldn't believe his country needed him to this extent. He didn't expect, nor did he receive, the least bit of sympathy from Colonel Fulbright or anyone else who was present at the meeting. It appeared to David, they cared not whether he had ever jumped from an airplane or even what his opinion on the matter might be.

David tried to remember where the Seeker said his family's farm was located. He remembered being told there was a waterfall the Seeker played in when he was a boy so one had to be fairly close. Also that it was in a small creek that flowed into a larger river just north of their farm. The Seeker said the farm was on the east slope of a hill, allowing good morning sun and adequate drainage for their grapes. With this information and a day studying Colonel Fulbright's topographical maps and reconnaissance aerial photos David decided on the probable farm. He committed to memory the lay of the land, distances, landmarks, and the compass coordinates going from one to another. Later, he told the pilot where the target drop should be but was informed by the plane's navigator it would be pretty much a lucky accident if he and Paul were dropped any closer than a mile from any particular point. They would do their best.

The flight went fairly smoothly. The small British Mosquito reconnaissance airplane sneaked into France over a desolate part of her southern coast, stayed away from populated areas, and flew at a high altitude. Everyone aboard breathed oxygen through mouth-pieces attached to flexible tubes. The plane dropped to twelve thousand feet at the place they thought approximated David's target. When word came that they were approaching the drop-off zone David had already decided he would just walk to the fuselage door, snap his chute onto the drop line, pull the door back, and jump out. The parachute was rigged to open on its own. He could do this.

Paul was so laid back he slept most of the way. When the green light came on he stretched, stuffed his beret in his back pocket, and nonchalantly walked over to David. Like a funeral director, he took David lightly by the elbow and said it was time. Before David knew what was going on Paul had him at the fuselage door, both of their lines snapped, and told him to yell "Vive la France," before shoving him out.

The night was cold and thin and dark. David couldn't get any air into his lungs. Hurtling through a black nothingness, David's heart lodged in his throat. His eyes watered, his stomach turned, his pulse raced as he surged at break-neck speed down, down, down. Stygian black, the night sucked up everything it touched.

David and Paul were only forty yards apart when they landed, David in a tree and Paul in the river. With the help of the sound of rushing water and the swishing of the tree branches the night enveloped them into tiny cocoons of isolation, letting neither know what happened to the other.

Paul, entangled in his parachute harness, died when it dragged him under and, gasping for air, his lungs filled with water. David, high in a tree, swung to and fro, his feet not touching anything of substance. After a while his pulse rate slowed and he tried to figure a way down. He unfastened his parachute and, holding on, used it to swing to a stout enough branch to hold his weight. He had to climb higher in the tree to free the chute. When he had it yanked free and wrapped into the smallest bundle he could, he stuffed it under his shirt. With his jaw set and without looking down, he slowly descended the tree, jumping the last eight feet.

David lost the French military pistol Colonel Fulbright gave him. After burying his parachute, he spent several minutes with a tiny flashlight searching around the base of the tree. When he decided he couldn't waste any more time he tossed his extra cartridges into the river and went looking for Paul. Eventually he came to the conclusion Paul must have landed in the river and been swept away. Time was precious. He had to go on by himself.

Two hours after midnight David made it to the farm he had picked from the maps and photos. It fulfilled the necessary criteria. If it wasn't the Seeker's family farm, surely they could head him in the right direction. At this point his inability to speak French was his most debilitating constraint. He decided to hide in their barn until the occupants of the house were up and about. David pushed one side of a double door entrance open just enough for him to slide in. He listened for sleeping animals and, not hearing any, he made a comfortable cubbyhole in the front corner, hidden from anyone's view by bales of stacked hay. He soon descended into a fitful sleep of dreams and dreads and problems unsolved.

David awoke to two excited people arguing. He peered over a bale of hay at an old man and a young woman each trying to convince the other to let him or her have the item. He couldn't understand a word they were saying but the gist was easily determined by their actions. They needed to stash the sack. First the woman stuck it behind a door and then the old man retrieved it and placed it flat down in a corner and positioned a tire directly on top. The woman then slid it out from under the tire and turned around toward the front opening of the barn. Two uniformed German soldiers came in, laughed, walked up to the gentleman and girl, and snatched their treasure.

Removing the sack, they held up a painting. One soldier slapped the other on his back and headed to the barn opening with the stolen goods. The second soldier grabbed the woman when she tried to run after the man with her painting. The retreating soldier, as he exited the barn, said something in German to the man now holding the woman's wrist. The old man picked up a piece of firewood and lunged at the soldier who was now ripping the clothes off the woman. She sobbed, trying to keep her dress together. The soldier slapped her, then let loose for a moment as she brought her hands to her face. He then turned and buried his fist in the face of the charging old man just below his right eye. The old man dropped the firewood, fell back, and melted into the floor motionless. The German turned to the woman, slapped her once more for good measure, and finished ripping her dress and slip away. She stopped resisting, silently shaking with terror.

David quietly stepped from his hiding place, picked up the dropped firewood, and crashed it into the back of the German's skull. With a strong grip David rolled the dead soldier onto the barn floor. The girl was shaking and couldn't stop. She had her hands over her face and when David tried to help her up she began beating them against his chest. He let go of her arm and then offered back her torn dress and slip. She paused, took a good look at David, then began whimpering something in French. David shook his head and went to see about the old man. The woman threw down her clothes, ran to David, grabbed his arm, and started pointing to the front opening of the barn. The other German soldier would be returning in another moment. David laid down the old man. He hadn't had time to see if he was still alive. Of course the woman was right. They'd all be dead if the soldier returned and found them tending to the old man with a dead comrade close by.

David dragged the German behind a stall gate then, laying down his ungainly weapon, stacked four bales of hay close to the barn door. The girl was making an exaggerated motion for him to look through a knothole. With her standing behind him he could see through the knothole that in front of the house sat an open, jeep-like vehicle only larger than any of ours. It contained a driver and an officer and right behind was a large truck with a driver sitting in the cab. The soldier who had absconded with the painting emerged from the back of the canvas-covered truck and went around to talk with its driver.

The woman was now looking out another knothole. She grabbed David's arm and pointed to the house. David understood she was suggesting they had probably spread out when arriving with a few going to the house and two going to the barn.

The German soldier was now coming back. David thought the returning soldier most likely wanted to molest the woman after his friend had finished. David, clutching the piece of firewood, ran to stand behind his four bales of hay. The soldier entered, yelled something in German, and walked toward where he had left his friend and the young woman. He stopped when he saw a brown leather boot extending from under a stall gate. He paused a moment then turned and ran back toward the front opening. David stepped from behind his four bales of stacked hay and met the man just shy of escaping. David swung the firewood, knocking the German to the ground. Leaning against several more bales of hay to David's right was a pitch fork. With one foot on the soldier's chest David reached for the implement and used it to stab the German in the throat. The man died when one prong severed his spinal cord.

David turned and asked how he might get into the house without anyone seeing him. "You . . . you are English?"

"American. I've come to see a man called the Seeker. Presumably your brother."

"Yes, he is. His name is Philippe. Come with me. We'll circle around the servant's quarters and go in through the cooking area, but I want to see about my father first."

"Do you speak German?" David tried to avert his gaze from her pert and firm figure pushing against pale green underwear. He was not doing a very good job.

"Not as good as English. Do you mind turning the other direction? I'm almost naked here." She told him her name was Genevieve. When they had decided the old man was not dead, just unconscious, Genevieve told David he was her father and was too old to take on such a big German. He had fought in the previous war and still considered himself a French soldier.

Genevieve led David out the back of the barn and around another small building, obviously empty, with its door open. He skirted the building after looking in to make sure it actually was empty, arriving at the back door of the main house. David told Genevieve she should stay outside while he went in. If two were sent to the barn then at least two and maybe more had been sent to the house. She reluctantly agreed then told David he would be entering through the kitchen and that she kept knives stuck in a block of wood just to the right of the stove. David thanked her and cautiously crept in.

The sky was starting to come under the influence of a sun still below the horizon. The stars were dimming as David's eyes adjusted to the first vestiges of daylight. However, the kitchen was still dark. He kept to the walls. At the stove he found the knives and grabbed a small paring knife and a hefty carving knife. From somewhere off to his right and deeper in the house he heard a man rifling through papers and yelling something to a soldier in another part of the house. The door leading from the kitchen was a swinging door. It creaked when David pushed it open. However, the German soldier in the next room was making so much noise himself, going through an antique desk, he was oblivious to everything except what he was doing. David squinted as he left the dark kitchen for the lighted parlor area. He silently walked up from behind, grabbed the top of the man's head pulling it back, and slit his throat all in one fluid motion. Blood gushed as the body slumped to the floor.

From the second floor he heard another man yell something. David wiped the blood from the knife on his pants leg and crept up a curved staircase. So far none of the soldiers had been carrying weapons. They were not expecting trouble. They were just retrieving priceless objects of art from the old, the infirm, the women left after the men had been sent to work in German factories. But he couldn't take that for a given. He had to be prepared for any eventuality so he quietly ascended the stairs expecting the man upstairs to be packing a weapon.

No one on the landing. No one in the first bedroom. From a second room a soldier emerged wearing a woman's earrings, necklace, and frilly hat. He was laughing until he saw David in the doorway of the first bedroom holding a large knife. The German picked up a chair and ran straight at David. In the ensuing struggle David dropped the carving knife but had the presence of mind to kick it away from the clutching reach of his adversary. The man was strong, probably knowing one of them was going to die. He gripped David's right wrist with one hand and David's throat with his other. David gouged at the man's eyes. With his left foot David stepped on the man's boot and pushed with his body. With his foot pinned the man fell backward with David now on top. David grabbed the German's throat with both hands and started squeezing the life from him. Genevieve came to David's back and began hitting him with clinched fists.

"You don't have to murder him. He's just a boy. This senseless killing's got to stop."

With the German almost unconscious David relaxed his grip and sat back to look more closely at the scantily dressed woman ravaged by a German one moment and pleading for the life of another in the next. What was with her? There were still three more left and he knew for certain the officer would be carrying a pistol.

"Miss, what's going on here?"

The German soldier had turned on his side with his elbow on the chair cushion and his head in his hand. His other hand was massaging his throat as he made several deep hacks spewing forth bloody spittle.

"I don't think the indiscriminant killing of every German man, woman, and child is the answer." She looked down at the soldier and shuddered. To David she said, "The Gestapo has received orders to confiscate several listed works of art and to send them to Berlin. Our painting was on their list. When they took Charlemagne's Bell, Father Dominique got a glimpse of the list and called us to say they were headed our way for father's Toulouse-Lautrec. The officer outside is Gestapo and these are just recruits he got from the German Army to do the dirty work. See," she pointed at the soldier who was now sitting up, "he doesn't have the Gestapo death-head insignia on his shoulder or lapel."

The soldier looked wild-eyed around the room. David retrieved the carving knife and apprised his captive, with gestures, of his situation. The man put up no further struggle. David gave the paring knife to Genevieve and told her to cut some lamp cord so they could tie his hands. She left and returned in a few minutes with several feet of a stout electrical cord and a black notch in the blade of the paring knife. David sat the man in a chair and tied his hands behind his back to the chair. He had to think. It was still three to one and the officer would be particularly troublesome. He told Genevieve they needed their captive to yell down to the officer asking to have one of the drivers sent up. He needed to say something like he had found an item too heavy to lift. She agreed and spoke in a soothing manner to the young German soldier. She then stopped and, with a hissing sound, drew her finger across her throat. The soldier nodded.

David walked to one of the front windows and quietly raised it, keeping the curtain between him and the window. He then grabbed the back of the chair the German was tied to and tilted it so that the front chair legs and the soldier's feet were off the floor. David then dragged the chair and the soldier to the window so that the soldier had to lean sideways to yell through the opening. Genevieve whispered something in German and the soldier yelled out a condensed version. She kicked his shin and said she didn't know what he said but it wasn't what she told him to say. David grimaced and stuffed a rag in the soldier's mouth.

In a moment the driver of the officer's auto was striding toward the front door. David was down the stairs in a flash. When the unsuspecting driver walked in David was standing behind the front door. David shoved the door to and grabbed the man. It was over fast with the driver spewing blood from his carotid artery and sucking air through a severed windpipe. Soon he was sinking to his knees and falling to the floor. Around his waist he had a brown leather strap with a covered holster holding a Lugar. David took the gun and instantly knew how to end the ordeal.

With Genevieve still in the remnants of her underwear she watched David from the top of the stairs. David stared back. She was silhouetted by sunlight entering through an opposing window. David backed toward the kitchen, turned, and ran outside, past the servant's quarters, around the barn, and came upon the truck from behind. Taking off the safety, he made sure the gun was loaded. Then bending at the waist, he crept to the opened passenger window. He rose and shot the driver in the back of the head while the man was looking in the direction of the house. David pivoted and pointed the gun in the next instant at the Gestapo agent. He was gone.

David ran between the two vehicles to the front stoop of the house. Slowly he opened the door and, standing to one side, peered with one eye into the silent front sitting room. A few feet in front of the stairs stood the German SS officer holding Genevieve by her hair. He had a gun pointed at her temple. He said something in French.

"*Ich bin Amerikaner.*"

"All right then, throw down your weapon and step inside. I won't shoot you. We'll make a trade. You let me drive off with the truck and I'll leave you and the girl alone, never to return, or even to report how you ambushed my men."

David had to have time to think. "How do I know you'll keep your share of the bargain?"

"You don't. You'll just have to take my word for it—the word of an officer of the Third Reich."

"Okay. Here's the gun." David tossed in the carving knife. It made a clattering sound on the wood floor as it landed and slid behind a lamp table. He then stepped into the doorway, pointed, and fired. The Gestapo Officer had been distracted by the knife and, when David fired, was looking to see where the thrown weapon had landed. The bullet traveled true to its mark and blew a small hole in the German's forehead and a sizable hole where it exited at the back of his skull. He fell to the floor still clutching Genevieve's hair. She fell on top of him. Snatching the gun, she jumped up hysterical. She started brandishing the gun at David, holding it high in the air, and shaking it.

"I could've been killed. You could've missed and he would have blown my head off."

David pulled the trigger, firing a second round, this time just over Genevieve's right shoulder. The girl's eyes got big, then wild. She dropped to one knee and fired back striking David in the pelvic area. She then jumped behind the divan.

David lay in the doorway. The old man stepped over and, with one hand holding his head, said in French, "Genevieve, what are you doing? Give me that gun. He shot the German coming at your back with a knife. He wasn't shooting at you."

Genevieve looked behind where she had been standing. The soldier from upstairs had somehow gotten her paring knife, cut his bindings, and come downstairs.

"Oh, Papa. I've done such a bad thing."

Her father groaned, "Help me get him inside. I've got to get hold of Philippe."

Genevieve ran to the doorway. David was now sitting up. "I've been fighting pretty much non-stop since last July, not receiving the first scratch, and now I get shot by a girl pacifist in pale green underwear."

"Shut up." Genevieve took his arm and, with the help of her father, got David to a standing position, then inside to their divan.

"I think I'll be all right, but I have to see Philippe."

The old man muttered something and offered David his cane.

Genevieve said, "I've got to get our painting out of the truck. Can you walk? If you can, I'll crawl in and hand it to you." To her father, she said in French for him to call the village doctor to see about David's little wound.

"Miss, as much as I'll hate to miss the sight, I think you should put on a dress or something before you crawl into their truck."

Dressed and outside, Genevieve swung the tailgate of the big truck open and jumped inside. She pulled back a big tarp, threw it outside, and yelled to David, "There's at least a dozen paintings in here, one small statue, and the bell. We've got to get these out and hide them in the barn. Will you help me?"

David grumbled and told Genevieve to hold on while he pushed both sides of the barn's double front doors open. Back at the truck he removed the dead driver and gingerly got into the cab, then slowly backed it toward the opening, getting the tailgate about two feet shy of the posts on either side. A few minutes later Genevieve had spread the tarp in the center of the barn and started handing him the stolen treasure from the truck's cargo hold.

"What about the bell? Is it all that important?"

Genevieve gave him a stern look. She said, "That bell was given to our church by three angels in December of the year 800 AD. It was rung at noon on Christmas day to commemorate the crowning of Charlemagne as Emperor."

"Then I guess we better figure some way to get it down and out of sight." David looked at the massive bell on the edge of the cargo bed. Evidently, when they first managed to get it loaded the men had decided that was good enough. The farther back into the bed they moved it the farther forward they would have to move it again when it had to be unloaded.

"Do you have any stout rope? We'll need two: one about seventy-five feet and the other twice that long."

David backed the officer's vehicle beside the truck and at a right angle. When Genevieve returned dragging two long ropes David had her tie one end of the longest rope around the car's rear axle. The other end he swung over a yardarm sticking out from the barn high up near its roof line. The yardarm was a normal conveyance used to drag bales of hay, or other heavy items, up to and then pulled through a second floor opening to be stored. Normally, a farm-hand used the pulley on the end of the yardarm but David thought the weight of the bell would be too much at the end of a six-foot yardarm, so he positioned the rope over the yardarm up against the barn exterior planking. He had Genevieve attach the loose end of the rope, with a clever knot he patiently instructed her to tie, to the bell's ears that would normally rest in a cradle, allowing it to swing when rung.

    David pulled the officer's vehicle away from the truck until the rope stretched taunt. Then a bit further and the bell tipped and rose. Suspended in air half in the truck bed and half out the bell hung directly under the yardarm. He took the shorter rope and wrapped one end of it around the middle of the bell. With the loose end of the rope he walked into the barn, shoved the two dead soldiers out of his way, and encircled it one time high up around a stout cylindrical post in the center of the barn and directly behind the tarp holding the other works of art. He then walked back to the truck, letting the taunt rope slide through his hands, and tied it's end to the truck's carriage. When he pulled the truck forward the bell swung toward the center post. Then he had Genevieve get into the officer's vehicle. He told her to put it in neutral keeping her foot on the brake and, as he pulled the big truck forward, she was to let off on the brake so that the smaller vehicle would roll back. In this manner they worked the bell into the recesses of the barn and eventually directly over a bare spot on the tarp. Genevieve then slowly backed up a few more feet until the bell came to rest beside the piece of bloodied firewood. David untied the rope from around the middle of the bell and untied the rope's other end from the big truck. He then untied the rope from the top of the bell and from the smaller vehicle. David looped the two ropes and tied them off with a loose end, then he drove both vehicles to the front of the house while Genevieve put the two ropes back where she had found them.

    Back in the barn, they wrapped the paintings and small statue in protective gunnysacks and stacked them beside the bell. On top they arranged bales of hay. When they were finished they stood back and admired their work. David decided to break open another bale and spread the loose sections in a hap-hazard arrangement just to make it look like the stack had been there for several months.

"How did the angels come to deliver the bell?"

"Our church was finished being built in the previous year but it lacked a bell. The bell tower was there but no bell. When the Pope let word out to his churches that he would be crowning Charlemagne at noon on Christmas Day he asked for them all to commemorate the occasion by ringing their bells. Our Father prayed for weeks that a bell would be delivered. Then, around the middle of December, a wagon came into town pulled by two oxen. It was escorted by three men wearing silk costumes—the likes of which no one had ever seen before. Also, they didn't speak a language anyone could understand. They went about their work of installing the bell, then left.

"It's made of bronze with no foundry markings and has the most mellow and clear sound when being struck. The Father said it must have been angels who delivered it. The authorities in Rome said they didn't send one and no one outside of our area was even aware we needed one. Over the years the church has been rebuilt two times. Each time the repositioning of the bell and ringing it consecrated the new building."

"Well, I'm glad I had a hand in saving it."

"David, you're so resourceful. I'm sorry I shot you. How do you feel?"

"If it were not for the occasional pain, we would suffer from the loss of that great joy we feel when it has subsided." David wondered where he had heard that and for what reason he now repeated it. There were times when he truly astonished himself.

Genevieve looked incredulously at David. She was speechless.

Back in the house Genevieve introduced David to her father, Pepe. The old man had a sizable swelling on the right side of his face. His eye was completely closed. However, he profusely shook David's hand, kissed his fingertips, held them out at face level, and said something which Genevieve interpreted for David as, "You were magnificent."

Genevieve told David to remove his pants. David looked at her in disbelief. She reached out, took him by his hand, and led him to a massive dining table. There she unbuckled his belt, pulled out his shirt, unfastened his pants, and pulled them down. She made David sit on the edge, then lean back. From his dangling feet she took off his shoes, socks, and lowered pants. She then raised his feet and swiveled him around so he was now lying prone on the table waist high. Pepe retrieved a cushion from the front sitting room and placed it under David's head before retiring to the divan to let his throbbing head rest. Also he didn't want to see whatever his daughter was up to.

Genevieve told David his underpants would have to go. David's face blushed bright red. She said there wasn't much blood but without being able to see the wound she couldn't dress it. David squirmed. She left, returning a moment later with a small towel. David groaned, removed his last vestment of modesty, and covered himself as best he could with the kitchen towel.

Genevieve poked and prodded, gently caressing the wound from all sides. She noticed how his flesh quivered when she traced around the area with her fingernail. With David squirming and shying from her touch she thought she had better stop. In French she said to herself, "I am so naughty."

"The bullet is deep inside. All I can do is pour alcohol over it. That'll kill any infection until the doctor comes." She adjusted David's towel. "Of course, the alcohol will burn. I could pat the area with a wet cloth or maybe blow on it."

David looked around for Pepe. "I'd feel safer if I waited for the doctor in the barn."

Genevieve gazed at his little-boy, worried face and winked.

Surely the doctor would be here shortly thought David. Moments later he arrived. Stepping over the dead driver, around the officer, and past the man beside the desk and the one draped over the railing at the bottom of the stairs he shook his head and said "My, my. What do we have here?" then quickly assessed Genevieve's preparation. He asked David what happened. David looked at Genevieve and said he was under the spell of a witch. The doctor glanced at Genevieve then at David. He laughed and proceeded to examine the wound.

Eventually, he gave David a hefty dose of morphine. Genevieve gave the doctor all the particulars while David descended into unconsciousness. The doctor opened his black bag, retrieved a few tools, dipped them in a sanitizing jar, and made a small incision at the wound. He probed around looking for the bullet. It had pierced David's pelvic bone, broke off a piece, and was hiding somewhere in the soft tissue. He couldn't locate the troublesome projectile and finally had to lengthen and deepen the incision. He now could pull back more of the tissue and give himself a larger discovery area. The bullet was soon found behind the broken piece of pelvic bone. He removed it using a pair of needle-nosed pliers. Thirty minutes later the doctor had removed the broken bone fragment, sutured the incision, and cleansed and bandaged David's entire right hip.

While they waited for David to revive, Philippe and two more resistance fighters came, loaded the dead German soldiers, and headed off to dispose of the two vehicles and the seven bodies. They left behind several cans of precious gasoline for Pepe to hide.

That afternoon Genevieve prepared a meal. The doctor suggested Pepe break open a bottle of his hidden cognac. He said David would be in a lot of pain soon and he couldn't spare anymore of his meager supply of morphine. David would have to endure. He had made a sizable cut to find the slug and a generous dose of cognac applied every so often was the only thing he could determine that would dull the senses and was in decent supply. Pepe said he had been looking for a good reason and suggested Genevieve ask David if he would join him. They'd get drunk.

The doctor said David should not be moved for two or three weeks and then for only short walks. His wound would be slow to heal. He asked Genevieve what she planned on saying to the Germans when they came looking for the missing men and their trucks.

"I'll give it some thought."

"Also, you'll have to come up with an excuse for harboring a person who doesn't speak French, who's been shot, and Pepe here, who looks like he got into a fight with a gorilla." The doctor turned to David. "Son, are you allergic to anything?"

"Bees. I don't know of anything else."

"Pepe, in the morning you'll need to take a sack to one of your hives and bring back a couple of bees." Receiving a nod in reply the doctor turned back to David and asked, "What kind of reaction do you have?"

"I swell up, my heart-beat races, and I have a hard time breathing. It lasted for about four or five hours."

"It lasted?"

"Yeah, I've only been stung once."

"Okay, Genevieve here's what we'll do. I'll put a quarantine sign on your front door. When they drive up let David stick his hand into Pepe's sack. You'll need to talk to them for a couple of minutes to let David's reaction get going, then let them see David, and usher them out the door as soon as you can. You'll have to inject him with this syringe. He should be back to normal in a few minutes. Just pray David doesn't have a severe reaction." The doctor turned to David, "I'll put two syringes in the refrigerator. When they drive up Pepe will bring you one of the two syringes while Genevieve is helping you get stung. Hide the syringe somewhere handy. If you get to the point where you can't breathe you'll have to give yourself an injection. Be sure and squirt out the air first." The doctor paused, looked down, and then said, "David, you can't wait to the last minute to give yourself the injection. It'll take a few minutes to get into your system and you could die in the meantime from suffocation."

David was coming off the effects of the morphine and the pain was very similar to the time he got hit in the chest by a hundred-mile-an-hour fast ball in high school. Pepe saw the pain in David's eyes and poured him a generous measure of cognac.

That night Philippe came in to see David. "You did a number on those Germans. I'm proud of you. How did you learn to shoot like that?"

David's head was reeling. He had finished one bottle of cognac with Pepe and now was working on another by himself. Pepe was asleep in a chair and Genevieve had gone to bed earlier after spending most of the evening cleaning up the blood and putting her house back in order. She also had a headache from worrying about what she was going to say to the Gestapo.

"Philippe, I have a message for you from General de Gaulle. Get me a piece of paper and I'll write it down. It's in code."

"So they chose you to get it to me because no one knows what I look like. That pig Barbee killed Jean Moulin in interrogation last year. He was the only other person."

"Please, Philippe."

"Sure, buddy. Here."

David wrote the best he could then read it. Philippe made marks in the margin of the paper so he could decipher David's scribbling.

"Hillbilly, you look terrible." He looked around the room. "I'll be in touch. We'll be in the woods tomorrow when the Germans come. If there's any problem we'll take them out. You go back to sleep. You sure made a hit with my family." With that he turned off the lamp, picked up his father, and carried him to the master bedroom.

The next morning, Pepe brought in a fresh sack of bees. Genevieve cooked breakfast then proceeded to pull up a chair to David's bed. She laid her make-up on a bedside table. Pepe brought in a bowl of ink he had made from crushed black walnut husks. Genevieve dipped a wash cloth in the blackened water and dabbed David's hands and wrists up to his elbow. She then opened his nightshirt and did the same to his neck and upper chest. To his face she used rouge to draw blotches and mascara to add black centers. She slicked his hair with pomade, sprinkled him with sickly perfume, pulled the curtains shut, and lit several candles. She fixed Pepe in a similar fashion on a cot in the corner of the room. Genevieve put everything away and they sat waiting on the inevitable.

They were not disappointed. At ten a.m. a car drove up with a driver and two German Gestapo officers. Pepe handed David the sack of bees while Genevieve ran downstairs for a syringe. David stuck his hand in the sack. Pepe had filled the sack with bees and David was stung several times before he could get his hand back out. Pepe twisted the top of the bag closed, jumped onto his cot, and pulled the covers up to his head and over the sack of bees. David hid the syringe under a corner of his pillow and waited. He was already feeling tight around the throat. Last time he had been stung only once and had swollen up grotesquely. By the time his parents had gotten him to the hospital he could hardly breathe. This time he had been stung ten, maybe twelve times.

The first Gestapo officer knocked on the door. Genevieve opened it only a sliver. In impeccable French she was asked if they might come in. Genevieve answered that the house had been quarantined and it wasn't safe for them to enter. The German pushed open the door, shoving Genevieve against the wall. He briskly walked in and was followed by a second, and junior, officer. Genevieve regained her composure and walked to the kitchen asking the men if they would like a cup of tea. They looked at each other then at Genevieve.

"How do you have tea? No one has tea or coffee."

"My tea is herbal. I boil roots from the sassafras tree and mix in different flowers. It tastes quite good."

"I think we'll pass." The second officer left the kitchen and started wandering around the house. "We're looking for a party of two vehicles and seven men who should have come by here early yesterday morning. Did you see them?"

"Yes, they were here. They took a painting."

The second officer burst into the room and whispered something into the first officer's ear. He turned to Genevieve. "Tell me about this quarantine."

"The doctor doesn't know what it is. He said it could be smallpox. You gentlemen should wash when you leave and have your clothing fumigated. The disease has already started to affect my father's mind. If it is smallpox they'll both be dead within a week."

"Why aren't you infected?"

"Some people have a built in immunity. It affects different people in different ways. Other than that I do not know. The doctor said we have not had a case here since he's been practicing so he's not sure. Would you like to see them?"

"We are not as gullible as you might think. Could this not be a ploy to keep them from being sent to work in our factories?"

"My father is too old and my brother is exempt. He attends Sorbonne University."

"Show them to us and we'll make up our own minds."

Genevieve walked slowly up the stairs. Halfway she stopped and said, "Don't get too close. Occasionally they have coughing fits and, if you get spit on . . . well, just don't get spit on."

When they reached the room she opened the door from the hallway. Both German agents looked in. David's head was swollen to twice its normal size and he was wheezing. The candles were giving the room an eerie glow. When they looked at Pepe he laughed and pulled the covers over his head. The second officer tugged at the first officer's sleeve. The first officer pulled away and walked confidently into the room and to Pepe's bed. He snatched the covers back.

Pepe released the bees. They headed for the officer. They didn't like being contained in the sack and felt threatened by the man towering over them. They chased him out of the room, down the stairs, and out the front door.

Genevieve took the second man to one side and said, "I speak a little German. When the men came for the painting they talked freely with each other thinking they couldn't be understood. They found my father's stash of cognac and proceeded to drink several bottles before loading the remaining bottles on their truck. One of them mentioned a meeting with a Spanish art collector for sometime last night. They couldn't remember what the signal was. I took it that the signal was coming from a ship or large boat moored in a deserted harbor. Anyway, they thought they would get enough money for the items in their truck to be rich and live in neutral Spain for the rest of the war. They were happy."

"Honey, did you say they found my cognac?"

"Yes, Papa. They found it all, both cases."

"Oh. Woe is me. I need that cognac. How will I make it through this nightmare?"

"I'm sorry, Mademoiselle. I'll inform my superior. Do you need anything?"

"No. Just leave before you become infected."

He hurried out the door and off they drove. Genevieve ran to the refrigerator, grabbed the second syringe, and ran upstairs to inject David. He was unconscious and not breathing. Pepe sat on a chair beside David's bed.

"Genevieve, he tried to give himself the injection but fell against his pillow unconscious so I gave it to him. I hope he'll be okay."

Genevieve put the back of her hand under his nose and against his mouth. She said, "I can feel only the slightest movement of air. Maybe it will be enough." She reached under the covers and placed her hand over his chest. "His heart is racing." Using her fingernail she flicked off the stingers she found still attached to his hand then gave him a second injection. "I hope his body can handle it." Pulling up another chair they waited.

After two hours and no change in his condition, Genevieve went downstairs and put two pans of water to boil. She needed to wash David's clothes she had hidden. After looking them over she decided to toss them and to give him some of Philippe's. After all they were about the same height.

Genevieve took a pot of hot water and several washcloths upstairs. She pulled back David's covers and redressed his wound, sponging him as she went. It took her an hour to give David a sponge bath and to change his nightshirt. The make-up came off easily but the black walnut stain would remain for several days. David was still unconscious, but clean, when she retreated to the kitchen.

Soon, Pepe came charging down the stairs saying David was awake and asking for her. She ran her fingers through her hair, took a quick look in a mirror, and ran up the stairs two at a time. David said he would like something to eat.

That afternoon Pepe and David drank two more bottles of cognac. Genevieve removed all the candles, opened the curtains, fixed a decent meal, and sat in a rocking chair in a corner of the room reading a book.

Gerard was the head of the local Milice. He received the report of the two Gestapo agents and wondered if Pepe and Philippe were really as sick as the report suggested. The Gestapo officers found the truck and jeep hidden behind sand dunes on a deserted stretch of the coast. No sign of the pilfered art or of the thieves themselves. Gerard committed the particulars to memory before filing it away.

Over the next few days David and Pepe put the cognac to good use. One afternoon Pepe took out a thick pad of paper and had Genevieve ask David to talk about his participation in the war. He had always dreamed of being a writer and here was his hero. He just needed the story.

Pepe also had Genevieve ask David for permission to use his war experiences in a book. David said, "Sure, as long as you give me an autographed copy."

David told about his trip to North Africa on the HMS *Queen Elizabeth*, capturing the two Gestapo agents with Philippe, and observing the men in the war room making tactical decisions. He told them about the invasion of Sicily and Italy, of fighting up to the *Gustav Line* at Mount Cassino, and being stranded on the beachhead at Anzio. He didn't have to embellish his story—Pepe did that. When he said he carried fifty pounds of gear, Pepe wrote seventy-five. When he said he captured three German soldiers or ten Italian soldiers gave themselves up, Pepe wrote down David shooting dozens before the scant few remaining surrendered to keep from being annihilated. He didn't even mention his fear of the tanks but Pepe wrote down how he single-handedly attacked those same tanks with grenades he placed on their treads and how he climbed on top and waited for someone to open the locked hatch to come out and repair the damage. Every now and then Genevieve looked to see what her father was writing and shook her head in disbelief. She was appalled at men and their penchant for war.

A month went by and one afternoon while Pepe was in one of his fields tending grapes, David asked Genevieve why she tried to save the German soldier wearing her jewelry after another had molested her.

She thought for a moment then pensively said, "David, he was not at fault. I was studying psychology before the war broke out and it's my belief that armed combat provides some psychological need for men. Do you have animals?"

"A dog. He died of old age just after my enlistment."

"Well, dogs don't have a problem reconciling the fact that they are a dog, a terrier or spaniel, and Fido all at the same time. They fulfill their need to be unique and individual and their need to be affiliated with a group. Man on the other hand has a problem dealing with these same issues. On the one hand he wants to assert his uniqueness, his individuality, his articulated oneness with his need to be accepted by the tribe, to be a part of a larger whole.

"This conflict between his need for individualization and his need for affiliation causes internal turmoil and tension. It's my opinion that combat and putting his life in peril is the only activity that allows man to satisfy this dualistic need."

"Genevieve, you are amazing. I know of only one other woman who could captivate my interest as you do."

"Did you love her?"

"Yes, I did—still do. But she had higher aspirations than what I could provide. She waited till almost time for me to be shipped overseas before writing to tell me I wasn't good enough."

"It sounds like you were not meant for each other. The easiest way to get over a lost love is to find another."

That evening, a few hours after dark, Philippe showed up. He slapped David on his back and said the Allies had landed on the coasts of Normandy. The Resistance was presently blowing up bridges and train tracks to keep the Germans from mobilizing their forces from all around France to counter attack. David asked if that was the message.

Philippe said, "No. General de Gaulle will be asking General Eisenhower to consider bestowing the honor of liberating Paris on the French troops. If he allows it General de Gaulle will walk down the Champs Elysees once the city has been secured and give a speech. He wants us to walk with him to show the members of the Communist Party, whose headquarters is in Paris, how big a following he has."

"Philippe, that's wonderful."

"David, there is another item of news. A badly decomposed body has been found a few miles downstream. He was wrapped in a parachute and carrying a French military Pistol, model 1928, with six loaded clips. Are you connected?"

"Yeah, we parachuted in together. He was to help me. I had never parachuted before nor do I speak French. I landed in a tree and he must have landed in the river. I looked for him."

"The authorities are trying to determine what he was doing here. If there is any problem a woman in Gerard's office will be notifying whoever might need a warning. She has our number. I hope you don't get a call until I get back. Of course, by then, Gerard will be stripped of any authority he might have anyway."

After six more weeks of recuperation David was walking with the aid of Pepe's crutch and enjoying the autumn. He knew his leg was not healing properly but hesitated to say anything. There was no medicine anyway and the doctor was in the custody of the Milice. One evening, as they sat in the garden listening to the crickets chirp, David asked Genevieve what would be her psychological solution to war.

"David, what do you call the German soldiers?"

"Krauts or Jerries. I think we called them Heinies in World War 1 . . . or, maybe it was Huns."

"By giving them a name you link them together. It makes killing them easier if you see them as one big enemy instead of lots of individual enemies. By doing this, some even feel it's okay to kill women and children, after all they're just Krauts. They do the same to you. The Americans are called Yanks and the British, Tommys. Philippe says that on the Russian front no one is taken prisoner. The Russians shoot every last German they capture and the Germans shoot the Russians. Women, children, and the elderly are simply collateral damage of no consequence one way or another."

"First I think we need to achieve a general awareness. We need to look for indicators that tell us we're heading into a war-like situation and we need an arsenal of diplomatic weaponry to divert our compulsions."

In the house, the telephone rang.

"Genevieve, you have a brilliant mind. I have a friend back home like you. I can sit and listen to him talk for hours. His observations are razor sharp and his keen wit keeps his newspaper prospering. He and I went to school together. He's the smartest man I know. You may be the smartest woman."

"I accept the compliment. However, I would prefer to be thought of as pleasant to look at."

David reached out and took her hand. "Genevieve, I think you're beautiful."

Pepe came running out of the house carrying a lighted flashlight. "Genevieve, ask David if he can ride. We have to go. Gerard found a parachute and a gun like the one on the man they found in the river. He's heading here with some of his men to talk to us."

After being informed of the situation, David asked, "Pepe has a car?"

"It's not much of one and he's not a very good driver but he has a lot of fun trying. You'll probably get stuck a few times, maybe, run into the fence or off the road, but it's all he's got and he says you have precious little time to use it. Go get your things. He'll want to leave as soon as he gets it running."

"All I've got is a fountain pen and that German Lugar. They're up in my room."

Pepe held his beret and ran to the run-down shed at the back of his property. Over his shoulder he yelled, "Genevieve, we need sandwiches."

In twenty minutes Pepe had the hay removed, the distributor cap replaced, the tank filled with gas, and two large metal cans strapped to the back of Philippe's Italian roadster. It hummed to life and Pepe pulled up to an astonished David.

"Genevieve, that's an Alfa Romeo racer."

"Yes, I know. It's actually a 6C made in 1930. It cost Papa a mountain of francs but it was worth it. He used it to induce Philippe to enter college so he could be a doctor. He's now the envy of all his friends and the most eligible bachelor in the area."

"Get in. Get in. We don't have time to waste. Genevieve, you got those sandwiches?"

"Yes, Papa." She handed Pepe the sandwiches and turned to David, "Something to remember me by." She bent down and kissed David with a slightly open mouth. With her teeth she bit his upper lip then ran her tongue under it, comforting it, caressing it.

Pepe gunned the throttle and Genevieve pulled away. David was sweating, his breath in short gasps as he thought of Genevieve wearing pale green. Pepe pushed down the clutch, shifted into first gear, and gave a nudge on the accelerator. Away they sped.

"Philippe told me to take you north and east if Gerard came looking. He thinks your unit has come to France through Marseilles and headed north along our eastern border. That's only two hundred miles but we have to take roads not frequently traveled and for the first ten miles I won't be using headlights." Pepe gripped the corner post holding the windshield and looked at David. "You better hang on."

David only understood a few of the words Pepe said but figured everything out during the first couple of minutes—especially the bit about holding on. He thought about all the things that had happened to him so far in this war and now he was speeding along a narrow winding road in a bright red racing car without lights. A crazy Barney Oldfield was trying to hold on to the steering wheel and speed-shifting like they were racing in Monaco's Grand Prix. He felt the adrenalin rush. He liked Pepe. He might have to come back after the war ends. Pepe would need help getting his vineyard up and running. Then, of course, there was Genevieve. There were lots of possibilities.

CHAPTER 19—FRANCE
Northeast France – Late July 1944

Pepe was a better driver than Genevieve had led David to believe. They raced along in the dark, turning corners just before running off the road. Pepe must've traveled these roads before. There's no way a man in his sixties could drive a car this fast, by starlight, and not hit something or spin off the road unless he knew the road he was traveling. David was mighty thankful when Pepe decided they had traveled far enough to turn on the headlights.

When the sky lightened with the breaking of day, David was able to give Pepe an appreciable look. He was sporting a red beret, a navy silk scarf, and black kidskin racing gloves. Clutching and down-shifting gears when entering corners, accelerating through and up-shifting on the straight-aways with barely a perceptible lurch, Pepe and the machine were one. David was impressed. Pepe might have been a race-car driver in his youth.

Occasionally, Pepe veered to the side of the road, pulled out a map, said a few undecipherable words, and continued. About mid-morning, they started running into burned-out hulks. There were tanks, overturned jeeps, wrecked troop trucks, destroyed artillery pieces, and dead soldiers. Pepe stopped when he came upon a small group of soldiers wearing surgical masks, placing dead GIs onto stretchers, and loading them in a large covered truck. Pepe motioned to David that they needed information.

"Pardon me, what Allied unit passed through? I'm so sorry. Which way have they headed?" David had seen the blue insignia with the Indian head and the three arrows designating a soldier from the 180th Infantry Regiment on the man just loaded onto a stretcher.

The soldier looked at the racing car and what he thought were two Frenchmen. All he could do was point.

David asked, "You with the 45th?"

"Yeah, we're the Grave Registration detachment. We retrieve fallen soldiers."

"Do you know where the 180th might be?"

"Just follow this road north."

Pepe picked up the direction pointed. In a few minutes he was accelerating up the road. There were signs of battle in every town they passed: burned vehicles, bombed homes and buildings, temporary floating bridges, bodies in the ditches, dead animals, and blasts of artillery fire in the distance.

Pepe stopped when they reached the military support detachments. He was told he could go no further. He shook David's hand, handed him his cane, and waved good-bye as he turned and headed home. David asked a medic how far it was to the 180th. The medic looked at David's cane and suggested he have an Army doctor look at his leg and then a jeep would take him on to his unit. David's wound was infected. He knew it by its color and its smell. He should've been further along in the healing process by now.

That night Colonel Fulbright came in to the makeshift hospital ward and found David. A clerk sat down a duffel bag of David's personal items and pulled up a seat for the colonel and one for himself. The colonel asked how his trip had gone and if he found the freedom fighter General de Gaulle had sent him looking for.

David narrated the events that occurred during the past couple of months while the clerk wrote furiously on his tablet. In a few minutes most of the men in the ward were sitting up on their bunks listening to the story. When David finished the colonel congratulated him on a job well done, gave him the insignias for his promotion to sergeant, slapped him on his back, and said how proud he was that David was in his command. The men in the ward started clapping, bringing the nurses in from their duty stations to see what was going on. Colonel Fulbright told David to stay with the medical detachment until his wound healed enough to rejoin his unit.

Two months later and with the wound finally getting better, David gathered his things and sneaked out to join his buddies. He hobbled north toward the town of Epinal where he understood the 180th was currently located. A passing jeep gave him a ride to the outskirts of town.

Epinal was divided by the Moselle River running from the northwest to the southeast. The river was fast-flowing and eighty feet wide with vertical stone walls rising on both sides from the water. After the Franco-Prussian War the French decided they needed a line of defenses to stop future German encroachment and built a fortress line of prepared cities including Toul, Verdun, Nancy, and continuing on through Epinal to Belfort. The Huns had sacrificed hundreds of thousands of soldiers in an unsuccessful effort during World War I to take Nancy and Verdun by storm. They never reached Epinal.

The Moselle River was spanned by numerous bridges, all of which had been totally or partially demolished by the Germans who were determined to stop the advancing Seventh Army. They mined the streets and placed massive road blocks with machine-gun support in strategic intersections. The Germans dug in. Here they would make a last-ditch effort or die trying. They had three infantry battalions and were reinforced with artillery, mortars, and dual-purpose anti-aircraft guns. They were evenly matched against the three battalions of the 180th. The 157th was crossing the Moselle north of town and the 179th was crossing south. It was up to the 180th to take the town.

David came to a wooded area. A sign read *Bois de L'Homme Mort*. He later found out the sign roughly translated to "The Woods of the Dead Man." The 180th was just a mile further north.

Captain Marcinko was surprised to see David. "Are you my reinforcements?"

"Yes, sir. Sergeant Calhoun reporting for duty, sir."

"At ease, Sergeant. It's good to see you. Did you have a nice vacation?"

"I wouldn't recommend it in the summer, sir, but the fall is beautiful."

"Sergeant Calhoun? Old Fussbucket gave you another field promotion, didn't he? You blackmailing him or something? Never mind. I don't want to know. Your buddies have dug in behind that water tower. Right now they're cleaning up the last Germans on this side of the river. It's been house to house for the last two days. We haven't been able to get across the river. Every time we try the Germans open up on us with their 88s. I tell you I been dreaming about those 88s.

"You had any chow today? Go get something to eat. I think we'll be fording that river tomorrow. That'll be all, Sergeant Calhoun."

"Thank you, sir. It's good to be back." David saluted, spun around, and headed out the door.

That night Gino, Little Billy Jenks, Boyd, and all of David's friends wanted to know what had happened on his jaunt into occupied France. When they heard about Genevieve, Boyd let out a howl. The Alfa Romeo brought forth some ooh-la-las as well. Afterwards, Gino gave David a stack of letters—most from Gabriela.

"Man, do you ever write her?"

"Who?"

"My sister. You numbskull."

"Sure I do. How do you think I rate so many letters? I'm just not completely over Rose."

"You think she still prays for you?"

"You know, Gino, I think she does. Someone's looking out for me. I've had some mighty close scrapes and all without a scratch until I scared this French girl half to death. She lowered to one knee, palmed a Lugar, drew a bead, and shot me inches from my . . . in the pelvic area."

"What do you think she was aiming at?" Gino waited a moment and when no response came he continued, "I guess you do have someone looking out for you. And you're looking out for me."

The next morning Colonel Fulbright arrived in a jeep and asked if they were waiting for an order to cross the river. Captain Marcinko told him he was just in time to see that very feat. The colonel suggested he would go see if the bridge was passable while the captain got his troops ready. Getting close to the bridge, the colonel heard bullets whistle by and casually walked back to Captain Marcinko's headquarters. He said they needed to go upstream and find a wide sweeping curve where the water would be the shallowest for fording.

By noon, the last platoon was crossing the waist-high water when they were spotted by the Germans. Instantly they started receiving automatic fire. The two platoons already ashore unleashed a furious barrage of small weapon fire as the platoon in the water splashed frantically to shore. Word was sent back requesting more ammunition; meanwhile, the men with extra shared.

It was a cook who heard the request. He formed a detail from the company mess and headed out. On the way they received a few potshots but nothing substantial. The men of the 180th were glad for the re-supply of ammo and rations. Thanking the cooks and mess help, they continued to canvass the area. It was a slow process as the Germans fought valiantly. A few surrendered, a few retreated, and a few fought until they lay dead at their posts. It took two days of intense fighting before Epinal was secure.

The 180th continued north just inside the French-Swiss border and south of the town of Fremifontane. David's friends carried his gear, leaving him to negotiate his way with the black cane and an occasional arm. There were minor skirmishes at every little town along the way but it was at Fremifontane where the Germans waited.

After five days of hard fighting, the Germans were still firmly entrenched in the town. In fact, they had yet to show the 180th how many men and arms they were up against. On October 6, 1944 the First Battalion was engaged with the Germans in Autrey, a small town north of Fremifontane. Early that morning David and the Second Battalion relieved a tired Third Battalion. The Third had been deployed to the east of town and had several days of hard combat under their belts. The Second Battalion's Companies E and G advanced toward the town to pick up where the Third Battalion had left off. David and Company F were held in reserve.

Company F set up their headquarters in a stone house in the midst of several sections of plowed fields surrounded on three sides by a dense forest. David volunteered to man the observer's post on a small knoll south of the farmhouse. The land was flat with David's hill the only spot affording a propitious view.

"Gino, you ever call in coordinates?"

Gino was digging their foxhole wider and deeper. He surveyed the area and wondered how long he'd have to fight. Some men were already being shipped home. The Army had devised a point system based on a man's marital status, number of dependents, wounds sustained, days of combat, and number of major conflicts participated in. He and David had built up a lot of points in the latter two areas but very few in the former three. It looked like they'd be there until it was over.

"No, never have. Shouldn't be that hard though."

David sat his binoculars down and picked up the radio headset. "This is Fox Company at the Perch. Do you read?"

Over the speaker came back, "Bright as day, Fox Company. You boys enjoying this fine autumn morning?"

"Yeah, it's just peachy. Have you zoned in on anything yet?"

"We can hit your headquarters . . . uh, the Hound, and come pretty close to the Perch."

"Well, let's not hit either of those two targets just yet. How many yards will a click get me?"

"Twenty with the mortars and fifty or better with the howitzers. We can give you half clicks if you need more precise targeting."

"We'll see. Have a cup of coffee on me. Fox Company out."

"171st Artillery out."

"Damnit, David, you've got to be the consummate GI. Of course you can't run, can barely walk. And that knife of yours drags the ground like a saber. Life magazine would make you its poster boy if we could get them a picture." Gino threw out another shovel of dirt.

"How deep you plan on making this hole?"

"Deep enough that I can sit down and read my letters and feel safe doing it."

The morning passed. At eleven-thirty David saw someone darting from one tree to another directly behind headquarters in the woods.

"Hound, we got action to your north, in the edge of the woods."

"Thanks." A pause. "First Platoon, check it out."

"We're on it."

David came back over the radio, "Hound, there's tanks. Should I call in artillery?"

"That's what you're there for."

"Artillery, this is Fox Company. We need howitzer fire 6 clicks north of the Hound."

"Roger that."

Sixty seconds went by, then several blasts from David's back ended with explosions to his front, lighting up the field just short of the woods.

"Artillery. Redo at 8 clicks."

This time the explosions were in the first expanse of the woods. David saw more action as a tank came into view from the tree-line left of headquarters.

"Hound . . . bandits to your left. Artillery, we need howitzers ten clicks left of the Hound."

"Roger."

The advancing Germans were met with machine gun fire from several positions and David kept calling coordinates. Gino got his light machine gun ready but the targets were too distant and so far his and David's position had not been compromised. Suddenly tanks and infantry came through the tree-line to the right of headquarters and bullets started flying over David's head.

"Gino, I think these guys mean business and now they're plenty close. Artillery, mortar fire ten clicks right of the Hound and keep those howitzers firing."

"I'm shot."

David looked at Gino. He was lying in the bottom of the foxhole toward the back. "Damnit, Gino."

"I'm sorry, bro. It's just in the arm but I can't fire the weapon."

"Can you stand?"

"Yeah, but the arm hurts like the dickens."

"You call in the coordinates and I'll man the gun."

Gino used his good arm to climb to his feet and took over the radio. David got behind the machine gun and started blasting. Fighting continued until three in the afternoon when the Germans, having sustained all the resistance they could tolerate, retreated into the woods.

"Artillery. Cease firing. They're high-tailing it for Berlin."

"Roger. You guys sustain many casualties?"

"Yeah, one here at the Perch."

From the Hound they heard, "Perch, we got a medic coming your way."

David helped Gino remove his shirt. "Not much blood. However, you'll not be throwing curveballs for a while. Guess you'll have to work on a change-up."

"Hell, man, I was first base. They needed me in the lineup for my glove and the fact I could hit the ball out of the park."

"Sit down. I'll keep a look for a while. You'll probably be heading home from that million-dollar wound."

"Think so?"

The medic bandaged Gino and said sick bay was full and Gino needed to stay at the Perch if he could. In the afternoon, Little Billy Jenks brought replacement ammunition. He told them Boyd had been killed. He got it in the head. Never knew what hit him.

All three were upset. Boyd was the first of their tight group to be killed. There had been lots killed but not from their group. Not from the ones who stormed First Battalion's headquarters and captured Colonel Wilson. Not from the ones who fought Handsome Harry.

David was keeping a wary eye on the woods. "Here they come." He picked up the headset and said, "Artillery, we got activity in the woods left of the Hound. I need howitzers ten clicks to the left and two past."

"Roger."

Little Billy Jenks muttered, "I'm outta here." He jumped out of the Perch and ran down the hill. A tank emerged from the right of the Hound and started firing its heavy machine gun at Little Billy. The shoeshine boy ran for all he was worth, zigzagging toward his comrades.

"Artillery, I need mortars 8 clicks right of the Hound and three short."

"Roger."

David manned the machine gun but the tank was beyond the gun's range. He fired anyway as both he and Gino yelled at Little Billy to run. Run!

Little Billy's down. Like a rag doll shaken by a dog, several more rounds pummeled his limp body. Tears streaked down David's face.

Into the headset, Gino hollered, "Artillery, mortar fire nine and a half clicks right of the Hound and three short."

The blasts came in on target and the tank was hit by flying shrapnel. Smoke and fire, then the center hatch opened and out staggered three soldiers. They ran for their lines with the last man cut down by machine gun-fire from a position behind the Hound.

This time there were many more Germans, more tanks, more infantry, more *chutzpah*. David fired the machine gun, Gino called in coordinates, and the Germans advanced. They were everywhere.

Over the radio came, "This is the Hound. All hands fall back and form a defense 1500 meters south of the fence."

David kept firing. Gino was down again. The German tanks advanced. Fox Company retreated. David stood up, punched his fist high in the air, and yelled, "Come on, you bastards."

Bullets whistled past on all sides, one struck the forward tripod of the machine gun. From a lifeless Gino, David took the headset. "Artillery, I need all your mortar fire 8 clicks north of the Perch. They're closing in on me. Howitzers, 4 clicks north and two to the left. Mortars, now 6 clicks past the Perch."

David aimed the air-cooled machine gun, he fired until his weapon quit vibrating, loaded another strip and started in again, and then, a few minutes later, loaded another. "Mortars, 4 clicks past the Perch. Howitzers, 2 clicks past and 1 click left. They're almost here."

David kept firing his weapon until the barrel started smoking. It jammed. He then grabbed his Garand and fired 8 rounds, yanked out the clip, slammed home another, and let her rip. Two more clips then empty. No more clips.

"Artillery . . . bring it down on me. They're here."

A Panzer tank stood thirty yards in front of David's mound. Artillery rounds were exploding all around. The German officer swiveled his cannon and lowered it on a straight line at David. David glared at the cannon, turned to Gino, bent over, and said, "Gino, its time to go." Gino's eyes were glazed, his body limp.

The tank fired. Dirt, machine gun, binoculars, a spade, and a shoe flew through the air. David's hill was gone. The Perch was no more. Smoke and dust settled. The tank moved forward, stopped, its hatch opened, and a small man stood up with his head and shoulders outside the tank. He saluted two crumpled bodies in a shallow grave then continued on against the retreating Company F.

The German infantry passed. One man looked at the two bodies. Three legs and one arm stuck out from the rubble. He turned to the man beside him. "Did you see that dog? He would've taken off my head had I gotten any closer to those bodies."

The second soldier muttered to himself, "*Dummkopf.*"

Three hours later it was dark. A big black dog pawed at the dirt. He uncovered a face, then an arm. He stepped over the face and licked it. He pawed at one of the arms. David stirred. He struggled to right himself. A piece of shrapnel was embedded in his leg. Slowly he pulled it out. It was cold to the touch. Must've been out for hours, David thought. Can't hear. Something in front. A wet tongue licked away dirt still clinging to David's chin.

"Balder? Is that you? It is you. Damn, I'm dead."

Captain Marcinko was taken prisoner, but Company F rallied behind Sergeant Geiger and began slowing the German advance. The Third Battalion came up to help and the Germans stopped to regroup. They would continue at first light, but now the Allies were much stronger and would be ready.

David pushed more dirt away, the dog moved off a short distance, and David stood up. More wounds but they didn't hurt. He pulled a piece of shrapnel from his side. Reaching down to Gino he said, "Come on, Gino. We didn't make it. We got to go see God."

Gino didn't move. David pulled away the dirt until he uncovered Gino's body. He reached down and pulled his best friend up and over his shoulder. Carrying Gino, he started walking after the dog. Funny, he didn't limp anymore. And he couldn't hear a thing.

The dog walked into the woods. He stopped every so often for David to catch up and then walked forward again. David saw little flickers of fire every so often. The dog walked in a zigzag pattern, first one way, then a turn, and on in another. Hours passed. David marveled at his ability to slowly trudge along behind his dog without getting tired. No blood seeped from his wounds.

They came to the edge of the woods and walked across a plowed field, the dog just a few yards in front. The black hound walked up to a man and sat down. A hand came down and caressed the dog's head. The dog vanished. From where the dog had been the man looked at David.

"It's me Lord, David . . . and, I've brought Gino." David slowly fell to his knees then tumbled sideways to the ground still clutching Gino's lifeless body.

David awoke the next day in the back of a truck with an IV tube sticking out of his arm. A medic came over and said something but David couldn't hear what he said. He shook his head and pointed to his ears. The medic nodded and, taking out a piece of paper, wrote, "We're hauling you to Reims. To a hospital. You'll be headed home soon."

David grabbed the paper and scribbled as fast as he could, "I'm not dead?"

The medic laughed and said what David thought was, "No."

David scribbled again, "What about Gino?"

"The man you brought in is not dead but there's little hope. He lost a lot of blood and has several severe wounds. I don't think he'll make it."

"Where is he?"

"He's still in sickbay. He couldn't be moved."

David lay back on his stretcher and wept.

CHAPTER 20—PARIS
City of Light – Early August, 1944

With a smile on his face Pepe waltzed into the kitchen. "Genevieve, my dear, I was just thinking about David. That was some kiss you planted on him. You probably had your eyes closed and couldn't see his. They were as big as saucers. You would be married by now had you been as amiable to one of our fine young French men. I just thought you ought to know."

"Father, do you not know? David's French."

"What?"

"His mother's maiden name is Sinclair."

That afternoon Pepe had a taxi come to his house and drive him to the Catholic church in town. He wanted forgiveness for his sins and, after he received absolution, he had a small matter to discuss with the priest.

"Hello, Pepe. What brings you out this wonderful autumn afternoon?"

"Father Dominique. I need to confess my sins."

"Yes, my son. Come into the confessional."

Suddenly, Pepe felt very old. It took both hands to open the door of the confessional. He staggered in and sat in the dark recesses. Father Dominique slid back the wooden partition leaving only a mesh screen separating them.

"Forgive me, Father, for I have sinned. It has been four years and three months since my last confession. During that time I have slept with five women, lusted over numerous others, used the Lord's name in vain, stolen gasoline from the German occupiers, and I have kept a great secret from you, Father Dominique."

"And what might that secret be?"

"Well, you were entrusted with a magnificent religious antiquary. But it was stolen from you by the heathen Germans."

"Yes, that is so. I have prayed hard and many times for its return. They had to pry my arms from it when they carried it to their truck. I have grieved so much my clothing doesn't fit. Continue, my son."

"Father, the German soldiers came to my house for my Toulouse-Lautrec to put with your bell and the other stolen treasures, but I fought with them."

"I did not know."

"I have Charlemagne's bell in my barn."

"You what?"

Father Dominique jumped up and hit his head on the low ceiling of the confessional. "You have the bell?"

"Yes, Father."

"Pepe, take me to it." Father Dominique lurched out, looked up, and said, "Thank you, Lord." He yanked Pepe's door open and said, "Well, man, let's be about it. You needn't keep me waiting any longer."

"But, Father. What about my sins?"

"They are absolved. You fought for the Lord and he forgives your transgressions."

"Even the five women?"

"Yes, well, we need to talk about them. Are they five different women or was it one woman and you slept with her five times?"

"Five different women, several times, numerous times each."

"Was it one of the women several times and then later another woman and so on?"

"No. For several years, it was all five."

Father Dominique grabbed Pepe by the arm. "At the same time? In the same bed?"

"Really, Father, you must think me some sort of libertine. I've kept them separated, each one not knowing about the others. My biggest problem, besides keeping them apart, is remembering what I've said to each."

"My, my. What a lot to forgive. You'll have to say the Rosary and ten Hail Marys. Are they members of the church? You'll have to ask their forgiveness as well. Though, I'll help you with that."

When they arrived at Pepe's house, Pepe paid the taxi driver while the priest ran into the barn. Genevieve and Pepe sat on a bale of hay as Father Dominique tossed one bale after another in a mad rush to unearth his beloved bell. In a moment, and almost out of breath, he pulled back the covering of half the tarp.

"Thank you, Lord. Thank you, oh merciful Father." Father Dominique wrapped his arms around the upper portion, the most slender part of the bell. Tears ran down his cheeks. Presently, he composed himself and said, "So, Pepe, tell me how this came to be. Did you fight the Germans by yourself?"

Genevieve came over to the bell and flicked off a few stray strands of hay. "Father, it was David who fought the Germans. He's the real hero. They were having their way with me and David saved me from them. He saved the bell also, of course. After Papa came at one of them with a piece of firewood—I think they would have killed him after they finished with me—so you might say David saved him as well."

Pepe looked at the paintings wrapped in oiled canvas and stuffed in gunny sacks. He opened one up, gave a gasp, and reached for another. "These are old-world masterpieces. We need to get them cataloged and a list given to the authorities. There's going to be some mighty happy people when they find out what that young man did for them. Here, let's take them to the house."

Sitting at the breakfast table, Genevieve told Father Dominique how David single-handedly defeated the Germans, how she shot him, and how they all fooled the German investigators.

"What a wonderful story. Pepe, you ought to write that down. You and I can deliver it to the authorities in Paris with the list of what he saved. They should give the boy a medal or something. By the way, how the devil did he get the bell unloaded and moved to the middle of the barn? Surely he wasn't strong enough to lift it by himself. I mean, it took all six of those burly Germans to get it loaded."

Genevieve paused a moment then said, "I'm not sure. He had me go after rope and, when I came back, he had it sitting right where it is now. He was sweating like he had done some magnificent feat and he had this proud look on his face. I just assumed he picked it up and carried it there."

Pepe reached over and put his hand on Genevieve's arm. "Honey, that bell weighs a thousand pounds or more."

Father Dominique raised his hand high in the air. "Please, bear with me. The Lord can cause miracles to happen. I believe he gave this young man superior strength. He was probably with David—that is his name, isn't it? He was probably right beside David. Did you say the young man shot the Gestapo officer between the eyes from twenty feet? I have to believe a miracle happened here and David was the instrument the Lord used." With that said, Father Dominique lowered his hand.

Pepe walked to his desk and retrieved a box of stationery, his pen, and his notes concerning the information David was coerced to give and Genevieve to translate. He came back to the table where his daughter and the priest were sitting and asked Genevieve if she would help him with the details as he was out cold until she shot David and hid behind the divan.

Father Dominique went to the barn and covered the bell. When he came back he said that he would make arrangements for workers to replace the bell in its tower. He asked if he might help with writing the story for the authorities. He had always wanted to write a secular novel but his position had not allowed it.

With the facts listed, Father Dominique and Pepe started fashioning a story. Pepe exaggerated David's fighting ability and Father Dominique magnified his intent. Soon the story was so fantastic neither thought anyone would believe it. Father Dominique said, "We need to make him more human. Add some emotion. Put in a love interest."

For the next few hours they turned it into a lurid romance. Father Dominique said, "Let me see. How about this, 'The mere touch of his hand sent a warming shiver through her body.'"

"I like it, but this passage here could be improved. Let's make it, 'piercing the dark interior of the barn, rays of sunlight on his sea-blue eyes shone like bits of gleaming porcelain.'"

"That sounds good, Pepe. Did he have blue eyes?"

"I don't know. Let's ask Genevieve."

"Yes, he did. And they were so dark you could lose yourself in them."

"Oh, that's good."

"You know, when he lifts the bell, we need to put down what the woman's thinking."

"Father, the woman is my daughter."

"That's true. Why don't we take some artistic license and have her be your servant? You know, that dark-haired beauty with the grey eyes. We could put in whatever we wanted about her."

"Yes, she was a looker. She came along right after Selene died. When I was feeling depressed she comforted me and lifted my spirits. She made me think everything was going to be all right, that I'd live through it."

"Let's not name her. We'll just describe her and mention that she was employed here."

Father Dominique stood up with his paper and said, "How's this: 'She watched David struggle to his feet lifting the gigantic bell. His stance emphasized the force of his thighs and the slimness of his hips. His muscles rippled under his thin shirt. It quickened her pulse. With steady hands and bare muscular arms, he enveloped the bell. A quick jerk and he stood defiantly holding onto the massive object. As he slowly walked to the center of the barn, she could see his body quiver from the weight. Sweat from his brow trickled down his face. Without the slightest sound he lowered the bell onto the tarp and fell to the ground beside it, blood started oozing from his wound.'"

"And then for the woman. 'She ran to him. 'Oh, David, David darling, you're shot.' With her slender fingers intertwined in his hair she lifted his head and placed it in her lap. 'You were so brave. You killed so many Germans; you saved me and our town's heritage. You are my hero. You are France's hero.' Her breasts gently caressed his cheek. He didn't want to move, but he had to for there were other matters to attend to.'"

Pepe looked at the priest from the corner of his eye. Genevieve shook her head. Father Dominique said, "What? You don't think I can have an imagination? I've vowed celibacy but it doesn't mean I don't think about it. I mean, I don't do it on purpose, it just kind of slides in sideways. You should see the lengths some of our female parishioners will go in an effort to see me blush."

Genevieve fixed their evening meal and the priest stayed the night. They worked until midnight embellishing, revising, and rephrasing their story to make it agree with the facts. The next morning they were up working on it when Genevieve came downstairs to cook their breakfast. Later that day, Pepe said they were now working on the other chapters in David's military efforts against the Germans in Sicily and Italy. By the evening meal they were just about finished with the fifth and final chapter. Next, they were going to make a condensed version. Then, with a list of the treasures, they planned to take both versions to Paris.

Father Dominique said he couldn't leave until after services on Sunday. He wanted to be the one to ring the bell calling his flock to worship. But if Pepe would wait on him, he'd like to travel to Paris and put in his opinion to those in charge. Pepe said they needed to wait until Paris was liberated but that shouldn't be too long according to Philippe.

The next day a truck pulled to the Martel barn and several happy workers toiled for a couple of hours to get the bell into the back. They could not understand how one man could have managed it by himself. They left thinking this American was one strong yank.

A few weeks later, on August 25, 1944, Pepe was eating his noon meal in the Vichy hotel cafe with Odette when someone rushed in and said, "Paris is free and General de Gaulle is walking through its streets saying as much. Turn on the radio. It's all on the radio."

Odette turned the power knob, adjusted the volume, and sat beside Pepe. She held his hand under the table while everyone listened to the announcer talk about the general's walk down the Champs Elysees. How sniper fire made everyone run for cover but the general walked upright through the streets daring anyone to shoot at him. Millions of people had turned out. They lined the sidewalks, filled the streets, gathered on rooftops, and hung suspended sideways from lamp posts. Now, standing on a balcony of the Hotel De Ville, General Charles de Gaulle walked to the microphone and waited for the bedlam to die down.

> "Paris! Paris outraged! Paris shattered! Paris martyred! But Paris liberated. Liberated by herself, liberated by her people, in concurrence with the armies of France, with the support and concurrence of the

whole of France, of fighting France, the only France, the true France, eternal France."

The general paused as the crowd clapped, cheered, and began to chant, "De Gaulle, de Gaulle, de Gaulle."

That night, Pepe told Odette he had to go to Paris.

"When will I see you again? It was a month this last time. You know, you could just move in. I'd take care of you."

"Baby, I can't. I have another life you know nothing about. The best I can do is to come and see you when I can. We talked about all this our first night together." Pepe walked to the dresser and started packing his clothes.

"Henri, don't pack. It's comforting to me to smell and touch what you leave behind. Sometimes I put on one of your shirts. It makes me feel like you're here, in another room, down the hall, or out to get the paper. I can give you money to buy new clothes. Here." Odette reached into her purse. With tears streaming down her cheeks, she held out a wad of bills.

"Odette, you are my one true love. I'll be back. I don't need your money, though I'm touched by the gesture. I own quite a bit of land and have made good investments, I have plenty of money. After the war we'll do some traveling. Have you ever been to Lucerne? Geneva?"

"No. But I'll go anywhere with you, Henri. Any time."

"I have to leave." Pepe started putting his clothes back into the dresser. He held up a folded shirt. "I'm not a big man, but still, my shirts are too big for you. Do you wear my pants as well?"

"No. When I wear your shirts I don't wear anything else."

"Nothing?"

"Nothing."

On a Monday morning Pepe pulled up to the rectory in the red Alfa racer. He had on a black beret, white cashmere scarf, and black leather jacket matching his black leather racing gloves. The priest emerged with a small suitcase containing two changes of clothes and some toiletries. He took one long look at the sports car and another at Pepe. He wished the Catholic hierarchy was more progressive in their choice of transportation supplied and clothing required.

He walked around the vehicle and gave an appraising low whistle. He then tied his suitcase on the back with the two cans of gasoline and jumped in. Finding a surprising amount of leg room, he stretched, and said, "Let's go to Paris."

On the way they rehashed their plan. The first stop would be the Hotel De Ville where the provisional government had established temporary headquarters. To the newly appointed authorities they would give the particulars about the treasure and about the young man who had saved it. From there, they intended on going to the biggest newspaper in France and see if they might be interested in printing the story.

The authorities looked at the list, listened to their story, wrote down the particulars, and said they would see what they could do. An hour later in a plush newspaper lobby the receptionist listened to their pitch and ushered them into a lower management office and introduced them to an overworked, underpaid staff editor.

Pepe opened his valise and pulled out a group of papers from the chapter where David carried the bell. "Young man, an American GI visited my farm before the Allied invasion needing help finding a particular resistance fighter for General de Gaulle. He was dressed in French peasant clothing and walked in on a fleecing by two truckloads of nasty German soldiers. One was molesting my daughter. I had already been knocked unconscious. This is the story of what he did. Father Dominique and I have obtained the relevant facts and written them down. Do you think your paper might be interested in printing the story?"

"Let me see what you've got."

Pepe handed the young man the excerpt from the final chapter. He and Father Dominique sat back in their chairs as it was read.

"Is this true? How could one man lift a thousand pound bell and carry it twenty-five feet?"

Father Dominique said, "It is true. The bell does weigh that much. It's Charlemagne's bell. No one actually saw him lift it but the truck it was sitting in wouldn't fit through the barn opening. The woman was gone for only a few minutes while she retrieved a rope. When she returned the bell was in the center of the barn sitting on a tarp and The

Calhoun was nearby, too exhausted to move for several minutes. We took some liberties with the woman to enhance the story's appeal."

"What about all those Germans? You don't even have him armed until the driver knocks down the front door."

"We know. That's pretty unbelievable. We thought about changing it but decided that if the man could actually do it we ought to be able to convey it to the reader."

"And this list of art treasure. I think you gentlemen are wearing a sheep's mantle."

Pepe reached for the sheaf of papers. He replaced them in his valise. "Here is what we're offering and the terms are available until nine o'clock tomorrow morning. Five chapters. You just read about a third of the final one. We want ten thousand francs for chapter one. You get all the rights to that one chapter only. We have a condensed version that will be made into a magazine article so your rights do not extend further than the chapter purchased and as it is worded. I suggest you purchase it and see what your readers have to say. If their response is like I think it will be, you'll want the rest of the chapters. However, at nine tomorrow morning we will leave to call on your competition and the first one with the money, and a desire to increase his circulation, gets the story. We might even sell one chapter to each newspaper. So when one of your competitors prints chapter one, and another prints chapter two, there might be several in line to purchase chapter three and all will increase their circulation to your detriment."

"Gentlemen, that is preposterous. We're not going to pay that kind of money for anyone's story. Good day."

"We're staying at the Grand Hotel de Champagne should you change your mind," said Pepe. "It's on the corner of rue Jean-Lantier and rue des Orfevres"

"I know where it is, thank you."

Once they were ushered out the door, the reporter got on the phone and talked with the Louvre. Then he called the government authorities at the Hotel De Ville. In less than an hour he was walking down the hall to the head editor's office.

The next morning a courier arrived at the Grand Hotel de Champagne with a note saying the newspaper had reconsidered and was willing to pay twenty thousand francs for all five chapters. There was a check attached. Pepe looked at his watch and said it was five minutes until nine and at that time the offer would be rescinded. The courier promptly folded the note, put it in his jacket, and handed Pepe a second note. This one said that the newspaper would like to purchase chapter one for the ten thousand francs but could not purchase any more until it could determine the public's response. The check was attached. Pepe removed the check and gave the courier chapter one. It was all done rather fast, leaving Pepe and Father Dominique wondering if they had priced it too low.

They checked out of the hotel and went to the next newspaper's office. After showing the receptionist the check from the first newspaper they were promptly ushered into the owner's private office. It was the same scenario as the preceding day. They let him read about the fight at the Martel farm and recovering the treasure. They said that the first newspaper had purchased chapter one and today chapter two was for sale for fifteen thousand francs.

"But, sir, you sold chapter one for ten thousand francs."

"Yes, we did. And after he runs it, he will want to purchase chapter two for whatever we ask. We're just giving you the opportunity to pull yourself up even. The price of chapter three is going to be determined by the response given the first two. If you don't get in on it now you won't be allowed to bid on further chapters."

"Gentlemen, you are swindlers. Pardon me, Father. Maybe I should say you are astute negotiators. Might I have some time to think about it?"

"The offer will stand until nine o'clock tomorrow morning. We can be reached at the Hotel Ritz."

The next morning Pepe and the priest were downstairs at seven for breakfast. They both snatched up copies of the paper containing chapter one and immediately turned to see what their story looked like in print. Pepe read it three times before he folded his paper and sat back in his chair as proud as a new parent. Father Dominique was also proud and spent quite a bit of time thinking what he would be doing with his portion of the proceeds. The way Pepe was handling things he might have enough to completely remodel the rectory. But what he really wanted was to purchase some land next to the church. He thought the church grounds should be extended and improved with gardens, winding walkways, water fountains, and more space added to the cemetery.

At eight a.m. the owner of the second newspaper walked in with a copy of his competitor's paper under his arm. He handed over a check and said chapter two would be running in his paper on the following day and he would also like to purchase chapter three. Pepe pulled out a chair and asked the man if he would care for a cup of coffee. A little agitated by the fact that Pepe was not running to bring him chapter three, the man reluctantly sat down.

"I'm sorry but chapter three has already been sold. Chapter four will be available for sale here tomorrow morning at nine. We have not determined the price but it will be a fair one."

The man left, wondering if his paper could afford to carry any more chapters of Le Calhoun. Pepe and Father Dominique promptly headed to the third newspaper and sold chapter three for 17,500 francs after showing the man the two previously received checks.

That afternoon they traveled to the part of town where the illustrators worked. They talked one into sketching scenes to match the story line of chapter one of the condensed version. Pepe and Father Dominique had the man draw Le Calhoun with a strong jaw, piercing dark blue eyes, and a foot taller than the Germans he routinely killed. He carried a Browning Automatic Rifle called a BAR that Pepe had in a picture. He used it to routinely knock out tanks, machine-gun nests, and entire squadrons of the most villainous-looking Neanderthals their artist was capable of drawing. The illustrator added captions to the bottom and sides of the pages with blurbs of words coming from out of the mouths of the characters depicted. It took most of the day for him to achieve a level of artistry satisfactory to Pepe and Father Dominique. They left with him working away and saying he would have the first chapter completed by the end of the week.

That afternoon Pepe called the first newspaper and told the head editor chapter four would be available for sale the next morning at nine at their new lodgings in the Hotel Ritz. The newspaper man said he had people all over town looking for them. He would be there and he would have that next chapter.

At eight a.m. all three newspapers were represented at the hotel café when Pepe and Father Dominique entered. They were seated at different tables and each was more than a little agitated by the presence of the other two. Pepe and Father Dominique pushed two tables together, arranged the necessary number of chairs, and beckoned their guests to join them after ordering a sufficient quantity of coffee and pastries.

Pepe pulled chapter four from his valise and set it on the table. The head editor from the biggest of the three papers quickly picked it up and began reading. Pepe asked if there was an opening bid. The smallest of the three said, "My paper is prepared to offer the outrageous price of 25,000 francs." He promptly snatched the chapter from the hands of the largest paper.

The second paper said, "I'm authorized to go as high as 40,000 francs." He held out his hand for the chapter.

The largest paper adjusted his glasses, reached inside his coat, produced a check, and asked, "Can either of you gentlemen better 50,000 francs?" He looked at each in turn, wrote the check, picked up chapter four, and said, "I guess we'll do this same thing tomorrow morning for the final chapter, number five." He turned to Pepe, handed him the check, and said, "Thank you Mr. Martel, and you, Father." With chapter four in his briefcase, the man from the biggest paper left two bewildered newspaper executives and two ecstatic authors.

Pepe leaned over the table and said, "Why don't you gentlemen pool your resources. The Father and I don't have any problem granting both of you equal rights." Pepe motioned to Father Dominique that it was time for them to be about their business. They departed leaving the two snickering and planning how they would show the big guy.

Later that morning they picked up the illustrations done so far and headed to a magazine office. Pepe told the head editor about the arrangement he had made with the three newspapers and then handed him the illustrations for the first chapter of the condensed version. By that afternoon they had a contract for the production and an advance payment of royalties for all five chapters to be produced in comic books starring Le Calhoun.

The next morning there were four newspapers represented, with the big guy doing battle with first one then another of his competitors. When the bidding finally stopped, the large newspaper had won again but was having to shell out 125,000 francs for the final chapter. He told Pepe he had hired two new receptionists to handle the number of calls and the people walking in off the street wanting more information about Le Calhoun. He showed them this morning's paper with the headline of "Le Calhoun to receive *Croix de Guerre*." The story went on to say the authorities had confirmed that the exploits of Le Calhoun were true. They were trying to find from the Allied Command where he might be fighting and for the rightful owners of the French treasures he had saved.

Later that same morning Pepe and Father Dominique exchanged their newspaper checks for two cashiers' checks—each for half of the total amount earned less the amount they had already spent on expenses and additional funds for their pockets. Pepe exchanged the advanced royalty check from the magazine producer less what was paid to the illustrator for a cashiers check payable to David Calhoun. In the future the illustrator's payments would be made by the magazine.

Father Dominique looked at his check for over a hundred thousand francs and decided he might buy the land, add the improvements, and still have money left for remodeling the rectory. He asked Pepe if they might stop by one of the book stalls before heading back. Pepe suggested they pick up cigars and spend some time at the thermal baths as well.

CHAPTER 21—THE TRIP
Springfield, Missouri - October, 1944

Carson was sick. He couldn't swallow. Rose made him gargle with salt water but that was a fiasco with him choking on some and spitting out the rest. She held him in her arms and paced back and forth trying to provide comfort. Worry came easy. Things had not been going Rose's way for a long time but she had to be strong. Carson needed her. Something had to be done. She walked into the hall and called a taxi to take them to the hospital. Sitting in her chair and holding tight the only person left who really mattered, Rose waited for the cab.

In the emergency room a nurse tenderly removed Carson from his mother's trembling arms and carried him to an examining room while a clerk asked Rose for the required admitting information.

"Mommy. Mommy." Carson choked out as he rounded a corner and lost sight of his mother.

The physician on duty looked down Carson's throat with a small flashlight. He held down the little boy's tongue with a wooden depressor. Carson squirmed and looked to his mother for help.

"It's all right, Carson. He just wants to have a look-see. He won't hurt you. Just be a little patient. Everything's going to be okay. He's going to make you well."

In the best bedside manner he could muster at two o'clock in the morning, the doctor told Rose that Carson had an acute case of tonsillitis. They would need to get the infection under control with antibiotics and then remove the swollen glands through surgery. Carson needed to stay at the hospital so the nurses could drip the antibiotics through a tube directly into his blood stream. Rose was welcome to stay in the room with the patient.

Three days later Carson had a routine tonsillectomy. While they were at it they also took his adenoids. Two days after that they took his mother's money. She left with another sack of drugs and a drugged-out feeling that without money she and Carson had been cast to the wolves.

Before Carson got sick Rose had cashed her routine money order from Jesse. After that first letter, giving her address in Springfield, Jesse sent a money order for a hundred dollars the first of every month. Rose had slowly spent her savings and was now down to using the unearned funds to pay their rent and purchase the few groceries and toiletries she and Carson needed. Mrs. Patterson would understand.

Mrs. Patterson didn't understand. Rose only had enough money to pay half of their monthly rent the previous month and couldn't pay anything this month so Mrs. Patterson told Rose she would have to find somewhere else to live. There were people waiting, with money in hand, for Rose's room.

Rose packed the few clothes they had and two glasses in her suitcase. In her make-up bag she placed a few pieces of flatware, Carson's toy tractor, and the two farm implements he attached and dragged around the floor. The bag had been emptied of make-up long before. Holding on to Carson's hand they left the apartment building not knowing where to go. She had to figure something out. If she could just get her stamina back she could get a job. It seemed like she was so weak. The slightest bit of work and she had to lie down. She slept almost as much as Carson.

The once empty make-up bag was now heavy. From the corner of the suitcase extended a portion of clothing she used to drag it along the sidewalk. They had gone only a few blocks before she led Carson to a park bench and sat down.

"Mommy, I'm hungry."

"I am too, honey. What do you think we ought to do about that?"

"Mommy, do we have anything to eat?"

"No, Carson. We'll have to get a handout at a church or something. Come on, let's go. We'll not accomplish anything sitting here waiting on our lunch to be delivered."

A voice from behind her said, "Ma'am, I occasionally go to the All Saints Missionary Church. They give free meals to those in need. In fact, I was just about to head that way. Would you care to join me?"

A shabbily dressed old man walked around the end of the park bench. He grinned and said, "It's not far. I guess ten blocks or so. If you will permit me, I'd be happy to carry your suitcase."

Rose held on to Carson and thought the old man would probably take the suitcase and run. Well, what if he did? There wasn't anything in it worth stealing. She held out her hand and said her name was Rose and her son was Carson.

The man shook her hand and said he was glad to make their acquaintance. His name was Skeeter. He picked up the suitcase and said, "If I walk too fast, speak up. Something about food makes me want to run."

Before they arrived at the church Skeeter was carrying the suitcase, the make-up bag, and holding on to Carson's hand. Carrying only her purse Rose walked slower and slower, willing herself to put one foot in front of the other. Skeeter told her it was just another block. She said she needed to sit down. Then she saw the church at the far end of the block and kept trudging behind Skeeter and her son.

At the church there were several people just like Skeeter who had come for a free meal. Some of them knew Skeeter and shook his hand or asked how he was doing but Skeeter didn't have time to talk; he wanted to know where the pastor was. He set their luggage behind the front door and put Carson and Rose in line.

Soon Rose saw him talking to a much younger man. In a few minutes Skeeter and his friend walked over to Rose and Carson who now had steaming bowls of soup containing potatoes, corned beef, and cabbage. Beside the soup sat glasses of tea in the middle of small puddles of water. Skeeter introduced the younger man as Pastor Gideon—the minister responsible for the free meal.

"I'm Rose Potter and this is my son Carson. Thank you so much for the food. We appreciate your generosity."

"I can't take the credit. I just do what the Lord wills." The pastor looked around, mentally calculating how many were in attendance. In a moment his thoughts were back to the present situation. "Is the boy all right? He doesn't seem to like the food."

Rose placed her hand on Carson's small shoulder. "He had his tonsils removed two days ago and just needs to let the food cool a bit."

Gideon reflected a moment. "I'll be right back. Maybe I can find him something a little more soothing."

Across the table from Rose and Carson, Skeeter sat down with his bowl of soup and glass of tea. "He's a real nice chap. We listen to him preach a bit. It's worth it. He's good to us. For some of us, this is the only food we'll get and his preaching is good for the soul."

The preacher came back with a tall glass of milk and cup of tapioca pudding. To Carson he said, "You might like this while you wait on the soup to cool." He set the milk down and handed Carson the pudding.

"Mrs. Potter, have you a place to stay? Are you new in town?"

"Well, to tell you the truth, I used our rent money to pay for Carson's hospital bill. I haven't been quite up to speed lately and haven't been able to work. So I guess the answer to both questions is no."

"I can offer you and the boy a place to stay while the two of you recuperate. Mind you, it's not the Ritz or anything."

A frown came across Rose's face. However, she perked right up and thanked Pastor Gideon profusely. For the next couple of months Rose helped the pastor operate his soup line and cleaned the sanctuary and other rooms of the church. She and Carson took up residence in a small building the church used to store gardening supplies. Gideon rearranged everything so that she and Carson had about the same amount of space as in their previous tiny apartment. Now, with regular meals, Rose started to get her health back and maybe even put on a little weight. She was so skinny. Until the pneumonia she had always been the picture of health, but since, she had steadily lost weight. Then when the letter from David came, breaking her heart, she had sunk even lower and eventually siphoned her will to live from Carson.

Jesse looked at the letter. "Return. No forwarding address. Aw, hell. It's Rose's monthly money order." He sat down. Maybe it was time for him to break his promise. She had been gone almost two years. The sheriff gave up looking a long time ago. Bill had hired three different detective agencies but they didn't fare any better. And they interviewed everyone in town. One agency even followed Rose's trail to St. Louis. For a while the police there had her picture pasted all over town but nothing came of it. The bus driver had retired and, being single and without a family, no one knew where he had gone.

Jesse wrote Rose numerous letters but never received a reply. He couldn't write a check or her dad would find out, so, for these many months, he had sent money orders hoping they found the person they were addressed to. But now his latest money order had come back. She must have moved without giving a forwarding address. Who could he talk to?

Jesse got in his car and drove to Lee Mountain. Emily was the person to talk to. She was the most level-headed person in town—maybe the whole county. When Jesse pulled in front of the Calhoun house, Jed and Emily were sitting in their rocking chairs on the front porch. They were excited to see Jesse.

"Have you heard from him?" Emily pleaded. "Does anyone know when he'll be arriving?"

"No, ma'am. He's still somewhere between London and New York, but I've got some other news I think you need to know about."

Jed and Emily looked at Jesse and when they decided he wasn't going to blurt it out, Jed went inside for another chair while Emily went inside for a round of iced tea, both leaving Jesse standing by himself on the front porch.

When everyone was comfortable Jesse told them what happened the night Rose left: how she was the one David bought the locket for, how Bill found it, and how he became so enraged Rose decided to leave. He told them she purchased a bus ticket to St. Louis but got sick and only made it to Springfield. He'd been sending her money every month but this month the letter was returned. Jesse told them he thought someone ought to go to Springfield and bring her back. She and her dad would, more than likely, make amends and Rose needed her family. Jed and Emily were her family as well. He told them she and David would probably be getting married when David returned—with or without Bill's consent. And there was another important person in the equation. Rose left pregnant. So, unless she lost the baby when she was sick, there was a child to take into consideration. Their grandchild.

Jesse said he'd promised not to tell anyone but he didn't think he could be held to that any longer. It was time for someone to go get Rose. David was coming home. He'd be here any day and Rose needed to be here when he stepped off the bus. Jesse said he would go get her himself but his dad was in intensive care and he couldn't leave.

That night Jed and Emily planned what they would do. Jed's truck wasn't up to the trip. An automobile trip was out of the question anyway since Jed's gas ration quota would not be sufficient for the entire trip. He would take the bus. Springfield wasn't that far—one day at most. The next morning Emily put clothes and toiletries for Jed in a sack and they headed into town. At the general mercantile they bought a proper suitcase and repackaged the sack. At the bus station Jed bought a ticket for Springfield and kissed Emily goodbye, saying the next time he saw her he would have their daughter-in-law and grandbaby.

Emily waved as the bus pulled away from the curb. She then turned and walked down the street to the First Bank and Trust of Dancing Deer. This was the second time she had been in Bill's bank. The first time was when she and Jed signed their farm as collateral for the horses that were slaughtered because Jed's black stallion tested positive for hoof and mouth disease. This time she looked at the building more closely and was impressed with how beautiful it was and how plush the carpeted walkways were. The wooden floors, teller windows, and window moldings all glistened from being polished with lemon-scented oil. Emily stood on the blue marble entrance and thought this truly is the most impressive building in town—it and the Ritz Grand Hotel and Ballroom.

"Emily! Emily, my dear. I'm so glad to see you." Bill held out his hand.

"Bill, we have to talk."

"Come into my office. We'll talk till our jaws hurt." Bill held the door open and they walked past Carla, his personal secretary.

"Hold all my calls and reschedule any appointments." Bill led Emily to one of the two wingbacks in front of his desk. He sat in the other. "Do you want to go first or shall I?"

"Bill, Jed just left on a bus to find Rose. He has an address in Springfield. Our truck wasn't in good enough shape for the trip and . . ."

"Rose is in Springfield? How do you know?"

"I can't tell you that. I probably shouldn't be telling you this except Jed doesn't have much money and I don't know how he'll get around or how long it will take to actually find Rose. She's not at the address he has. She's moved. He's just going to try to find her before the trail goes cold."

"Well, why is Jed going after her?"

"Because when she left she was pregnant with our grandchild."

"Our grandchild?" Bill paused a moment while he sorted through this new information. "Is David . . . Oh, Jesus." Bill sank into his chair holding his head in his hands. After a moment of silence he jumped up from his chair and blurted out, "I've been such an idiot. How long ago did the bus leave?"

"Fifteen or twenty minutes."

"Emily, will you excuse me? I'm going to catch that bus and drive your husband to Springfield. We'll do this together. Will you be all right by yourself?"

"Oh, sure. The girls are there."

Bill ran from his office. As he whistled past, over his shoulder he told his secretary he'd be in contact. He ran out the front door right into an elderly woman. "Oh, I'm so sorry!" Bill held the door for the woman then raced straight to his car. Before he got there he stopped dead in his tracks, turned, and ran back into the bank to the head teller.

"I need a thousand dollars . . . twenties and a few fifties. Tell Jennifer . . . Carla. She'll make the proper postings."

Bill stuffed the money into his pocket and jolted again through the bank's front door. At Big John Lynch's he used coupons from three different ration books to fill his car and flew out of town on the highway going north and a little east. Forty miles down the road he hijacked the bus.

"Jed, get your things. Those Messerschmitts won't have a thing on the Packard today."

Jed reluctantly had the driver retrieve his suitcase. In a matter of minutes they were sailing down the highway toward Springfield. "Bill, how'd you find out?"

"Man, it's all over town. Everyone knows. They just don't know where—and neither do I. Say Jed, I want to apologize to you. I've not been a kind person to you these past few years. You, on the other hand, have been a real gentleman—the kind of man I should have been. You've done well providing for your family and raised some damn fine kids. I just hope I haven't completely ruined my relationship with Rose. She means everything to me."

"If you're coming clean, what can you tell me about the hoof and mouth episode?"

"The horses I sold you did not have the disease. But I did play a part in it. I have grieved over the baseness of my actions and will do whatever you think is fair to compensate you for your losses."

"I thought so." Jed turned and looked out the windshield. Presently he said, "I have no need for your money."

"I can do other things. How about a new house for you and Emily?"

"How about you watch where you're going? I don't think these roads were made to travel at these speeds. Who's going to rescue Rose if we're in a ditch somewhere?"

"Okay, you can be in charge for a while."

A few miles down the road they stopped to get something to eat in the town of Wind Springs. The town diner's parking lot was full with only one parking space was available. A green Plymouth pulled up at the same time as Bill. However, Bill didn't hesitate and took the space. The other car was full of hoodlums and they became agitated at Bill's aggressive driving. The driver got out and hulked behind Bill's car—waiting. Bill walked up to him and handed the man a twenty-dollar bill. He told the man he'd like to pay him for any inconvenience he may have caused. Dumbfounded, the man pocketed the money and headed back to his car of jeering comrades.

Inside, Bill and Jed waited on a table. Eventually, they were seated by a front window and began looking over the menu. Outside, the Plymouth had not been able to find a place to park and two men jumped out and started to push the Packard from its stolen space.

"Jed, order me whatever you're having. I'll be back in a minute."

Bill looked around the parking lot to see if there might be something he could use as a weapon. One truck had scraps of lumber in the back. He stepped on the back bumper and grabbed a short length of two-by-four. Taking long purposeful strides Bill walked to where two men had their shoulders against his car. Pushing, with their feet firmly planted and their backsides against the Packard's front bumper and radiator grill, the two men were using all their weight trying to move the recalcitrant vehicle. With the stick Bill walloped hard the ankle of a man charging at him from the back passenger door of the Plymouth. The man hollered, picked up his foot, and, dripping blood on the gravel, danced around on one leg while holding his throbbing foot. The other two left the front of Bill's car, they separated by a few feet, and came at Bill from different angles.

Inside the restaurant, the patrons gathered by the front windows fully expecting the three rough-looking men to pulverize the nice-looking man in the blue sports coat. Jed decided to order but couldn't get the waitress to come to his table. She saw him waving his arms, took a quick look out the window, and hurriedly walked over to Jed's table.

"Ain't you going to help your friend? Them's the Bonds boys. They'll kill him for sure."

"He ain't my friend and he deserves a good whipping. However, I don't think them Bonds boys know who they're up against. If it looks like they'll be doing any major damage to . . . uh . . . my friend, then I'll go help. But really, there's only three of them."

Outside, the first of the two approaching men took a swing. Bill ducked and rammed the butt of the stick into the abdomen of the second man leaving the first thinking about taking a second swing. The second man doubled up in pain. The first man clinched his fists waiting on an opening. He'd show this dandy you can't buy your way into his town.

Bill used his stick to whop the back of the second man's thigh while he was bent over at the waist holding his stomach. Bill got the stick caught on the man's pants and had to yank hard to pull it free, ripping the man's pants. The second man stumbled forward and fell to the ground holding his leg with one hand and his stomach with the other. Bill looked down. There was something wrong with his stick. It had two nail heads sticking out toward the end. Bill left the second man laying at his feet and the first man now moving backward, to walk to the man he hit first who was still sitting in the gravel. This adversary had removed his shoe and sock and was caressing an injured ankle. Bill used both hands on his two by four to strike the hurt man hard in the arm he was using with palm down on the ground to keep himself propped upright. The man yelled in pain, let go of his foot, and grabbed his arm—which now hung limp at his side. He fell on his side crying. Back at the green Plymouth the second man had regained his feet and was now leaning against Bill's Packard holding onto the radio antennae. Bill slammed the piece of lumber down on that man's right foot at the spot where the shoe tongue ended.

With every swing of the two-by-four the crowd cheered. These three had a reputation for making trouble. The waitress turned to Jed, "Why doesn't he do something to that brute just standing there?"

"Who knows? He probably has him scared to death and will let the other two take care of him later."

Bill looked at the two men wallowing on the ground and casually walked over to the one not yet touched. The man backed up until he bumped against his own car. He reached into his pocket and pulled out Bill's twenty. Bill leaned close, whispered something in the man's ear, and swiftly smashed the butt of the stick between the man's legs. It thudded against the car fender, crushing anything that might have been hanging in its way. The man let out a hideous howl and slumped to the ground. Laying on the loose gravel, he had both feet sticking high in the air, shaking.

In the restaurant there was a collective, "Ow." one exclamation of, "Good God," and another, "Oh, hell no."

Bill walked to the truck and tossed the stick back where he found it. All three men were writhing in the parking lot, moaning in pain, and holding different parts of their bodies.

Inside the restaurant Bill found Jed casually looking over the menu. The waitress walked up to their table and set down two glasses of water. To Bill, she said, "Sugar, them's the Bonds boys. Their dad's our chief of police."

Bill stood up, took out his wallet, and put ten dollars on the table. "In that case, we better be moseying on down the road."

"Where you gents heading?"

Jed stood up and said, "Little Rock."

Back in the car Bill drove out of town heading west—away from Little Rock which was south and east and away from Springfield which was north and east. When he cleared the city limits he turned on a minor county road and started criss-crossing back in the general direction of Springfield.

"Bill, what made you do it?"

"I was stupid. I convinced myself that I loved your wife and you stole her. It was revenge, I guess. I wanted her to think I was the better man and that she had made a bad decision marrying you. Like I say, I was stupid. You have every right to hate me. I wouldn't blame you in the least. But, I'd like to make it up to you. Jed, I could buy you those other two farms. Then you'd own the whole blooming mountain. You could rename it Calhoun Mountain. Or, maybe, you'd like a new car, a herd of horses, more cattle—anything. You name it."

"Let's put all that on a back burner. Emily and I have each other and everything else is just things. When David gets back we'll both be pretty damn happy. If David and Rose do get married, maybe you could do something for them."

"Hell, man, I'm going to do that anyway. Jed, I've changed."

"Well, we better not tell those Bonds boys what you used to be like."

As the miles whizzed past, Bill started feeling good about the entire situation. He sensed that finding Rose, owning up to his misdeeds, and releasing his anger on those toughs was the start of a new life.

"Bill, you ought to do something for the city. Buy that thermal spring from old man Ridley and build a city park, plant some trees, install water fountains, rebuild and extend the sidewalks. How about letting the farmers start a co-op? You could donate that new farmer's market to them. Give them discounts at your Feed and Seed Store. Buy an organ for one of the churches. Fix the clock on top of the county courthouse. You could make a career of public works—all anonymously, of course."

When they pulled into Springfield later that evening they stopped at a restaurant and ate. It was their first meal for the entire day. Jed asked the waitress how to find the address Jesse had given him. She drew them a map on a napkin. After hurriedly gulping down their food, they more or less ran to the Packard. With Bill driving and Jed navigating they soon found the apartment. Mrs. Patterson told them she had not seen Rose for almost three months. The last time, she and the little boy were walking hand in hand down the street dragging a suitcase.

"Tell me about the little boy," Bill asked.

"Oh, well, he's a cutie. Never seems to cry much. Plays with that little tractor thing all the time. Does everything his mother tells him. He's talking real good and knows lots more words than others his age. He's got blond hair and the prettiest blue eyes."

It was dark when they left Mrs. Patterson's boarding house but they still drove around trying to get a feel for the city. After a couple of hours they checked in at a downtown hotel. In Jed's room they tried to come up with a plan.

"Jed, do you think she has a job? I mean how does she eat? Where does she get her money? She couldn't have socked away enough to last two years. Her mother promises she's not heard from Rose—so she hasn't sent her any money. What do you think?"

"I think Jesse's been sending her money every month—maybe, David as well. When she was evicted from the boarding house Jesse's check was returned and that's how I found where she was. I don't think she's had much money. You know she's been real sick. Jesse said she had pneumonia in both lungs—could've lost the baby."

"Oh, my God. I should have been here."

"Bill, she was running from you."

"That's sick, isn't it? What makes a man fly off the handle like that? You know, I tried to keep them apart. All I could think was that another Calhoun was stealing something belonging to me."

Bill looked out the window at the downtown buildings of Springfield, Missouri. "If she doesn't have money maybe we should start by checking the shelters."

Back in his room Bill called his secretary at her home. The next day they got off to an early start. After a fast breakfast, they started cruising the city looking for shelters for the homeless. They drove up and down the residential streets of Springfield. When they found themselves in a shopping area they stopped so Bill could buy clothes and toiletries. By the end of the day they knew their way around Springfield but they were no closer to finding Rose.

That night, Jed suggested they check the hospitals and then the churches. They had an early breakfast the next morning and headed to the first hospital. After leaving the second hospital with no new information, Bill suddenly stopped the car. He jumped out and hurried over to an old man going through a trash bin. Jed watched as the old man started pointing down the street. Bill gave the man a bill from his wallet and excitedly got back into the car.

"He said there's a church not far that gives out a meal everyday to the poor. He said a woman with a little boy helps serve the food."

When they got to the church several people wearing tattered clothing were loitering about. Bill parked the car. They walked inside the fellowship hall next to the church and saw her. She was stacking plates.

Bill walked up briskly and stood right in front of his daughter. Rose looked up from her task, saw her dad, and started crying. Bill walked around the table to her. She put her arms around his waist and cried into his shoulder.

"It's all right, honey. Everything's going to be all right."

Gideon walked over. "Is anything wrong? Here Rose, here's a napkin." He held out his hand to Bill and to Jed. "Welcome to the Lord's house. I'm Pastor Gideon."

"I'm Bill Potter, Rose's father, and this is Jed Calhoun."

Jed shook hands with Gideon, "Pleased to meet you, sir."

Gideon turned to Rose. "Rose, are you okay? Darling, can I get you anything?"

Bill's face turned ashen as he and Jed looked at each other, trying to find solace in their new friendship for this latest development. Bill asked, "Might I have a few minutes alone with my daughter?"

Jed removed his jacket and asked if he could help serve the meal. A line had developed.

"Sure. I still have to bring more food from the kitchen."

Bill and Rose walked outside. "Daddy, everything's such a mess. Do you know about Carson?"

"Only what a fine little boy he is."

"He's just like David. Oh, Daddy. David's going to be a priest." Rose started crying in earnest with this latest admission.

"Honey, I don't think David's going to be a priest."

"Yes, he is. He wrote and told me. He said for me not to write to him anymore. He was going to give his life to Christ and help the poor in North Africa."

"Well, you see, Rose. David didn't actually write you that letter."

"What are you talking about? I still have it. I threw away his others but I kept that one."

"Rose, I wrote that letter, signed David's name, and put it in your mailbox at Jesse's newspaper. I thought somehow it would finally make it to you and I was trying my best to break you and David up."

"David's not going to be a priest? But he didn't write to me anymore."

"Well, you see, Rose. That's another thing, I wrote to David like I was you and told him you had fallen in love with someone else. Rose, I've been a blatant fool. Can you ever forgive me? David still loves you. He's been shot in France, treated in a hospital in Reims, then sent to an evacuation hospital in England. He's heading to Dancing Deer right now. He'll be arriving any day and you need to be there when he steps off the bus. We're all going to be there."

"How bad was he shot? Is he going to be all right?"

"According to his letter to Jesse, which got printed in the paper, he was accidentally shot by a French woman he'd just saved from some Germans. Then he was shot a few months later by a tank. He said he's going to be okay but would have to walk with a cane for awhile."

"Daddy, Gideon's asked me to marry him."

"I thought as much. Do you love him or do you love David?"

"Gideon's a fine man. He plays with Carson." Rose paused, looked down, and then after a moment she said, "But I love David."

"Good. Get your things and . . . where's the boy? We'll leave as soon as you can get packed. No. Don't pack anything, just get Carson and his toy tractor. I'll buy you all new stuff. Whatever you want. Whatever the Packard can hold. And we've got to find a toy store. Let's hurry."

"Daddy, I can't leave Gideon like that. Let me talk to him." Bill had his arm on Rose's shoulder when they walked back into the fellowship hall. Rose stopped, turned to her dad, and said, "That was a detestable thing you did."

"Yes, I know. I'm embarrassed. I plan on spending the rest of my life making it up to you and David—and my grandson."

Inside, Gideon and Jed were serving a long line of people. Rose took Gideon's arm and led him out of the hall. Bill removed his jacket and started scooping soup.

After everyone was fed, Bill and Jed took the pots into the kitchen. In the dining area several volunteers scraped off the food residue, stacked the plates, and separated the glassware and silverware. When the tables were wiped, the chairs re-arranged, and everything washed and put away, Bill and Jed stepped out front to wait for Rose and Carson.

When Rose emerged she was holding the hand of a beautiful little boy. Jed placed Rose in the front passenger's seat while he and Carson got in the back seat. Jed planned on playing farm with Carson and his tractor all the way to Dancing Deer. Bill put Rose's empty luggage in the truck of the Packard.

As the car pulled away from the curb, Gideon watched through a window. He wiped at a tear slowly making its way down his cheek.

CHAPTER 22—DANCING DEER
Dancing Deer, Arkansas – December 1944

With Jed aboard a bus heading to Springfield and Bill in his car trying to catch the bus, Emily decided to go to the library before heading home. As the old Calhoun truck puttered down the street Emily saw the banner the town put up welcoming David home. She brimmed with pride for her son. Some of the lamp posts and most retail window displays were decorated with red, white, and blue paint. Some even sported pictures of David supplied by the paper. Creighton's Jewelers was set for the biggest sale in the history of the store to commence the day after David arrived.

Several months ago the Army had notified Jed and Emily that David was missing in action. Emily thought the worst but Jed consoled her saying David was okay. If anything, he was a prisoner and would be released when the war was over. The way the Allied forces were winning battles and the way the Russians were advancing toward Berlin from the east and everyone else from the west it would be only a short while before the Germans surrendered.

Jesse had written about him as now missing after being sent on a secret assignment. The entire town started sporting grim expressions. A cloud of despair had descended. Then, in early November, the Army said he had been found but had been shot. They had him in a hospital in Reims, France, and then in Plymouth, England, and would be releasing and returning him home as soon as his wounds healed sufficiently for travel. He had been awarded the Army's prestigious Distinguished Service Cross.

Jesse eventually received a letter from David saying he was in London and would be coming home through Russellville after he visited his friend Gino's parents and sister, Gabriela, in Syracuse. He said he would be bringing home a surprise for everyone. Jesse printed David's letter in the paper and, after a week of thought, sent someone to Russellville with David's picture. The man sent was charged with checking each passenger getting aboard any bus coming to Dancing Deer. He was supposed to see if, when David did get on the bus, he had a young lady with him. He was also to immediately call the newspaper. The town would have its warning and be ready.

If David was bringing home a new bride, well, there are fireworks on Independence Day and there are fireworks on the first day of the year, but they would pale in comparison to the fireworks David would be setting off if he stepped off the bus with a wife.

At the library Emily hugged Nadine and asked how Rupert was coming on his cabinetry shop. Nadine told her Rupert was having a hard time finding the saws, drills, and other tools he needed. He had placed classified ads in the Kansas City, Little Rock, and Dallas newspapers. Responses were just now starting to come in.

Then the door burst open and an excited Faye Spencer rushed in. Out of breath and spitting as she talked she blurted, "Mrs. Calhoun, I saw your husband's truck outside. Is he here? There's some people just got off the bus and are looking for anyone who knows anything about David."

"Miss Spencer, I'm driving the truck. What are you talking about?"

"Just come with me. It's the biggest story of my career. These people are from France and they want to know about David. The man's a hero."

"David's a hero? Our David?"

"He's not just our David any longer. These French say he's their David. They've got artist's renditions of him fighting twenty to thirty Germans at once with nothing but a piece of firewood. They say he saved a young girl and an entire town's treasure from the German Gestapo. Somehow, he lifted and carried a gigantic bronze bell off a German truck and into a barn. He did that after the girl he saved shot him in the leg with a German officer's pistol. I tell you, it's the biggest story this town's ever seen."

Carla wrote, by hand, a short note to *The Marsden County Meteor*, enclosed a cashier's check, and dropped it in the local mail slot at the post office. Bill told her to write the letter anonymously saying she had driven through Dancing Deer and found the city to be picturesque but needed more trees. She stopped at the bank and got a cashier's check for three thousand dollars for their purchase. Carla was also instructed to find a tradesman who specialized in repairing large clocks in high places. She had a long list of things to do. What in the world had come over her boss? Everything he asked her to do had to be hush-hush. This certainly wasn't like her old boss. In the past, the nasty things he did were hush-hush and the good things he did were done for publicity. She thought she liked her new boss better—or were these new things actually nasty even though they appeared to be good?

There was also a letter to the County Agricultural Extension Agent. Bill needed him to see if he could get a movement started to organize the farmers into a co-op. If he could, Bill planned on donating his new farmer's market to them—land, building, and improvements. Potter . . . donate. Can you believe it? The words didn't ring true when used in the same sentence.

Nadine put a sign on her desk saying she'd be back shortly. She and Emily walked up the street right behind a fast-paced Faye Spencer. In front of *The Marsden County Meteor* several groups of people congregated in little circles. At the center of each circle were a couple of people getting names and setting up interview appointments. Along with the Dancing Deer natives, Emily thought she had never seen so many Claudes at one time in one place. The scent of lilac permeated the air. Faye wondered if her flirty sister would consider this to be heaven with so many handsome Frenchmen kissing hands and speaking poetry in an indecipherable language.

When they approached, Jesse said in a rather loud and commanding voice, "Ladies and gentlemen, this is David's mother."

What had been a rather noisy gathering suddenly became quiet. Jesse took Emily's arm and said to the people standing by, "Please continue. I will apprise Mrs. Calhoun of the situation and—if she agrees—a limited number of interviews will be granted."

Inside Jesse's office, Nadine and Emily sat on plush leather chairs. To Faye, leaning against the door, Jesse said she could take notes but any use of those notes would have to be approved by him. With a smile, he looked at Emily. "Mrs. Calhoun, it appears David has achieved some sort of mythical status with the French. He's bigger than life to them. They needed a hero and this Pepe Martel and Father Dominique have given them a fantastic story with David playing the leading role.

"I don't know how much is true. Certainly not the part about David carrying a thousand-pound bell from a large truck inside a barn but it does appear he killed a number of German soldiers who were sexually assaulting Pepe Martel's daughter, Genevieve. They want to award David the *Croix de Guerre* and plan on staying until he arrives and the medal presented.

"In the meantime, they'll be interviewing anyone who has a story about David to tell. They're not interested in the mundane stuff, but anything exciting, home-spun, or eccentric. It helps if it's true but that's not important since they're just relating what's been told to them. That's what sells newspapers. They're prepared to pay handsomely for the stories. What do you think?"

"I don't think I can invade David's privacy for money."

"Well, look at it this way. David will need to start earning a living soon. If he works for someone then there's no problem, but if he's like his dad he'll want to be his own boss. For that, he'll need venture capital. Any number of people will be more than happy to loan it to him but if we work this just right you can refute any inaccuracies given and hand David your proceeds to start whatever career he wants—without him having to borrow from an outsider.

"Here's what I propose. We give two interviews at your house. The first tomorrow morning to answer any questions they may have. You tell them the truth about what a nice guy David is, how hard he worked when he had to go harvest other people's crops, how he learned his back-woods savvy, and what his personality is like. You know, what makes him David. Then after everyone else has had their say and they have written their articles you'll give them a second interview and set the record straight on anything you believe someone else has said that was inaccurate. I don't believe anyone will say anything bad about David but someone might say something that lacks complete honesty."

"Jesse, you were David's best friend. I know you'll look out for his interest. So, if that's what you recommend, that's what we'll do."

"Okay. Faye, you escort the two Mrs. Calhouns back to the library. Go out the back way. I'll go out the front and start to negotiate with the newspapers for the fee they'll have to pay for the two interviews. Altogether, there's four of them. Oh, and just for your knowledge, they don't refer to him as David but as 'The Calhoun.'"

Jesse got up from behind his desk and turned toward Emily, "Each paper will want to bring a photographer to your farm tomorrow morning and I'll have to invite the French diplomat who's going to give David the award. If you would have some pictures handy, maybe a playbill for that *Romeo and Juliet* performance, and anything else you think they might find interesting. They'll probably want to take pictures of your house, of David's room, the barn and animals, where Balder's buried, and of the surrounding forest. You know, I think this will work just fine. Be sure and have an ample supply of iced tea and strong coffee."

That afternoon, Jesse interviewed the reporters from the four newspapers and the official from the New Orleans' French Consulate. To each reporter he offered copies of his pictures of David and the letters he had received. In return he asked for them to give him copies of the stories they would be running. They agreed, knowing not everything would be exactly true, and it was a professional courtesy to allow someone to counter with a corrected version.

They had already found out about the locket, the hoof and mouth fiasco, his years spent harvesting other people's crops, and Balder. Soon, the residents town-wide were scratching their heads, desperately trying to remember anything the reporters would pay to hear.

The next day on top of Lee Mountain, Emily displayed the pictures she had and told them as much as she could about David without saying anything he might have objected to. The man from the French Consulate gave Emily copies in English of the stories already run in the French newspapers. They awaited her response.

She read them and the interviews with people on the scene. She then looked at the pictures. "Is this all true? I mean, how could anyone have picked up that bell?"

The diplomat replied, "We don't know for sure. But somebody picked it up and moved it inside the barn. The two members of the resistance said the truck had been unloaded when they arrived and the only ones who could have done it were Pepe, who was sixty and lying down inside with a large knot on his head, Genevieve—his eighteen year-old daughter—and the Calhoun. But he had already been shot by Genevieve. She says she helped him unload the smaller treasures then went after rope. The Calhoun did the heavy lifting with a bullet in his hip. Genevieve said when she returned with the rope the bell was sitting on the tarp in the middle of the barn—that's twenty-five feet from the closest point he could've gotten the truck.

"The truck was too wide to fit in the barn opening so we don't know how he got the bell in except to have man-handled it in some way. Pepe's story did exaggerate the number of dead soldiers. The two members of the resistance said they disposed of seven Germans. But still, he was only one man and was unarmed until he coaxed one of the drivers into the house carrying a pistol. I've got to say, Mrs. Calhoun, we believe every word—adjusting Pepe's number down to seven of course."

One of the reporters added, "Mrs. Calhoun, tell us about his allergic reaction to bee stings."

"We weren't aware of that until we went harvesting in the summer of 1933. He got stung while picking peaches and we had to take him to the emergency room. It took a big chunk out of our earnings to pay his medical bill."

"What about his marksmanship?"

"He learned that from his father. Since we had to spend the summers traveling from one crop to another there wasn't any way we could have food put away for the winter so my husband and David had to kill wild game. Wait a minute, that's not exactly correct, a neighbor did bring us smoked beef and pork that first year. If I remember correctly, David's father paid the man back with venison."

"Where is your husband, Mrs. Calhoun?"

"He should be back any day. He's on a personal trip to Missouri."

Jesse suggested they take their pictures.

Later that morning the diplomat thanked Emily for her hospitality, and said he thought they had plenty of information for the time being. Of course, there was still one interview left but that would wait until just before they left for France.

The next morning, Friday, Jesse opened the letter with the cashier's check for three thousand dollars. He thought, now here's a story and went to find Faye Spencer. The receptionist found him first. He had a telephone call from Russellville.

"He's here. He's here. And he's with a good-looking woman. I got a picture. Want me to try and beat the bus back?"

Jesse shrugged his shoulders, "No, we wouldn't have time to get the picture developed and no one here would know her anyway. Just come on back and enjoy the party." Jesse called Emily for the second interview.

CHAPTER 23—COMING HOME
Reims, France – November 1944

The cart slowly wound its way from bed to bed. Creaking with each turn of its casters, the cart announced its arrival. It held rubber hammers, syringes, stethoscopes, tongue depressors, plastic tubes, clean linens, surgical masks, and extra pens. Attached to its side were three clipboards holding patient lists, medication instructions, and death warrants. A nurse herded the cart and at each stop along the way she took and measured life signs, the cart was a medical station.

"Wake up, Mr. Calhoun. I need to take your temperature. Here, put this under your tongue. Mr. Calhoun, I know you can hear me. That lame excuse of losing your hearing won't cut it. We have to bathe you this morning. You're to receive your medal today." The head nurse reached out and shook life back into David.

A man rolled up in a wheelchair with a comic book on his lap. "Is he the Calhoun?"

The nurse said, "The one and only. They say he fought an entire battalion of Germany's best trying to save his company. He fought them to a standstill, by himself, while his buddies ran for their lives. Germans descended on him from three sides eventually overrunning his position. His last battle was a solo against a Panzer while most of what was left of the German infantry closed in. They left him for dead but he walked out carrying the body of his best friend." The nurse looked at a clipboard at David's feet. "Wake up, Mr. Calhoun."

David stirred. He asked, "Where am I?"

"Well, let's see. You're in an Army hospital in Reims, France. You've been hit by shrapnel, and in a couple of hours you're going to receive the Distinguished Service Cross for valorous action in imminent peril."

David sat up and shook his head. "You're mistaken. I'm in Dancing Deer. I'm getting married today. You probably want that guy over there." David reached out his hand and pointed to an empty bed.

"Now really, Mr. Calhoun. Yesterday you said you were fishing with your dog. This isn't going to hurt. I'm not going to give you a shot."

"You must've already given me a sedative. I'm groggy. Go away."

Another wheelchair rolled up and one man walked over pushing a rack holding an IV solution. "Is he really the Calhoun?"

The man in the first wheelchair said, "Yep."

"Sir, would you autograph my book?" The man tethered to the IV held out a comic book and pen.

"Leave him be until I finish getting his vitals. Then you can pester him all you want. If any of you would like to give him a bath you'll have to get in line. There's plenty of nurses who've already signed up for that detail."

"I can take my own bath, thank you. May I see that book?"

"Yes, sir. Uh . . . should we refer to you as the Calhoun?"

David stared at the cover. It was titled The Calhoun, Book One and had a picture of an American GI holding an Italian soldier off the ground by his throat. He flipped through the pages. It detailed everything he and Gino did in Sicily, except for purchasing the hotel. The main character was similar to himself, except his features were more exaggerated. "Where'd you get this?"

"They're everywhere. I'm going to buy the others when I get paid. They just became available in English but the locals have had their own version for weeks. I'm told there are five different books. Last month your story was written with more detail in several Parisian newspapers."

The second man in a wheelchair asked, "How did you get that bell into the barn? Did you lift it? Did it really weigh a thousand pounds? I've got to know."

"The bell? Well, that was interesting. I didn't want to bother with it as it was so big but when I was told its history, somehow I had to get it secured. Does one of these books talk about the bell?"

"Yeah . . . uh . . . yes, sir. And about all those Germans guarding it."

"Mr. Calhoun, you really need to take your bath now. The brass won't take it very well if you're not ready on time."

The nurse pulled back his sheet and helped him to his feet. David had a bandage around his chest and another on his leg. Slowly they made it down the hall. Every eye followed David and the nurse.

When they reached the toilet facilities, David brushed his teeth and asked for a few moments of privacy. Soon a young nurse came looking for David and asked him to follow her to a chair where she told him to sit. She began stropping a razor against a leather strap. In a few minutes she had neatly lathered his face and expertly scraped it off. Another nurse arrived saying it was time for his shampoo and haircut. She made him lean back, putting his neck on the edge of a porcelain basin. She lathered his hair twice and after the second rinse she toweled him dry and gave him a haircut with a razor. She said she'd finish after his bath.

A slender nurse in her twenties took David's elbow saying it was her turn. She helped David into a tiled area where he sat on another stool. As she turned on the water to a handheld umbilical cord and got the temperature warm to the touch she said, "David, tell me again about Dancing Deer. Are you sure bears come into town during the night to go through people's trash?" She then helped David remove the remainder of his clothing and the gauze bandages as he told her more wild tales of his hometown.

"Did you lose?"

"No, David. I won."

The nurse bathed him with a soft spray and sponge. She was careful around his injured areas and patted him dry before applying new bandages. David was impressed with the pampering he was getting. Moving her hair to one side she asked if he hurt anywhere. If he needed his neck or back rubbed. If he would like to lay down while she massaged anything that ached.

Later that day Colonel Fulbright, the sergeant-major, and a couple of captains awarded David the Distinguished Service Cross. He was told that it wouldn't be long before he would be heading home. His old unit had already crossed into Germany. In fact, it wouldn't be that long before they were all heading home. As a last gesture he gave David, Pepe's black enameled cane with the silver tip and the silver handle cap. He said he'd sent a squad of men to the Perch to retrieve David and Gino's personal items. The cane was sticking straight up like a marker.

A clerk who had been writing everything down coughed. The colonel took the hint and said, "Oh yes, and here's that medieval knife you've been hauling around."

David took the knife, slowly he slid it from its calfskin sheath, and ran his thumb along its blade. From the corner of his eye he saw the look on the colonel's face. He slid the knife back inside its scabbard and said, "Colonel Fulbright. I'm going home. Would you find someone who needs a good-luck piece and give it to him?"

"Son, I know just the man." The colonel held the knife to his side as his clerk jumped up to buckle the belt around his officer's waist.

Colonel Fulbright turned to the photographer and suggested that after taking the picture of him giving the Calhoun his medal another picture could be taken of the Calhoun turning over his hand-to-hand combat piece to his commanding officer.

"Sir," one of the officers raised his hand, ". . . before we have those pictures taken someone should probably clean it. It looks like there are blood stains on the handle, in that groove going down the edge of the blade, and on the bottom half of the scabbard."

"We'll do no such thing. This knife is almost sacred."

Several nurses had gathered off to one side and were filled with admiration for the man they had been taking care of for the last few days. The nurse who had bathed him started making plans to visit Arkansas after the war was over. She reasoned that Dancing Deer shouldn't be that hard to find; not with a celebrity like David living in it. She'd locate David and tell him she needed to examine his wounds. It was just a routine follow-up. Then she'd ask where a girl could get a good meal. Everything would fall into place. She was a smart girl and had finally set her goal for life after the war.

When the brass left, people started milling around David's bed. They all wanted his autograph and for him to tell them about his exploits—especially about the bell and how many Germans he had killed with the Bowie.

A doctor came over and asked one of the nurses hovering around what was going on. He decided David needed to be transferred to England. They had to restore order; to get the nurses back to work. That afternoon, David was loaded on a transport plane with a dozen other patients. He was escorted by the nurse who had bathed him. Once again a beautiful and slender woman with a mission had been able to orchestrate events to her benefit. It happens all the time, all over the world. They headed to a hospital in England.

Pepe handed Genevieve the newspaper. He watched her face as she read the article on the front page. Her pulse quickened. Her face flushed. Her eyes grew big. "Oh, Papa, David's in the hospital. I've got to go to him. They won't know how to take care of him."

Genevieve jumped from her chair and ran up the stairs two rungs at a time, toward her room. Tears streamed down her face. Pepe finished his *café nationale* and went to the barn for Philippe's car. This might be the last time he would get to drive it. Philippe wanted it back. He had called from Paris and said he would be picking it up on his next trip home. With the roadster parked by the front door Pepe went to Genevieve's room. She was packing her things.

"Papa, will you drive me?"

"Honey, you know I will."

That afternoon Genevieve and Pepe walked through the ward where the clerk said David was placed. He wasn't there. She asked the head nurse where she might find David Calhoun. The nurse told her he had been transferred to Plymouth, England; from where he would be heading home in the following week.

"How bad hurt is he?"

"Not bad. He couldn't hear for a couple of days. His ears had suffered from the percussion of an explosion close by. His hearing came back after the swelling went away. He had received shrapnel in his back, side, and leg, but there was nothing life threatening and when his wounds heal to where he can sufficiently take care of himself he'll be discharged."

That night Pepe and Genevieve discussed what their next step should be. Genevieve was adamant about going to David. She told her father she loved David; he was the only man for her. Pepe suggested he go to Paris and get them visas for America and find out from the authorities exactly where David lived. He said he'd always wanted to see the English Colonies. Genevieve said that David had informed her he was from a little town called Dancing Deer in the state of Arkansas—somewhere in the middle of the country.

Pepe spent the next week taking care of the details. He made a trip to his banker, received a letter of credit that could be used at any international bank, a second cashier's check for the comic book royalties for David, procured their visas, secured transportation on a freighter, and purchased a money belt to carry the large amount of American currency he planned on frittering away. This was going to be a great vacation for him and he was going to have a great time with his daughter. She would never again be able to say he gave his son preferential treatment. He even found time to spend two nights with Claudette.

Before they got out of Springfield, Jed told Bill he wanted to telephone Emily. She might have some word on David. And he wanted to tell her they had found Rose and Carson. They stopped at the bus station where Jed located a bank of private telephone booths. When he emerged he informed everyone that Jesse had a reporter at the bus station in Russellville who would call the paper when David arrived. "Also there were French reporters who had shown up and were asking people for information about David. He's to get a French award for saving a girl's life and a bell from the Germans."

Bill handed Jed a Baby Ruth. He had spent the time while Jed was on the telephone at the candy counter with Carson and everyone was now eating Baby Ruths.

Rose asked, "Do we have time for me to get my hair done and to buy some make-up?"

Bill said, "Sure. We also need to find you and Carson some new clothes."

That afternoon they were back on the road. Rose sported a new-do and they had found clothes and toys for Carson. Rose was disappointed in the dresses available for her. She said her clothes back home were of better quality. Bill talked her into purchasing a new dress and pair of shoes just in case her old clothes didn't fit. He thought she had grown taller and a bit thinner. She did like the feeling of having something new to wear.

When the road approached Wind Springs, Bill got edgy and Jed began looking at the map to see if there was a decent way to go around. Rose asked if they might find a diner to stop for supper.

Bill and Jed said, "No" at the same time.

Jed added, "There's a nice restaurant in the next town. We had a bad experience in Wind Springs the last time through. If it's all right with you we'll just sail on past Wind Springs to that next town."

Bill hunkered down in his seat. Jed turned his back to the window and they drove through town five miles an hour below the posted speed limit. The highway went past the police department where several policemen were standing by the front door, obviously waiting on a black Packard. Bill wiped the sweat from his forehead and then noticed in his rear-view mirror a police cruiser pull out from the police station and change lanes to close in on the Packard. The cruiser stayed with them to the edge of town. Bill swore to himself that if he got out of there he'd never grace their doorstep again.

Pepe wanted to stay awhile in New York City. He thought they might head to Arkansas by way of Niagara Falls and then on through Chicago to St. Louis. That way they'd come in through the back door. There was so much to see. He wondered if Genevieve would know they had made a wrong turn, if they saw the Grand Canyon or Yellowstone on the way.

Genevieve decided she had better take charge of their travel itinerary. She wanted to get to David as soon as possible. In New York City they caught a train south to Georgia and then turned west toward Little Rock.

"Papa, did you know David has three sisters? Also, he thinks his father is one of the smartest people in the world. He told me about some of his father's inventions. You'll like him. He used to make whiskey when he was a boy. He had to quit because it's against the law."

"It's against the law to make whiskey in America? What kind of country is this?"

Pepe and Genevieve hired a car in Russellville and arrived in Dancing Deer a couple of hours before dark. They were impressed with all the trappings the town was putting up for David's arrival. One group had a ladder they moved from one street light to another. They decorated each with red, white, and blue paint. The retail stores tried to outdo each other with one patriotic window display after another.

The driver from Russellville told Genevieve, Dancing Deer was the home town of David Calhoun, a hero of the war. He was scheduled to arrive any day and the town was preparing a big celebration. They've been stringing lights for over a week. I imagine, before the day is over, they'll be dancing on the sidewalks. He dropped them off at the Ritz Grand Hotel and Ballroom.

Before taking Rose and Carson to his house Bill drove Jed to Lee Mountain. It was late on a Thursday night and everyone in the car but Bill was asleep. Everyone in the house was also asleep. Quietly Jed tiptoed to the bedroom. He slipped off his clothes, slowly pulled the covers back, and slid in beside his wife.

In the cool darkness he heard, "Did you think I wouldn't know when you lay beside me?"

"No, I knew you'd know. I love you, darling." Jed reached for Emily. He cradled his wife of twenty-something years in his arms and thought about his returning son. Life was good.

The next day was Friday and the first day of the school holiday for Christmas. However, Jed's children did not get to sleep in as everyone got up and dressed early. Emily and the girls wanted to go into Dancing Deer to see Rose and meet Carson. Breakfast was a swift affair and everyone loaded into Jed's truck and headed down the mountain. Along the way Emily told Jed about the French newspaper reporters and how David was a French hero.

Pepe and Genevieve ate breakfast downstairs in the Ritz Hotel Bistro. There were several French newspaper people present and Pepe felt right at home listening to muffled French coming from several tables. Genevieve looked through the latest edition of *The Marsden County Meteor*. She read everything that related to David, the Letters to the Editor, and the upcoming sales at the local retail establishments. In the Letters to the Editor, the readers wanted to know who was spending money on their town. Someone had bought trees, had a clock fixed on the county courthouse, and there was talk of public restrooms soon to be built. Also there were rumors of other improvements in the works including wider sidewalks, water fountains, and a new park.

"Papa, let's walk around town. I want to see Creighton's Jewelers."

Rose and Carson were used to getting up early so when Rose came out of her bedroom she was astonished to see her father had breakfast prepared and was reading the paper with a cup of coffee.

"Rose, honey, I've learned to do a lot of things myself these past two years. Have you decided whether you're going to wear the locket out or in when you go into town?"

"I really haven't given it much thought. But out, definitely out. I'm tired of hiding it because of what someone might think. He gave it to me and I'm proud of it and of him. I'm going to wear it out and I'm going to town and walk up and down the sidewalk so that everyone will have a chance to see it."

The telephone rang. Rose ran and picked it up on the second ring. It was Jesse. He said he was glad she was back as David had made it to the bus station in Russellville. After a short layover David would then be departing for Dancing Deer, arriving around noon. Jesse asked her to come down to the newspaper's office as soon as she could and to bring Carson. He asked if Emily would be coming by as there was no answer when he rang her home. Rose didn't know.

Moments after hanging up the doorbell rang and when she opened it there was Jed, Emily, and David's three sisters. Rose hugged Emily and the girls. She introduced Carson to everyone and told Emily to call Jesse. David was in Russellville and would be arriving at lunchtime. Emily went into the living room as everyone else went into the kitchen where Rose started pouring orange juice for Carson and the girls.

Bill asked, "How did you come up with the name of Carson?"

"It's Mr. Calhoun's middle name. I found it at the courthouse."

"Does that mean the next one will be named Carrington?"

"No, probably not."

Jed bounced Carson on his knee as the girls watched. When Emily finished talking with Jesse she walked into the kitchen and said,

"Jed, honey, I need to go into town and have the second interview with the French newspaper men." She ran her hand through Carson's blond locks. "Young man, you look just like your dad and, probably, his dad."

"I know, I thought so too. I was startled when I first saw him. I thought he was going to ask me to take him fishing. Bill, can the girls ride in with you? Emily's turned journalist on me."

"It would be my pleasure. Take a cup of coffee with you. Those French like theirs so strong it spends most of the time arguing with the cup."

The girls suggested that Rose should get ready as they would get Carson bathed and dressed. This was going to be a special day. They were all looking forward to seeing David's expression when he was first told about Carson.

Back in town Jesse had a list and he called everyone on it. He also had a cub reporter go tell the town merchants when David would be pulling up. A second reporter carried a sign telling the people on the sidewalk. Jesse went outside to make sure the town's decorations were finished. He then walked to the Ritz Grand Hotel and Ballroom to let the French newspaper men know so they could start making plans for the final interview, their presentation, and their departure. He opened the door for a striking woman he had never seen before. She nodded thank you as she came through followed by an older man just about the same height and weight as he. Inside, he found the newspaper men and the one diplomat drinking their coffee. They were happy to finally put the finishing touches on their efforts and several looked at their watches to mentally calculate the minutes to David's arrival. They handed Jesse copies of their latest articles on David. Jesse spent a few minutes reading them through before handing them to Emily when she arrived.

Genevieve and Pepe walked down the street looking in the shop windows. It was what the locals called an Indian Summer. There had already been a frost but this day was short sleeve weather in the seventies. Christmas was in less than two weeks, the end of the war in Europe was in sight, and the town hero was coming home. They were ready. Everyone was in a festive mood.

Creighton's Jewelers had David's picture in their newspaper advertisement and when Genevieve and Pepe entered the store they saw a life-sized picture of David making a purchase. Mr. Creighton said he had a big sale planned for the day after David arrived but had decided to start it early. If there was anything they wanted to see he would be giving substantial discounts. Genevieve asked about the picture of David.

"Well, that's a big mystery. David bought the locket just before he shipped out and no one knows who it was for. I sold it to him myself. There's been a storm of controversy with more than one young lady claiming she has it, but so far no one's been able to produce it. I have lockets similar. Would you like to see?"

The door opened and a young man poked his head in saying, "David will be here at twelve-thirty."

Genevieve looked at her watch. It was almost noon. She looked out the window to see people hurrying by. She grabbed Pepe's arm and looked up at Mr. Creighton. "Thank you, sir. I think we'll be heading toward the bus station to get a good place to watch."

Jesse asked the paper's photographer if he had his camera ready and if his tripod was in place. It was just a short walk from the bus station to the courthouse right down Main Street. Everyone had agreed that the grounds in front of the courthouse would be the best place for the presentation. The town had set up several hundred white wooden folding chairs, built a platform, and installed a portable address system for the occasion. After the interview Jesse and David's parents went to Jesse's paper to wait for Rose and Carson.

Rose strode into the newspaper's office as confident as ever. She introduced Carson to everyone present and received quite a few stares at the locket. Her friends had no trouble putting two and two together. Faye stumbled onto the truth when she asked Carson if his daddy had gone to war.

"My daddy's coming home today. It's a Christmas present to me from Jesus."

Jesse told the group, "In fifteen minutes everyone needs to start heading to the bus station or to the courthouse. The bus will be arriving in just thirty more minutes." He turned to Rose. "May I speak with you in private for a moment?"

In his office Jesse said, "David thinks you married another man." He let that sink in for a moment, then continued with, "When the reporter called he said David was bringing a woman with him. Rose, he may already be married."

Rose fell into Jesse's chair. "I should have guessed." She lowered her head into her hands and started crying. Jesse handed her his handkerchief.

Between sobs she managed to stammer, "My father wrote David and me counterfeit 'Dear John letters.' His ploy broke up the relationship. Jesse, what am I going to do? What am I going to tell Carson?" More tears welled up in her eyes and flooded down her cheeks.

"I don't know, Rose. You really can't blame David, he didn't know. In my last letter from him he said he had a surprise for everyone and we know he went to Syracuse before coming home. It's my guess the woman is Gabriela, Gino's sister. Of course there is also a nurse who's decided that David is her special assignment."

"I can't go to the bus station. If he's chosen someone else thinking I didn't love him, he needs to think it was the right thing to do. Would you please ask my dad to come in?"

"Sure."

In a minute Bill appeared and asked what was the matter. Rose wiped the tears and told him that they may have been too late. Bill went over to Rose, got down on his knee, and said, "Rose, I'm so sorry. It's all my fault. I wrote both of those letters and I don't know how to undo the sorrow I've caused. What can we do?"

"If he's married, or is about to, I think I ought to go to Boston. We'll not let anyone else know I was here. Go get David's family. I'll tell them." Through the doorway she motioned to Jesse.

With one hand on the edge of the door Bill turned back to Rose and said, "Rose, I'll stay with you." He then walked over to Jed.

To Jesse, Rose said, "Here's what I want. If he has another wife, or a woman he plans on marrying, I won't cause him any pain. It means he's gotten over me. In that case, I'll go on to Boston and live with my mother. Can you see to it that your employees don't tell anyone what happened?" Rose slipped the locket inside her blouse.

"Yes, I can. Rose, you are a brave woman. Will you stay here while I go to the bus station to find out the truth of the matter?"

Jesse walked tow where his employees had congregated. Jed, Emily, and the three girls came into Jesse's office. Rose told them what she had decided and all the women cried together. Emily hugged Rose like she was already her daughter.

Jed said, "David should know about his son. No one should keep that away from him. Rose, you got to choose between Pastor Gideon and David. Don't you think David should be given the same opportunity?"

Rose started crying in earnest. Between sobs she managed to get out, "I don't know what to do. Everything's so confusing."

In the meantime Jesse told his employees with so much emotion there wasn't a dry eye in the house. With Rose still talking to Jed and his family, the employees of *The Marsden County Meteor* left for the bus station.

In a few minutes the Calhouns also started for the bus station.

When the scenic-cruiser entered the outskirts of town, an attractive woman put her hand on David's knee. "Are you the one the town's celebrating?" Just as she said that she saw the banner.

David was dumbfounded. People were two and three deep on both sides of the street. They cheered, whistled, and threw confetti high in the air. When the bus pulled up to where it normally loaded and unloaded passengers, it had to wait for the bystanders to clear a way.

The driver opened the door and Sheriff Sherman Shodtoe got on before anyone could get off. He said, "We want everyone but David here to get off first." At that the other passengers started unloading.

The sheriff sat down next to David and said, "Me and the police force are here to escort you to the courthouse where you'll be presented with the keys to the city. Also, there are some foreign people here and they want to give you an award as well."

Outside the bus, the crowd was getting impatient for their hero. David's family was excited that David was home and nervous at the possibility of his bringing a new wife. They were also worried Rose was about to have a nervous breakdown.

Rose's friends at the newspaper didn't know what to think. They all loved Rose but a story is a story. The people have a right to know, but then again, you can't get the story out if you're unemployed. A particular cloud of despair hung around them *en masse*.

All the passengers got off. The reporter from Russellville nudged Jesse. "That's her."

"Who?"

"That's her. She's the woman who was hanging on to David at the bus depot this morning."

Faye broke from the crowd and ran to the woman. They hugged. "Katy, I'm so glad to see you. I wasn't expecting you till next week."

Faye's sister, Kathryn, looked around at the throng of people. "I know. But once I made up my mind I couldn't wait. I'm sure glad I didn't miss this."

Jesse clapped his hands in exhilaration. At the top of his voice he yelled, "Yahoo." He then looked around at the people staring at him and slapped his employee with the good news on the back. "Lordy mercy! Is this a good day or what?"

The crowd picked up the cheering as David and Sheriff Shodtoe emerged from the bus. Jesse broke through the line and ran to David. He gave him a big hug and said, "You bring anybody?"

"No. I've not brought anybody. What's going on, Jesse?"

"What's your surprise?"

"I've got these comic books you've got to see."

"That's great, buddy. Rose is waiting for you at the newspaper." Jesse stepped back to let that sink in. David's family pushed through. There were plenty of hugs and kisses and tears.

To the sheriff, Jesse said, "On the way to the courthouse, if you could detour the procession by the newspaper's office to pick up someone, I can guarantee a positive article on your performance."

The sheriff yelled for his deputies to block off Main Street and the side street to the newspaper's office. Jesse told the band conductor of the slight change and they headed off. The procession was led by the band marching to the percussion of the drums. David and his family were followed by the sheriff, his deputies, and the city police. Two hundred spectators tried to keep up.

Reaching the second intersection the band began playing "The Baby Elephant Walk." From Main Street they turned toward the newspaper's office where Jesse had already run and was now inside and out of breath. Rose asked what was happening. Jesse told her to go outside, Everything was just fine. Everything was fantastic.

Rose stepped outside to wait. In only a moment the band changed from percussion only to a lively and happy tune and came around the corner bringing the love of her life. In front of the marching columns of band members David hobbled forward. Rose was so deliriously happy she danced with the music as she hurried to David. Bill and Carson followed close behind. When David saw Rose he started to run toward her but couldn't. One leg wouldn't move as fast as the other and it was painful for everyone there to watch. Rose ran to him, stopping just before knocking him down.

"Rose, you're beautiful. I thought you were married and living in Boston."

"I thought you were a missionary and helping the poor in North Africa."

"What?"

"Don't worry, darling. None of it's true. I'll explain everything later. Do you remember me telling you to go win the war and I'd take care of everything here? That children have a way of unifying? Well, David, here is your son, Carson."

"I have a son?"

"Yes, and he looks just like you."

David bent down and picked up Carson. He hugged him, tussled his hair, and sat him back down on the ground. "Carson, son, I'm going to kiss your mother."

David kissed Rose, then lifted her off her feet. They twirled around in the street until they were both dizzy.

Bill came up holding out his hand. "Welcome home, Son."

David shook Bill's hand then picked up Carson and sat him on his shoulder. With one hand steadying his walk with Pepe's black cane and Carson holding onto his ears, David held Rose's hand with his other and they walked together in the procession back to Main Street and on to the courthouse. When they neared the presentation area the band began playing "As The Saints go Marching In." It was the cue to throw more confetti. At the bottom of the steps to the platform David gave Carson to Rose and he stepped up and walked as steady as he could with Pepe's cane to the center of the stage where a microphone was placed.

Bill placed Carson on his shoulders and winked at Faye Spencer. Kathryn smiled back as big as she could and nudged her younger sister. "That handsome man with the little boy just winked at us."

Faye smiled at Bill. "He's the richest man in town. He owns the bank and the Ritz Grand Hotel and Ballroom. He's also the biggest scoundrel in town, but he's making headway."

"Is he married?"

Faye looked at her older sister. She was just coming off a bad marriage and had come to Dancing Deer to recover. She'd always been a flirt. "He's off limits."

Kathryn showed Bill another big smile. To Faye she said, "Faye, honey, no one's off limits until they're married."

Jesse leaned against the backdrop behind the stage platform and marveled at how magical everything had turned out. As he looked out over the audience he could hear the diplomat say what a wonderful person David Calhoun was and how important he was to the people of France.

Off to the left fringe of the crowd Jesse saw the pretty woman from the hotel. She was crying. He took out his handkerchief, stretched and refolded it, and then walked briskly to where the attractive woman sat.

"Please, Miss, may I be of assistance?" Jesse held out the Irish linen handkerchief.

"*Merci.*" Genevieve took the handkerchief and dabbed at her eyes. Her make-up was a mess. She had been crying since David ran up to the woman he thought had spurned him.

Jesse stared at the young French woman. He said, "*Du rien.*"

She countered with a smile. "That's very funny. How did you learn to speak French?"

"From a book. What's the matter with it? Did I mispronounce something?"

"Oh no. You just put the accent on the wrong syllable. It sounded a little odd."

"Well, you speak wonderful English. Are you French?"

"*Oui.*" She held out her hand. "My name is Genevieve."

Jesse had to steady himself. He held onto her hand. "Genevieve Martel?"

"Yes. How did you know?"

"Mademoiselle Martel, my name is Jesse Bell. I run the paper. And I just have to say that everything David said about you is true—in spades."

"What did our David say?"

"He told me he had met the most captivating woman in all of France and that she was smart and beautiful as well. He suggested that, after the war, he and I should make a trip to France where he would introduce her to me. He said he and her brother, Philippe, would tell war stories and have her father write them down."

"I see. Well, Mr. Bell . . . may I call you Jesse?"

"Please."

"Well then, Jesse, David must have thought you and I would become great friends."

"Yes. I think he's intuitive that way. And you have come to America to see him?"

"Yes. I thought he needed me."

"After the ceremony, may I take you to lunch and then show you around our pleasant little town?"

"Only if you will allow my father to accompany us."

Astounded, Jesse asked, "This is Pepe Martel?" He paused, then turned to Pepe, and said, "*Bonjour, Monsieur Martel. Je m'appelle Jesse Bell.*" Jesse held out his hand.

Pepe shook Jesse's hand enthusiastically. "*Enchante, Monsieur Bell.*"

To Genevieve, Jesse said, "I would be honored to have the pleasure of you and your father's company."

On the platform the French diplomat draped the ribbon holding the medal over David's head and kissed him on both cheeks. Into the public address system he finished his speech with "*Vive Le Calhoun.*"

The audience echoed it back two more times: "*Vive Le Calhoun. Vive Le Calhoun.*"

David dropped his cane and had trouble reaching to the platform to retrieve it. Carson, now standing beside his grandfather, broke ranks from holding Bill's hand and ran to the center of the stage. He picked up the cane and handed it to his father. There were tears in his eyes as he held out the smooth, black stick. With one hand David accepted the cane and with the other he tousled Carson's hair. The crowd roared in approval.

Pepe leaned to Genevieve and whispered something. She shrugged. He nudged her again. In French she said, "Oh Papa, you are incorrigible." She turned to Jesse and in English said, "My father wants to know if you will introduce him to the tall redhead standing beside the photographer?"

The End

Author Bio
Ron Lambert, an examined life

As an accountant in a small West Texas town, I spend my days studying the bank statements and tax returns of other people's businesses. I classify, summarize, and display their financial transactions in some meaningful format. I love creating order out of chaos.

I'm middle-aged and twice married—with the second blessed from heaven. Four grown children, their children, two bobbing tails of barking energy, and one sly cat round out my cache of treasure.

Over the years I have operated two retail stores, several service businesses, one ranch, and one restaurant. I have been prosperous and poor, with wild fluctuations in between. At present, being neither rich nor poor, I consider my status as deeply entrenched in middle class—a term bandied about by politicians and economists.

In an effort to restore my youth I purchased an old sofa on two wheels. For the past ten years, I have occasionally strapped sacks of clothes, maps, and a compass that doesn't seem to work onto the back cushion. After kissing my wife I set out for adventure and story. Usually, after only a week or so, I realize what I left behind was more important than what I set out to find and drive a day and a night hell-bent-for-leather back home.

I then settle into an old and comfortable routine. I read a few books, attend a few plays, daydream of new horizons, and plan my next adventure. I kept a journal on my first excursion. It was such an exhilarating experience: rewriting the journal and incorporating the pictures I took, that I became intoxicated to the point I wrote a novel.

At present, with pen on fire, I'm scratching out the ending for my seventh book. I'll win prestigious awards and be asked to speak at the local library if someone would read what I have written.

If you're looking for an evening spent with colorful and mesmerizing characters, if you want to immerse yourself in a rollicking good story, enthrall yourself to the point of madness, go two days without bathing, then have I got a story for you.

ADDITIONAL NOVELS
Continuing the Dancing Deer Series

Soon all will be available on Amazon.com and at our corporate office in trade paperback and e-book formats.

Dancing Deer (Book 1)
    Dancing Deer is the embodiment of small-town America. When asked, she sent her sons to war. This is the story of The Calhoun—one of those boys. It's also about the men he served, the men he fought beside, the men he fought against, and the women who loved him.
    There is the French Resistance, the German Gestapo, Anzio Annie, *Midge at the Mike*, the *Gustav Line*, and the Forty-Fifth Infantry campaigning from Sicily through Italy and France pushing back the formidable Germans. But this story is so much more.
    Find a comfortable chair and settle in with a great new book. You won't be disappointed.

The Last Dance (Book 2)
    Bill Potter is charged with murdering his Friday night squeeze. His bumbling lawyer steps out of a dead-end job of contracts and leases to save Bill from being strapped to "Old Spanky." Bill's wife returns after a twenty year absence to muddy the waters and it's up to her and Pepe, the womanizing Resistance fighter and WWI spy from France, to solve the case.

The Measure of a Man (Book 3)
    A group of Cuban immigrants decide to barnstorm the Midwest, entertaining the towns they come to with a game of ball. When they get to Dancing Deer the men on the city council con Bill Potter into a wager for more than they can afford to lose. Bill's position is that the Men from Dancing Deer will prevail. With a team of misfits and one win

under their belts Bill goes in search of a new manager. His ex-wife is traveling throughout the Western US with Pepe, the French womanizer. She knows more about ball than anyone and he has to convince her to come back and once again save him from the wolves at the door.

Lost in Appalachia (Book 4)

Dancing Deer's Chief of Police is lost in the mountains of West Virginia. Suffering from an injury, he can't remember who he is or why he's lost. Two kids take him in and hide him from a determined fiancée. She offers a big reward and the chief thinks he must have committed a major crime for someone to pony up such a large bounty.

Christmas in Dancing Deer (Book 5)

The Catholic church is consolidating its orphanages, but the children don't want to be separated. They come up with an alternative plan to present to the church council but then the women of Dancing Deer bring the orphan girls into their homes for the holidays. The boys leave on their own in the snow and spend a night with a burdened bank robber in a desolate cabin.

Beggarman, Thief (Book 6)

A story of a bank robber who finds his moment of epiphany in a shack with seven lost little boys. He goes home after twenty years on the lamb to have Christmas with his family and to right his wrongs. But he finds his past is in hot pursuit and the new life he has found is in jeopardy. He runs away in the clutches of a pretty lady evangelist who is taking her show on the road to the very town where he committed his last crime.

Toe to Toe with A Drunken Philosopher

This is really one story in three parts. First we have the high school philosophy teacher who has to resign his position much as Aristotle had to when the authorities in Athens came looking for him. Part number two is of an indigent Irish family who emigrate from the Emerald Isle. The little Irish boy in the family grows up to become a priest. Then the third part pits the philosopher and the priest in a contest of wits.

Order Form

Book Name	Qty	Price	Extension
Dancing Deer	☐	$17.95	_____
The Last Dance	☐	$15.95	_____
The Measure of a Man	☐	$15.95	_____
Lost in Appalachia	☐	$15.95	_____
Christmas in Dancing Deer	☐	$15.95	_____
Beggarman, Thief	☐	$15.95	_____
Toe to Toe with a Drunken Philosopher	☐	$15.95	_____

Sub-Total _____

Sales Tax (for Texas purchases)   @8.25% _____
Shipping: $4.00 for 1st Book
$2.00 for each Additional Book _____

Grand Total _____

Would you like your book(s) autographed?   Yes ☐   No ☐

Would you like your book(s) gift wrapped?   Yes ☐   No ☐
To_____ From_____

Order Form (continued)

Name _____

Shipping Address:
    Street or PO Box _____

    State and Zip _____

Telephone _____

Payment:
    Check Enclosed ☐

    Credit Card:
        Discover ☐

        Visa ☐

        MasterCard ☐

Card Number _____

Expiration Date _____

Code (on back) _____

Keep Credit Card Information for future purchases ☐

Order Form (instructions)

Boxes   Place quantity or checkmark (X) where applicable

Mail Completed Form To:
>Printers Guild Publishing, llc
>425 Spring Street, Suite 101
>Columbus, Texas 78934-2461

Or Fax Form to:
>(979) 733-0015

Or Call-In Your Order:
>(979) 732-2962

For Pick-Up:
>You are welcome to come by our office in the Stafford Opera House at 425 Spring Street, Suite 101, Columbus, Texas to pick up your shipment and save shipping costs or to talk with the author. Please call (979) 732-2962 to make sure someone will be there.

Security
>We do not share any of your information with anyone. We do not keep your credit card information unless you check the box allowing us to do so for future purchases.